ALICE HEARTS WELSH ZOMBIES

Cover design and illustration by Mave Gibson

Library and Archives Canada Cataloguing in Publication

Dunn, Victoria
Alice hearts Welsh zombies / Victoria Dunn.

Issued also in electronic format.
ISBN 978-0-9812612-4-9

I. Title.

PS8607.U553A45 2012   C813'.6   C2012-901944-5

The Workhorsery
132 Heward Avenue
Toronto, ON
M4M 2T7
www.theworkhorsery.ca

MIX
Paper from
responsible sources
FSC® C011825

10 9 8 7 6 5 4 3 2 1

ALICE HEARTS WELSH ZOMBIES

By Victoria Dunn

THE WORKHORSERY

To Mom

Contents

Alice Visits the Mailroom for the Very First Time

"Good morning, Alice, we have…"

Alice spun around in her office chair. "Good morning, Welly. So nice to see you! How was your post-mission R and R?"

"… a new assignment." Welly leaned over her desk and added a 'Don't forget, Odyssey is a paperless organization' memo to the teetering pile of papers beside her computer. "My furlough was fine, thanks for asking."

"Just fine? Where'd you go? I went to British Columbia to visit all the New Age communes where I grew up. Except the one that's now producing 'organic pornography', whatever that means. Anyway, it was an awesome month of communing with nature." Alice frowned at Welly. "I bet you spent your time off buried in some dusty old museum."

"I did visit the British museum, but it's not that dusty."

"Welly, that museum's in London, half a mile from your front door! After six weeks chasing a magician through the sewers of Lichtenstein, you deserved a real break. You should go somewhere different and have fun. You do know what fun is, right?"

Alice had worked with Welly for almost six months now, and not once had she seen him completely unwind and enjoy himself.

She was genuinely concerned he might have forgotten how.

She took in Welly's overpriced but conservative three-piece grey suit, and his almost certainly overpriced but conservative hair cut. His only rebellion from the image of a respectable gentleman circa 1955 was his refusal to wear a tie. Hardly surprising, Alice thought, given the number of people who'd tried to strangle him.

"Vacations are also a good time to experiment with your look," Alice added. "You might notice something different about me." With a flourish, she pointed at her head.

Welly sighed. "Yes, your hair is significantly shorter and less colourful than usual."

"My hairdresser said if I had one more chemical treatment, it would fall out. So she cut off all the damage and left me with this new, sophisticated, I'm-over-twenty-five-now look."

Welly glanced at his watch. "As I said, significantly shorter and less colourful. Now, we really do have a new... "

"Okay, so it's brown and boring." She tilted her head. "Like yours."

"... assignment, and our first order of business is visiting the Mailroom."

That got Alice's attention. She glanced nervously at the pneumatic tube that delivered mail to her desk. The sounds she'd heard coming out of it had been disturbing. And there were rumours that were even more troubling.

"Why do we have to go to the Mailroom?" she asked. Odyssey International's Head Office was a vast and sprawling complex, most of which she hadn't explored. The historic library was at the top of Alice's list of places she wanted to visit. Whereas the Mailroom was at rock bottom because it sounded like it was inhabited by the living dead.

Which was a ridiculous idea, of course.

"We need to consult the Mailroom chief. Ken has rejected all forms of modern communication; he believes they're dehumanizing or some such nonsense. Seeing him in person is a great deal quicker than writing him a letter."

Considering some of the weirdoes Alice had met since joining Odyssey International, Ken sounded relatively harmless. She'd worked with Mick in Medical, who was a lunatic, and she was partnered with Welly, who despite his good looks and dreamy British accent, was mad as a hatter.

Welly rested his briefcase on her desk and opened it. "Of course, we'll have to be armed." He took out a large, heavy-looking, black Taser with an enormous, yellow cartridge over its muzzle.

"Oh no, it's your job to be armed," Alice said. "I'm the one who goes around being all psychic."

"Sensitive," Welly corrected, using the Odyssey-approved term.

"Whatever. Anyway, I doubt I could even lift that... thing."

"Beautiful, isn't it?" Welly caressed the Taser. "Shoots up to six darts in parallel trajectories, and has a laser beam option for sending electroshocks through ionized streams of air. Lady Jane did herself proud on this upgrade." He rustled through his briefcase and took out a smaller device. "Now, this Taser requires physical contact to stun, but only for two seconds instead of the usual five. Also, there's an attachment I can get for you that can charge a net electrically to —"

Alice held up her hands. "Please, just tell me why we need Tasers to go to the Mailroom. It's not like I've needed to be armed to the teeth to visit other sections. Although it'd probably be a good idea when going to see Mick." And the Admiral, she thought, but nobody ever said anything bad about the boss. Not where he might hear it, anyway.

"We're not allowed to use deadly force in the Mailroom," Welly said, with an air of grievance.

"Are the Mailroom staff armed?"

"No, but I'm sure Ken would love that. He's a raving nutter."

"Uh-huh." Alice took the smaller Taser from Welly and stuffed it into her purse. Tired of craning her head back to look up at Welly, Alice stood. This improved matters, but only slightly. She wasn't short, but even in heels, standing next to Welly always made her feel tiny. Alice was never sure if she liked that or not, but then she couldn't decide if she entirely liked Welly either.

"Earth to Alice?"

"Oh, yes, I'm ready," she said. Alice straightened her new, bright yellow summer dress, part of her whole 'I'm over twenty-five' makeover, and grabbed her purse. "At least, as ready as I'll ever be." She followed Welly as he headed for the stairs at a brisk pace. Like all doors in Head Office, the one to the stairwell was decorated with the corporate logo; an art deco Greek sailing ship with a wide-open eye on its prow. In Alice's opinion, it was a nice design that had been thoroughly ruined by the garish company colours of orange and turquoise. 'Odyssey International' was emblazoned above the logo, and below was the motto, 'Conservo Pondera', Latin for 'maintaining balance'.

"Is the elevator broken again?" Alice asked.

Welly glanced back and nodded. "Some fool in Maintenance tried to fix the wiring without removing the protective spells first."

Alice shuddered. She'd learned about the dangers of touching magically charged things without adequate preparation during her training on Survival Island. After seeing one trainee lose a hand, she'd never broken the rules again.

Well, almost never, she thought. Recalling the time she'd rubbed that black cat's fuzzy belly on their last mission. But really, how was she supposed to know that touching a magician's familiar gave the man unrestricted access to your most embarrassing inner thoughts?

After going down what felt like the twentieth flight of stairs, Alice began to wonder just how big Head Office really was. She hadn't been allowed to explore it thoroughly, but she knew the Admiral's office was on the top floor.

The next floor down belonged to Borislav and his private army of security guards. And the level below that was Mick's lab of healing and human experimentation. Underneath Medical were the Offensive and Defensive Technology labs, also known as 'Guns and Germs'. Alice suspected they'd organized things that way in order to make it easier to ship the wounded employees from Guns and Germs up to Medical.

And then there was her own section, which so far in Alice's experience was all about rounding up stray unicorns and getting far too familiar with demons and rogue magicians. Her business cards read 'External Investigative and Enforcement Division', but not even Welly could explain exactly what that meant.

And with that, Alice realized she'd exhausted the limits of her personal knowledge about Head Office. Somewhere below her own floor she knew there was a research library and offices belonging to accountants, lawyers, and the custodial staff, but she'd never been allowed in any of them. There were rumours of an Odyssey jail somewhere in the lower levels, and Alice supposed something had to happen to criminal magicians who weren't accidentally tripped into magma pits. She was still embarrassed that her biggest contribution to saving the world had been a complete fluke.

In any event, she was quite sure she and Welly had already passed all these places, and every level of the enormous parking garage as well.

If parking was in the basement, she thought, the Mailroom must be in the sub-basement. Or possibly the sub-sub-sub-basement. Alice checked her lucky Hello Kitty watch. They'd been walking for at least fifteen minutes.

"Can we take a break?" she asked Welly, plaintively.

"Almost there!"

Alice sulked. If she'd known about today's trek down into the depths, she would have worn sensible shoes. But advance notification wasn't part of Odyssey's corporate culture.

What was part of the corporate culture, however, were numerous strict and occasionally baffling rules. Only wear Odyssey-approved underwear (no lucky Hello Kitty panties allowed). Sweep out your cubicle every New Year's Eve. No unauthorized pregnancies for the ladies or impregnations for the men. The newest version of the Odyssey Employee Handbook was forty-seven volumes long and would take the better part of a decade to read. So most sections opted to print up the rules specifically pertaining to them on helpful posters.

Alice knew they must be close to their destination when she spotted a poster detailing in pictograms how to correctly use the pneumatic mail tubes without losing important limbs in the process. The blood dripping from the arm stumps of the unlucky stick man in the poster was needlessly graphic, she thought.

Finally, Welly stopped at a landing and opened a door. Before Alice could breathe a sigh of relief, she spotted two of Borislav's security guards at the end of the short hall. Their creepy, all-black uniforms and menacing assault rifles were never a welcome sight. The huge metal doors behind the guards' desk looked like the entrance to a supervillain's lair.

As usual, one guard was male and the other was female. Male/Female pairings were the standard at Odyssey, especially in Security and Alice's own section. The practice was supposedly part of 'maintaining balance', although Alice felt it was old-fashioned to believe men and women were automatically opposites. But this belief was far from the only old-fashioned thing about Odyssey.

"Wellington and Alice from Section Five," Welly said, by way of introduction. "We're here to see Ken."

The male guard typed their names into the computer, while the female guard began waving a turquoise and orange metal wand over Welly's limbs. The embroidered white and black badge on her shoulder read: *Dura lex sed lex.* The law is hard but it is the law, Alice mentally translated and shuddered.

Now it was Alice's turn to be scanned, and the static charge caused by the wand made the hairs on the back of her neck stand up. A warm, tickling sensation followed the wand's path over her body, and Alice felt like she was being irradiated. If she was, that would explain the rule restricting pregnancies, she thought.

"She doesn't match her photo," the man said, stabbing a forefinger at the monitor. The woman gleefully slammed down the scanner and shrugged her rifle off her shoulder and into her hands.

"She's the only Alice in Section Five," Welly said, impatiently. "Alice Murphy, look it up."

"Really," Alice added, keeping her eyes on the armed woman. "This happens every time I dye my hair. Okay, I know what you're thinking, my hair doesn't look dyed, and you're right, this time I went for a new, sophisticated, I'm-over—"

Welly cut off her nervous babbling. "Just compare the scan results to her employee record."

The male guard did some quick typing and frowned darkly at the monitor. Alice felt sweat break out on her forehead, but didn't dare wipe it away.

"Confirmed," the man said, disappointment in his voice. "Alice, Section Five. Both of you are cleared for the Mailroom." The woman slung her rifle back over her shoulder with a sigh.

"Thank you," Welly said, coldly. "Is Ken in?"

The male guard rolled his eyes and smirked. "Not like Kenny would let us inside to check."

"Kenny?" Welly raised an eyebrow. Alice watched, curious. Almost everyone here went by their first name, but this nickname didn't sound complimentary.

The woman sniggered. "As in, 'You killed Kenny, you b—'"

"Save the explanation." Alice jumped in before the guard could swear. "*South Park* is way past Welly's time. He hasn't watched TV since the nineteen-seventies."

"And save the attitude," Welly said, glaring at both guards. "Now, let us in please." His tone was polite, but it was clearly an order.

"It's your funeral," the woman growled, as she hit a large, red button. Emergency lights began to flash down the length of the hall, and a loudspeaker crackled to life. "Warning, doors to Mailroom are open. Warning, doors to Mailroom are open."

Alice sidled closer to Welly. "Um, the rumours about the Mailroom, they're not true, are they?"

"Which rumours?"

Welly took out his Taser and walked through the doors as soon as they were open wide enough. Alice hesitated a moment and then followed, not wanting too much distance between them. She didn't like to think of herself as a damsel in distress, but Welly was supernaturally strong.

She blinked rapidly as her eyes slowly adjusted to the dimmer light inside the Mailroom. From the stories she'd heard, Alice had expected some sort of demonic hellscape. Instead, there were green plants hanging from the ceiling, a pleasant smell of vanilla in the air, and small fountains burbling at regular intervals along the walls. Alice was impressed by how healthy the hanging plants appeared to be, as she'd been under the impression nothing could grow inside Odyssey's Head Office.

She'd brought in an African violet once to brighten up her desk. By lunchtime, the plant had caught fire and exploded. She still occasionally found fragments of charred petals in her computer keyboard.

Ahead of them was a large poster declaring in bright orange letters, 'Odyssey International is an equal opportunities employer.' Another poster cautioned in red, 'Respect our employees. Severe penalties are enforced for hazing.' Yet another read... Alice frowned. "*Little House on the Prairie* TV Night?"

Welly shrugged and led her further into the Mailroom, toward a huge conveyer belt carrying boxes and envelopes of all sizes. The belt fed numerous smaller conveyors that were sorting the mail by size and sending it down chutes into bins marked with Odyssey's sailing ship logo. Eight staff members in turquoise and orange overalls were slowly moving the filled bins onto large steel carts. Once full, the carts were pushed through a beaded curtain into another room. Despite the machinery, the noise was muted, and a mellow ballad could be heard playing in the background.

"The music sounds vaguely familiar," Alice said.

Welly nodded. "Barry Manilow."

"Who's Barry—Oh my God!"

One of the staff had dropped a bin, and now turned in the direction of Welly and Alice to retrieve the scattered mail. He had no nose and his dislocated jaw hung open, wagging with every move. He moaned, and his eyes rolled back into his skull.

"Alice, don't blaspheme," Welly said, calmly.

"But that's—A zombie!" Alice gasped.

"Yes, but where are the human supervisors?" Welly asked, waving at them with his Taser. "Ken has no respect for standard safety precautions."

Alice stared at the zombie who was now joined by another. This one still had her nose, but had large bald patches on her very pale skull. Both zombies wore heavily padded overalls, which covered all of their bodies except for their heads. Even their hands were covered with thick, orange mitts, which were now interfering with their ability to pick up the mail.

"This can't be real," Alice said. "Zombies are figments of George A. Romero's twisted imagination. This is Odyssey's Mailroom, not the set of *Night of the Living Dead, Dawn of the Dead, Land of the Dead, Survival of the Dead,* or *Lap Dance of the Dead!*"

Welly spared her a concerned glance. "I don't think it's healthy to watch so many of that kind of film."

"And I don't think it's healthy to have zombies in the Mailroom!" Alice resisted the urge to dissolve into hysterics.

"If I had my way," Welly growled, "every last one of them would be chucked in the incinerator."

Another staff member entered the room. He wore similar overalls, but no mittens and he looked very much alive. He headed toward the overturned bin, but Welly flagged him down.

"We need to speak to Ken right now."

The young man looked over at the now four zombies trying to pick up mail with their padded mitts. "I'm not sure. He's very busy."

"Just tell Ken the acting head of Section Five is here. That'll light a fire under him."

"Uh, okay." He skittered away. He'd seemed very nervous, but Alice figured if she worked with a bunch of the undead she'd be jumpy too.

Now all eight zombies had stopped working and were milling around the overturned bin. Alice was surprised by how non-threatening they seemed. Instead of acting like bloodthirsty cannibals, they appeared to be just confused and more than a bit OCD.

"So you throw around your rank and Ken jumps to attention?" Alice asked, not taking her eyes off the zombies.

"Hardly. Ken hates me."

She gave him a knowing look. "What did you do?"

"It's nothing personal," Welly said. "Ken hates all Enhanced Agents. Don't worry, he isn't as unreasonable when it comes to Sensitives such as yourself."

"I wasn't worried, but you still haven't told me why Ken hates Enhanced Agents."

"Because Enhanced Agents treat my Mailroom like a twenty-four-hour practical joke shop," a tall, thin man announced. His blond hair was thin and straggly, but was more than made up for by his thick, drooping moustache. In his cowboy boots, faded blue jeans, and unbuttoned, embroidered denim shirt, he looked like a very unhappy rhinestone cowboy.

"Every month," Ken continued, in an irate tone, "Enhanced Agents sneak in and steal fingers and ears to stick in each other's coffee. Last December, twelve zombies were kidnapped and decorated as Christmas trees."

Welly raised his free hand to his mouth. Alice would have suspected he was hiding a smile, if she didn't know him better. Welly rarely smiled for any reason and certainly wouldn't at rule-breaking.

The Twelve Days of Corpsified Christmas were before Alice came to Odyssey's Head Office, but she was all too familiar with Enhanced Agent hijinks. Not only were Enhanced Agents stronger, faster, and longer-lived than the average human, they had triple the testosterone. And that included the women, Alice thought, remembering how the adorably petite Enhanced Agent Lei had tried to strangle the six-foot-plus Welly after he'd changed her vacation schedule.

"And let's not forget the year before," Ken growled, "when several zombies were decapitated and their heads used as Halloween jack-o-lanterns!"

Alice took a deep breath and tried to send out calming energy. Her trainer on Survival Island had referred to this as the Kumbaya approach to conflict management. A big part of her job as a Sensitive was keeping all the testosterone-fuelled squabbling under control.

"I had nothing to do with that incident," Welly said. "And if you bothered to remember, I exiled both Frankel and Washington to the branch office in Outer Mongolia."

Kumbaya, my Lord, Kumbaya.

"Under protest, as I do remember," Ken shot back. "And just

like all Enhanced Agents, you kill zombies every chance you get!"

Ooooh Looord, Kumbaya.

"Of course I kill zombies. Anyone with a scrap of common sense would kill zombies, instead of dressing them up and treating them like people!"

"Enough!" Alice shouted, stepping between them. "You're both giving me a headache and—Eep!"

"What is it?" Welly asked, raising his Taser.

She pointed at the floor. A finger was lying there, a metre away from where they were standing.

"Damn it," Ken cursed, and scooped up the finger. "Scott, are they all wearing their safety mitts? How many times do I have to tell you..."

As Ken stormed over to the unfortunate Scott, Alice let out a sigh. She'd learned a lot about picking up on other people's thoughts and feelings, but so far all her attempts to manipulate their emotions had been a complete letdown.

Alice looked at Welly, who was fingering his Taser with an unsettling gleam in his eyes. "Can you please behave like you're civilized?" she said.

"I am civilized," Welly said, offended.

Ken returned, his face red. "Now, take your damn—"

"You really shouldn't use that word," Welly interrupted. Before he could launch into his all-too-familiar lecture on the evils of swearing, Alice intervened.

"So Ken, what inspired you to hire zombies for the Mailroom?"

Both men looked taken aback by her enthusiastic question, but Ken recovered first. "Zombies suffer from diminished mental capacity, but that doesn't mean they can't lead full, productive lives." He shot a nasty look at Welly.

"But why sorting mail?" Alice asked, forcing Ken's attention away from her partner.

"Unfortunately, only a few zombies can handle complex tasks. However, this Mailroom is highly automated, with computerized scanning and sorting, so the zombie mail clerks just handle the heavy lifting and filing. Of course, I also encourage them to develop hobbies and other interests, but nothing too stimulating. Overstimulating a zombie is never a good idea, I'm sure you'd agree."

There were now three human staff members in the room, and they'd managed to get all but one of the zombies back to work. The last zombie had walked into a corner and apparently couldn't turn around. He was chewing on a Boston fern and its macramé holder. Alice wondered if that qualified as a zombie hobby.

Ken needed no further encouragement to continue lecturing Alice and Welly. "Many of the zombies who work here are very fond of Laura Ingalls Wilder's *Little House* series. Of course, most of them can't see well enough to read anymore, but they really enjoy the series on our two-hundred-inch plasma TV." Ken pointed to Alice's yellow dress. "Zombies really like bright colours too, but be warned they don't always understand the concept of personal space, especially if overstimulated."

Alice swore to herself she'd wear black if she ever returned to the Mailroom. However, she decided to say something positive, to keep Ken on his even keel. Welly appeared willing to let her take charge for the moment, and she was beginning to feel like a real Sensitive, building consensus and promoting harmony between people. This was why Odyssey had recruited her from her old job as a telephone psychic. She always knew exactly the right thing to say.

"Your zombies are so laid-back. They're not at all what I imagined the living dead would be like," Alice told him. She watched as a very large woman disentangled the plant-chewing zombie from the macramé hanger. "I keep expecting them to start moaning. Brains, brains, brrraains!"

"Stop that!" Ken said, sharply.

"Why—" Alice began, but then noticed the zombie closest to them had started repeating "brains" over and over again. Soon, all of them were droning the same word, and the effect was more than a little disconcerting. Her confidence vanishing as quickly as it had arrived, Alice backed up, closer to Welly. To be honest, she hadn't been a very good telephone psychic.

Ken went over to them and started a new mantra, chanting, "Peace, peace, peace."

One after the other the zombies slowly followed his lead, abandoning "brains" for "peace". Now it was as if the Mailroom had been taken over by zombie hippies. Alice heard Welly make a disgusted sound under his breath

Not for the first time, Alice wished she'd majored in science or business instead of English and classical literature. People with sensible university degrees didn't work for Odyssey. They had normal jobs, sane bosses, and living co-workers.

Ken came back and fixed her with a disapproving glare. "Zombies are very prone to peer pressure, so you have to be careful what you say or do around them. Of course, I'd expect negative cultural stereotyping from an Enhanced Agent, but I really hoped for better from a Sensitive."

"You call them zombies," Alice countered, stung. "So you're asking for stereotyping."

Ken sighed. "We're trying to reclaim the word 'zombie' as a positive label, but it's been an uphill battle. I tried alternatives like 'life-impaired' and 'differently living', but they just led people to assume zombies are dead."

Alice mouthed the word 'assume' to Welly. He just gave her a smug 'I told you he was a raving loon' look in return. His hand was flexing on his Taser.

"'People of decomposition' and 'virally abled' were more accurate labels, but they never caught on," Ken continued, sadly, "giving me little choice but to help my staff reclaim their proud heritage as zombies."

"And you'll have more joining this misguided movement of yours," Welly broke in impatiently. "There's a reliable report of a Stage Two zombie outbreak in Wales. I'm going to need you in the North Atlantic Briefing Room in an hour."

Before either Ken or Alice could respond to this announcement, an alarm sounded in the next room.

"What's happening?" Alice asked.

"A.A.'s mailed another bomb to Odyssey," Ken growled, stomping off.

Welly followed Ken, and Alice tagged along after him. "Alcoholics Anonymous is bombing Odyssey? What did we ever do to them?" she asked.

In the next room, a metre-high beige cabinet was emitting the klaxon sound. Alice barely heard Welly's response, "A.A., in this case, 'Agitators for Antichrists'."

"Hang on, antichrists?" she asked, but if Welly heard her, he gave no sign. He was on high alert, checking exits, while simultaneously keeping an eye on the zombies in the room behind them.

Ken was consulting the computer display on top of the cabinet. "It's a confirmation, definitely an explosive!" he shouted at Scott, who looked like he was going to faint.

Alice was feeling pretty tense herself, but she was less worried about the bomb than she was about the agitated zombies who were milling about the room. Their numbers had grown too. Human staff were trying to herd the zombies away, but they kept coming back to gape at the howling cabinet.

A zombie missing both of his ears lurched toward her, and she jumped back with a frightened squeak. Welly instantly levelled his Taser and fired.

The earless zombie went down, and two others close by also fell to the floor and began to jerk spasmodically. The remaining zombies stampeded in multiple directions, ignoring the shouting human staff.

As Welly disconnected the used Taser cartridge, Ken abandoned the bomb detector and elbowed his way through the zombies. He swung at the Taser in Welly's hand with a package of mail. "Get out, you barbarian! Get out, get out!"

"Don't forget, the North Atlantic Briefing Room. Not the South Atlantic, the North." Welly attached a new cartridge to his Taser.

Enraged, Ken drove Alice and Welly out into the main room and toward the metal doors. "If I ever see you anywhere near my Mailroom, I'll take your Taser and—"

"The meeting's in one hour!" Welly shouted back.

"I'll be there, but not for you! I won't let you near those poor Welsh zombies!" Ken pounded a large red button, and the metal doors slowly opened, adding to the cacophony of sound and light.

Welly strode out through the doors. Alice heard a dull whump behind her, and a shockwave sent her stumbling after Welly into the hall.

"Have a nice visit?" the female guard asked.

Alice ignored the guards' laughter and focused on her relief at getting away from exploding mail and rampaging zombies. She was also grateful to be away from all those little fountains. The sound of trickling water made her want to pee.

Alice caught up with Welly on the stairwell and was glad his Taser was out of sight. "There are zombies in Wales?" she asked.

He nodded. "And it's vital we get them cleared out of there before the World Bog Snorkelling Championships next week."

"The what?"

2

Ken Introduces a Friend

Every mission officially began with a formal briefing. Alice wasn't sure if this was an Odyssey rule, but it was definitely the way Welly liked to run things.

Sometimes he'd even conduct budget analyses, feasibility studies, and other old-fashioned corporate rituals, but Alice hoped that zombies gone wild in Wales would merit a speedier response. Entirely too much of her career at Odyssey so far had been spent helping Welly do paperwork.

Then again, Alice thought, when things did get exciting, it was usually because someone was trying to kill her. Alice looked forward to the day when she'd achieve a happy medium at Odyssey between dying of boredom and dying at the hands of a sex-crazed slime demon.

Fortunately, the North Atlantic Briefing Room was more interesting than the other beige, boring conference rooms they'd used before. Like the rest, it was plastered with posters instructing employees to never accrue overtime and to always burn their finger and toenail clippings. However, the space had been recently redecorated, with new turquoise chairs around an orange conference table and several framed photographs on the walls.

Welly was ignoring her, so Alice got out of her chair and indulged her curiosity. Most of the photos were of disaster zones, like the Mount St. Helens volcano in Washington and the Tunguska explosion in Siberia. If the small engraved plaques beneath the frames were to be believed, both of these events were caused by irresponsible magicians later arrested by Odyssey.

Alice paused at one photo depicting a grinning man standing with his arm around the shoulders of a grey-skinned alien. The agent was gesturing thumbs up, and behind him Alice could see a sign that read 'Area 51'. Alice peered at the plaque under the picture hoping for an explanation, but all it said was, 'Enhanced Agent Tom Endicott, b. 1962, d. 2010*'. Puzzled by the asterisk, Alice searched until she found a tiny upside-down notation on the plaque, '*Recycled 2011'.

"Um, Welly, why are we recycling dead agents? And how could you recycle—?"

"No! Absolutely not!"

Startled, Alice turned around, but Welly wasn't shouting at her. Ken had arrived and was standing just inside the room with arms crossed and thunderclouds in his expression. But he wasn't the cause of Welly's outburst either.

Teetering in the doorway was an ancient, desiccated zombie. If it hadn't been wearing the same turquoise and orange padded jumpsuit as the zombies in the Odyssey's Mailroom, Alice would have thought there was an unwrapped mummy on the loose.

"You are not bringing that thing to this meeting," Welly snapped at Ken.

"Dave isn't a thing," Ken said. "He's the head of Mailroom Recruitment and has every right to be here."

"What's this?" a new voice asked from the hallway outside. "A traffic jam in the doorway?"

"Hi Mick!" Alice called out.

A hand waved at her from behind Ken and Dave. "So near and yet so far, my precious platypus," the head of Odyssey's Medical Section opined. "Divided by cruel prejudice."

"Zombies attending meetings is strictly against Odyssey's rules," Welly informed Ken.

"There's no such rule," Ken snapped. "If there was, there'd be a poster about it in every meeting room."

"He has a point—" Alice began.

"Right there!" Welly pointed at a poster at the far end of the room.

'Humans only at Odyssey meetings,' Alice read. 'Sole exception: Annual board of directors' meeting.' She frowned. Banning zombies from meetings didn't explain why a Minotaur with a bad case of mange was eating the stick figure on the poster.

Ken's face was turning red. "That rule has nothing to do with zombies. Dave's as human as you are and just as much of a man."

Dave's jaw dropped a little, giving Alice the distinct impression he was smiling.

Alice walked over to where Welly was seated and brought out her fortune-cookie arsenal, "A wise man knows that life is too short to waste… "

Dave suddenly lurched forward out of the doorway and careened into Ken.

"Hey, no shoving!" Ken protested, stumbling further into the room.

Dave made an agitated sound, and Ken immediately turned around, took hold of Dave's mitts, and made soothing noises at him.

"Life isn't short," Mick said, the author of all this chaos. "However, it is too much fun to waste standing in hallways."

As always when Mick entered a room, Alice felt like everyone else around him faded into monochrome. He was skinny and long-limbed, and his bright red dreadlocks commanded attention. He was also black, a gorgeous blue-black without a hint of brown. Alice tried not to stare, embarrassed that she found his skin colour so fascinating. She often wondered where Mick really came from, for while he claimed Australia was his home, he didn't have an Australian accent. Or any kind of accent at all, as far as Alice could tell.

Mick's choice in clothing provided no hint of his origins either. Today, he was wearing a pristine white lab coat over a bright Hawaiian print shirt and matching shorts. He had a neon orange messenger bag slung over one shoulder. Barefooted, he looked like a mad scientist on an island vacation.

"You painted your toenails turquoise. They look great!" Alice said.

Mick smiled broadly. "And you cut your hair and went back to your natural colour. It's definitely a new, sophisticated, I'm-over-twenty-five-now look."

Welly cleared his throat. "Ken, remove the zombie so we can start the meeting."

Ken took a deep breath, puffing out his chest. "If Dave's not welcome, you can count me out too."

Alice could feel the tension build between the two men, both waiting for the other to back down. She sensed that Ken was concerned about the Welsh zombies, but he also figured he had Welly over a barrel. Ken's thoughts seemed rational, except for his conviction that Dave was not only human, but an indispensable Odyssey employee as well.

Mick grinned. "Alice, I bet you five dollars these two resort to fisticuffs before this mission is over." He dropped his messenger bag on the table, and its contents clattered loudly. "Five Australian dollars. I don't have any Canadian currency on me."

"No bet," Alice said, tightly. If she didn't calm Welly and Ken down right now, they'd be throwing punches before the mission even began.

C'mon guys, Kumbaya? For me?

"By all means, send a replacement," Welly told Ken. "As long as it's someone who has a pulse and won't waste our time by rabbiting on about zombie rights."

"It's a waste of time talking to someone as close-minded as you," Ken shot back.

Welly stood up abruptly, pushing his chair back from the conference table. Alice had jumped out of the way just in time. "Better close-minded," Welly growled, "than a zombie-huggi — "

"Kumbaya, kumbaya, kumbaya!" Alice shouted.

Both men stared at her, stunned into silence. Dave leaned against Ken and whimpered. Mick blew her a kiss.

"I mean, enough with the fighting," Alice said. "Or I'll leave you both behind — whoa." She swayed on her feet.

"Are you all right?" Welly asked, sounding concerned.

"Just a weird head rush," Alice said.

Welly was immediately beside her, guiding her into a chair. "I'm not an invalid," she complained, but part of her liked the attention.

Welly sat down beside her. He looked at Ken, then Dave, then sighed. "I call this meeting to order." From the resignation in his voice, it was clear he'd decided to give in on the issue of Dave, at least temporarily.

To his credit, Ken didn't gloat over his victory. He pulled out a chair across from Alice and steered Dave into it.

As Ken pushed the chair back in, Dave tipped forward and his face hit the table with a thud.

"Hey, hey, hey!" Mick protested. "Don't damage that nose." He placed a fat, white candle in the middle of the table.

Ken sat Dave back up. "Are you okay, pal?"

Dave didn't appear perturbed. His eyes stared at nothing in particular and his nose twitched.

Welly cleared his throat and began reading from a computer

tablet balanced on top of a stack of yellowing files and papers.

"Right, let's begin. Friday June twenty-eighth; ten-hundred forty-two hours Head Office time; meeting to address a potential Stage Two Zombie Outbreak in Wales. Meeting chaired by myself, Wellington, acting head of Section Five. Also present, Alice, Sensitive from Section Five, Ken from the Mailroom, and his pet zombie named Dave."

"Hey!" Ken protested, but was ignored.

"Also present, Mick, head of Section Three, until Odyssey sees fit to hire a real doctor. Mick, will you please sit down!"

"Don't get your knickers in a twist." Mick rummaged around in his bag, and pulled out a small yellow box, opened it, and took a deep sniff. The lettering on the box, over a picture of stacked biscuits, proclaimed the contents to be cornmeal. "A very good year," Mick commented.

Alice's eyes kept straying back to Dave. There was something not quite right about him, and not just because he was a walking corpse. Keeping her gaze on him, she reached across the table and grabbed her laptop, Giles the Fourth. Alice felt more secure behind the screen, even though it wouldn't provide much protection if Dave got bitey. Then again, Dave's jaw looked like it might fall off at any moment. Alice took a deep breath and tried to relax.

"We'll forgo the standard pre-mission tarot reading, as Alice still hasn't replaced the deck she lost in Italy." Welly gave her a pointed look.

"I'm on top of it," Alice lied. As if any deck could replace her lucky Hello Kitty tarot cards, she thought.

"Now, to the first and only item on the agenda," Welly continued. "There's a report of a possible zombie sighting from... Le-le-wry-tid Wells in Wales."

Mick laughed. "What town was that again?"

Welly gave him a dirty look. "It's a Welsh town, so naturally it has more consonants than any sane man can pronounce. It's spelt

L-l-a-n-w-r-t-y-d W-e-l-l-s."

"Llanwrtyd Wells?" Ken asked, making the name sound more or less as it was spelled.

"Close enough," Welly said, ignoring Mick's snicker. "Suffice to say, it's the smallest town in Wales. Reputedly the smallest town in Great Britain as well, with a population of just over six hundred." He put the tablet aside and tapped the stack of files in front of him.

"Wales," Mick said. "I think Just Sanji won the office pool for where the next zombie outbreak would occur." A bottle of alcohol, several plastic cups, and a box of cigars had joined the box of cornmeal on the conference table.

"If I ever find out who runs those travesties," Ken jabbed a forefinger at Mick, "dismissal from Odyssey will be the least of their problems."

Alice tuned out the bickering and returned her attention to Dave. Sparse strands of dark curly hair stuck up from his leathery scalp. Two blue eyes had sunk most of the way into his skull, and his lips were pulled back into a permanent grin. Dave's nose, on the other hand, was pink and completely mobile. More mobile than a normal nose, Alice thought, as the tip of Dave's nose suddenly lifted straight up by itself.

"Do you like it?" Mick asked, glancing over at Alice. "I'm very proud of that nose." He reached into his lab coat pocket and pulled out a lighter. Sparking it, he lit the white candle.

"Mick," Welly said, in a tone of great forbearance. "What are you doing?"

"You remember that nose, don't you?" Mick asked Welly. "I believe you were quite familiar with the original owner." He picked up the box of cornmeal and poured its contents out in front of the burning candle.

"Tom Endicott was a good man and a good Agent." To Alice, it sounded as if Welly was speaking through clenched teeth. "And

I don't appreciate being reminded that his remains were used in one of your Frankenstein experiments."

Oh no, Alice thought, appalled. Tom Endicott was the name of the Agent in the Area 51 photo.

"Oh pish posh," Mick said. "Tommy wasn't going to be using his nose again after the bad day he'd had." He began running his right index finger through the cornmeal, creating thin, straight lines.

"Wait a minute," Alice said. "You actually took someone's nose and stuck it onto a zombie's face? Oh my God, you did! You recycled Tom!" She clapped both hands over her own nose.

"Alice, stop calling on deities," Welly said. "Especially during staff meetings."

"Tracking is Dave's passion," Ken said. "When his nose fell off, he became very depressed. That donor nose gave him a whole new lease on life."

Dave groaned and flailed a little as he started to tip sideways. Ken straightened him. "I keep telling Maintenance to buy chairs with safety harnesses. They never listen!"

Mick had finished drawing a square in the cornmeal, and was now working on a cross design in the centre. "Modern zombie research is very exciting," he said to Alice. "And it helps that all of you have signed your bodies and souls over to Odyssey in perpetuity."

Alice found herself wishing, not for the first time, that she'd read the entire Odyssey employment contract before signing it. Or any of it, really. Sure, they'd upgraded her psychic abilities, which was very nice, but if she'd known beforehand the process involved brain surgery, she would have refused. Odyssey had also installed a tracking device without telling her where it was in her body. Alice wondered if someday her picture would be up on a wall, with the notation 'recycled' after her date of death.

"Know what?" Welly said to no one in particular. "I'm going

ahead and holding this meeting all by myself." He picked up a file folder from the stack in front of him and opened it. "Here we have a map of Llanwrtyd Wells. Pity it was printed in the eighteen-eighties. But those sorts of misunderstandings are bound to happen when your research section is run by a mad medieval monk."

Mick spread his hands over the candle, and the flame appeared to grow brighter. "Baron La Croix, standing at the crossroads between life and death," he said. "We most humbly request your assistance in our current endeavour. Namely, finding lots of zombies, the fresher the better."

Baron La Croix? Alice wondered. Mick changed deities the way other people changed their sheets. She vaguely recalled the previous month's deity-du-jour had been some sort of sexy Native American Earth Goddess. Mick had made Alice sit through a sweat lodge ceremony before he would certify her as physically fit.

"Her name's Nokomis," Mick said. "And you're right, she's quite the babe."

"Mick, eavesdropping is rude!" Alice cried out, offended. She was supposed to be the official team psychic, not him.

"This is ludicrous," Welly said.

"Pleased to hear it," Mick said. "The Baron is renowned for his quirky sense of humour." Opening up the wooden box on the table, he asked, "Cigar, anyone?"

Alice shook her head. Few things in this world smelled more disgusting to her than cigars. Ken's zombies, on the other hand... Alice sniffed the air, grateful she still had her own nose. No, she hadn't imagined it earlier. Ken's zombies all smelled like vanilla.

"I don't want Dave exposed to anything that might further compromise his breathing," Ken said.

"He doesn't breathe," Welly said. "He's a zombie."

"Of course he breathes," Ken said. "He just breathes very slowly and shallowly."

— 25 —

Alice stared at Dave, trying to see some sign he was actually breathing. Other than the late Tom's extra-mobile nose trying to fold itself over to one side, she didn't see anything. Concentrating harder, she tried to pick up any thoughts or emotions from Dave, but the surface scan revealed nothing.

Just to be sure, Alice shifted her to focus onto Ken and immediately picked up on his fondness for Dave, who he thought of as a real, live person. It was sad, she thought, that Ken wasn't able to accept the fact that his zombies weren't human anymore.

Mick put the cigars back in his bag and opened up the amber bottle. "Rum, anyone?" He licked his lips in anticipation, his shockingly bright blue tongue briefly visible.

"A little early for me," Alice said. Although, she thought, since Head Office was located somewhere between dimensions of time and space, waiting for the sun to be over the yardarm was pointless. "Changed my mind. Yes, please."

Ken also took a cup. Dave's nose twitched, and he made what sounded like a disapproving moan. While Ken whispered something into the space where Dave's left ear should have been, Mick held a rum-filled cup out to Welly.

Welly grumpily waved off Mick's offer of a drink. "Brother Placidus also gave us a brief report on the history of Llànwrtyd Wells." Welly opened a dusty folder and read aloud, "In seventeen thirty-two, whilst strolling through the Welsh wilderness, the scurvy-riddled vicar of Llanwrtyd came upon a foul-smelling spring. Observing the spring, he saw an extraordinarily healthy frog leap out. Inspired, he promptly drank of the waters of the spring and was cured of his scurvy."

"Wow," Alice said, after a sip of rum. "That vicar must have been seriously desperate if he was wandering around the countryside drinking out of stinky springs. It's like getting yourself irradiated in the hopes you'll end up with superpowers instead of cancer." She placed her cup out of the way and double clicked the magical incantation on her computer's desktop that allowed her laptop to access the Internet interdimensionally. Moments later, the Odyssey International browser page popped up. "What did you say the name of the town was?"

"Ll-lan — Llanwrtyd Wells," Welly said.

"Ll... What?"

He cleared his throat. "Llanwrtyd Wells."

Alice pushed her laptop across the table to him. "Just type it into the search bar. I'll see what I can find on Ll-lan... welly Wells."

As Welly typed, he said, "Getting back on track, there's a probable Stage Two Zombie Outbreak in Wales. I'm rating this a Rough Weather Emergency." He returned the laptop to Alice.

"Rough Weather?" Ken asked. "Rumours of zombies don't usually rate more than Turbulent."

Alice continued to search online, as she didn't care what the emergency level was so long as it was below Stormy. Odyssey had thirteen different levels, all nautically themed and difficult to tell apart. All Alice bothered learning was that the metaphorical seas were never calmer than Choppy, which meant the usual stray unicorns and teens making magical mischief, while anything Stormy and above meant death and destruction.

"The report was from a very reliable local source," Welly said. "I tried to get the Cardiff branch office to confirm the sightings, but once again they're ignoring Head Office."

"Hey," Alice interrupted. "Bog snorkelling is real!"

"Yes, as I told you the World Bog Snorkelling Championships are next week, July sixth and seventh to be precise, which is why we need to return to business."

"It's hilarious," Alice added. "People put on snorkels and costumes, and then really try to swim the fastest in bog water. I bet they stink for days."

Mick was now leaning back in a chair, an unlit cigar in one

hand and a plastic cup of rum in the other. "The town also hosts a fantastic Saturnalia Beer Festival every year. Mustn't be missed. The Man versus Horse Marathon is a lot of fun too, and the horse doesn't always win."

"This is the coolest town ever," Alice said, clicking on more links. "They've combined running and mountain biking with bog snorkelling to create a triathlon. Plus they've merged mountain biking and bar hopping in an event called the Saturnalia Wobble. I bet they're more than wobbling before they're done."

"Most appreciated if you could find something actually useful for our assignment," Welly said, grumpily.

"Because learning about scurvy-curing springs was so—Check it out, I found a train schedule."

"A rail schedule?" Welly sat up.

"Looks like La-la-welly Wells has its own stop on something called the Heart of Wales line." Alice blinked at the screen. All these double-el Welsh names looked the same, but the 'Wells' was clear enough.

"Let me see that." Welly pulled her laptop away from her. "Swansea. This rail line goes to Swansea. If this outbreak gets out of hand, the zombie plague could infect half of Wales inside a week."

"Plague is a very pejorative word," Ken said.

Welly stood up. "Everyone get your gear together. We're leaving now." He turned toward Ken. "Let me make this perfectly clear. You will not, under any circumstances, bring a zombie along on this mission."

"I never said I would," Ken said.

Dave moaned.

*

Life would be easier, Alice thought as she followed Welly down yet another flight of stairs, if she had a job that didn't require her to keep an emergency overnight bag in her desk. Travelling around the world for work had sounded fantastic when Alice had joined Odyssey. But saving the world from magical mayhem meant there was never anytime for shopping, sightseeing, or watching gorgeous sunsets on romantic beaches. Plus potential boyfriends didn't appreciate you ditching them at the last-minute and refused to believe that you really did have to stop someone from cracking open the earth's crust in Lichtenstein of all places.

Tired of these depressing thoughts, Alice asked Welly, "Shouldn't we wait for Mick and Ken?"

"Thankfully, we won't have to travel with that pair," Welly said, with feeling. "As heads of their respective sections, they need to make preparations for their absence, so they'll meet us there."

Alice hoped Ken wouldn't be leaving the easily terrified Scott in charge of the zombies. No one would get any mail for a week. Mick's Medical section, on the other hand, would operate far smoother without him, and his long-suffering staff would probably throw a party the minute their boss left headquarters. "You didn't leave Lei in charge of our section again, did you?"

"Not to worry. I told her that if she killed any of the support staff this time, accidentally or otherwise, I'd have her transferred to Security."

Lei was an Enhanced Agent as scary as she was tiny. "Good," Alice said. "I really miss Brad. He made the best coffee."

"Did you remember to pick up a new Oddfone?" Welly asked, changing the subject.

"Lady Jane wouldn't give me one. She said I'd lose my head if it wasn't attached, and until she figured out how to surgically implant the Oddfone, I'd have to be content with squandering regular cell phones."

Lady Jane looked like a sweet old lady, but she ruled Guns and Germs with an acid tongue and an iron fist. Her mechanical hand had flattened many an unwary staff member who'd been careless with Odyssey equipment. Alice, fortunately, always knew when to duck, but being psychic hadn't protected her from Lady Jane's industrial-strength sarcasm.

"It's completely unfair," Alice complained. "If you hadn't been strung up by the bad guy over a lava pit, I wouldn't have dropped my Oddfone into the magma."

"Do you want me to talk to her on your behalf?" Welly asked.

"No thanks. I don't want to be lectured again about her precious waterproof, shockproof, but alas, not volcano- or idiot-proof Odyssey phones. From now on, it's your job to call for help."

"Never work," Welly said, in a serious tone of voice. "I lack both your decibel range and flare for the dramatic."

He was teasing her and she knew it. She considered punching him, but she'd only end up bruising her knuckles. Enhanced Agents were dense in more ways than one, she thought.

Alice snickered to herself, and Welly glanced at her suspiciously over his shoulder.

"What?" she asked, innocently.

Welly shook his head. "Have you been keeping up with your mental exercises?"

Alice made a face. "I'm no good at that touchy feely shi—um, sherbet."

"An important part of your role as a Sensitive—"

Alice interrupted him. "And I still think Sensitive's a dumb name. Hi, I'm Alice and I'm Sahn-si-teev. What the heck is wrong with psychic?"

"—is the ability to positively influence the emotions of people we come in contact with during the course of our assignments."

"I'll just tell them the love of their life is closer than they think, and it'll make them so happy they'll do anything we want." At least, Alice thought, they weren't trekking down to the Mailroom again. Although the fact that the parking lot was above the Mailroom was yet another bit of Odyssey weirdness.

"What if you have to convince someone not to kill me?" Welly asked.

"I hope your will is up to date," Alice said. "How many floors does Head Office have?"

"That depends."

"Depends?" Alice asked. "On what?"

Welly shrugged. "It's complicated."

She should have guessed. Everything about Odyssey's Head Office was too complicated to completely comprehend. If you didn't know exactly where a section was, you'd never find it. All of the outside windows showed different views and were not to be opened under any circumstances. And the biggest puzzle was how time worked inside of Head Office. People entered from multiple time zones, and yet everyone arrived simultaneously at nine in the morning Head Office Time. Furthermore, it didn't matter if you chose the New York exit or the branch office in New Delhi; when you left Head Office at five in the afternoon here, it would also be five p.m. there.

Alice knew trying to understand these mysteries was a quick route to a migraine, so she avoided thinking about them. Besides, the one time she'd suggested to Welly that they could travel a few hours back in time by entering through Ottawa's door and immediately leaving through the Vancouver exit, he'd demanded she swear an oath to never, ever try it. Given that Welly was not a man who scared easily, she'd assumed the consequences of messing around with time were somewhat dire.

Welly stopped in front of a steel door marked 'W'. "We're here," he said, and pulled it open. Alice found herself stepping into familiar surroundings. Concrete pillars lined the parking spaces, and asphalt ramps spiralled away on either side of the lot.

Welly headed straight for his car without hesitation. Welly always knew exactly where he was going no matter where they were. Maybe, thought Alice, an infallible sense of direction was part of being an Enhanced Agent. She wasn't jealous, even though she sometimes had problems keeping left and right straight.

In her opinion, Welly's enhancements were not enough to make up for the fact he was constantly being shot at, perforated, and burnt to a crisp. And yet some six decades ago, Welly had actually volunteered to join Odyssey, straight out of the British Army. No one had tricked him into signing Odyssey's employee contract unread while he was hypothermic in the hospital, recovering from having nearly been swept over Niagara Falls. No, that had been Alice's introduction to Odyssey's recruitment tactics instead.

Knowing Welly, he'd read every last one of the papers they'd asked him to sign, including the small print about never being able to quit and the possibility of having your nose recycled. And then for some insane reason, he had gone ahead and signed them.

"There she is," Welly said. He patted the silver Aston Martin's hood with affection. "How are the garage gnomes treating you?"

Alice never knew when to believe anything Welly said. His enhancements also made it hard for her to pick up on his thoughts, and he had a very dry sense of humour. Garage gnomes, she thought, sounded even less likely than zombies in the Mailroom.

On the plus side, Alice thought, as she climbed into the passenger's side, driving anywhere in Welly's car was an almost sinful pleasure. He'd spared no expense, from the surround sound system to the red leather bucket seats.

"I missed you, beautiful," Welly said.

Alice missed the days when he'd been too self-conscious to talk to his car in her presence.

"The magic's gone," she said.

"What?" Welly asked, sounding concerned.

"Never mind."

Welly started the car, and within a few minutes, they were driving around a complicated series of interlocking spirals which eventually resolved into a succession of helpful signs labelled

'Cardiff, Exit 42'. Alice restrained herself from pointing out that forty-two was the answer to life, the universe, and everything. They'd run across quite a few forty-twos in their last assignment, and Welly had gotten progressively grumpier each time she'd brought it up.

Welly pulled up beside a small booth. There was a turquoise-striped, orange-spotted wooden bar blocking the road. Alice presumed the exit to Wales was on the other side, but she couldn't see anything past the barricade except darkness.

"Delta!" Welly cursed.

It only took Alice a few seconds to translate. Delta, letter D, damn. Welly was fluent in NATO phonetic alphabet swearing. She peeked past him at the attendant's booth. It was empty with a piece of lined notebook paper taped to the window.

The handwritten note read, 'Gone out. May return. May not.'

"Foxtrotting Cardiff!" Welly pulled his Oddfone out of his jacket pocket. "Lilith, patch me through to Mick, will you?"

The f-word, Alice thought. My goodness, he's testy today.

"Mick," Welly growled into his Oddfone. "The Cardiff exit is down."

Alice heard an indistinct reply on the other end.

"Right," Welly said. "Couldn't see fit to inform me, could you?"

Another pause.

"Because that would take all the joy out of existence. Got it." Welly sighed. "We'll head for London instead... No, we're absolutely not taking the Belfast exit. I don't care, we're taking the shorter route from London to Cardiff. And Mick, find some shoes and wear them. Both you and Ken will meet us at the Red Lion, Parliament Street, in an hour. We need to discuss our cover identities. Lilith, please inform Ken of the change in plans promptly. And remember, promptly means in the next five minutes, not whenever you feel like it during the next three weeks." He hung up.

"What's wrong with Belfast?" Alice asked. "I'll have you know some of my relatives came from there."

"Before sensibly moving to Canada."

Alice rolled her eyes. There was no reasoning with Welly when he was in a mood. She looked again at the flimsy bar separating them from Wales. "Why don't we just lift it up and drive through?"

Welly gave her a horrified look. "Are you mad?"

"What?" Alice asked. "Would we end up in another dimension? Or travel back in time?"

"Neither," Welly said. "You'd simply be dead."

"What about you?" Alice asked. She'd seen firsthand just how hard Enhanced Agents were to kill.

"I'd rather not think about it," Welly said, backing his car away from the Cardiff exit. "Ever been to London?"

3

Mr. Snuggles is Not Pleased

"Alice, step lively!"

Alice stopped admiring herself in the reflection of a London shop window and picked up her pace, trotting after Welly. Except, she told herself, no one ever trotted in brand new, black leather Mock Martens boots. All the style of Doc Martens at half the price.

For once, Alice didn't care that she had to take two steps for every one of Welly's lengthy strides. In these boots, she was strutting her stuff. Sexy, dangerous, an Odyssey International Girl of Mystery...

Someone grabbed Alice's arm and brought her to a sudden stop, nose almost touching a shiny red phone booth.

"For the last time, watch where you're walking," Welly said, releasing her. "If you keep admiring yourself in shop windows, you'll end up with a flattened nose."

Alice stared at the phone booth. "Do people still use these? Doesn't everyone have cell phones now?" She peered through the glass at the giant, retro phone inside.

"The tourists would be heartbroken if we didn't keep a few." Welly took hold of Alice's shoulders and moved her out of the way just as a plump woman in walking shorts yanked open the door of the phone booth.

As Alice followed Welly down the street, she could hear the woman saying to her husband, "Oh, Ralph! You have to take a picture of me inside this darling phone booth!"

"This isn't a sight-seeing tour," Welly reminded Alice. "Or a fashion show."

"There's no need for sarcasm," Alice said to Welly. "Since I'm not going to be colouring my hair anymore, I have to find another way to express my individuality."

In truth, Alice had always dreamed of owning a pair of Doc Martens. Now her and Welly's cover identities as Mick's bodyguards had finally provided the perfect excuse to buy a pair of knock-offs. Alice couldn't understand why anyone would pay full price when the Mock Martens in the discount store looked practically identical.

"Never noticed you having difficulty expressing your individuality," Welly said, dryly.

"That's because you've made a fetish out of conformity."

Welly had refused to abandon his awful unicorn-hide shoes or his boring, grey three-piece suit. But his stubbornness hadn't stopped Alice from making him take her shopping after a loud argument over the humanity of zombies got Welly and Ken thrown out of the Red Lion. In addition to the Mock Martens, she'd bought black jeans, a matching jean jacket, and a dark purple T-shirt. Alice felt like she should have a heavy metal soundtrack following her down the street.

Plus it didn't hurt that zombies weren't attracted to dark colours, she thought. Her bright yellow, zombie-bait dress was now buried at the bottom of her overnight bag.

Still, Alice tried to ignore all the tempting reflective surfaces around her. She wanted to be a proper Sensitive and fulfill her very important role of looking after her Enhanced Agent.

Everyone assumed the stronger Agents were there to protect their psychic companions, but the long-term survival of un-partnered Enhanced Agents was poor. They took too many risks and had a knack for getting dismembered by demons or accidentally embedded inside glaciers. Alice had heard rumours there were a couple of Enhanced Agents currently circling the Earth in low orbit. So she knew she needed to return her focus to the mission and protect Welly from himself as best she could.

They turned a corner and Alice heard a friendly shout. Looking away from the bright red, double-decker bus rolling down the street, she saw a grinning Mick sprawled across the hood of Welly's car. He looked like he was auditioning for the part of a bikini-clad girl in a car commercial, except thankfully, Mick was fully dressed. He'd abandoned the Hawaiian look for a black top hat and tails with a purple silk shirt. Shaded, round eyeglasses perched on his nose and a silver tipped walking stick was resting across his knees.

Alice leaned close to Welly. "What exactly is Mick supposed to be again?" she whispered. A real bodyguard would know this sort of thing and Alice wanted to stay in character.

"He's the lead singer of an internationally famous calypso steel drum band," Welly said without lowering his voice. "Mick, get off my car!" he bellowed, clearly caring more about his beloved Aston Martin than staying undercover.

Alice belatedly noticed Ken standing nearby, hands in his pockets. He was wearing a dingy brown serape over his denim outfit and holding onto a dirty, green backpack. Ken looked like a homeless American cowboy lost in London.

"It's a pan not a drum, mon," Mick said to Welly, not moving a muscle.

"Drop the fake Jamaican accent," Welly said to Mick. "Your passport for this trip says you're an American. And don't make me shift you myself. Because you know I will."

"It's a tragedy, mon," Mick opined, laying it on even thicker. "I've always felt a special connection to da Islands. Jah is all." He slid gracefully off the car, took Alice's hand and kissed it. "Alice, my winsome wallaby! Have you decided to join me in the worship of the Baron La Croix?"

Welly sighed, irritably. "The nearest island you have any connection to is New Zealand."

"What?" Alice asked, confused by Mick's question.

"Australia is a merely a very big island," Mick told Welly. To Alice, Mick said, "You're wearing purple and black, my dear. These are the Baron's colours. And may I say, you look charming."

"Australia's a continent," Welly corrected.

"All of the continents are big islands floating on an eternal magma ocean. It's beautiful, mon. Jah is good."

"You don't look or sound like an Australian aboriginal, no offence," Ken said, crossing his arms and leaning on the roof of the car.

"Get off my car!"

Ken removed his arms quickly.

Alice blinked. Ken looked... guilty? She shook her head. It was probably the moustache, she told herself. Moustaches always made people look like they were hiding something. Besides their upper lip.

"No offence taken," Mick said to Ken, his Jamaican accent instantly vanishing. "As there's a good reason why I don't. Back before I joined Odyssey, I went on a dreamwalk. Technically, I wasn't the one dreamwalking, but..."

"Save it for the drive," Welly said. He pointed his keys at the car, which beeped.

"You know, flying would be faster," Ken said, a shade too enthusiastically.

"Why on earth would we fly when we can drive?" Welly asked, opening the driver's side door and climbing in. "It'll only take a couple of hours. This isn't North America, mind. Everything's closer together here." He carefully shut his car door.

Alice stared at Ken. Something definitely wasn't right about his demeanour, and it had nothing to do with his moustache. She was about to ask him what was wrong when she caught a glimpse of her reflection in the car window. Suddenly, she remembered Mick's comment about the colour scheme of her clothing. "I didn't choose purple and black for the Baron," she told Mick. "I picked these colours because they make me look menacing."

Mick snickered.

Alice crossed her arms. "They do!"

Mick's snickers turned into peals of delighted laughter.

Alice glanced down and realized her pink kitty watch was in full view.

Welly leaned out the open window and ordered, "Stop playing around and brush off your shoes before you get in my car."

Alice obediently brushed off her new boots before climbing in the passenger side. Being intimidating was easy for the guys, Alice thought, as Ken and the still-giggling Mick slid into the back seats. Certainly, no one ever tried any funny business with Welly, not even when he was stripped down to his underwear.

"All of you, pay attention," Welly said, holding up one finger. "This car is not a rolling restaurant. No one eats in my car, no one drinks in my car. She's not your personal ashtray either. There will be no smoking—Mick, that includes anything herbal or sacred. If it results in smoke, ash, or any kind of debris, it's not welcome in my car."

No one would mess with Mick either, Alice thought, because he radiated crazy-person vibes so strongly. While Ken... Okay, they'd agreed to make him Mick's personal secretary instead of a bodyguard, but only because he refused to carry a weapon, even a Taser. Alice sensed he had some sort of ethical objection to violence in general and guns in specific. But he had lots of experience ordering around the living and the dead, so even he radiated more authority than she did.

Alice looked down at her new, not-very-intimidating boots. Oh well, she thought. At least Welly had equipped her with a Taser, now hidden in her oversized purse. Although Alice really hoped she'd never have to use it.

Other than on Mick, she thought, glaring at him.

Mick beamed at her. "It would be an electrifying encounter."

A loud "Foxtrot!" beside her startled Alice out of her fantasies of stringing Mick up by his exceptionally long toes.

Welly yanked his key out of the ignition.

"What's wrong?" she asked, but Welly was already out of the car and under the hood.

Confused, Alice turned to her travelling companions. "What's going on? Wait..." She narrowed her eyes at Ken, who was very tense and staring determinedly out the window. His secret was perched right on the top layer of his mind, practically screaming at her. "Why on earth are there spark plugs hidden in your bag?"

"Someone's been mucking about with my car!" Welly roared from outside.

Ken flinched and then waved his hands frantically at Alice, trying to mime silence.

Mick laid one long finger on the side of his nose. "Alice, my dear, how do you feel about flying?"

Before Alice could answer, her door was open, and Welly was hauling her unceremoniously out of the car. "My spark plugs are gone!"

"Uh, yeah, I know," Alice said, trying to stall for time. As his partner, she should tell him Ken had his precious sparkplugs. But if she did, there was no telling what Welly might do to Ken.

The Admiral would be very unhappy if an Odyssey employee was dismembered on a public street, Alice thought. And Welly wouldn't be the only one who'd pay if he provoked one of the

Admiral's infamous temper tantrums.

"Tell me who did this," Welly demanded. "It would have taken time to mutilate her engine like this, enough time to leave an imprint behind of their malicious little minds. I want you to tell me who it was, where they are, and then I'm going to make sure they never do it again."

Why on earth did Ken sabotage Welly's car? Alice couldn't see Ken, but she could feel his panic pushing against her mind. It felt like he was shouting, "Don't tell!" in her ear.

"Um…" Alice said. There was no possible way she could tell Welly. The Admiral's reaction to the resulting mayhem aside, there was no guarantee Mick could put Ken back together properly. Ken might end up recycled like poor Tom Endicott. While Ken would probably be okay with having his body parts grafted onto zombies, she wasn't.

Mick exited the car and stretched languorously. "The Agitators for the Antichrists have been on a campaign of petty annoyance against Odyssey lately. Stealing spark plugs sounds like their kind of caper."

Welly looked at Alice. "Well?"

Alice bit her lip. Ken had climbed out of the car and was trying to hide behind Mick. Both of them were clearly in on the plan, which was worrying. Still, she thought, they were all on the same side, so how bad could it be?

Alice peered under the hood of Welly's car, trying to look as if she had a clue where the sparkplugs would have lived. "Oh, you're right, Mick," she said, trying to sound confident. "There's… Agitated Antichrist vibes all over this engine."

"Antichrists," corrected Mick, helpfully. "Never forget, there's more than one."

Alice ignored him. "While your vehicle is experiencing roadblocks in the short term, the long-term outlook is positive." The one nice thing about being a Sensitive, even a not particularly talented one, was people tended to believe her so long as she sounded like a fortune cookie. "Success is right around the corner."

"Great, another delay," Welly growled, closing the hood of his car. "Wales will be overrun with zombies by the time we get there."

Alice relaxed and realized she'd been holding her breath. Welly could be scary when he was mad.

"Actually, there's a direct flight from London to Cardiff," Ken said, nervously tapping the roof of the car.

"Get off my Foxtrotting car!" Welly snapped. "Why do you all insist on treating her like a piece of furniture?" He took off his jacket, revealing a rather large gun strapped to his ribs, and buffed some invisible scratches off the hood with his sleeve. Alice was grateful there were no bobbies in sight. She hated talking police out of arresting Welly.

"What an excellent idea!" Mick said, brightly. "We'd shave hours off the trip."

Alice decided Mick and Ken must have concocted the plan to steal Welly's spark plugs in order to force him to abandon his car and fly. Mick was right; it would definitely save a lot of time. Plus hours on the road with Welly micromanaging Mick and Ken's every movement inside his precious car wasn't appealing in the slightest.

"I think we should fly," Alice said. "A fresh start will put you on your way."

Welly looked at each of them in turn, then sighed. "Very well," he said. "Since you're all dead set on flying, we'll fly. But as soon as we've dealt with this zombie menace, A.A. is next on my list. We've been ignoring them for far too long."

Welly flipped open his Oddfone. "Lilith... Yes, that's right. I need someone to come and pick up my car. Send along a cab, too. And make it a licensed cab! I'm not a tourist and I don't care to be taken on a scenic tour of London."

Alice shook her head. Lilith was so going to send them an unlicensed cab.

Closing his phone, Welly patted the hood of his car. "Don't worry," he told it. "You're better off safe at home, and I promise I'll take you on a good long spin when I get back."

Alice checked to see how Mick and Ken reacted to Welly treating his car as if it was sentient, but as far as she could tell neither of them found anything odd about his behaviour.

*

It was outrageous what being Odyssey employees allowed them to get away with regarding weapons and equipment on airplanes, Alice thought as she climbed the rolling stairs to the plane. Welly made some phone calls, flashed some ID, and the next thing she knew their party had been escorted right past Security.

Below her, Alice saw baggage handlers tossing luggage into the belly of the plane. "Careful with that!" she shouted, as a plastic pink cat carrier went flying, but the handlers wore large ear protectors and likely couldn't hear her. The cat's yowl was probably inaudible over the engines, but it was loud as an emergency siren in her mind. Alice winced, resisting the pointless urge to cover her ears with her hands.

Welly had once tried to explain how Odyssey's travelling privileges had come about. However, it had been a ridiculously complicated scheme involving magical persuasion, diplomatic immunity, and the Admiral taking a sizable bite out of the Secretary-General of the United Nations. Alice decided she really didn't need to understand the process so long as it worked.

After all, Alice barely understood Odyssey's overall mission of 'maintaining balance'. Despite numerous long-winded attempts, Welly had never managed to satisfactorily explain to her exactly what they were supposed to be balancing. She suspected he didn't really understand either.

Alice nodded at the friendly brunette flight attendant as she stepped inside the plane. She could still feel the enraged cat's emotions, as if it was sinking its little needle-sharp teeth right into her brain. Alice would've happily blocked out the kitty's conniption, but Welly had specifically instructed her to remain open to psychic impressions.

Alice was dubious about the prospect of flying in a propeller plane, but according to Welly, the Bombardier Q400 was the epitome of aeronautical engineering. In fact, once Welly had discovered the plane they would be on, his mood had improved considerably.

The cabin was bright and spacious, and there was so much legroom that Welly had taken the window seat without argument. As Alice sank into her plush seat beside him, she couldn't deny it was very comfortable. Mick had insisted Ken get the window across the aisle. She didn't need to read his mind to know Mick had no intention of remaining seated throughout the half-hour flight and wanted free and easy access to the aisle.

For her own part, Alice hated window seats on planes. Not because she was a nervous flyer, she reiterated to herself. The copiously sweating man two seats behind them, who had already buckled up his seat belt even though the plane was still stationary, now he was a nervous flyer. Alice just didn't want to be reminded that she was high up in the air, and plane windows undermined her happy illusion that the plane was rolling safely along a super-long runway. Only half an hour, she reassured herself as the engines revved up. Just a nice short hop over to Cardiff. Then we'll rent a car, check in with the branch office, and drive to that unpronounceable bog-snorkelling town.

That thought reminded Alice that there was something she still didn't understand about the whole let's-sabotage-Welly's-car charade. "Who are the Antichrist Agitators?" she asked.

"Agitators for the Antichrists," Welly corrected. "Their goal is to pave the path for the rise of the Antichrists. Their strategy so far consists of being as irritating as humanly possible."

"How can there be more than one Antichrist?"

"The term 'antichrist' appears only in the Epistles of John," Welly said, "in both the plural and the singular. Therefore, it stands to reason that during the End Times, there will likely be more than one."

Mick stood in the middle of the aisle. He'd taken off his sunglasses and was surveying the plane with interest. "Church of England, through and through," he said to Alice.

"Mick, stay in your seat," Welly ordered. "We're taking off soon."

"Never fear, we won't be going anywhere for awhile yet," Mick said, strolling casually toward the back of the plane.

At that precise moment, the engines died.

"What?" Welly said. Standing up, he tried to flag down a flight attendant. "Miss? Miss!"

"Can I help you, sir?" a young man in uniform asked. "My name is Darryl." He had bright red hair and a friendly smile.

"Ah, Darryl. You're a... steward?"

Alice winced. She could clearly hear the 'ess' Welly had chopped off the end of the word.

"Yes sir. How can I help you?" Darryl asked, his voice phlegmy. It sounded like he was fighting off a cold.

"Can you tell me if there's a problem with the departure?"

"Actually, there will be a slight delay. Nothing serious. I understand there's been a bit of an incident with the baggage."

Alice felt a sudden flash of panic from Ken, and she glanced across the aisle to see him staring horrified at Darryl.

"What kind of incident?" Welly asked, darkly. "Was it sabotage?"

"No, I don't believe—"

"Don't be silly," Alice said to Ken. "It's not the Agitators. And it's not zombies, either. Boy, have you got work on the brain! It's just that darn cat. I tried to warn them. You can't toss a cat carrier around like it's a sack of laundry."

Darryl looked startled. "Who told you about the cat?"

"Excuse me!" an elderly woman with large, round glasses called out from a few rows back. "Did someone mention a cat? My Mr. Snuggles is on this flight. Is everything okay?"

Darryl shot Alice an exasperated look. Walking back to the old lady, he said, "Can I ask you to come with me to the back of the plane? We need to confirm a few things about Mr. Snuggles. Has he recently had a rabies jab?"

"Who's Mr. Snuggles?" Ken asked, when they were gone. "And what are they jabbing him with?"

"I told you, he's a cat," Alice said. "He's also an escape artist. She should have named him Mr. Houdini. They'd better not get too close to him because he's pretty mad. Good thing he's had his rabies shots."

"So that was the incident with the baggage?" Welly said. "An escaped cat?"

Ken sank back into his seat with a sigh of relief.

"Yes," Alice said. "And they're looking in totally the wrong place for him."

Welly took out his Oddfone. "Where is he? The sooner they catch him, the sooner we can get this plane off the ground."

Alice closed her eyes and tried to locate Mr. Snuggles a.k.a. Mr. Houdini. Here kitty, kitty, she thought.

Then she caught a flash of blood-soaked glee which completely destroyed her focus.

"Ew! He just caught a pigeon!" She opened her eyes. "I'm sorry, I know it's the circle of life, but the breaking of little bones and squishing of guts... It's really nasty. And you know something else? Mr. Snuggle's not scared or lost. He just wants to kill things. Lots of things. I've changed my mind; his name should be Mr. Manson."

Welly put his Oddfone back inside his jacket. "Hopefully they won't delay the plane very long over a missing cat."

"A psychotic missing cat," Alice corrected, raising her psychic shields. Welly wanted her to stay alert, but there was no point when all she could pick up was caterwauling and the death screams of pigeons.

*

Welly's optimism had been misplaced. An hour and a half later, the flight attendants were handing out small packets of peanuts and apologizing profusely for the ongoing delay. Alice glanced over and noticed Mick had wandered off again.

"Is he talking to the passengers again?" Welly asked, a hint of despair in his voice.

Alice carefully lowered her shields. Mr. Snuggles must have calmed down or wandered out of range because she could no longer sense him. There was no point trying to directly access Mick's mind; Alice knew from experience he was completely unreadable. Whenever she tried, all she ever picked up was 'The Girl from Ipanema' playing in an endless loop in his brain. But she could easily sense the reactions of the people Mick interacted with. "Yep, he's telling the elderly couple on their honeymoon that his Tropical Beat music will give them an extra special wedding night."

"Tropical Beat music." Welly shook his head.

"So far he's told the two nuns that he plays Island Rhythm Band music and it will help them get closer to God. The two teenage girls sitting behind us were told that his Jump Up music will be a great addition to their workout routine. And then he told the skinny man with the huge wife that his Calypso music can drown out the screaming matches between his wife and his mother. Oh, and he told the two Muslim businessmen that they should invest in Soca music. Plus, I think he's handing out autographed brochures."

"It's rude to eavesdrop," Mick appeared beside her.

Alice jumped in her seat. "Darryl thinks you're from Mars, not the Caribbean," she blurted out. Random acts of honesty were one of the annoying consequences of being psychic.

"I know," Mick said, eyes gleaming behind his shaded glasses. "I'm dying to find out why." He waved at the red-headed steward just exiting the cockpit. "Why Mars instead of Venus?" Mick called out, practically bouncing to the front of the plane.

"You really shouldn't encourage him," Welly said, opening a hardcover book.

"I know. But on the bright side, he's stopped posing for pictures." During Mick's first tour of the passengers, almost all of them had taken cellphone photos with him. Including the two nuns. "And he's no longer promising free copies of his Soca/Calypso/Island Rhythm workout DVD, Jump Up, Fat Off."

Welly sighed. "It was too much to hope Mick would keep his cover story straight."

"To be fair," Alice said, "I think all those different names he gave for the music he plays might just be synonyms. And it could be worse."

"How exactly?" Welly asked, without looking up from his book.

"The plane isn't full, so that's fewer people for Mick to freak out, right?"

"Hope springs eternal." Welly turned a page.

Despite the protracted delay, Alice was grateful Mick and Ken had cooked up this scheme to fly. At least here Mick had an entire plane to roam. The thought of being trapped for hours in Welly's car with the hyperactive Mick made her shudder.

Alice got up on her knees and looked around the plane. Scattered throughout the cabin were around fifty people. Welly had told her this plane had capacity for seventy-eight passengers, three flight attendants, a pilot, co-pilot, and over fourteen cubic metres of baggage space. Welly was always very reliable when it came to specifications, if a bit too detailed. Alice had zoned out when he'd started to wax lyrical about the Goodrich tricycle-type landing gear and anti-skid brakes.

Mick was still chattering at Darryl. As far as Alice could tell, Mick was trying to examine a bandaged finger, and his help was being firmly refused. Good instincts, Darryl, she thought. Mick might want to transplant the injured finger onto Dave or some other lucky zombie.

Alice sat back down and thumbed through the magazines in the seatback pocket. She'd already finished the book in her overnight bag, *The Day of the Triffids*, and was getting bored. She leaned over toward Welly. "What are you reading?"

"None of your business."

Alice lifted the book up and read the cover. "*Little Zombie on the Prairie!*"

"Keep your voice down," Welly said.

"I didn't think parodies were your cup of tea," Alice said.

"It's not a parody," Welly said sternly. "It's one of Laura Ingalls Wilder's unpublishable books."

"Unpublished?"

"Unpublishable due to its content," Welly corrected.

"It's an excellent, firsthand observation of a zombie outbreak," Ken said, looking across the aisle from his window seat. "Wilder provided very detailed descriptions of all stages of infection. *Little Zombie on the Prairie* is a sympathetic, heart-warming treatment of zombies."

"Too sympathetic," Welly grumbled.

"It's a bit of tearjerker," Ken continued, "especially the death of

Zombie Mary."

"You guys are pulling my leg," Alice said. "As if anyone would ever cry over the death of a zombie."

Ken made a rude sound and disappeared back into his own book. She heard him muttering, "Pleased to meet you: *Neis cwrdd a ti*."

"No, no," Mick said, sitting back down beside Ken. "It's a long 'A', *neis cwrdd â ti*. And you may want to use the formal instead, which is *neis cwrdd â chi*."

"Just how many languages do you know, Mick?" Alice asked.

"Why would I want to count languages?" he asked in return.

"Peanuts, sir?" A bleach blonde flight attendant held out a packet toward Mick. The badge on her navy vest read, 'Hi, my name is Shelly. Fly Me!'

"Excellent." Mick snatched the packet away from her. "The Baron La Croix loves peanuts. Twenty packets should be enough, plus some grilled corn and hot peppers if you have any."

"Mick," Welly said, sternly. "Stop harassing the stewardess."

"That's 'flight attendant' not 'stewardess', you dinosaur," Alice hissed at Welly.

Welly ignored her. "Are you certain there's no trouble with the engine?" he asked Shelly, not for the first time.

"Yes sir. They've simply had some difficulty loading the baggage. I'm sure we'll be cleared to fly in no time." Shelly gave Mick an uneasy look and moved on.

"Did you see her name tag?" Alice asked. "'My name is Shelly. Fly Me!'"

"What's wrong with that?" Welly appeared genuinely puzzled. "Fly Me Airlines is the name of the company. And the male stewardess had the exact same thing on his name badge."

Alice rolled her eyes. "As I said, you're a dinosaur." Thanks to his enhancements, Welly appeared to be in his mid-thirties, but Alice knew he was a lot older than he looked.

"Did you fall in love with prop airplanes when you were fighting in World War Two?" Alice asked him.

Welly turned another page in his book. "I was too young to fight in the Second World War. Instead, I volunteered for the Korean conflict, and one day I'll tell you a story about the little Cessna Bird Dog that could. But right now you need to do a deep scan of the passengers."

Alice looked around the cabin. Everyone, except Mick, looked perfectly ordinary. "Why do I —" she began.

She was interrupted by a pleasant series of musical notes, followed by a pleasant, male voice. "Ladies and gentlemen, this is your captain speaking. I'm pleased to announce that our flight has been cleared for departure. We will be arriving in Cardiff in approximately forty minutes. Thank you for your patience, and thank you for choosing to Fly Me."

Ken glanced across the aisle at Alice as the engines roared back to life. "They finally found the cat?"

"Of course not," Alice said. "And trying to track him down with that drug-sniffing dog is only going to end in tears and recriminations."

— 4 —

Darryl Should Have Taken a Sick Day

Twenty minutes into the flight, Welly put his book down with
a disgusted sound. When Alice looked up from her magazine, he
asked, "Have you done a deep scan of the passengers like I asked
you?"

Alice put away the magazine and folded her arms. "No, I haven't.
Because if there's trouble, the information will pop into my head.
Whether I want it to or not." And sometimes with more gruesome
details than she ever wanted to know, Alice thought, remembering
Mr. Snuggles and the murdered pigeon. She didn't see the point
of actively looking for more.

"Relying on vital information to pop into your head could get
you killed and get me horribly injured," Welly said.

Alice also avoided deep scans because they were far more
unpleasant than just scanning the surfaces of people's minds.
It was one thing to pick up on what people were thinking and
feeling. It was another thing entirely to dive into their minds and
risk drowning in a miasma of emotions, thoughts, and memories.

Plus that level of psychic exploration meant using Odyssey's
biotechnology, something Alice tried to avoid whenever possible.

"The flight's almost over," Alice protested.

"Landings are just as dangerous as taking off," Welly insisted. "Trust me, you don't want to be surprised by a possessed passenger or a mentally disturbed magician during the approach to the airport."

Alice sulked for a couple of minutes, and then remembered she was trying to act like a professional these days. And Welly, as the acting head of Section Five, wasn't just her partner but also her boss.

"Oh, all right," Alice said, and closed her eyes. "*Om mani padme hum.*"

"Must you do that?" Welly asked, in a pained voice.

"Don't knock tradition," Alice said, not opening her eyes. "*Om mani padme hum.*"

"Must you do it so loudly? You're drawing attention."

Alice eyes snapped open. "Do you want me to do a deep scan or not? Because I'm perfectly willing to watch you get horribly injured. Over and over again, if necessary."

"See, Ken, I told you," Mick said. "They bicker like an old married couple."

"Shut up, Mick!" Alice and Welly barked in unison.

"Excuse me," the brunette flight attendant interrupted. "Is everything all right?"

She was older than the other two flight attendants and radiated authority. Her badge said her name was Bronwyn.

Much to Alice's annoyance, Welly gave Bronwyn one of his extremely rare winning smiles. "Thank you, we're well taken care of."

"Glad to hear it, sir. But I'm going to have to ask all of you to keep it down. You're disturbing the other passengers."

Alice frowned. Bronwyn had a good decade on her, but there wasn't a sign of grey in her undyed hair. And she made her polyester navy vest and skirt uniform look tailor-made to show off her curves.

"Terribly sorry, won't happen again." Welly gave all three of them a stern look. "Will it?"

Ken and Mick managed to look completely innocent. Alice doubted she appeared anywhere near as guilt-free.

"Thank you, sir," Bronwyn said, distracted by something at the back of the plane. Alice peeked over her seat and saw the male attendant waving for attention. And coughing.

"If there's anything you require," Bronwyn said, "don't hesitate to ask."

"Thank you, Bronwyn." Welly leaned into the aisle and watched her walk away until she pulled the curtain across the kitchenette.

Alice fixed him with a dirty look. "What?" he asked.

"Nothing," she grumbled. And it was nothing, Alice told herself. She didn't even like Welly, so why should she care that he never looked at her with that sort of interest or treated her with that kind of respect. Besides, just like Bronwyn, she had a job to do.

Closing her eyes again, this time Alice chanted much more softly, "*Om mani padme hum.*" The mantra itself didn't matter; it just helped her focus on the Sensitivity Amplifier 3000 Odyssey had installed in her brain. When she'd first found out that Mick had inserted a neural implant into her amygdala, she'd freaked out. However, there was no denying that with training, the amplifier had made her psychic abilities more reliable and far reaching. "*Om mani padme hummmmm.*"

Visualizing her brain as a brightly coloured diagram, Alice quickly found the amplifier hidden inside her temporal lobe. She knew that the actual implant resembled a tiny bed of nails, but thinking about the pointy electrodes piercing her amygdala would only induce a panic attack instead of increased psychic abilities. So her trainer had told her to envision the Sensitivity Amplifier as a bright yellow dial that she could turn to the desired setting. Right now, it was set at only two, and she visualized turning it all the way up.

The scent of burnt toast let her know that she'd successfully dialled her amplifier to eleven. Alice took several deep, slow breaths and visualized a large, freshwater lake. Once it was clear in her mind, she overlapped the image of the lake with the airplane's cabin.

Alice now imagined she was floating just above the lake's surface, able to see where the water eddied and flowed around the passengers. Here and there the water rippled, but she recognized that as the confusion Mick was leaving in his tow. Whirlpools meant trouble, though, and one was circling the large woman and her skinny husband.

Alice took a deep, slow breath and visualized cautiously dipping her toe into the whirlpool.

If he didn't bring his bleep mother every bleep place we go I wouldn't have to bleep...

Alice yanked her metaphorical toe back. She was glad she'd taken her trainer's advice and downloaded the PG-13 filter.

She floated over the lake that was the plane's cabin, but didn't sense any other significant disturbances. The nuns were praying for Mick's soul while a bunch of young men at the back were laughing over some brochures. However, there was some choppiness near the back kitchen area. Alice followed the disturbed water and, behind the curtain, found Darryl talking in an agitated manner to Bronwyn. He was right in the center of a very large and very dark whirlpool.

This isn't going to be fun, Alice thought, as she forced herself to wade in. Anxiety gripped her immediately, closely followed by strong feelings of fear and confusion. Darryl's mental state was melting down, and Alice's was being dragged down with it.

I know this shit sounds crazy, Darryl said to Bronwyn, the words echoing in Alice's head. *Why do you think I waited over an hour to tell you? And okay, I've got the flu, but this wasn't a hallucination. This is serious shit! There's an ancient mummy back in the baggage compartment and it bit me!*

Alice snapped back into her head. "Shit!"

"Alice." Welly frowned at her. "I've told you to say Sierra instead."

"No, this is serious shit," she said, her voice shaky from the rapid transition out of her trance. Alice's emotions and thoughts were tangled up with Darryl's, and it was difficult to separate the two.

"Are you all right?" Welly asked.

"Yes, no, maybe..." Alice took a deep breath, dialled down her amplifier, and visualized all of Darryl's emotions and memories draining out of her body. "There, that's better." She met Welly's eyes and added, "We're doomed."

"You're not making any sense," Welly said, looking genuinely concerned.

"Okay, just don't kill the messenger. Darryl was bitten in the baggage compartment." Alice took a deep breath. "Bitten by Dave."

Welly sprang to his feet and wheeled on Ken. "You brought a Foxtrotting zombie on a Foxtrotting plane?"

"That's why you stole Welly's sparkplugs," Alice said to Ken, with sudden realization. "So you could smuggle Dave onto the plane."

"And you Foxtrotting sabotaged my car!" Welly's face was rapidly turning a shade of red Alice had never seen before.

This is all my fault, Alice thought. Waiting for important information to magically appear in her mind wasn't a great way to do her job, after all. But when the alternative risked frying irreplaceable brain cells, what was she supposed to do?

Ken stood, his expression not the least bit repentant. "I can't do my job without Dave!" The overhead compartment didn't provide quite enough room for him to stand up straight, which made his defiant stand less impressive than it might otherwise have been.

Mick's maniacal grin didn't help either.

"After today you won't have a job!" Welly shouted. "I'll Foxtrotting make sure of it!"

"You both need to sit down and calm down immediately." Bronwyn was back and she looked ready to spit nails. Alice saw Darryl just behind her. He looked pale and sweaty.

Welly flashed his ID at Bronwyn. "I'm sorry," he said, his voice quieter but still forceful. "We need immediate access to your baggage compartment. It's a matter of international security."

Darryl grew rapidly paler. "Baggage compartment?" he squeaked and sneezed twice.

"All right," Bronwyn said after a moment of consideration. "But I won't have you upsetting the other passengers. Am I clear?"

Alice quickly scanned the surface thoughts of the nearby passengers and was relieved to find that all of Welly's Foxtrots had sown confusion instead of panic. Several of them were wondering if they'd really heard the crazy British man say something about zombies.

"We're calm," Alice assured her. "Really, really, really calm. I promise."

Bronwyn began to lead them to the back of the plane. Welly went first with Alice following immediately after him.

"There's absolutely no risk," Ken insisted from behind her. "I sealed Dave's casket myself inside the mandatory plywood and corrugated cardboard air tray with double-locking plastic buckles. There's no way Dave could get loose."

"I should have suspected something when you insisted on this particular flight," Welly growled. "The only direct flight from London to Cardiff, you said!"

"But it's true," Ken said. "This is the only direct flight."

Welly glanced back at Alice. "And you! How much did you know about this?" He sounded betrayed.

"I didn't know anything!" Alice protested. "I only made up the bit about the Agitators because I didn't want you to hurt Ken."

"Trust me, I'm going to hurt Ken."

"I was just an accessory after the fact," Mick said, cheerfully from behind Ken. "I loved the idea, but I was busy with my own preparations back in London."

"Keep your voices down!" Bronwyn shouted

"I swear, it was already open when I went back there," Darryl babbled ahead of them. "It must have happened in baggage handling. I'm sure Fly Me will compensate you for any damage."

The two attendants, Welly, Alice, Ken, and Mick pushed through the curtain and rounded the kitchenette.

"I paid one hundred and twenty-five dollars, and followed every rule about shipping bodies by air," Ken shouted. "It's a foolproof system!"

Bronwyn opened the door, and they all piled into the large baggage compartment. Alice saw a broken cardboard cover— 'Handle with Extreme Care' emblazoned on it—propped up against haphazardly stacked luggage. Further back, she could see the remains of a thick plastic bag surrounding a bright red, wooden casket with an open lid.

"But not an idiot-proof system," Welly said, darkly.

He unholstered his Taser and pointed it at Darryl's chest.

"Welly!" Alice cried out. "You can't Taser Darryl!"

"At this low altitude, I can safely put a bullet in him without fear of causing decompression," Welly said, calmly. "So I can certainly Taser him."

"You can't Taser someone just for being curious," Alice protested.

"He's a zom—I mean, he's infected. He needs to be subdued."

"What the hell is going on?" Bronwyn yelled. "I don't care if you are from Interpol; put that Taser down right now!"

Alice's first thought was that it was completely unfair for Welly to have a fake Interpol ID when she didn't. Fortunately, her second thought was more helpful.

"Welly, if you Taser Darryl, the other flight attendants will arrest you for air rage. And that would put Mick or Ken in charge of this assignment. Do you really want that?" Behind her, in the passenger compartment of the airplane, she could hear someone asking what all the commotion was about.

"First off, you're next in command. Second, I'm not raging, and even if I was, I rather doubt two stewardesses—sorry, two flight attendants—would be enough to nick me."

Ken stood in front of Darryl, his arms spread. "If you Taser him, you'll have to Taser me too!"

"With pleasure," Welly said. "Considering the way you've abused my car today."

"This is ridiculous!" Ken shouted. "Dave is not a biter! Darryl, show me your injured hand." He turned to face Darryl.

The flight attendant remained frozen in place, eyes fixed on Welly.

Alice could now hear at least two passengers in the kitchenette behind them, demanding to know what was going on. Bronwyn pushed past her and stuck her head of the baggage compartment door. "Go back to your seats. Immediately!"

Ken grabbed Darryl's right hand and tore the bandage off his index finger. "See, Dave barely broke the skin, and Stage Four zom—infected are hardly—ah, infectious. You'd have to have a compromised immune system for a nip from Dave to infect—"

Darryl let loose a hacking cough.

"You were saying, Ken?" Welly asked, mildly.

Alice took a deep breath and brought out the big guns. "Welly, remember how the Admiral reacts whenever Odyssey Agents get in the news?" Behind her, she could hear the passengers arguing with Bronwyn.

"Oh yes," Mick chimed in, "I especially loved the time the Admiral used Agent Juergen Kress as a Tiki torch for the annual barbeque. Took several years off Juergen's life expectancy, but he had a gorgeous all-body tan for months."

Welly paled and he slowly lowered the Taser.

Bronwyn turned in the doorway. "I'm reporting this incident to the captain and co-pilot." She pointed directly at Welly and fiercely added, "If you dare use that Taser on Darryl while I'm gone, I'll have you up on charges the moment we land in Cardiff." Alice could hear Bronwyn chivvying the passengers back to their seats, as she marched out of the kitchenette. "No, there's no terrorist attack," Bronwyn said. "Don't be ridiculous!"

Alice closed her eyes and leaned against the closest bulkhead, feeling giddy with relief. Sure, there was a zombie on the plane, but everything was under control. All they had to do was close up Dave's casket, ensure Darryl didn't wander around infecting anyone, and in no time at all, they'd be safely landing in Cardiff. Alice re-opened her eyes and immediately tensed up again. "Ken!"

He glanced at her. "What?"

Ken had taken Dave out of his casket. He was now running his hands over the zombie's limbs, giving the impression of a very gentle police frisking.

"At least Bronwyn didn't see Dave," Alice said. She shook her head. Was she the only sane Odyssey employee on this plane?

Dave wasn't wearing his orange and turquoise jumpsuit anymore. He was dressed in jeans and a leather jacket. Strangely, these normal clothes and the blue sneakers on his feet only served to make him look less human, not more.

Alice peered closer at Dave. "Ken, is that duct tape on his hands?"

"Duct tape is far more effective for reattaching fingers than stitching them back on." Ken straightened the collar on Dave's jacket and stepped back to admire his work. "Zombie skin is very fragile, so suture thread has an unfortunate tendency to pull right out. Next thing you know, you're knee deep in fingers and toes."

"Oh," Alice said faintly, remembering the finger she'd seen on the Mailroom floor. "I didn't realize you could just stick them back on."

"They do lose some functionality, but…"

"Ow!" Darryl yelped.

Grateful for the interruption, Alice turned to see Mick operating a hand-held machine she'd never seen before. It looked like a Star Trek tricorder and even made the same trilling sounds she remembered from the original show. Although Alice didn't remember Spock's tricorder ever having a big retractable needle at one end.

"Easy does it, now." Mick helped Darryl sit down beside an empty, hot-pink kitty carrier. Darryl looked impossibly pale.

"Don't worry," Mick continued. "Light-headedness and confusion are normal in Stage One zombism. It's also a pretty standard reaction upon first seeing a zombie. It'll only take a moment to find out which case applies to you, my dizzy friend." Mick fiddled with some dials and the machine began to hum a tune. It sounded suspiciously like Star Trek's opening theme.

Darryl was staring wide-eyed at Dave. "Am I hallucinating?" Darryl asked, in a shaky voice.

"Hallucinations aren't a usual symptom," Mick said, crouching beside him. "However, if you're infected, you may actually faint during Stage Two. But don't be concerned; at that stage, your brain is only moderately damaged. Loss of consciousness is caused by the significantly reduced blood flow to your outer extremities."

"What are you talking about? I have the flu!"

Dave's nose began twitching rapidly. He pointed at Darryl. "Whoof!"

"Yes," Ken told Dave. "Very good."

Alice stared at Dave. "Um, Ken, did Dave just bark?"

"He can only make limited sounds because of the decomposition of his lips and tongue," Ken answered. "He's just letting me know that Darryl is infected. Dave's priceless in situations where blood tests are impractical." Ken smiled, pride in his expression. "You're priceless, aren't you, Dave?"

Dave rocked his head up and down, letting loose a blissful moan. He reminded Alice of a pleased puppy. A mummified puppy who didn't have a tail to wag, but a happy puppy, nonetheless.

A loud ululation from Mick's machine made Alice jump and Dave howl.

"Sorry," Mick apologized, "I'll turn it to vibrate, shall I? There, that's better. Now, let's have a look-see at the test results." He pressed a button and peered closely at the small screen at the top of the machine. "Ah, good news, Darryl!"

"Good?" Darryl managed, his arms wrapped tightly around himself.

"Oh yes," Mick enthused. "You're a zombie. Only Stage One, but isn't that—oh dear, he's fainted. Could be Stage Two, I suppose."

"Oh God," Alice said. "The plane's going to crash." She pointed at Ken with a shaky finger. "And it's my fault because I didn't scan you when you stole Welly's spark plugs!"

"Don't overreact, a couple of zombies on a plane is no reason to panic," Ken said.

"No, of course not, how silly of me," Alice muttered. She suddenly realized that something else was wrong. Welly hadn't corrected her when she'd called on God. She looked around, but her partner was no longer in the baggage compartment.

"Wakey, wakey," Mick said, gently slapping Darryl on the face. Darryl groaned and flailed his arms. "That's the stuff!" Mick said. "Practice now, you'll need these skills for later."

"I've flown with zombies before," Ken said, "and no one died or even got seriously injured."

Alice narrowed her eyes at him.

"Okay, there was that one nun, but it was completely accidental.

Dave was only Stage Three back then and just wanted to chew on her prayer beads."

Mick stood up. "Ken, can you take care of Darryl for a bit?"

"What? Yes, of course," Ken said. Ignoring Alice, he went over to the semiconscious flight attendant, followed by Dave. Ken gently propped Darryl up against a bulkhead, while Dave sniffed his red hair.

Mick tucked his tricorder into his messenger bag. He then hopped over the remains of Dave's cardboard and plywood shipping container, and left the baggage compartment.

"I should go find Welly," Alice said.

"Your partner's a thug," Ken said, frowning.

"Not always," Alice said, feeling too emotionally drained to be angry anymore. "Most of the time, he's very kind and considerate. He'd also save your life even if it meant risking his own." She frowned. "But zombies seem to bring out the worst in him. And he loves his car. You should really give him back those spark plugs."

Alice found Mick and Welly talking quietly in the kitchen area. Welly looked extremely unhappy.

"Don't overreact, things really aren't that bad," Mick was saying. "Yes, Darryl's infected, but the chance of him having passed it on to anyone else on this plane is miniscule. Stage One zombism isn't very contagious. But if you want, I'd be happy to check all the passengers to make sure he didn't gnaw on anyone."

"No." Welly shook his head. "I think we would've noticed that."

"Besides," Mick continued, blithely, "even if our brand spanking new zombie did infect one or two passengers, there's no need to panic. The vast majority of zombies are never diagnosed. They just quietly rot away in the comfort of their own homes without ever passing the virus on. Sad, really."

"I know," Welly said. "I wouldn't have us investigating this rumour of zombies in Wales if it weren't for the benighted Bog

Snorkelling Championships raising the risk factor. Alcohol in combination with zombism frequently triggers the formation of mobs. Not to mention tourists could spread the infection far and wide, and Swansea's in the direct line of fire."

"Still, a full-blown zombie outbreak in Cardiff could be fun." Mick grinned and clapped his hands. "We could just lose track of Darryl after we land, you know."

"We're here to stop an outbreak, not cause one," Welly said sternly. "I suppose I should be grateful you two didn't try to stuff Dave into the trunk of my car."

"That was plan B."

"Or smuggle him onto the plane as an extra passenger."

"Plan C! Want to try guessing what Plan D was?"

Welly shook his head again. "You will quarantine Darryl and have Ken take him directly back to headquarters as soon as we're on the ground."

"Party pooper," Mick said. He then looked thoughtful. "The baggage area isn't really isolated enough for a quarantine. I wonder if anyone would notice if we jammed Darryl into one of the overhead compartments? They're incredibly roomy."

Alice was relieved they weren't planning to Taser everyone on board and take over the plane. So much so, that even Mick's idea of stuffing a zombie in with her overnight bag didn't worry her much.

She slipped past Welly and Mick and peeked through the curtain. A sea of puzzled, concerned faces stared back at her. Evidently some of the shouting had been audible in the rest of the plane. Alice peered over their heads, looking for the nervous flyer who'd been sitting behind her and Welly. She winced. He appeared to be crying.

A cell phone suddenly appeared in her line of vision and flashed. She glared at the young man holding the phone. "Do you mind!"

"I've got university to pay for," he said, as he checked the picture on his phone. "If we're going to be on the evening news, I want to have something worth selling."

His seatmate, who was wearing a soccer jersey, punched his shoulder. "I still say I heard them say something about zombies."

"Yeah, what's that about?" the student with the phone asked Alice. "Speak clearly, the recorder on this isn't that great."

Alice saw the blonde flight attendant, Shelly, heading down the aisle straight for her. "No comment at this time!" She jumped back from the curtain. "Incoming," she warned Mick and Welly.

Welly brushed past Alice and blocked the only way into the baggage compartment. Shelly came through the curtains and squeezed by Alice and Mick, her arms full of blankets. Shelly tried to walk around Welly, but he extended his arm, stopping her dead in her tracks. Alice could sympathize; walking into Welly felt like bumping into a tree.

"I'm sorry," he said, "but for security reasons, I can't allow you back there."

"I don't know who you think you are, sir," Shelly said, "but Bronwyn told me to take these blankets to Darryl. She didn't want to deal with you again and I don't want to deal with you now. But you have no legal right to prevent me from doing my job, so stop trying."

Mick pushed up against Alice. "Brava!" He tipped his top hat to Shelly. "I say we give her an all-access backstage pass."

Alice shoved Mick back. It was getting very crowded in the small kitchenette. "Welly, we don't want to make Bronwyn come back here or we'll all end up as the main course at Odyssey's next barbeque."

"Fine," Welly said, in a resigned tone, and pulled back his arm. "Be my guest," he told Shelly.

As she sailed past Welly, he grumbled, "Stewardesses were so much easier to handle back in the day."

Alice grimaced at him and he sighed. "Yes, I know. I'm a dinosaur."

Predictably, there was a sharp scream from the baggage area. Shockingly, it was followed by a soft "whoof".

"That wasn't Dave, was it?" Alice asked, hoping she'd imagined the second sound.

Mick looked as surprised as she felt, whereas Welly just looked puzzled.

On the other side of the curtain, Alice heard one of the university students asking, "Did someone scream?"

She yanked the curtain open. "No one screamed. Everyone's fine. Can't you tell the difference between a squeaky door and a scream?" Alice put as much conviction as she could behind the words and felt an unexpected surge of energy. But it rapidly dissipated, leaving her feeling light-headed, as if she'd just driven her brain a hundred and twenty kilometres per hour in a forty zone.

The passengers looked confused. The student with the cell phone slowly sat back down, frowning.

Alice closed the curtain. Welly and Mick had already disappeared into the baggage compartment. She joined them and pushed past Mick to see what was happening. Dave was standing in the middle of the room, his nose twitching up and down as well as side to side, and his duct-taped hand was pointing directly at Shelly. She'd dropped the blankets and looked on the verge of fainting.

Mick pulled out his bizarre tricorder and waved it up and down in front of her. "Tell me, Shelly, have you recently exchanged bodily fluids with Darryl?"

"What the hell is that thing?" she gasped.

"This is the Med-Trekker IV," Mick replied, tapping several buttons. "Think of it as a portable surgery, pharmacy, and laboratory, all wrapped up in one shiny, user-friendly box. It slices, it dices, and more importantly for you right now, it does blood tests." A needle popped out of the machine, and he jabbed Shelly's right shoulder with it.

"Ow! No, I meant that—that horrible thing!" Shelly pointed at Dave.

"Don't pay any attention to ignorant people, Dave," Ken said, soothingly.

"Oh, him," Mick said. "Costume party for the upcoming Bog Snorkelling championships. He's sure to win. Now focus, Shelly. Have you had any kind of intimate contact with Darryl here during today's shift? Kissing, licking, biting—anything like that?"

Shelly couldn't tear her eyes away from Dave. "Don't be disgusting. I've been trying to stay clear of Darryl all shift. He's spreading the flu like the plague. He should never have come to work today."

"Work," Darryl mumbled. "Money... needed money... work."

Ken took one of the blankets Shelly had dropped and wrapped it around Darryl. "Stage Two, this fast," he said, sounding very concerned.

"I'm sure he's already given the flu to half the passengers, and of course, he's sneezed all over me and Bronwyn. God, I hate my job!"

"You're in enough trouble, young lady, without using the Lord's name—" Welly began.

"She was having sex in the bathroom," Alice blurted out. She blushed when everyone turned to stare at her. "It's true and it's not the first time, either. Shelly's done it in tons of airplane bathrooms, and ew..." Alice shook her head, trying to dislodge the image of Shelly's latest escapade using the anti-bacterial soap. Sometimes Alice wished she wasn't psychic. "I'm never using a bathroom on a plane again."

"So she got infected after being intimate with Darryl," Ken said. "That makes sense. Zombism is often sexually transmitted."

"I didn't have sex with Darryl!" Shelly protested.

"She hates Darryl," Alice said, "but really likes the blond guy in the back row." She narrowed her eyes and concentrated on Shelly. "Except you don't, not really. You just enjoyed having sex with a hot guy on company time. You don't even know his name."

Shelly's mouth had dropped open during Alice's speech. Now she snapped her jaw shut, and the look of astonishment on her face was replaced with outrage. "You pervy little peeper! I'll have you know I don't have to stand for this abuse! You wouldn't last one minute in my job. I've been spat on, vomited on, pinched, kicked, and if I had a euro for every time I've heard, 'Darling, I'd love to fly you!' I could buy up this pathetic airline and change its fu —"

"The Baron is a mighty Loa, in all his aspects," Mick said, awe in his voice. The Med-Trekker IV was shuddering violently in his hands. "I'll make so many libations to you."

"What are you babbling on about?" Welly asked.

"The zombie virus has gone airborne!"

5

Alice Learns What Goes Up Must Come Down

"**Z**ombie?" Shelly squeaked, her attention fixed back on Dave.

Everyone else was staring at Mick. "What did you say?" Ken and Welly demanded in unison.

"The virus has gone airborne," said Mick, sounding pleasantly surprised. "Anyone on this airplane with a compromised immune system could get zombified without direct contact with an infected person. Which means, Shelly," Mick shook a finger at her, "you should always make your Mile High partners use a condom. But on the bright side, your boring little dose of the clap is now a spectacular case of zombism."

"Talk about unsafe sex," Alice said.

"What's going on? Are you all insane?" Shelly sounded on the verge of hysterics.

"Interesting discussion question," Mick said, "but a bit off topic."

"Right, listen up!" Welly barked. "Ken, you sit on these two zom—infected and make sure they stay back here with Dave until the plane's ready to land. Mick, you—Mick, leave Shelly alone—go remotely scan the passengers with the Med-Trekker and give me your best guess as to how many of them might be infected. Pipe down, Ken. Dave cannot go up front to help. And Mick, you will not talk to the passengers, administer blood tests, or manhandle them in any fashion."

"Alice," Welly continued. "You come with me, we're returning to our seats. We're going to be very calm and collected, and you're going to ensure everyone around us is too."

Welly gave both Ken and Mick a hard look. "You two are chiefs in your own bailiwicks, but I'm team leader here and now. Anyone who disobeys my orders will be Tasered, am I understood?"

Mick grinned. "All look, no talk." He bounded out of the baggage compartment.

Ken nodded, grimly.

"I'm still here!" Shelly shouted at them.

Alice was glad to make a quick escape from the hold, leaving Ken to explain things to Shelly.

"Who's going to calm me down?" Alice asked, as Welly led her back to their seats and the wide-eyed stares of passengers on either side of the aisle.

"We've been hijacked, I know it!" a woman cried out. "They're holding the flight attendants hostage."

"No, one of them's here, but she just passed out!"

"I heard something about a plague!"

"Hail Mary, full of grace, the Lord is with thee..." That was one of the nuns.

Someone sneezed. "I don't feel well."

The nervous flyer jumped to his feet as they passed him. Without breaking stride, Welly slapped a hand on his balding head and forced him to sit back down.

Dropping heavily into his seat, Welly pulled out his Oddfone. Instead of sitting beside him, Alice stood on her toes, trying to pry open the oxygen mask compartment. "How can I get into this thing?" she said, scratching at the edges.

Welly pulled her down. "Stop that. The oxygen mask won't be released unless the plane decompresses which isn't going to happen." Into the phone, he said, "Lilith, patch me through to Borislav, straight away."

"How could something like this happen?" Alice wailed. It wasn't fair, she thought. She was going to die boyfriend-less, or worse, become a zombie and end up dating Dave.

Welly placed one finger over her mouth. "Loose lips sink ships," he whispered. "We don't want to alarm the civilians."

Alice could barely hear him over the sound of civilians being alarmed all around them. The nervous flyer behind them was up again and demanding to know where the parachutes were. She pushed Welly's hand away with difficulty; it felt as heavy as concrete. "When you start using phrases you learned as a soldier back in World War Two, I get alarmed!"

"It was the Korean— Borislav, I'm on commercial flight number 4242, Fly Me Airlines, London to Cardiff. Two zombies in the hold and an unknown number of passengers infected."

"Talk about loose lips," Alice muttered.

Welly shot her a dirty look. "Yes, and we'll need a clean-up team to meet us when we land."

The thought of Borislav meeting them at the Cardiff airport made the small hairs stand up on the back of her neck. Alice hoped she wouldn't have to talk to him, although he'd never been anything other than polite to her, even after garrotting her boyfriend.

Ahead of Alice, an elderly woman listed into the aisle, and her husband asked her if she was okay. Alice watched as the woman clumsily reached up to pat his arm. Then she sneezed.

"It's so tragic," Alice whispered to Welly, tears prickling in her eyes. "They're on their honeymoon!"

"Alice, send out calming energy," Welly ordered sharply, the Oddfone still pressed to his ear.

"I can't! I don't have any to spare."

Behind her a snack cart lurched down the aisle. "Peanuts? Drink?" Bronwyn asked, with way too much intensity in her voice.

"That's odd," Welly said. "There weren't supposed to be any snacks on this flight."

"Pray for us sinners now... sinners now ... and..." One of the nuns lost her place in her prayers.

"They gave us peanuts while we were stuck on the tarmac," Alice reminded him.

"That's different," Welly said. "They were trying to stave off a passenger revolt."

"Excuse me, Miss," said a voice behind them. "I asked for a diet cola."

"Peanuts?" the flight attendant replied. "Drink?"

"Oh no, I think she's infected too," Alice said.

"Infected?" the teenaged girl sitting directly behind Alice asked. She stuck her cell phone in the air and took a picture.

Her friend grabbed her arm. "Don't do that! The radiation from your phone could crash the plane."

"She said that woman's infected," the teenager insisted. "Infected with what? What's going on?"

"It's the title of my new album," Mick said, rejoining them. He mimed giant letters stretching across on a rainbow arc. "Infected. In red on a black background. With tap-dancing lab rats underneath."

He lowered his voice. "This is the voyage of the damned, as far as compromised immune systems are concerned. The delay before take off gave Darryl's flu virus plenty of time to set up shop, and there's more than one case of incipient liver disease. Hard drinkers, this bunch."

"Cut to the chase, Mick," Welly growled. "How many?"

"Hard to tell, but of the forty-eight passengers, I'd say twenty are showing signs of infection. Plus there could be more who are asymptomatic. FYI, two of the uninfected young men in the back row are planning an assault on the baggage compartment to rescue Darryl and Shelly."

"Possibly as many as twenty," Welly said into his phone. "No, I can't arrange to land somewhere more discreet!" He snapped the Oddfone closed and stood up, stepping over Alice. "Mick, stay out of trouble. I'll take care of our would-be heroes."

"How could the zombie virus spontaneously go airborne?" Alice whispered to Mick. She imagined microscopic zombie viruses floating around in the air and wondered how many she had already breathed in. She tried holding her breath.

Mick leaned over to speak directly into her ear. "Sometimes, when two viruses love each other very much, they rent a tastefully appointed cell, put on some mood music, have a few drinks, and then swap genetic material. Really, it's not so very different from us. Except zombie viruses will swap genetic material with absolutely anyone. They're quite promiscuous."

"This has happened before?" Alice asked.

"Oh, the zombie virus has ordered room service with everything from chicken pox to ebola, but I've never had a confirmed case of it going airborne before." Mick rubbed his hands together. "And it's happening right now in a closed system with re-circulated air. Isn't it marvellous? Just think of all the fresh blood samples I'll get." He straightened up and glanced in Welly's direction. "As soon as Mr. Spoilsport lets me take them."

Instead of heading straight to the back to deal with the students, Welly had stopped in the middle of the aisle. He was staring at his watch. "Foxtrot!"

"What now?" Alice yelped.

Welly strode back to their seats. "Mick, sit down." Mick ignored him and headed for the back of the plane instead. He had to climb over a seat to get past Bronwyn and her snack cart. "Peanuts!" she yelled after him.

As Welly retrieved his Oddfone from his jacket pocket, he said, "We should have begun our descent ages ago."

Leaning over Alice, he looked out the window, craning his neck. "It's not there." Welly opened his phone.

"What's not there?" Alice didn't dare look for herself.

"Cardiff," Welly said, in a low worried tone. "Or Newport or even Bristol. There's no telling how long we've been off course." Into the phone he said, "Lilith, tell Borislav he's got his wish." Welly concentrated for a moment and then began rattling off map co-ordinates.

Alice didn't have time to wonder how Welly knew their longitude and latitude. For just at that moment, the plane lurched and the teenagers behind them shrieked, then giggled. A seat belt sign started blinking above Alice's head.

"Omigawd, we're going to die!" one of the girls squealed. She sounded thrilled by the possibility.

"Omigawd?" her friend asked, sounding very confused.

Bizarrely, the nervous flyer was finally calm. From what Alice could hear, he was speaking rapidly into his phone about black op helicopters and government conspiracies.

The intercom came to life. "This is your captain speaking. We will be encountering some turbulence." After a brief pause, he added. "Please fasten your lap straps." Another pause. "And return all trays to their upright positions. We will... be encountering some turbulence."

"He sounds really confused," Alice said. Not that she could blame the poor pilot. She was feeling quite confused herself. As well as terrified and traumatized.

"Has he been infected?" Welly demanded, grabbing her shoulder.

"How would I know?"

He glowered at her.

"Oh right," Alice said. "I'm the Sensitive." She closed her eyes and attempted to focus. "*Om mani padme hum*."

This time, Alice didn't waste a minute on New Age visualizations of lakes, but went straight for the cockpit. To her inner eye, the pilot looked out of focus, as if he was a poor colour photocopy instead of a real person. The co-pilot was sharper, but he was slumped over his controls, breathing shallowly.

Alice steeled herself and then visualized grabbing the pilot by the skull.

It suddenly felt like her own mind was coated with thick, damp cotton wadding. She tried to think, but words and phrases jumbled around with no rhyme or reason. All she knew was that she had to land the plane, but memories of so many different landings inundated her, making it impossible to focus.

The plane lurched again, throwing Alice back into herself just as her butt left the seat for a brief moment. She squeaked in fright and grabbed her armrests. "All trays to their upright positions!" she blurted out.

"Alice?" Welly asked.

"The pilot's a zombie," she gasped.

All around her she could hear the other passengers saying, "Zombie?"

"For real?"

"Zombies aren't real!"

"It's a zombie plague!"

"All trays to their upright positions," the captain said.

Welly bent down and tightened her seat belt. "What about the co-pilot?"

The plane did an odd sort of sideways shimmy, eliciting another series of shrieks from the teenage girls. Alice shut her eyes tightly. "I don't know. I think he's unconscious."

Alice felt Welly straighten up and opened her eyes. "What are you doing?"

"I need to get into the cockpit and land this plane." This time when the plane bounced, Welly's head hit the ceiling. "Delta!"

"The cockpit door's locked," Alice protested. "You'd hurt yourself breaking it down, and you don't even know how to fly a plane, do you?"

"I can fly a Cessna," he said.

"And if we were in a teeny-tiny two-seater that'd be useful!" Alice raised her voice. "Does anyone here know how to land a real plane?" she asked the cabin at large.

People began to scream.

"For the love of Golf, Alice!" Welly snapped.

The captain's voice came back on the intercom. "Unfortunately, I... miscalculated the landing," he said. "We will circle the airport to have another go."

"I don't see an airport!" the still-nervous flyer cried out. "Where's the airport?" He stood up again and began stumbling toward the back of the plane.

"Sorry," Alice said to Welly, but he didn't respond. He was staring at the rear of the plane. "Get away from that door!" he shouted.

Alice twisted in her seat as Welly charged past her down the aisle. The nervous flyer was at the rear exit, yanking frantically on a bright red handle. Welly grabbed him by the back of his collar and pulled him away from the emergency exit. The man flailed, clawing at the air and grabbing at the seats. Alice saw one of his shoes go flying, right over Welly's head.

"You'll depressurize the plane!" someone shrieked.

"Don't be ridiculous!" Welly bellowed, his forearm locked around the nervous flyer's throat. "We don't have nearly the aaaaaltitude!"

The plane swooped forward, as if it was on a roller coaster, and this time all of the passengers screamed in perfect unison.

"Encountering turbulence," the captain said.

The plane tilted sideways and then righted itself.

"Trays upright," he added.

"We're all going to die," Alice said, covering her face with both hands.

"Don't you be ridiculous either," Welly said, shoving the considerably-more-than-nervous—and now gasping for air—flyer into his seat and buckling him in. Welly's hair was a mess, and the right breast pocket of his suit jacket was torn. "The vast majority of passengers survive crash landings if they behave calmly and sensibly."

Alice took a deep breath and reminded herself that she didn't actually have a premonition of anyone dying. Just of the plane crashing into the Welsh countryside, and at this point, you didn't have to be psychic to figure that out.

Ken lurched down the aisle and slammed into Welly. "Dave's secure," he said, breathlessly.

Welly grabbed him and pushed him down into his seat. "Strap yourself in," he said, over the cacophony. "I don't want you to die before I have a chance to kill you myself!"

Ken obeyed. "I got Shelley to buckle up in one of the jump seats in the back."

"What about Darryl?" Alice asked.

"Mick took care of him while I had words with two punks who thought I was a kidnapper. Idiots."

"Knew I forgot something," Welly muttered to himself.

"Approaching the runway," the captain said, distractedly.

Alice could now see the ground clearly through Welly's window. There was no runway. No houses or trees either. Just lots and lots of green land, all bunched up like a blanket on a messy bed.

The other passengers abruptly stopped screaming. It was as if everyone in the plane was holding their collective breath.

An old lady said, "Okay. I'm okay."

"Peanuts?" Bronwyn asked.

"Omigawd, omigawd…"

"Hail Mary?"

Welly pushed past her and buckled himself in, blocking the view. "Thank goodness," she said.

Then Welly's hand hit the back of her neck and pushed her head down. "Grab your ankles," he ordered.

"Wait," Alice said. "Where's Mick?"

"Trust me," Welly said. "Mick can take care of himself."

"Everyone, please lean forward in your seats and wrap your arms around your knees," Shelly called out, her voice high and tight with fear. "Note the emergency exits at each end of the plane."

I forgot to note the emergency exits, Alice thought. She tried to turn her head, but Welly's hand was still on her neck.

"Brace for impact!" the captain shouted.

"Brace!" Shelly echoed.

And immediately after, Alice could hear Bronwyn call out from the back of the plane, "Brace!"

There was a sudden drop, followed by a bounce up and a thump down. Alice had just enough time to think, Wow, are we on the ground already? That wasn't so bad.

Then the plane's nose tipped forward forty-five degrees.

"BRACE! BRACE! BRACE!"

*

Every time Alice had flown anywhere, she'd imagined dying in a plane crash. But she'd envisioned a big, fiery splat. It would be very sudden and very hot.

This crash wasn't sudden or hot.

This was a long, agonizing slide down the side of a hill into a ravine, followed by a loud crunching noise from the front of the plane.

The airplane seat dropped out from under Alice with an ominous groan of tortured metal. She felt the cushion beneath her come loose. Then she slammed back down and her knees hit the seat in front as the back of her chair folded forward, crushing her under its padding. Alice flailed helplessly, only to be grabbed by a strong hand and shoved back against her seat.

Wait, no. Not her seat. Somehow she was on the floor. Or the ceiling. Which way was up again?

In the midst of all the chaos, a familiar voice was shouting at her. Something about a door. Alice coughed, her eyes stinging. Smoke was coming from somewhere. She tried to sit up and banged her head on something hard. Grabbing it, Alice realized she was holding onto an armrest, which meant she did know where the floor was after all. Relieved, Alice suddenly remembered that Smokey the Bear always recommended staying low to the ground in fires. She flattened herself against the carpeting.

Head toward the door, the voice insisted. Alice confusedly recalled there was an emergency exit at the back of the plane. She groped her way down the tilted aisle on her hands and knees, cursing herself for paying absolutely no attention to the safety instructions. All she could remember was the useless part about the seat cushion functioning as a floatation device.

And her knees hurt! Why did her knees hurt so much?

Suddenly, the person who'd been manhandling her and ordering her around inexplicably decided to shove her down and crawl right over her. Before Alice could protest this treatment, the darkness in front of her cracked open, and her senses were flooded with warm sunshine and fresh air.

Air? Air!

Coughing, Alice crawled down the angled floor toward the door, only to be pinned back against the bulkhead by an all-too-solid arm. There was a hiss followed by an acrid, rubber smell, and then suddenly, a wall of incandescent yellow dropped down in front of her eyes and unfurled into a slide.

Before Alice could react, she was lifted and dropped out the door onto the inflatable escape chute.

Alice plummeted toward the ground. She shrieked and then gasped as she tumbled off the end of the slide onto muddy grass.

Almost instantly, another person landed on top of her. She struggled free, only to find herself face to face with a glassy-eyed teenager.

"Are you okay?" Alice asked.

The girl giggled hollowly, and it was one of the eeriest sounds Alice had ever heard. Abruptly realizing she was nose-to-nose with a zombie, Alice scrambled backward. The girl giggled again, just as a second teenager slid down and they both rolled several feet away together. Giggling.

Alice looked up. The plane had skidded to a stop against the side of a large hill. The front wheels had collapsed, and the nose was crumpled flat against the ground. Against the hillside, a broken wing stuck straight up in the air, the propeller missing. On the other side, behind the one intact wing, was the cheery yellow slide. She could see Welly in the doorway, smoke billowing around him. He was extracting passengers from the interior as fast as he could, disappearing and reappearing with people in his arms.

For a moment, she was distracted by the sight of his gorgeous heroism. Then he pitched an old lady onto the slide as if she was a sack of refuse. "Careful, oh careful!" Alice tried to shout. Her throat felt tight and not much sound came out.

Welly took more care with the lady's husband, but Alice knew it wasn't because he'd heard her. It was because the man wasn't a zombie. Probably wasn't a zombie, she amended, coughing. The inside of her throat felt like it had been exfoliated by a smoky loofah. Who knew what toxic chemicals she'd breathed in?

Alice climbed slowly to her feet, every muscle aching. She

staggered and bent down to rub her knees. Then it occurred to her that she was standing in a small valley surrounded by zombies and her Taser was somewhere back on the plane.

"Don't worry," a cheerful voice said behind her. "They're nearly all Stage One and far too disoriented to form a mob."

Alice felt several of Mick's dreads brush her cheek as he leaned in close to whisper in her ear. "I still wouldn't recommend chanting 'brains' around them."

Alice blinked. "Mick, you're alive!" Her voice sounded almost normal this time.

"A bit slow on the uptake, my worried wallaroo?" Mick looked as if he had stepped off the plane in perfect comfort. His tall top hat was still in place, and his tailcoat was unrumpled. Even his shoes were pristine, despite being planted in the middle of a muddy field. His walking stick had disappeared, but otherwise, there was no indication he'd just been in a plane crash.

"I was worried; you weren't in your seat when we crashed."

"Oh, I shared the casket with Dave," Mick said, putting on his sunglasses. "Remarkably roomy and comfortable."

The strangest image flashed into Alice's mind. Instead of Mick and Dave snuggled together in the broken shipping container as the plane went down, she saw Mick plastered spread-eagled on the ceiling of the kitchenette like a giant, leggy tree lizard.

Unable to cope with Mick confirming this vision, Alice wailed, "I don't understand any of this! Is everyone on the plane a zombie? Are they going to eat our brains? Am I a zombie?" Because if confusion was one of the early symptoms, Alice had it in spades.

For that matter, so did everyone else. Some passengers were slumped on the muddy ground, while others wandered around aimlessly, either in stunned silence or crying.

"I think I broke my leg," a man said, nearby.

A hand grabbed Alice's arm, making her start. "Help me and I'll explain what's happening."

Alice turned to find Ken regarding her with urgency. He looked the way she felt: rumpled, muddied, and bruised. She felt reality stabilize a little bit. Compared to Mick, who was still grinning at her, Ken was positively sane. "What about Welly?" Alice asked, pointing back at the plane.

Ken didn't bother looking up. "Enhanced Agents are very good at looking after themselves." He coughed and cleared his throat. "But the newly zombified aren't, so I need you to help me separate them from the uninfected. Some of the infected might also need first aid as well as crisis counselling."

Alice glanced around. From what she could see, it wasn't only the zombies who needed first aid or counselling. The nervous flyer was walking in agitated circles, around and around. One of the university students was trying to pull his buddy's leg straight. His friend screamed and then told him in no uncertain terms to leave it alone. "Call nine-one-one and get me a doctor!"

"You're such an American," his friend said, standing up and crossing his arms. "It's nine-nine-nine or one-one-two here, and there's no point because there's no cell phone service."

"Yeah, well, you're a Welsh bastard, and don't you dare touch my leg again."

"I'm okay," a quavering woman's voice insisted. Alice saw the old man standing over his elderly wife, helplessly. The woman smiled serenely up at him. "I'm okay." Her leg was sticking out at a right angle to her body and looked a lot worse than the American student's shin.

Ken went to them and gave her husband a reassuring pat. "Don't worry, she's not feeling any pain right now. We'll get that leg fixed up in no time." To Alice, he said, "Now that the fire's out, I want all the zombies and the potentially infected kept near the plane. The others can go over there." He pointed at the muddier half of the field.

Alice glanced up at the plane, and sure enough smoke was no

longer billowing out the open door. There was no sign of Welly.

She looked back and saw Mick sneak behind Ken's back and jab his Med-Trekker's needle into the old man's arm. He yelped.

"Mick," Alice scolded. "Welly told you not to manhandle anyone."

"I demand to know what's going on!" the old man shouted. "What's wrong with my wife? Why can't she feel her legs?"

"I was ordered to leave them alone during the flight," Mick said to Alice. "But now we're safely on the ground, so everyone's fair game." He pushed a button and a needle poked out of the Med-Trekker. Before Alice could react, he stabbed her with it.

"Ow! That better be a clean needle."

"Why won't anyone answer my questions?" the old man demanded.

"New needle every time," Mick said, patting his medical monster. "This baby holds up to three thousand hypodermic needles, seventy-five scalpel blades, and twenty-five sterilized catheters."

"Get away from me," Alice squeaked, but Mick had already moved on to his next victim, one of the Muslim businessmen.

"I'm okay," the old man's wife said, sweetly.

Ken had also left her side and was now arguing with the skinny man who'd been traveling with his wife and mother.

"I'm not leaving her," the man said. "Especially not if she's sick. She's my mother, damn it!"

"And I'm not leaving him," his much larger wife said. "Roddy can't look after himself. He'll just bugger everything up... Oh, I feel dizzy."

Suddenly she keeled over, knocking Roddy's mother off her feet. They both tumbled into the mud.

Ken frowned. "She might be infected too."

The skinny man bent over the two comatose women, slapping their cheeks in turn. "Agatha! Mom! Wake up!

Ken ended up letting them all stay in the zombie group.

"Chances are good Roddy's been exposed to the virus anyway," he told Alice. "He's just not showing symptoms yet, or his immune system might actually be able to fight it off." Ken's tone of voice clearly indicated which scenario he was rooting for.

A crawly sensation was working its way down the back of Alice's neck. She felt like thousands of microscopic zombie viruses were trying to find a way to colonize her cells and start making sweet, sweet love to each other. "But you said back on the plane it was difficult to catch."

"That's true when you can only catch it by exchanging bodily fluids. Under normal circumstances, only a chosen few get the privilege of becoming a zombie," Ken said. "Regrettably, some of the passengers who breathed in the virus still won't get sick, but only if they maintain a strong, healthy immune system and they're kept separate from the infected." He paused. "Now that there's an airborne variant, I'll have to be extra careful about screening my Mailroom staff. Maybe I should get an infra-red scanner installed in the main entrance to measure body temperature."

"Uh oh," Alice said, pointing over his shoulder. "Bronwyn's wandering off."

Ken captured Bronwyn by the back of her collar and steered her into the zombie herd. "Brace," she said. "Brace, brace."

A middle-aged zombie in a Hawaiian shirt turned toward her. "Brace," he said, agreeably.

"So many Stage Two," Ken said worriedly. "I really need to get them safely back to Head Office soon."

"What are all these stages you guys keep talking about?" Alice said, shooing the Hawaiian shirt clad zombie away from her.

As Ken organized the zombies, trying to make them more comfortable, he explained to Alice that there were five stages of zombification. Stage One was the initial zombie infection, which was hard to conclusively identify without a blood test or a zombie tracker like Dave. The person still appeared healthy and showed only minor neurological impairment. They were more obsessive-compulsive than usual, more confused, and a little too trusting.

Alice spotted Mick handing out brochures to the passengers in the potential zombie category. She overheard him saying to one older man, "You're either very gullible, my friend, or you're a Stage One zombie. Either way, you'll love my free Tropical Beat Date Night for Seniors."

Alice suddenly realized one particular zombie was conspicuous by his absence. "Where's Dave?" she asked, nervously glancing around.

"Safe in his fireproof box," Ken said. "Only the outer shipping container was damaged, and he has enough air in his casket to last for days."

Alice gave a sigh of relief. She didn't care about Ken's delusion that Dave breathed, as long as his corpse-like friend wasn't lurching around terrifying people.

Ken led Alice away from the pile of zombies and started herding healthier-looking people away from them. Alice's new Mock Martens were getting coated in mud.

"Is this how the zombie apocalypse begins?" The student desperate to make money was back. "Are all those people zombies? Are they fast zombies or slow zombies, and when do they start eating people?" He held up his phone, which was recording video.

"Shut up," Alice said. " There's no such things as fast zombies, I mean, zombies at any speed."

"Is it a government conspiracy to hide the existence of zombies?" the student persisted.

"Did someone say conspiracy?" the nervous flyer asked.

"If your partner was more reasonable, Dave could be a real help right now," Ken said. He was calm as if none of this chaos was happening around him. Grabbing the student by the shoulder, he shone a pen light into his eyes, measuring how well they tracked.

"Dave can sniff out even the earliest stages of zombism."

"Aha, you said zombism," the student crowed. "There is a cover-up!"

"You're not helping," Alice said to Ken. "It's one thing to use the zed word around the... um, zeds, but... Stop filming me!" She smacked at the student's phone, but he ducked away.

"It's a conspiracy!" the nervous flyer wailed. "It's a secret British government project to test a new biological weapon on Welsh civilians, and they're all part of it!"

"He's right," the student said. He was out of arm's reach now and aiming his phone at Ken. "I bet you guys engineered all of this to breed super zombies—super Welsh zombies!" He stared at his phone, looking frustrated. "I can't believe there's no mobile coverage out here. How am I supposed to upload any of this?"

"That's ridiculous," a nearby middle-aged British woman said. "It's that guy's fault we crashed." She pointed at a Middle Eastern man who was on his knees and single-mindedly repeating a phrase in a language Alice couldn't identify.

"That's insane," Alice snapped.

"Yeah, how racist can you get?" the student asked.

The woman propped her hands on her skinny hips. "Before we crashed, you and your friends said there were terrorists on the plane."

"That was before I knew about the zombie plague," the student shot back.

"Zombies don't exist. Terrorists do!"

"You're all wrong," Alice insisted. "The plane crashed because of the pilot. I mean, it wasn't really his fault, he just got sick... in his brain... like an aneurysm."

"I heard you say the pilot was a zombie," said a very disapproving voice behind her.

Alice turned and saw one of the nuns on the ground, holding the other one's head in her lap. The zombified nun was muttering,

"Hail Mary brace." The clear-eyed, angry nun shook her finger at Alice. "If you didn't want impressionable minds to believe this zombie nonsense, why did you spread the rumour…" The nun looked down at her fellow nun and chided softly, "Sister Luke, please stop gnawing on my rosary beads. Let us pray together instead."

Alice backed away from the nuns slowly. The nervous flyer was back to circling, though now he was staring up at the sky.

Ken tapped the Middle Eastern man on the shoulder and pointed at the uninfected group.

"He's just praying," he told Alice.

The nuns were praying too, but Ken sent them both into the zombie group. The healthy nun hefted Sister Luke to her feet, the sick nun still chewing on rosary beads.

"Is Sister Luke Stage Two?" Alice whispered.

"Yes, definitely," Ken said, not bothering to keep his voice down. "Stage Two is much easier to identify, although more difficult to manage. They often get locked into repetitive behaviour patterns, usually associated with something they do in daily life."

"You can almost see their IQ points dropping away, one by one," Mick commented, as he strode by in pursuit of another victim.

"They can also become aggressive, especially if they were in a state of high anxiety prior to infection," Ken said.

"Like her?" Alice asked, pointing to the nearby Bronwyn. She was still repeating, "Brace, brace, brace!" but it now sounded more like a satanic chant rather than a helpful suggestion. Even the other zombies were trying to avoid her.

"She's definitely getting there." Ken walked over and took Bronwyn's hands. Staring into her randomly rolling eyes he said softly, "I let go of my past and embrace my zombie future."

"What are you doing?" Alice asked, cautiously approaching them.

"Positive affirmations can ease the psychological stresses

zombies experience," Ken said. He then told Bronwyn, "Today I will embrace all that is beautiful in decomposition."

Bronwyn snapped her jaws at Ken, and Alice jumped back.

"Frustration is a big problem in Stage Two," Ken said to Alice. "So you need to be extra patient and understanding. I've created a pamphlet of positive affirmations for zombies. Odyssey won't let me distribute it to the general public, but you can have a copy if you want."

"Sure," Alice said, humouring him.

Turning back to the flight attendant, Ken said, "Zombie life is good. I am at peace." Keeping a firm grip on Bronwyn's hands, Ken sat her down with the other zombies. In a soothing voice, he repeated, "Peace, peace, peace..."

Ken's chanting was mesmerizing, and Alice found herself nodding along with the zombies.

"Bad news, my delightful dingo," Mick announced, breaking into her reverie.

Alice started to panic, envisioning herself—earless and noseless—working in Odyssey's Mailroom. But she quickly realized Welly would save her from such an unbearable fate and shoot her in the head. That thought was strangely soothing.

"She's not a zombie, right?" Ken asked, not looking away from Bronwyn.

"And she would have made such a cute one," Mick said. "Plus Agent Washington recently had a very bad day in Outer Mongolia, and her delightfully African-American nose would add some much needed colour to Alice's pasty Irish looks."

"Thanks a lot." Alice was so relieved, she only half-heartedly smacked Mick.

"You break it, you bought it," Mick chided her, before telling Ken, "You're not a zombie either, my moustachioed moloch, but that's hardly surprising. You'd have long ago started sorting mail with your staff if you were at all susceptible to this virus."

— 88 —

"Moloch?" Alice asked. "Did you just call Ken a demon?"

"No, I called him a harmless reptile that walks funny. Also known as the Thorny Devil, but don't let the name fool you. They are gentle and considerate lovers."

"With each other, right?" Alice asked. "Right?"

Mick waggled his eyebrows by way of answering before saying, "I've noticed that Odyssey personnel are statistically much less likely to be infected when compared with the general population. I'm working on a new theory, specifically to do with the possible presence of zombie cooties on interoffice mail, which means we can use your blood serum to help develop a vaccine. Of course, it could be the brand of coffee in the break rooms in which case..."

"Just who are you people?" one of the healthy-looking passengers demanded in a thick Welsh accent. She was a tall woman with a large purse clutched tight against her chest. "You're clearly not with Fly Me Airlines. I want to know who's in charge of this fiasco!"

Alice blinked. The purse was moving. And it appeared to have air holes. "Interpol, I think," she said, distractedly, staring at the bag. "But don't worry, help is on the way." The purse barked at her. Alice wondered if animals could catch zombism.

"I want answers as well." The skinny man waved a stick-like arm back at his mother and wife. They were sitting in a heap on the ground together, like two traumatized Pillsbury dough girls. "Look what you've done to them!"

Alice couldn't think of a single thing to say to him or the woman with the growling dog in her purse. Or the students who were arguing with the lady who insisted that accusing Muslims of terrorism was rational, not racist. Or the young man on the ground, holding his leg and making hurt noises. Kumbaya, she desperately thought at them all, willing them to calm down.

Instead, another irate passenger joined the group surrounding her and Ken, wanting to know why a strange moustachioed American was telling them where they could sit in a godforsaken field. Then a very rumpled businessman demanded someone do something about the crazy man stabbing everyone with needles.

Kumba-help, Alice thought.

6

Odyssey Arrives in Style

As if in answer to Alice's prayers, Welly walked up beside her carrying a large box. Instantly, the irate passengers stopped shouting at her and turned to stare at him, as if sensing that here was a real leader.

He reeked of smoke, and the right pocket of his jacket was hanging on by a thread, but otherwise he appeared undamaged. "There was a gas leak on the plane." His voice was a hoarse rasp, but that had no impact on his aura of command. "Several of the passengers have been in—er, affected by the gas. The authorities have been contacted and will be arriving very soon. For now, please take a water bottle, sit down and rest."

Water, Alice thought, diving into the box. Welly, I love you!

Mick appeared out of nowhere and peered into the box. "No, no, no," he said. "This won't do at all. I need caffeine. Coffee, an energy drink, or even a Cuba Libre, hold the rum." He strode back to the plane, muttering to himself.

Welly ignored Mick and handed out water to the uninfected passengers, spinning a yarn about natural gas causing visual and auditory hallucinations. He sounded very convincing, and they appeared willing to be convinced. Alice was too grateful to resent the fact that he was doing her job better than she had.

Alice took a long drink of water and let herself relax. Suddenly, she realized something sharp was poking into her ribs and had been for some time. She stuck a hand under her shirt and found a thin piece of metal. "It's the underwire of my bra!" Alice exclaimed, pulling it out. "The crash broke my bra. They sure don't warn you about that in the safety instructions."

No one took any notice of her.

"Will the plane explode?" the skinny man asked, nervously.

"The plane will not explode," Welly reassured him. "The fire started in the coffee makers and stayed mostly confined to the kitchen."

Alice gulped down some more water and glanced at the plane. There were only a few wisps of smoke escaping out of the emergency exit now. As she examined it, Mick emerged, carrying a large clear bag full of half-sized cans of cola and packets of peanuts. When she looked back, Welly was showing his fake Interpol I.D. to the woman with the purse dog.

"Every day, in every way, my body's holding together," several voices intoned.

Ken had all of the zombies and possible-zombies sitting in a circle and chanting affirmations in unison.

Mick strolled up and handed the infected nun a can of pop. "Drink," he urged her. "That's right. Drink it all down." As she drank, he stared at her intently, pushing buttons on his Med-Trekker. "Coffee would be better, but when life tosses you a grenade, you make do with mechanical hands."

The other zombies didn't appear to notice Mick's odd behaviour. The healthy passengers, for their part, had calmed down a great deal thanks to Welly's reassurances, and most seemed convinced that all the zombie talk was the result of gas fumes. Only the student with the cell phone was still agitated, but that was because he couldn't get any reception.

Alice felt ashamed. She hadn't dealt with the healthy passengers in any kind of constructive way, and Ken had been able to handle the zombies by himself. In retrospect, Alice realized she hadn't been much help on the plane either. Sure, she'd had a premonition they were going to crash, but way too late for it to be useful.

Alice told herself firmly that she'd have to do better from this moment onward. Unfortunately, she didn't know what exactly to do better.

She gazed at the student with the broken leg, but all of Alice's first aid training said, "Don't touch! You'll just make it worse." In fact, she could clearly hear her Red Cross instructor's voice in her head, saying those very words. For some reason, he'd liked to say it a lot.

Mick wasn't really helping anyone either. Having handed out all of the soft drinks, he was now busy walking clockwise around the circle of zombies, pausing periodically to throw what appeared to be salted peanuts over their heads.

"Mick, you're supposed to be a doctor!" Alice shouted at him. "Help these people!"

"I am." Mick flashed her a broad grin before continuing with his bizarre ceremony.

Ken disengaged himself from the chanting zombies, took the packets of peanuts away from Mick, and headed over to Alice. "The affirmations should hold them until Odyssey arrives."

"Why are some of them so much," she lowered her voice, "more zombie-ish than others? I understand Darryl hitting Stage Two first, but didn't everyone else get infected more or less at the same time?"

"Viruses affect all individuals differently," Ken said. "It could be any number of factors, from the health of their immune system to the strength of the strain they're exposed to. Some people speed through Stage One within minutes, others take hours, days or even weeks."

Welly joined them and asked Ken, "What's the status of the zom — infected?" His voice already sounded perfectly normal again, as if he hadn't been on a burning plane at all. Alice's throat still felt scratchy.

Mick bounced past them, his Med-Trekker warbling shrilly. "A cure! A cure! My kingdom for a cure!"

Welly gestured to Ken and Alice to move out of earshot of the passengers. "Mick is getting far too excited about his findings, and you know that's never a good sign. What's the status of the zombies?"

"This airborne virus must be particularly virulent variant," Ken told them. "Several of the passengers are in Stage Two already. Darryl could be Stage Three within hours."

Before Alice could ask what happened in Stage Three Welly said, "Then I'll deal with them now, before they start mobbing people." He reached into his jacket for his gun.

"Over my dead body," Ken snapped, grabbing his arm.

"That can be arranged," Welly growled, "especially if you don't let go right now."

Alice made a disgusted sound. "Oh, stop it, both of you! You sound like the Tough Guy facing down his Egotistical Adversary in James Patterson's latest, trashiest novel. Now Ken, let Welly go. You know you're only making matters worse by invading his personal space."

After a moment, Ken reluctantly unhanded Welly and crossed his arms sulkily. Then Alice turned on her partner.

She jabbed her finger into Welly's perfectly muscled chest. "You can't shoot a nun. It's a sin even if you're Anglican and not a Catholic." Alice winced and shook her finger. Would she ever learn to stop poking him in his granite-hard pecs, she wondered.

"Shooting a dead nun isn't a sin," Welly insisted.

"She's not dead yet!" Ken protested.

"I wasn't done!" Alice shouted. Then she continued in a quieter voice, "Welly, Ken's right, they're still people at this stage, not undead monsters."

"That's not what I said," Ken argued.

"Not. Done. Yet," Alice said, giving him a stern look. Then she turned her attention back to Welly. "And if you start shooting the zombies, you'll panic all the healthy passengers. Some of them could end up badly hurt or even infected because of you."

Welly let go of his gun and pulled his hand out of his jacket. Alice felt vindicated. She was useful after all, if only for subduing testosterone-fuelled overreactions. Still, it was a start.

"Shooting them would be a mercy," Welly grumbled. "Do you know what happens in Stage Three?"

"They get like Dave?" Alice asked.

Ken tugged at his moustache distractedly. He glanced back at the zombies, who were still sitting in their cozy circle. "I should check on Dave," Ken said. He walked toward the half-buried nose of the plane.

Welly didn't try to stop him. "Stage One is the initial zombie infection."

"I know all about that," Alice said. A cold breeze blew down the valley and she thought she could hear helicopters in the distance.

"Stage Two is borderline zombism. That's when they start to get dangerous."

"Yes, Ken told me. He just never got to Stage Three." Alice could definitely hear several choppers now, getting closer.

"Stage Three is..." Welly paused. "Do you hear that?"

"Yeah, yeah, helicopters," Alice said. "Tell me about Stage Three. Borislav's going to be here any minute."

"If you say so," Welly said, looking amused.

Alice ran a quick internal check, reminding herself about the importance of trusting first impressions. When it came to being psychic, it never paid to over-think. "It's definitely Odyssey."

The nervous flyer pointed at the sky. "Black ops! I can hear the black ops helicopters!"

Welly rolled his eyes. "Life is so much easier when our men are the first on the scene, even if Borislav's with them." He turned away from Alice and started walking toward the flatter part of the field.

Three helicopters crested the hill, and the nervous flyer began waving his arms wildly, trying to convince people to run for the hills. Everyone stayed put. The two large Chinooks overhead hardly looked like black ops helicopters as they were painted bright orange and turquoise. The small, black, five-seater following the two heavy transport copters was barely noticeable.

"Wait!" Alice called after Welly. "What about Stage Three? What does that look like?"

But even with his enhanced hearing, Welly couldn't hear her over the sound of the Odyssey helicopters landing on the far side of the field.

Moments later, Odyssey personnel were swarming over the scene, their black uniforms identifying them as Borislav's security forces. Security at Odyssey included external clean-up jobs as well as internal security. Alice knew 'clean up' was the Odyssey euphemism for a multitude of sins, including destroying supernatural property and tampering with witnesses.

Welly was in the middle of it all, shouting instructions which were largely ignored. Alice moved closer to the crashed plane, staying well back from the chaos. She knew Borislav himself was somewhere nearby, as the small, black helicopter perched between the two Chinooks belonged to him. However, Alice didn't expect to spot him in the crowd. Borislav had a way of blending into the background, even as the ominous impact of his presence was everywhere.

Soon, medical personnel carrying stretchers exited one of the Chinooks and began collecting the injured. Alice spotted the student with the broken leg being carried to the transport helicopter on the right. She also saw Ken helping the medics guide the zombies toward the helicopter on the left. The newly zombified appeared very willing to stick with their peers and obediently follow Ken.

Most of them were, at any rate. Shelly the flight attendant kept sitting down on the ground and trying to assume the crash position. Alice wondered if Shelly would like her new job at Odyssey anymore than her old one with Fly Me Airlines. Alice supposed there were worse fates than working in the Mailroom, although personally she'd rather die. Still, Shelly would get into less trouble there as there was no zombie equivalent of the Mile High Club in the Mailroom. At least Alice sincerely hoped there wasn't.

Alice frowned. Ken was guiding both Darryl and Shelly onto the left-hand helicopter. However, Bronwyn, their superior, was nowhere in sight.

Borislav's guards weren't having as much success herding the healthy into the helicopter on the right. Alice saw one pair confiscate the student's cell phone, and the angry young man took a swing at them. Two more guards came to their co-workers' aid, and tackled the student. The nervous flyer began to shout about police brutality, drawing more passengers into the conflict. Soon the four guards were surrounded, and the woman with the barking purse demanded to know where they were being taken.

Alice didn't catch the answer, but clearly it didn't satisfy, as more passengers began to yell at them and press in closer. Hoping to help calm things down, Alice began to walk toward them. She was only halfway there, when the skinny man shouted, "You're kidnapping my mother and wife!" He then shoved one of the female guards. She shoved back, and a general melee broke out. A woman screamed as a very agitated Chihuahua escaped from her purse and began running around wildly.

"Calm down!" Alice shouted, as she tried to push her way through the crowd. "Everyone calm the hell down!"

The uninfected nun blinked at her and nodded, "Calm down." She appeared to relax, but whatever spell Alice had put over her was broken when the dog darted up and bit the nun on the ankle. Alice dodged quickly to avoid the killer Chihuahua as the limping nun chased after it, yelling, "Spawn of Satan!"

Alice had to keep moving to avoid being knocked down and ducked just in time to avoid a leather briefcase flying through the air. She began to have second thoughts about wading into the crowd and turned to run.

And found herself face to face with Bronwyn.

"Brace," Bronwyn growled, baring her teeth.

"No! No bracing, bad zombie," Alice said, trying to back away, but there was no room in the growing free-for-all.

"Brace," Bronwyn insisted. "Brace, bra—!"

Her last 'brace' was abruptly cut off as Welly put Bronwyn in a headlock. Alice nearly collapsed in relief.

"Get out of here!" Welly barked at her, yanking Browyn off her feet, causing her face to turn blue.

"Don't kill her!" Alice cried out. "It's not her fault she wants to eat my brains."

Welly grimaced, but he loosened his chokehold. Bronwyn wheezed, "Brainnnnnss."

"Now get out of here," Welly ordered. He began to drag Bronwyn toward the left-hand helicopter.

Alice followed in his wake, protesting, "I'm your partner, not a damsel in distress who needs rescuing!" She paused, then added, "Okay, except from Browyn, but that's different, she's a zombie and…"

Suddenly, all thought was disrupted and everyone gripped their head, including Bronwyn. It was like a blast from an ear-splitting air horn, except there was no audible sound. Slowly, everybody turned toward the small, black helicopter in front of which was a stocky old man of unremarkable appearance, a bright orange Thought Disrupter 3000 held loosely in his right hand. Alice shivered. Borislav.

With a benign smile, Borislav slipped the small orange wand into his pocket and began to speak ponderously in a soft tone. The crowd hushed as everyone strained to hear his heavily accented words.

"We are Odyssey International Search and Rescue. We will take you to Cardiff Airport, your original destination. Ambulances will take injured to the University Hospital of Wales; all arrangements have been made.

"Do not be concerned about the passengers who became ill. They will receive very best of private medical care from Odyssey. Please, remain calm and I promise, very soon this will all be a happy memory."

Borislav bowed his head slightly and signalled to his people to resume their work.

The only statement that rang true to Alice was the last. This wouldn't be the first time Odyssey had modified peoples' memories to suit their purposes. "Welly, tell me Borislav isn't planning on making all these people disappear?"

When he didn't answer, Alice realized Welly was no longer nearby. "Welly!" she called out, suddenly panicked.

"Right behind you," Welly said, making her jump. "Sensitives should be more aware of their surroundings."

"Where were you?" Alice shot back.

"I had to dispose of Bronwyn," Welly said, frowning at his jacket now covered with dark stains.

"Not permanently?" Alice asked, apprehensively.

"Unfortunately, no," Welly said. "Dead zombies don't drool all over one's suit."

"That's great... I mean, sorry." Alice lowered her voice. "About

Borislav—"

"Not here," Welly cut her off and led her toward the crashed airplane, away from the passengers and Odyssey staff.

As they got closer, Alice saw the emergency slide had been detached and deflated, and was now rolled up neatly by the plane. Alice knew Welly had been compulsively tidying up the accident scene. Of more concern, someone else had jimmied open the second emergency exit near the cockpit. Before she could get worried, though, the culprit popped into her head.

"Ken's back in the plane," she told Welly. "He's looking for someone."

"Probably that Delta'd zombie of his." Welly snorted disgustedly. "Now, what did you want to tell me?"

"Tell you... right, Borislav." Alice glanced around nervously, but there was no sign of the Russian. "Um... he wasn't telling the truth about where he's taking the passengers. Nothing terrible is going to happen to them, is it?"

"Don't be ridiculous," Welly said. "Remember when you were airlifted by Odyssey from the nuclear bunker?"

"No, I don't remember," Alice shot back. "Mick messed with my mind, and forty-eight hours of my life was sucked out of my brain."

"There you go, no permanent harm done," Welly said.

It was a fair comment, Alice thought, considering she'd woken up in her apartment, which Odyssey staff had cleaned better than she ever had. Still, no one she knew had become a zombie during her missing days. Alice watched as the Chinook bearing the non-zombified passengers lifted off. "What about all the zombies' relatives? What will they be told?"

"After the memory modification, standard operating procedure is to tell them their relative moved to Africa and heroically saved the lives of several orphans before being eaten by a lion."

"A lion," Alice repeated, incredulously. "And what do you tell people who are from Africa?"

"That their relative moved to California and died in a wildfire, but only after heroically…"

"Saving a bunch of orphans," Alice finished, and shook her head. "That's terrible."

"Better than the truth," Welly said, fatalistically. He waved at Mick. Mick pointed at himself and raised his eyebrows questioningly. "Mick, stop playing games and get over here," Welly barked.

As Mick sauntered over, Alice watched as the remaining security guards spread out, searching the valley and the hillside, looking for any evidence that would need to be 'cleaned up'. The helicopter with the zombies had remained behind and was being used by Security to store debris. Alice supposed there was no reason to rush the zombies back to Odyssey's Mailroom. They'd have the rest of their afterlife to handle packages of occasionally exploding mail.

Mick gave Welly a mock salute. "*Oui, mon capitaine?*"

"Save it. I realize now I should have warned you away from the passengers after we landed. Now, was there any purpose to you jabbing all of them or were you just doing it for Sierras and giggles?"

"Not just a purpose, but one that will live down the ages!" Mick declared, slipping the Med-Trekker into his messenger bag. "Thanks to getting these samples at such early stages of zombism, I'm close to a cure. Oh, so very close!" Mick clapped his palms together and wiggled his fingertips like the mad scientist he was.

"That's wonderful," Alice said, feeling hopeful. Maybe the infected in the helicopter weren't all doomed to become Odyssey Mailroom employees.

Welly snorted rudely. "I'll believe it when I see it, Mick. Every single time there's a zombie outbreak, you promise the exact same thing."

"I'm hurt," Mick said, not sounding hurt at all.

Ken poked his head out of the plane's forward entrance and shouted, "Wellington, I need some of that brute, physical strength of yours!" For all that the tail of the plane was elevated, this door was nearly at ground level, thanks to the collapse of the front wheels.

"He only wants you for your body!" Alice called after Welly. She was giddy with relief now that the whole dreadful adventure was over. Somewhere back in London there was an old lady hugging a cat named Mr. Snuggles, claiming he'd saved her life by running away and forcing her to miss her plane. Alice knew exactly how she felt, having teetered on the edge of a zombie apocalypse, but instead escaping disaster by the skin of her teeth.

All's well that ends well, Alice told herself.

"Whatever gave you that idea?" Mick asked.

"Mick, stop invading my mind."

"Hardly an invasion, more of a drive-by peeking," Mick said. "So why do you think we're all done with zombies? Don't forget, our original mission was to investigate a credible zombie sighting in Wales." He gave his messenger bag a pat. "While this airborne strain is a gorgeous specimen, somewhere out there is another uniquely beautiful virus just waiting to be added to my collection. If it's compatible with the airborne virus, I might be able to marry them, and together with some coffee, salt, proper facilities, and the blessings of the Baron La Croix, we'll give birth to a bouncing baby cure."

"Marry the viruses to each other, you mean," Alice said, needing the reassurance.

"Of course, unlike bacterium, viruses refuse to marry outside their species. Terribly parochial of them, but there's no arguing with viruses."

Alice decided to join Welly on the plane. Long conversations with Mick were rarely fruitful and often alarming.

Still, it took a fair bit of courage for Alice to climb back into the plane. Once inside, she was relieved to discover it wasn't as scary as she remembered. Everything stank of smoke, but the air was clear now. She could see that all of the seats had disintegrated into heaps of cushions and snapped armrests.

"Everything's broken," Alice exclaimed. "This wasn't such a safe plane, after all."

"The seats are designed to collapse," Welly said. "They absorb the impact of landing. Leg injuries are still pretty common, but people's necks and backs rarely get broken anymore."

"Brace..." a muffled voice said.

"Is someone still in here?" Welly asked Ken. "I was sure I cleared the passenger section."

Alice clapped her hands over her mouth. "That's Darryl! We forgot all about him." She ran to the back of the passenger section, both men following her.

"I never forget a zombie," Ken said, sounding offended.

Alice lowered her shields and quickly scanned for the missing flight attendant, but his mind wasn't like healthy brains. His thoughts were even more confused than the pilot's had been, and Darryl had no idea where he was.

"Brace," he said again, and Alice suddenly realized where he was.

"You stuffed him in this overhead compartment, didn't you?" Alice accused Ken.

"No," Ken said, thoughtfully. "I suspect it was Mick who stashed him up there."

"We've got to get him out of there," Alice said, reaching for the catch.

Welly caught her hand. "We're certainly not letting him out," he said. "There's no reason to allow him run around loose, just so he can start biting us."

"I hate to say it," Ken said. "But I agree with Wellington this time. Darryl's safe where he is for now. I've already checked on

— 103 —

him, and he's in good shape."

"How did Mick manage to get Darryl into one of the overhead compartments without any of the other passengers noticing?" Welly asked aloud.

"It's amazing the hijinks you can get up to when everyone's distracted by a plane crash," Ken said.

"Brace…" Darryl said, sadly.

Alice felt sorry for him. "Poor guy, he's going to die soon, isn't he?"

"Of course not," Ken said. "I've been able to keep zombies alive for years. And when mummification is successful, they can survive for at least a decade or more. I'm extending their lifespans all the time."

Wow, Alice thought. Ken had completely lost his mind. He needed to spend more time with actually living people instead of zombies.

"Darryl isn't my main concern," Ken continued, leading them back to the front end of the plane. "The door to the cockpit got warped during the crash. The pilot and the co-pilot are trapped in there, and I need to be able to get to them. The pilot is certainly a zombie, but I don't know if he's been injured. I also need to check the condition of the co-pilot; he might have been infected too."

When they reached the door, Welly rapped on it with his knuckles, as if testing its composition.

"I wonder if Borislav's men have anything like the Jaws of Life," Alice began, when a precognitive vision flashed through her mind.

Alice cried out, "Don't do that!" seconds before Welly reared back and kicked in the door with an ear-splitting clang of metal.

"There you go," Welly said to Ken. "One open door. Have fun with your zombie mates."

"I don't know why you bring me along if you're not going to listen to me," Alice said, annoyed that one of her rare glimpses of the future had been completely wasted. "And it would be nice if you thought twice about a dumb macho stunt that's going to hurt your ankle."

Welly gave her a sharp look. "My ankle's fine."

"No, it's not," Alice said. "You'll wait until you think no one's watching, then you'll pull up your pant leg and strap the he—"

Welly held up one warning finger, interrupting her.

Alice rolled her eyes. "... And strap the H-E-double hockey sticks out of it."

"He's not here," Ken exclaimed, sounding very agitated.

"Who?" Alice asked.

"The captain," Ken said. "The co-pilot's dead, but the pilot's not here!"

"Foxtrot!" Welly exclaimed, pushing into the small cabin.

From the doorway Alice could see what had both men transfixed. The escape hatch in the roof of the cockpit was wide open.

7

Borislav Cleans Up the Welsh Countryside

"Lovely," Welly snarled. "Now I get the pleasure of informing Borislav."

Ken grabbed Welly's arm. "No, let me handle this!"

Welly yanked his arm out of Ken's grasp. "Look, I don't enjoy having to turn this over to Borislav," Welly said, in a restrained tone. "But procedure dictates when quarantine is broken—"

"The pilot couldn't have gone far," Ken said, desperately. "And Dave is out there tracking him."

"Dave's missing too?" Welly barked. "How the Hotel did he get out of his casket?"

Alice instantly knew how. "Oh Ken," she said. "You said you were only going to check on Dave, not let him out."

"He wasn't comfortable in—" Ken began.

"This gets better and better," Welly cut him off. "Two missing zombies. Borislav's going to skin us alive and feed us to the Admiral."

"Can you skin an Enhanced Agent?" Alice wondered aloud. Then she immediately wished she hadn't, as the answer popped into her head. "With a power sander. Ow."

"If you tell Borislav there are any zombies unaccounted for," Ken said, "he'll bomb this entire area and tell the Welsh authorities it was a wildfire."

Welly's expression clearly said he couldn't see a downside to that scenario.

"But you know it never completely works," Ken continued. "Every year they're massacring more zombies in California."

Alice could sense Ken was telling the truth. Or at least, he believed everything he said. Borislav was definitely ruthless enough to torch large swathes of the western seaboard of the United States, Alice thought. However, considering how fanatical Ken was on the subject of zombies, she doubted all California wildfires were caused by Odyssey's clean-up crews. Maybe just most of them.

"I've got a really strong feeling Ken is right about Dave tracking the pilot," Alice said. "And it'd be a shame to lose Dave." As zombies went, he was pretty harmless, except to overly curious flight attendants.

"No, it wouldn't," Welly said, glowering. "Losing Dave wouldn't be any kind of shame at all." He gestured through the cracked windows of the cockpit. "What would be a shame is losing all this beautiful countryside because a couple of the walking dead decided to go for a stroll."

"I hate that TV show," Ken said, suddenly.

"*The Walking Dead*?" Alice asked. "Okay, the pilot episode was like watching undead paint dry. And yes, then it became a soap opera with occasional cannibalism but it's still better than..." The thunderous look on Ken's face shut her up.

"*The Walking Dead* perpetrates and popularizes every disgusting stereotype about zombies, including the misleading and insulting title!"

"No, you don't get it," Alice said. "In the graphic novels it was very clear that the walking dead are the human survivors not—"

"Enough!" Welly barked. "We have bigger fish to fry."

Welly reached up and slammed shut the escape hatch. He then bent over the dead co-pilot and tore off his name tag. "When Borislav's guards check the cockpit, we need them to report that the pilot is dead."

"Good plan." Ken snapped his fingers. "I'll check and see if I can find an extra uniform. Darryl can stand in for the co-pilot. The condition he's in, he won't be able to tell them anything different. It should take Security at least three hours to get around to running identity checks."

Welly made a sound of approval as he dragged the co-pilots corpse over to the pilot's seat. "I have to say, using Darryl didn't occur to me. Not bad. Two bodies in the cockpit should allay even Borislav's suspicions, for a while."

"We're going to dress up a zombie?" Alice asked, faintly. Watching Welly manhandle the dead co-pilot was bad enough; the thought of getting that close to Darryl and his airborne virus pals made her feel twice as nauseated.

Ken gave her an impatient look. "Darryl's not a child. I'm going to assist him in dressing himself."

Welly strapped the corpse into the pilot's seat. "Ken, you're in charge of turning our zombie steward into a co-pilot."

As Ken left the cockpit, Welly added, "Alice, if you could—"

"Oh no, I'm not helping him," Alice said. "I'm going to get our overnight bags. You two can play macabre musical chairs by yourselves."

Alice re-entered the passenger area and felt a moment of despair looking over the wreckage. How could she figure out which overhead bin to look in when it was impossible to find where they'd been sitting? For that matter, her purse was somewhere under the seats which were now a pile of broken plastic and pleather.

Then Alice rolled her eyes. "You're a psychic, dummy," she admonished herself. Even before joining Odyssey, she'd been good at finding things. Especially if she'd had contact with the item or the person who'd lost it. One afternoon, Alice had found ten sets of lost car keys for people on a Vancouver beach before she got bored with the whole exercise.

"Come out, come out, wherever you are," Alice called out to her pink Hello Kitty hair brush, and immediately she knew which bin housed her overnight bag. Making her way through the debris, she was glad it was nowhere near where Darryl was stored.

Welly's collapsed seat had fallen into the aisle. Alice was about to climb on top of it to reach the undamaged bin when she spotted her purse partially buried underneath. She gave it a yank, only to have the strap come off in her hand. When she finally did dig it out, she discovered the top had broken off her lipstick, smearing everything inside in Bloody Merry Red. She decided to worry about it later and climbed up to retrieve the overnight bags. Fortunately, they appeared to have survived in better shape. Alice tied a knot in her purse's broken strap and slung the bag over her shoulder.

She would have been grumpier about the condition of her purse, except that retrieving her belongings had proved easy in comparison to the difficulties Ken was having several rows back, trying to extract the wedged-in zombie.

Due to the slight upward slant of the overhead bins, Ken had to push up on Darryl's shoulders first in order to pull him down. Mick might have also overestimated the roominess of the bins, Alice thought, as Ken freed one of Darryl's shoulders only to have the other one get stuck again.

"Brace," Darryl said.

"Doing my best," Ken muttered between grunts.

Alice wondered if Darryl had any clue what was happening to him. She took a deep breath and quickly scanned the zombie's mind. Unlike Dave whose brain had been empty, Darryl's consciousness was still there, if just barely. The newly zombified pilot had been overwhelmed by his disorganized thoughts, but

— 109 —

the flight attendant had only one thought circling the drain: brace for impact.

"Brace," Darryl said, as the top half of him was finally freed, and then added more frantically, "Brace, brace, brace!"

"Don't panic," Ken advised, but Alice suddenly realized why the zombie was freaking out.

"Careful, he's slipping out—" Alice began to warn, just as Darryl slid out of the overhead bin and bounced head first into several broken seats, knocking Ken over on his way down.

"Are you okay?" Alice asked, as she cautiously made her way through the wreckage to check on Ken.

"We're good," Ken said, pulling himself and Darryl up.

"Oh no," Alice gasped. A broken cup holder had embedded itself into Darryl's forehead.

"Damn," Ken said, mildly. "Alice, can you get Mick?"

"Get Mick to do what?" Mick asked, from behind Alice.

She jumped. "Stop it, stop it, stop it!" Alice shouted at Mick. "Or I swear I'm going to tie bells on you!"

"Bells?" Mick considered it. "Bone rattles would be more the Baron's style." He pushed past Alice and took a long look at Darryl. "My diagnosis is that's a cup holder."

"I know that," Ken said sharply. "Can we safely remove it?"

Mick took Darryl's head in his hands and tilted it from side to side. "I'd wait until he was back at Odyssey. It's not doing any real harm right now, especially as he's going to have poor impulse control and language skills once he gets to Stage Three anyway."

Mick stepped back and patted the zombie on the shoulder. "You'll be fine, my brainless bandicoot," Mick said, brightly. "The frontal lobe is highly overrated."

"Brr... brrr... brrrr...," Darryl managed, and then began drooling.

"Okay, time to get you out of those clothes," Ken said, unbuttoning Darryl's shirt. Then he paused and looked directly at

Alice. "I think Darryl would appreciate some privacy."

Not wanting to watch a zombie strip tease anyway, Alice picked her way back to the overnight bags. Once she'd hefted them onto her shoulders, however, a thought occurred to her. "Why aren't you asking Mick to leave too?" she called back to Ken.

Ken looked embarrassed. "Alice, you're a girl, and Darryl really doesn't know you that well so..."

"I'm going, I'm going," Alice said, marching as fast as she could up the littered aisle. Forget about catching zombism, she thought, if she stayed around Ken and Mick any longer she might catch craziness.

She stuck her head out the front emergency exit and found Welly standing just outside, talking to two of Borislav's guards. "You can go in after Ken has secured the scene and given you permission. Understood?"

"But Borislav..." the male one began.

Alice blinked. Was this pair the same ones who'd harassed them outside the Mailroom? She was ashamed to admit it, but most of Borislav's guards looked alike to her. Alice found it hard to focus on their individual features when they were carrying such big guns.

"Let me make this very clear," Welly said to the guards, his tone brooking no argument. "You clean up after the investigative team is done. We're not done yet. So you two trot along to somewhere you're wanted. Now."

They both gave him a dirty look, but obediently retreated. Alice decided they couldn't be the same ones as this morning, as the female guard wasn't nearly homicidal enough.

Welly helped Alice out of the plane. "We'll guard the door until Darryl's in the cockpit," he said in a low voice. He took his overnight bag from Alice; then reached for hers, too. She let him have it; they'd argued too many times in the past about his old-fashioned manners. Plus she had bigger worries right now.

"Borislav's not going to come over here and insist we let him in?" Alice asked. He terrified her, and for good reason. The first time Alice had met him he had levelled most of an industrial park. The last time she'd come face to face with him, he'd garrotted her ex-boyfriend with razor wire.

To be fair, her boyfriend had been trying to destroy Odyssey and was holding her hostage. Ultimately, Alice was grateful to get out of that sticky situation alive, but she was under no illusions that Borislav had been at all concerned for her personal safety. If her soon-to-be-ex-boyfriend had succeeded in blowing her head off, Borislav would have brushed off the bits of brain matter, arranged to have his suit dry cleaned, and gone about his day without a second thought.

"No, Borislav knows the rules," Welly said. "We're in the right here."

"That's a relief."

"Of course, if Borislav finds out we're accessories after the fact to a pair of zombies escaping a quarantine zone, we'll be lucky if he decides to personally discipline us."

"And if we're unlucky?" Alice asked, dreading the answer.

"He'll hand us over to the Admiral."

Alice shuddered. She'd only met the head of Odyssey International once, when she'd been formally inducted into the organization and partnered with Welly. The Admiral was a shape changer, who had an unfortunate propensity to shift form as his mood changed. He'd been particularly moody that day, Alice remembered.

"Maybe this isn't such a great..." Alice began, when Ken exited the plane with Mick in tow.

"Darryl's securely buckled into the co-pilot's seat," Ken said.

"And looking very snazzy in his new uniform," Mick added. "If zombies had sex, he'd definitely be getting lucky tonight."

"Darryl does appear to like his promotion to co-pilot," Ken

said. "It's probably a dream come true for him, as very few boys grow up wanting to be stewardesses some day."

"You're as bad as Welly," Alice said. Maybe it wasn't just coincidence that Ken looked like a cowboy who'd stepped out of the 1970s, she thought. Odyssey employees who spent too much time in Head Office aged slower than those who worked outside. She wondered if Ken regularly broke the rules about overtime. Welly's mother had, and as a result, she didn't look a day over eighty-five, although she was over a hundred now.

"I'm nothing at all like Welly," Ken said, giving her an offended look.

"Enough, both of you," Welly said. "Let's retrieve our AWOL pilot before Borislav realizes he's missing and annihilates the unspoiled beauty of Wales."

*

Maybe Welly's ankle injury was addling his brain, Alice thought, as she stood on a nearby hill, searching the surrounding area for any sign of the missing zombies. First of all, this part of Wales was hardly unspoiled, with a great big wrecked plane sitting right in the middle of it. Second, even the landscape unmarred by the crash was covered with gray-green scrub and not a single tree in sight.

Welly had climbed the steepest part of the hill where the plane had slid down, while she'd clambered up the gentle slope of one of the neighbouring hillocks. Mick had, not surprisingly, disappeared from sight, while Ken searched in the immediate vicinity of the plane for clues he claimed Dave would leave behind.

Borislav's guards were in the process of removing the singed and battered baggage from the plane. Alice felt a moment of anxiety when they dragged out Dave's broken shipping container and casket, but no one showed any particular interest in it. Along with the luggage, Dave's shipping material was loaded into the Chinook helicopter to haul back to Odyssey.

Alice took a deep breath, closed her eyes, and tried to locate the pilot psychically.

Om mani zombie hum.

Immediately, Alice sensed the mental confusion she now recognized as zombism and focussed harder to pick up the actual thoughts.

"Brace, brace, brace!"

"I'm okay, I'm okay, I'm okay…"

"Peace, peace, peace…"

"Brainnnnnnnnnnsss."

"For God's sake!" Alice opened her eyes. Instead of the pilot, she'd found the zombies down in the helicopter. She tried a couple more times, but couldn't reach through the interference caused by all the zombies she'd actually met in person.

Alice momentarily considered trying to sense Dave, but quickly dismissed the idea as a lost cause. The zombie pilot and the zombie passengers still had minds for her to contact, albeit damaged ones. But she already knew no one was home in Dave's skull. Alice could only assume when people died in Stage Three and became full-fledged zombies, their psyches didn't resurrect with their bodies.

"Dave? Here Dave!" Alice called out for lack of a better idea. "C'mon Dave, who's a good boy?"

She tried to remember if Dave's ears were still intact. Then again, she thought, even if the cartilage was still attached, mummified ear drums probably weren't very functional. Mick should have given Tom Endicott's ears as well as his nose to Dave.

She gave up and bent down to rub her knees. She felt tired, sore, a bit hungry, and very discouraged. Up to now, she'd assumed she could find anything. Zombies were more exotic than overnight bags or car keys, but working at Odyssey Alice had located all sorts of supernatural weirdness from unicorn horns to horny demons. Even when she'd worked for Amethyst Aura's Psychic Hotline, she'd found true love, although only for other people. Apparently, escaped zombies were the only things in the world—other than a non-homicidal date—that Alice couldn't find.

So much for being more useful on this mission, Alice thought, discouraged.

A sharp-pitched whistle pierced her fully functional eardrums. Alice looked down the hillock and saw Mick and Ken beside the plane's destroyed nose, waving at her. Even from this distance, she could tell Ken was very excited.

Alice reached the plane just before Welly finished limping down his far steeper hill. A glimpse of white bandage under his pant leg confirmed her earlier suspicion. Welly had indeed strapped up his ankle. Despite his enhancements, Welly managed to get hurt on every single assignment she'd been on with him. Alice promised herself she'd find a way to make him listen to her and be more careful.

"I've found the trail," Ken said as soon as they joined him. He pointed down the slope to where the valley curved to the north out of sight of the plane.

Welly examined the ground at their feet. "Where do you see the footprints?"

"There are none," Mick said. "Ken and Dave share a psychic bond. They're heterosexual life partners."

"There's no psychic bond and no footprints," Ken said, not disputing the 'life partner' designation. "I've trained Dave to leave signs for me to follow. See? He left one there, there, and up there."

They all looked where he indicated, but only Ken, apparently, saw anything.

"I told you it's a psychic bond," Mick said.

"You can't have a psychic bond with a zombie," Welly said,

testily. "Corpses don't have psyches."

"Corpses don't," Ken said as he began picking his way further down the slope. "But zombies do."

"Only when they're new," Alice said. "But I've scanned Dave's mind, and he's completely psyche-less." She met Ken's eyes. "No offence."

"Almost as if he was dead," Welly said, sarcastically.

"Zombies are not dead!" Ken insisted. "If Alice can't sense Dave, it's only because zombies at his evolved stage don't spend a lot of time thinking. They don't suffer from self-doubt or neuroses, and as a result—"

"Shush!" Alice interrupted, and turned around with a smile on her face. "Borislav," she said with forced brightness. "So good to see you!"

"Alice, it is always great pleasure to see you," Borislav said, as he approached them. He smiled at her, but it didn't reach his eyes. "However, I think you just told tiny fib."

"A fib?" Alice squeaked. She had to step hard on her urge to confess everything, including the time she'd stolen a toy lamb in kindergarten.

"No one is ever glad to see me," Borislav said, lightly. Then all geniality left his features as he looked at the men. "Wellington, Kenneth, do you not have mission you should be completing for Odyssey elsewhere?"

"I'm never glad to see you," Mick volunteered.

Borislav ignored not only Mick's words, but his entire existence. "Or are you two just here to make work for me? Perhaps find another plane to crash?"

"In fact," Mick said, his tone still light, "I sometimes think the world would be a better place without you."

"Mick, this isn't the time or place," Alice cautioned. Mick and Borislav's enmity was legendary.

"You're right, Alice," Mick said. "I was only kidding, anyway. I don't really think the world would be a better place without you, Borislav."

"Yes, we have a mission," Welly said. "In fact, we're heading off right now. I'd ask for a lift, but this is perfect hiking country. I thought I'd show Alice the Welsh mountains, and we could all use the fresh air and exer— "

Mick interrupted, his eyes glittering. "I think the universe would be a better place without you, comrade."

Borislav showed no outward reaction, but Alice shivered in the sudden chill that descended. The blades of the remaining Chinook began to spin, and within moments the helicopter rose into the air. Alice watched it fly overhead, wishing she was on it, even though it was full of zombies and security guards.

"Do what you like, Wellington," Borislav finally said. "You may even leave this creature behind." His grey eyes flickered over Mick with icy contempt. "As everything in this valley will soon be cleaned up."

Borislav turned his back and walked calmly to his private helicopter.

"Run!" Alice exclaimed. "He's already set the charges!"

"Foxtrot!" Welly grabbed her hand.

It felt like Welly was pulling her arm out of her socket as she scrambled to keep up with him. However, Alice didn't object. She knew what would happen if they didn't reach the other side of the hill in time.

Borislav's helicopter buzzed overhead, blaring 'The Ride of the Valkyries'.

Whoever showed Borislav *Apocalypse Now* should be shot, Alice thought.

Just as safety was in sight, Mick began to cheerfully count, "T minus five, four, three— "

"Hit the dirt!" Welly ordered, throwing himself and Alice forward onto the ground. She felt Ken land beside her, but didn't dare look up. Instead she buried her head in her arms.

The bright flash of light caused her eyelids to light up. A strong, loud wind pulled at their bodies as if trying to drag them down into the valley. The ground shook under their bodies, and Alice's stomach roiled. She was suddenly grateful there had been no meal on their flight.

After what felt like minutes, but was probably only seconds, the wind died and the earth stopped shuddering. She peeked out between her arms and saw Ken begin to move.

"Wait for it!" Welly barked, and Ken froze.

Alice knew what she'd find if she went back into that valley, or more accurately, what she wouldn't find. There'd be no evidence of any plane, no traces of explosives or radiation; at the most there'd be just some scorched earth. Within hours, all records would be changed and memories altered. Fly Me Airlines Flight Number 4242 would cease to exist.

All in the name of 'Maintaining Balance'.

Alice couldn't help wondering at times like this if she was really working for the good guys. Sure, Odyssey employed people like Welly and Ken who believed they were on the side of all that was right and honourable. But Odyssey also employed people like Borislav. Even Mick, who wasn't as scary on the surface, enthusiastically experimented on people, willfully ignoring the concept of informed consent.

A bird chirped. An insect buzzed. Welly released a deep breath. "Now it's safe."

Alice sat up and sneezed. She was covered in dust, but she was luckier than Ken. He'd landed in a mud puddle, and it had soaked his serape making it extra ugly, dingy, and brown. He muttered under his breath as he stripped it off and wrung out the dirty water. In Alice's opinion, it didn't help much.

Welly stood and then offered her a hand up. Alice didn't refuse, as her knees were really sore now.

"Try to get as much of the dust off as possible and don't breathe it in; it could be toxic," Welly said. "Then we need to step lively. Those Delta'd zombies have a head start on us." He took off his suit jacket and began to shake off the potentially poisonous plane particles.

Alice looked at Mick. He didn't have a speck of dust on him and appeared to have never taken cover in the mud and brambles. He was watching Borislav's helicopter fade into the distance, the strains of Wagner no longer audible.

Odyssey's methods were sometimes questionable, Alice thought, but she did agree wholeheartedly with its goals. Saving the world from demons, arresting (and occasionally melting) power-mad magicians, and now averting the zombie apocalypse. There was no way Alice was going to let the world end while she still didn't have a boyfriend.

"That crazy Cossack," Mick said as Borislav's helicopter disappeared from sight. He looked over at Alice and winked. "He's such a drama queen."

*

After half an hour of hiking over uneven ground, Alice was even less impressed with Wales's supposedly unspoiled wilderness. "So where are these mountains you wanted to show me?" Alice asked Welly.

He looked at her with a puzzled expression. "All around you."

"These... little folds in the ground are mountains?"

"Yes, mountains," Welly confirmed. "Hikers come from all over the world to enjoy them."

"No, no, no," Alice said, shaking her head. "These are not mountains. They're hills. No, they're hill-ettes. Speed bumps! If this place is popular, it's only because those poor hikers have never seen a real mountain range. I used to live in British Columbia, so I know what I'm talking about," she added, confidently.

"You've got no eye for natural beauty." Welly sounded amused.

"Where are all the trees then?" Alice asked. "That's natural beauty."

"There's a tree," Welly said, pointing at a bedraggled little bush clinging to the side of a steep slope. "Yes, the Cambrian Mountains are older than the Rockies and maybe a little worn around the edges, but they are still definitely mountains. Younger doesn't automatically mean better. Experience is a great deal more valuable than youthful ignorance."

"What are you talking about?" Alice asked, confused. "How can the Rockies be ignorant?" His sore ankle must be making him cranky, she thought. "But I suppose you find this place beautiful because it's your home and native land," she conceded.

"Wales is most certainly not my native land," Welly said, offended.

Alice was pleased she'd finally hit a nerve. She knew it wasn't fair, but roaming over the Welsh countryside after surviving a plane crash had definitely not been her idea. Someone had to pay for her aching knees and frayed nerves.

"Of course it is," she said. "Britain, Scotland, Wales — It's all part of the same island, right?"

"They're all very different!"

"Watch where you're going," Ken snapped at them. "You're compromising the scene."

Welly and Alice halted and stared at Ken.

"The scenery?" Alice asked, wondering if she'd misheard Ken. "Because this doesn't look like a crime scene."

Ken ignored her. He carefully placed his filthy serape on the ground and knelt on it. Then he slowly parted the dry grass with his hands, searching.

Alice sighed and looked at the ground around her. She didn't see anything unusual or criminal.

"Thought so," Ken said, fishing something out of the grass.

"Did Dave leave you another clue?" Alice asked, and Welly gave her a dirty look. "It doesn't hurt to humour him," she whispered at him. "You might try it sometime."

"Too busy humouring you all the time," Welly said, dryly.

Ken stood and showed off his prize. "We're definitely on the right trail."

"Oh God, it's a fingernail!" Alice felt ill.

"Alice—"

"No, no lecture about taking the Lord's name in vain," Alice cut Welly off. "He's holding Dave's fingernail."

"Actually, it belonged to the pilot. All of Dave's fell off long ago," Ken corrected. "Zombies have a bad habit of picking at themselves, so everyone keep an eye out for nails, hair, or fingers."

"That's it," Alice said. "If you guys want to play Hansel and Gretel with zombie body parts, go ahead. I'm going to lie down, rest my throbbing knees, and have a nap. Wake me up when the apocalypse is over."

"All you had to do was ask," Mick said, from behind her.

"What, I didn't ask…" Alice turned her head, just as Mick used his Med-Trekker to jab her with another needle. "Mick!"

"I didn't sneak up on you this time," Mick said. "So you have no reason to complain."

"Except you injected me with… What did you inject me with? Oh. Oh my."

Welly grabbed Mick by his lapels and shook him. "If you hurt her—"

"No, Welly," Alice said, "I'm definitely not hurt."

Welly reluctantly let Mick go and looked at her concerned.

But it was true; none of her hurt anymore. Alice felt like she'd taken several painkillers, had a long nap, and downed two double long espressos. "What is this wonderful stuff you've injected me with?" she asked Mick.

"Just a little 'pick me up' I brewed in the lab. I call it Jolt Four Locos for Five Hours Energy Elixir, and I've got more than enough for everyone. Side effects may include itchy, watery eyes, alien hand syndrome, and an irresistible urge to tap dance."

Ken shrugged and offered his arm. Welly just frowned at Mick and trudged on.

Alice caught up with Welly, thrilled with her newfound energy. "How's your ankle?" she asked, brightly.

"Getting better all the time," Welly said. "Are you sure you feel well? No bizarre side effects? Hearts palpitations and the like?"

"No, really. I feel great!"

"Delta." Welly's right foot turned on a loose rock.

"I can fix up your sore ankle, too," Mick offered.

"Stay away from me," Welly growled. "I don't want to wake up and find my toes grafted onto one of Ken's zombies."

Instead of denying the possibility, Mick just laughed.

8

Welly Discovers the Origin of Bog Snorkelling

An hour from the crash site, Welly and Alice got into an argument.

"I'm just asking for my overnight bag," Alice said, trying to pull it away from him.

Welly refused to let go. "We don't have time for you to change your clothes."

"I don't want to change my clothes," Alice protested. "I'm saving a fresh change in case I'm the one who falls into the bog. I promise, it'll only take a minute to grab what I need."

"We're going to fall into a bog?" Ken asked.

"Not you," Alice snapped.

"We don't have time—" Welly began.

Alice came to a halt and put her hands on her hips. "I just want to change my bra, okay?" She'd thought the remaining underwire had survived the crash intact, but part of it had snapped off and was now jabbing her. Not to mention, she was sick of only being properly supported on one side.

"I don't expect any of you to understand since none of you are C-cups. But I need to do this!"

All three men stopped dead in their tracks, staring at her. Welly looked consternated, Ken was blushing, while Mick appeared way too intrigued.

"Oh, for heaven's sake, you're grown men and this is the twenty-first century," Alice said. "Women have breasts, they wear bras, get over it!"

Alice began walking again, but then stopped. Part of why she hadn't been more useful on this mission was because she wasn't being proactive enough. And there was no time like the present to make changes, Alice thought.

Reaching under her purple top, she unhooked her bra, shrugged the straps down her shoulders, and pulled the whole thing out of her sleeve. Alice then took hold of the elastic shoulder straps, stretched them, and shot the bra into the unspoiled Welsh countryside.

"There," she announced. "Problem solved."

Mick clapped. "It's a new sport! Bog bra flinging!"

Alice looked at Ken, whose ears were bright red. "Lead the way, Ken. Go find some zombie spoor or something."

Her hippie mother would be proud of her, Alice thought.

After a few minutes, Welly fell into step beside her. "I..." He cleared his throat. "... may have been micro-managing a tad."

"Just a tad," Alice said. "That's okay, as long as you understand I will not be asking permission if I need to go to the washroom... that is, the closest straggly excuse for a bush."

"Fair enough," Welly said, good-naturedly. "As long as you agree to stop littering Wales with your lingerie."

"I'll try to resist the urge." Alice grinned.

"Who's going to fall into a bog?" Ken asked her.

Alice looked at him, confused. "What are you talking about?"

"You said someone was going to fall in," Ken insisted.

"I did? I don't remember that."

"With any luck, it'll be your zombies," Welly said to Ken.

Ken gave him a dirty look and marched ahead of them.

"You do realize, you just jinxed yourself," Alice said to Welly.

"Story of my life," he said.

"Damn it, Dave!" Ken cursed, stooping to pick up something from the grass. "I've told you time and again to stop chewing on the duct tape on your hands."

Alice looked away quickly, but unfortunately Ken was broadcasting his disappointment that duct taping Dave's fingers back on hadn't been a permanent solution. She swallowed hard and walked past Ken quickly.

Welly, however, halted right beside by Ken. "And I've told you time and again to not use that word."

"What word?" Ken asked, as he stood up. "Duct tape? Damn? What the hell is your problem with swearing?"

"Every time you swear, you risk drawing unfriendly attention from the supernatural and causing harm. When you damn someone, you could end up literally damning them." Welly started walking again.

"You just said damn," Alice said, when he caught up to her. "Twice!"

Welly gave her a long-suffering look. "But I wasn't swearing now, was I? It's the difference between having a conversation on differing concepts of Hell in the Protestant and Catholic faiths, and you telling that magician in Lichtenstein to go to Hotel."

"He didn't go to hell or Hotel or whatever," Alice argued. "He tripped and fell into his own lava pit."

"In the Book of Revelation, Hell is described as a lake of fire," Welly said, piously.

Alice rolled her eyes. "So you're saying that if I'd only darned him to heck, he would have stubbed his toe and fallen into his hot tub?"

"If you're not willing to have a serious discussion about this—"

Alice interrupted him. "No, I'm just not willing to feel guilty over a klutzy magician who tried to melt you in the very same magma he took a nosedive into!"

"I don't want you to feel guilty," Welly said. "Just be careful. I don't want you to risk yourself on my behalf."

"And what the Henry-Egbert-Larry-Larry is that supposed to mean? You risk yourself all the time saving my life, and I'm not even supposed to use a naughty swear word on your behalf?"

"I don't want you to ever risk your soul to save me," Welly said. He picked up his pace, leaving the fuming Alice in his wake.

"I'd risk a great deal more than that, you big dummy," Alice muttered to herself.

*

Half an hour later, Alice stepped in something disgustingly unidentifiable. She wiped the bottom of her boot against the grass with limited success. "This better not be zombie poop," she said. "Do zombies poop?"

"Yes," Mick said.

"No," Welly said.

"It depends," Ken said.

"Everybody poops," Mick insisted. "Even bacteria. Some of my best friends were bacteria," he added. "It's tragic how short their lives are, but it's also quite inspiring. No one lives for the moment like a bacterium."

"But only in Stage One will you ever see anything resembling an actual bowel movement," Ken said, ignoring Mick and speaking directly to Alice. "In Stage Two, the zombie virus revs up the infected's adrenal production, but conversely, it also slows down the autonomic functions of the body: heart rate, respiration, digestion. This results in chronic dehydration. Any matter still in the bowels dries up and mummifies inside the infected person."

"TMI," Alice said, faintly. Welly just rolled his eyes and resumed walking.

Ken picked up a stick and poked at the squished mystery poop.

"If you keep zombies hydrated and physically intact, there may be occasional leakage through the urinary tract," Ken continued. "An adult diaper will take care of any problems there, until Stage Three when decomposition of the soft tissues sets in. The external reproductive organs are always among the first to go."

"I really didn't need to know that," Alice said, appalled.

Ken tossed the stick away and began walking again.

"Fascinating," Mick said, skipping along beside him. "Are zombies at all prone to diaper rash?"

"I've never had any problems, but then I keep all my zombies well moisturized with Vanilla Body Lotion from The Booty Boutique. If you don't, their skin will start cracking."

Alice realized she'd never be able to use a Booty Boutique product again. Not with a nightmarish vision of Ken giving his zombies vanilla-scented, full-body massages stuck in her head. She quickened her pace until she was walking right next to Welly.

"Any more questions?" he asked.

"I was going to ask if there were plant zombies like Wyndham's triffids," she said, "but I've decided curiosity killed the cat."

"That reminds me," Welly said, glancing at his watch. "Almost nineteen hundred hours here, which makes it going on fourteen hundred in Ottawa."

Alice smiled. Welly usually took his mother out for tea on Friday afternoons. When he was on assignment, he'd call her instead. It also made perfect sense that talk of dead cats reminded Welly of his mother. One of Mrs. Wolfe's many hobbies was taxidermy.

Welly flipped open his Oddfone and addressed Odyssey's switchboard operator. "Lilith, patch me through to my mother, please."

The upside of the Oddfone was you never had to worry about getting a signal. You could be stranded on Everest or stuck at the bottom of the ocean, and the Oddfone would always give you a direct connection to Head Office.

"No, it's not a waste of Odyssey's time and resources, Lilith, and I know you wouldn't care if it was."

The downside of the Oddfone was all calls went through Lilith, Alice thought. Rumour had it that Lilith wasn't even human, but a demon condemned to inhabit Odyssey's ancient phone system for all eternity. Alice didn't really believe that, but it couldn't be denied that Lilith answered no matter when you called: twenty-four hours a day, seven days a week, three hundred and sixty-five days a year (sixty-six on leap years).

"I honestly don't care what you think of me," Welly said.

"Did Lilith call you a mama's boy again?" Alice asked.

Welly ignored her. "If she's not home, where is she? ... Of course, she'd want me to know... Who the Hotel is Patrick O'Higgins?"

"Your mom's on a date? Good for her!"

Welly gave Alice a dirty look. "I gathered from the name he's Irish," he growled into the Oddfone. "Forget it, I'll try later." He snapped the phone shut and jammed it into his jacket pocket.

Alice stopped walking, closed her eyes and visualized Mrs. Wolfe in her mind. "*Om mani mommy hum.*" It only took a few moments to track her down, as Alice had met with Mrs. Wolfe several times and eaten many of her world-famous sandwiches. "She's in a car," Alice said. "A man is driving her somewhere. Lots of rocks and trees, so really it could be anywhere in Ontario or Québec. Yes, it's definitely Patrick with her in the car, she's thinking about him. Oh my goodness, that's so sweet."

"What?" Welly asked.

Alice broke the connection and opened her eyes. "They met at Blessed Sacrament Church at a special Mass for widows and widowers."

Welly looked shocked. "That doesn't make any sense. Blessed Sacrament is a Catholic Church." With a frown, he began walking again.

Alice followed him. "So what?"

"Mum's an Anglican."

"Again, so what?"

Welly grimaced and picked up his pace. "You wouldn't understand."

"That Catholics and Protestants didn't socialize back when you were a boy? Unlike you, your mother's not letting extreme old age stop her from having a bit of romance in her life. Maybe you should try it sometime, it's not like I bite or anything—"

Welly stared at her, and Alice realized she'd let her mouth run away from her. "Just be happy for her," she muttered. She slowed her pace so she was walking behind him.

"The course of true love never runs smooth," Mick said, appearing beside her. "Have I ever told you about Phil? He was a heartleaf philodendron and truly one of the most romantic plants I've ever known. Ah, the love that dares not mulch its name."

Alice kept her eyes focussed on her boots. She had not just made a pass at her boss, she told herself. "Mick, I swear if you don't leave me alone, I will pummel you into the ground."

"Discretion is the better part of valour," he said, quickly retreating.

*

Over the next half hour, Ken appeared to slowly lose confidence in the trail he was following. He changed his mind several times and had them double back twice. Mick passed the time by darting in and out of the undergrowth, flushing out bunnies and chasing them. Despite his loud declarations that they'd make a tasty snack, he never caught any, to Alice's relief.

Welly, meanwhile, was doing a slow burn.

Alice found it difficult to keep her mind on the missing zombies. Instead, she obsessed over the idea of dating Welly. There was no denying he was handsome, dependable, and sexy as hell.

Unfortunately, Welly was also old enough to be her grandfather, an absolute dinosaur when it came to women, and her last office romance had ended with Borislav nearly decapitating her boyfriend with his garrotte.

On the plus side, Alice thought, Welly would be a lot more difficult for Borislav to kill.

"Is it possible to slit an Enhanced Agent's throat?" she asked.

Welly looked at her askance. "Rather not answer that," he said, slowly.

"I will!" Mick said. "It can be done, but to sever the spinal column, you'd need a lot more upper body strength and a good quality chainsaw. I recommend one with an ergonomic handle and vibration suppression, as you'll be at it for a while. I'm personally fond of the Husky Man gas-powered landscaping models, as you really don't need more than nine thousand rpm to cut through enhanced bones."

"Cheers, Mick," Welly said.

"Always glad to help," Mick said.

Welly shook his head. "Have you tried scanning for the zombies again?" he asked Alice.

"You're just trying to change the subject from chainsaws."

"Imagine that," Welly said. "Humour me for a change and give it another go."

"If I must," Alice said, with a martyred air. She slowed to a stop and closed her eyes. Alice reminded herself she'd been able to find Welly's mother on the other side of the ocean with very little effort. Surely she could locate some zombies who couldn't be more than a couple miles away at most.

"Here zombie, zombie, zombie..." Alice whispered under her breath.

After several minutes, she shook her head. "Nothing. No, wait. I think I might have found the pilot."

"Where is he?" Ken asked, eagerly. "You see, Welly, I told you zombies have brains."

"Don't call me Welly!"

"Shush everyone." Alice tried to focus. "I don't know where he is. He's very confused and low to the ground." She paused and frowned. "I think he's bleating."

"Bleating?" Ken asked.

"Sorry," Alice said, opening her eyes. "I think I found a sheep instead."

"You can't tell the difference between sheep and a zombie?" Ken yelled at her.

"Back off my Sensitive," Welly said, sharply, stepping between Ken and Alice.

"It's okay, Welly. He was a very confused sheep," Alice said, disappointed in herself. "Or is it a ram? What do you call a boy sheep?"

Welly glanced at his watch. "Ken, you have two minutes to find your pet zombie's trail or I'm calling Borislav myself."

Ken looked panicked. "I'm sure Dave left a clue here somewhere."

"You could just rely on your psychic bond with Dave," Mick suggested.

"For the last time, there's no psychic bond between us," Ken said, pacing back and forth, eyes glued to the ground.

"One minute, thirty seconds," Welly announced.

"Maybe not," Mick said. "But what do you have to lose by trying?"

"Okay, okay," Ken said. He took a deep breath and shut his eyes. "Dave, where'd you go, buddy? Give me a sign. Anything."

Nothing happened.

"One minute," Welly said.

Alice decided to help. She didn't believe in Ken and Dave's psychic bond, but she did believe in avoiding Borislav at all costs. "Don't think about Dave," she told Ken. "In fact, try not to think at all. Just relax and hold an image of him in your mind."

"Dave always says I think too much," Ken said. Alice watched as the tension left his body, and then he nodded. "Okay."

"Thirty seconds."

"You're not helping," Alice berated Welly.

"Quite aware of that fact."

Alice turned her back on Welly. "Ken, you need to believe, to know deep down inside that you've already contacted Dave. So all you need to do is just allow it to happen. Now take a deep breath in … and breathe out."

Ken released his breath, just as Welly announced, "Time, gentlemen. And lady."

"I've got it!" Ken said, pointing excitedly at a runty tree ahead of them, to their left. "Dave went that way."

"It worked?" Alice asked, shocked.

Ken ran to the tree and waved them over. "Look, these are his teeth marks! That was amazing, I never believed in all that mumbo jumbo…"

"Hey!" Alice protested.

"Sorry, Alice, but Dave goes on about psychics and astrology all the time." He shook his head in wonder. "Okay everyone, follow me." With a spring in his step, he headed off.

"It doesn't make sense," Alice said, staring at the bark. It did look gnawed at.

"Excellent coaching, my psychic possum," Mick said. "Maybe you shouldn't have been given a failing grade in Supernatural Communication for Dummies, after all."

"Not thinking was the only thing my instructor said I was good at," Alice said, still weirded out. "Maybe only one person needs a psyche to make it work?"

"Hurry up, people. Daylight's wasting!" Ken shouted at them.

As they followed him, Welly grumbled, "Tree was probably gnawed at by some sheep."

"As long as they weren't zombie sheep," Alice said. Then the image of herds of zombie sheep roaming the hills, terrorizing the locals, popped into her head.

Jogging to catch up with Ken, Alice anxiously asked, "Can animals become zombies?"

"It can be a problem with domesticated animals," Ken said. "Modern farming methods overcrowd stressed animals into cramped living quarters, making zombism easy to catch and spread. However, wild animals can usually outrun zombies. In the rare event of a zombie actually catching one, the animal almost never survives the attack." He paused. "Thank you for helping me find my centre back there. I never would have noticed those tooth marks otherwise. You almost had me believing I was psychic."

"Sure, whatever," Alice said.

"Outbreaks among wild animals can happen," Mick said, joining them. "Especially if someone was using — oh, let's say, bunnies — to train his favourite zombie to track for him."

Welly stopped walking. "I always suspected you were responsible for that debacle," he growled at Ken.

"What debacle?" Alice asked, looking back at him.

"The Great Zombie Bunny Invasion of nineteen eighty-three," Mick said.

"It's an urban legend," Ken snapped. "It never happened. Just because one drunk thought he saw a zombie rabbit staggering past him in one small corner of Minnesota, that's no reason to call it an invasion! I had everything under complete — " Ken stopped mid-rant and looked around at everyone staring at him. He rubbed the back of his neck and turned away. "The trail heads this way. Stay close."

Welly shook his head, sighed, and trudged after Ken.

*

Thirty minutes later, Welly fell into a bog.

One moment Alice was slogging along through the increasingly mucky mud and grass, congratulating herself for having the foresight to buy new boots. Then suddenly Welly pitched sideways, going down with a startled yell. He landed with a splash in what appeared to be a harmless, shallow puddle, but instead was a bottomless pit of dark brown mud, intent on sucking him down to the center of the earth, one limb at a time.

Or so it appeared to Alice. "Welly!" she screamed.

"Look out for water scorpions," Mick advised. "They're small, but vindictive."

Welly threw both overnight bags away and then tried to drag himself out using a clump of nearby grass. It came up in his hands, roots and all.

Ken tramped back to their group, looking irritated. "Didn't I tell you to stay close? You can't go wandering around in a bog."

Bog? Alice looked around. All she could see was green mossy earth, interspersed with slimy brown mud puddles. How the heck was anyone supposed to snorkel in this?

Welly grunted, his free leg kicking in the air as he tried to squirm up onto solid land. Except Alice knew in a flash there wasn't any solid land within his easy reach. She looked around for a branch to extend out to him, but there were none in sight.

Alice shook her head. What was she thinking? Welly was probably heavier than all of them put together. If she tried to pull him out, they'd both end up at the bottom of the bog. "Mick, help him!"

"Don't worry," Mick said. "Despite their appearance, ombrotrophic mires are extremely acidic. Even if there's a dead sheep or two down there, he could splash around all day without any risk of bacterial infection."

"That's not helpful!" Alice shouted.

Ken crossed his arms. "Hurry up," he told Welly. "Dave's getting further ahead with every minute you waste!"

"Your Foxtrotting pet zombie..." Welly paused. With a heroic effort, he flung himself onto his back, his trapped leg coming free with a disgusting sucking noise. "... is already at the bottom of this Foxtrotting bog!"

"Fat chance," Ken said. "Zombies are very light on their feet. The only way Dave would ever get trapped in a bog is if someone pushed him in."

"It's the dehydration," Mick added. "They're very buoyant."

Welly rolled over several times, coating himself thoroughly in mud. When he reached solid land, he climbed to his feet, his pants soaked and dripping. He was missing his left shoe, the tension bandage he'd wrapped around his sore ankle had vanished, and he looked deeply irritated. "Alice," he began.

"Oh Welly," Alice interrupted, slapping a hand over her nose. "You smell like rotten eggs."

"I'd say it's more of a locker room aroma," Ken said.

"You must have been in some pretty raunchy locker rooms," Alice said.

Welly cleared his throat. "If you're quite done, we — "

Alice shrieked, pointing at his shoulder. "There's a huge bug crawling on you!" It was a wicked-looking black thing with a long tail and oversized pincers.

"Water scorpions are hardly huge," Mick said. "That one's maybe twenty-two millimetres, tops. Did you know that they breathe through a snorkel?"

Welly knocked the bug off his shoulder without looking. "Alice!" he snapped.

She focussed on him, wide-eyed. "Yes?"

"You're going to walk up ahead with Ken," Welly said, as he retrieved their soaking wet overnight bags. "Make sure he doesn't lead us into any more bogs."

"Me?" Alice squeaked.

Welly appeared to have developed a tic in his jaw. Either that or he was grinding his teeth.

"Oh right," Alice said. "Because I already know where it's safe to walk, the same as I already know there's a road just past that next hill, even though we can't see it yet." Glimpses of the very near future always felt like déjà-vu, except the vu part hadn't happened yet. "Hey!" she exclaimed, realizing what she'd just said. "A fresh start will put us on our way! I mean, there's a road behind that hill."

She expected them to be happy with the news that they would soon be rejoining civilization, but everyone looked concerned instead. In fact, Ken and Mick looked far more worried now than when Welly had fallen into the bog.

"Are you sure there's a road over there?" Ken asked. "It's not just some farmer's sheep track?"

"Positive," Alice said. "It's paved and everything."

"Paved," Ken repeated. "Which means they may no longer be on foot."

"Hang on, are you saying zombies can drive?" Alice asked. The idea of Dave behind the wheel of a car was simultaneously funny and terrifying.

"Sadly no, their eyesight and hand-eye coordination aren't good enough," Ken answered. "It's a shame, Dave misses driving every day. However, zombies are perfectly capable of hitching a ride to the nearest hospital. Of course, sometimes they don't get there…"

"And neither does the Good Samaritan foolish enough to pick them up," Welly said. He rubbed his forehead with one muddy hand, and then started fishing around in his pocket for his Oddfone. "I'm obligated to call in," he said. "And I'm going to have to raise the emergency level. Well done, Ken. Your zombies are making a beeline for—"

"La-welly Wells!" Alice blurted out, excited. "That's a really cool coincidence, as that's where the original report of zom—"

All three men were staring at her.

"Did I say, cool?" Alice asked. "I meant, bad. Really, really bad coincidence."

9

Alice Makes a New Friend

Ken darted to the top of the hill and looked down. "There's a two-lane highway all right," he confirmed. "But there's no traffic, so Dave and the pilot could still be on foot."

Welly opened his Oddfone; brown water poured out of it and continued dripping off the end of his elbow as he lifted it to his ear. "Lilith, I'm raising the emergency level from Rough to High Seas. There are at least two zombies on the loose in Mid-Wales, last known location..." He momentarily paused. "Highway A forty-three just south of Llanwrtyd Wells... Llanwrtyd... I'll spell it for you, Lima, Lima, Alpha..."

Alice was amused that every time Welly spelled something, it sounded like he was swearing. She was wondering if any English curse words began with the letter 'l', when her attention snapped back to Welly.

"No, Lilith, I said loose zombies not losing zombies." His voice was calm, but his body was rigid with tension. "That's not true, we didn't lose... No, you cannot tell Borislav we lost two—What? Yes, of course you could tell him, but that's not the point!"

"Oh no," Alice breathed. She'd never met Lilith, in truth knew very little about her. But one thing everyone knew about Lilith was that she was the best telephone psychic Odyssey had. Way better than Alice had ever been.

"Listen here, Lilith," Welly said, regaining his composure. "If you breathe a word to Borislav, I'll inform him about the time you called him 'a jumped-up mall cop with delusions of Stalinhood'."

"She did?" Alice asked, impressed.

Mick nodded. "More than once. It's one of the many reasons why I love Lilith."

Welly made a rude noise. "You're not afraid of Borislav?" Then he paled. "You're really not?"

Alice usually had difficulty reading Welly's mind, but not now. Images of being skinned with a sander were competing with the Admiral's last staff barbeque. He was so unnerved that when Mick reached for the Oddphone, Welly let him take it.

"Hello Lilith, my love," Mick said. "As much as I agree torturing Enhanced Agents is entertaining, I really need Borislav to keep his Slavic nose out of my zombie cure-making business. So, I would consider it a personal favour... Oh, Lilith that cuts me to the core." Mick sighed melodramatically. "I suppose I have no choice but to tell the Admiral you called him 'a poor excuse for a high magician who couldn't defend himself against a standard shape-shifting curse'."

"Is Lilith suicidal?" Alice asked.

Welly shrugged. "Homicidal definitely."

"Are you sure you don't care, sweetheart?" Mick asked. "Then I suppose I'll tell the Admiral who was responsible for that standard yet highly effective shape-shifting cur— Yes, thought so... Here's Wellington, he'll iron out the boring details. Kiss, kiss." Mick handed Welly his Oddfone back with a grin.

Welly gave Lilith their coordinates, their ETA for Llanwrtyd Wales on foot, and the instruction to let Borislav do no more than set up the standard roadblocks for a High Seas Emergency. After he hung up, he said, "Smashing job, Mick. Never even heard a rumour about Lilith being responsible, how did you know?"

Mick smirked. "Lucky guess. I've known the lovely Lilith for a very long time, and it just seemed the sort of thing she would do. Shall we join up with Ken? I believe he's now checking the highway's asphalt for tooth marks. Should be fun to watch!"

Welly and Alice followed Mick as he bounded up and over the hill.

"But aren't you afraid Lilith will curse you?" Alice called after him.

Mick laughed. "What makes you think she hasn't already?"

Alice was still trying to come with an answer when they reached the highway. Ken was walking from one side to the other, looking desperate.

Welly sighed. "Any luck other than our usual?"

Ken frowned. "There may be signs further up the road."

"And Canada may one day win the World Cup," Welly said, dismissively.

"Hey!"

Welly ignored Alice's protest. "Listen up. We'll continue north toward Llanwrtyd Wells. For safety, we walk towards oncoming traffic as it'll be dark soon. First vehicle we see, we commandeer. Now, we've already made a dog's breakfast of this mission," Welly glared at Ken. "So let's not botch it up any further, if possible."

Alice could sense Welly's desire to rip into Ken for the whole airplane debacle as clearly as if Welly was shouting it. But all he said was, "Let's get a move on, shall we?"

This is what attracts me to Welly, Alice thought as everyone marched up the highway. He doesn't hold a grudge. He just deals with the situation at hand and lets bygones be bygones.

Without breaking stride, Welly pointed a finger at Ken. "Don't think for one second I've forgotten what you did to my car."

Ken threw his hands up in the air. "As if that matters

anymore!"

"It matters," Welly said, picking up his pace. "It matters a lot!"

"I've got your damn sparkplugs right here," Ken said, shaking his backpack at Welly. "I'll put them back myself, as soon as we get back to Head Office!"

"Stop swearing. And if you touch my car again, your zombie won't be the only one with fingers held on by duct tape!"

All right, Welly did hold grudges about his car, Alice conceded. But at least he hadn't harangued Ken about the plane crash. While Ken's foolish decision to bring Dave along had caused it, Welly was being reasonable and only blaming Ken for things under his control.

"And if we survive this mission," Welly continued, "I'm going to get you sacked for that stunt you pulled on the plane. All those civilian causalities are on your head, and anyone else your misbegotten zombie infects."

Alice grimaced. Perhaps she was shallow and only liked Welly because he was incredibly good-looking. Glancing over at him in his bog-soaked suit, Alice corrected herself. Incredibly good-looking most of the time.

"I'll take good care of all the new zombies in my Mailroom," Ken shot back. "They'll have a better life than anyone working under you."

Welly rubbed his face and muttered under his breath. He then looked over at Alice. "You're on the wrong side for oncoming traffic, you need to move to the right," he told her. "No, your other right." He walked over and guided her by the small of the back.

Despite the lingering 'eau de gym socks' encompassing him, Alice felt a tingle at the contact. Shallow and wanting a big, strong man to lead her around, she thought despairingly, like a lovesick girl from the 1950s. If this continued, she'd end up volunteering to be barefoot and pregnant, while Welly slaughtered zombies in the kitchen.

Embarrassed by this line of thought, she asked, "How can we be sure Dave or the pilot would head this way?"

"Zombies always head for the largest population centre possible," Welly answered. "Despite Llanwrtyd Wells's small size, it's the closest thing to an all-you-can-eat buffet in the vicinity."

"Zombies head for towns and cities because they're incredibly social creatures," Ken argued. "If one gets separated from the pack, they immediately try to rejoin it, or failing that, reach out for human companionship."

"So tearing our limbs off is just their way of giving us a hug, is it?" Welly asked, sarcastically.

As they began to argue again, Alice dropped back behind them. If they ever found Dave, Alice thought, maybe she should date him instead. Looks weren't everything, after all, and Dave seemed a nice, quiet, non-argumentative sort.

*

"I can sympathize with you now," Alice said to Welly as they trudged down the road an hour later. "You've got a twisted ankle. I've got a blister."

The sun was setting over a small grove near the end of the road, proving beyond any doubt that Wales did have trees. Alice still thought they were small, hunchbacked things compared to the over-muscled Canadian giants she was used to seeing in British Columbia's forests.

"Actually," Welly said, "my ankle is feeling fine." He'd taken off his remaining shoe and was now walking in his socks. The sulphurous odour he'd acquired after falling in the bog had faded to the comparatively inoffensive scent of wet dog.

Alice caught his arm, grimacing at the feeling of cold, sodden wool. She'd discovered it was always easier to keep up with Welly if she held on to him. She didn't know if it was because he slowed his pace to accommodate her, or if he was simply dragging her along in his wake, but either way it worked.

Ken was several meters ahead, still searching for a sign from Dave. Thankfully, this kept him sufficiently busy to prevent further bickering with Welly.

"Enhanced Agents heal remarkably quickly," Mick said, from behind them. "But like wild animals, they also possess an instinct to conceal their injuries. It's an advantage in the field, but a nuisance when it comes to experimenting on them."

"If Odyssey had a real doctor in charge of Medical," Welly said, brusquely, "we wouldn't need to 'possess an instinct to conceal our injuries'."

Alice glanced back. Mick was smiling as he drummed long fingers on his messenger bag. "A real doctor," he said, "as your limited mind defines the profession, wouldn't be as close as I am to discovering the cure for zombism."

"I've yet to see any proof," Welly said.

"Oh ye of little faith. The Med-Trekker IV is busy processing the blood samples I've fed it. Those results, combined with my natural brilliance and some really strong coffee, will deliver a proof even you won't be able to deny."

"It'll be a dark day, when you create that cure," Ken said, falling back to join them.

"What do you mean?" Alice asked.

Welly shook his head. "You really don't want to ask."

"Yes, I do. What's wrong with having a cure for zombism? Your Mailroom is..." Alice stopped in time, realizing that calling Ken's workplace a fate worse than death wouldn't be very tactful. "Your Mailroom is very nice, with the plants and fountains and such. But I'm sure the zombies from the plane would rather be cured than work there." Alice didn't add that she'd be less worried about getting infected if she had options other than death or postal employment.

"The invention of a cure risks devaluing the important contributions zombies have made to our society," Ken said, severely.

Welly snorted.

"Zombies have a great deal to teach us," Ken insisted. "About patience, acceptance, living for the moment—"

"I believe Alzheimer's disease already teaches us the joys of losing one's mind," Welly interrupted.

"Zombism is not a disease!"

Mick raised a finger. "Technically, it is," he said.

"It's not *just* a disease," Ken amended. "Zombies have their own unique culture, one worth preserving instead of curing out of existence."

"Hey," Alice said, letting go of Welly's arm and pointing down the road. "There's a house." Welly had been right, she really shouldn't have asked. Alice vowed she'd try to curb her curiosity in the future.

The small cottage looked normal enough: painted white, grey slate roof, tucked behind a low stone wall. Just off to the side was a wooden shed, and beside that, a farmer was chopping wood. Sheep dotted the rolling green hills behind him, completing the picture of pastoral bliss.

"It's all so cute," Alice said.

"Why would a farmer chop wood when there's hardly enough light to see?" Ken asked, tugging tiredly on his moustache.

Welly opened his jacket and checked the battery level on his Taser. "He's not chopping wood. He's hitting the chopping block repeatedly with his axe."

"Obsessive-compulsive chopping could mean he's Stage Two," Mick said.

Welly pulled out his gun and cracked it open, checking the bullets in the chamber.

"A revolver?" Mick asked. "How very retro of you."

"This," Welly said, snapping the chamber back in place, "is a Smith and Wesson forty-four Magnum, two hundred seventy millimetre barrel, double action, with a six round cylinder and a three-dot adjustable rear sight. Fire this beauty inside, and you'll peel the paint right off the walls. Fire it at a zombie, and you'll blow a hole in it big enough to put your fist through. Or take its head right off," Welly said with relish.

"There was a time when I carried one of those," Ken said, quietly.

Alice stared at him, surprised by this confession.

"As weapons go, it's a work of art," Ken continued. "But my experience working with zombies has shown me that we must evolve past the need for mindless violence."

"Trust me," Welly said. "I'm quite mindful when it comes to killing zombies."

As they got closer to the farm, Alice could see that the farmer wasn't swinging his axe with any kind of skill. Sometimes it hit the block edge on, but most of the time the axe landed on its side. Every few strokes the blade would get stuck and then the farmer would keep tugging at the handle until, by sheer persistence, he'd work the axe free.

"He's strong," Ken commented, admiringly.

The axe landed upside down and the business end of the blade bounced up, nearly hitting the farmer in the face. Alice winced.

"Or instead of shooting him, I could just let nature take its course," Welly said.

"I've got to stop him before he hurts himself," Ken said. He climbed over the low wall.

"Should we help him?" Alice asked, hoping the answer was no. Thankfully, both Welly and Mick appeared content to stand back and watch.

"Don't worry," Mick said. "Ken is the Zombie Whisperer."

"And the Zombie Wrangler," Welly added, re-holstering his

gun.

"Kenny," Mick said, with a snicker.

Welly frowned. "I still don't understand why that name's so amusing."

"Someday," Alice said, "I'm going to tie you to a chair and force you to watch all the TV you've missed over the past twenty-five years."

"My bondage experience with Alice is going to involve bells," Mick confided in a stage whisper to Welly. "She promised!"

Alice decided not to encourage him with a response.

During their conversation, Ken had crossed to the shed and propped open the door. The farmer pounded away at his stump without acknowledging him.

Ken now positioned himself directly behind the farmer. Just as the axe reached the apogee of its swing, Ken snatched it from the zombie. Dropping the axe behind him, Ken grabbed the back of the farmer's pants with one hand and took hold of his collar with the other.

The farmer's arms continued to swing up and down for several seconds before he realized something was missing. As Ken steered him toward the open door of the shed, the farmer began to flail wildly.

Mick suddenly jumped over the stone wall, brandishing his Med-Trekker. "Hold him there for just one moment! I need to get a sample."

"I'm not letting you use him as a guinea pig for your idiotic cure," Ken said, dragging the zombie steadily toward the shed. His eyes flashed with anger, but his tone of voice remained calm, almost soothing.

"Not at all," Mick responded, coming closer. "Guinea pigs are useless for science, they spontaneously combust with the least encouragement. Zombies are thankfully much hardier subjects."

"Back off, you're upsetting him," Ken said, as the zombie's head lolled to the side, jaws snapping.

"Don't worry," Mick told the zombie. "I just need to know if our pilot sneezed on you, Dave gnawed on you, or if a mystery zombie gave you the gift that keeps on giving."

"Ken, cooperate with Mick," Welly called to him. "We do need to know how he got infected."

Ken stopped in front of the shed. "All right, just hang on," he said, letting go of the zombie's trousers. Then he and the zombie fell backwards.

"Ken!" Alice cried out.

She needn't have worried, for the moment they hit the ground, Ken rolled on top of the zombie, pinning its legs down with his own. Ken then leaned an arm against the zombie's chest, using his body weight to prevent the zombie from breaking free.

"Hurry up, Mick," Ken said.

Mick crossed the remaining space between them with a one long stride and jabbed a needle into the farmer's arm. "Got it."

Ken immediately rolled off the zombie and scrambled to his feet. Before the farmer could react to his newfound freedom, Ken pulled him up by his shirt collar, and with one shove, propelled the zombie into the darkness of the shed.

Alice was very impressed. Ken had some serious skills when it came to zombie wrangling. She knew she'd never have enough nerve to try something like that, not in a million years.

Ken slammed the door shut and dropped the latch, locking the zombie farmer inside. Then he patted the door and said, "Don't worry. I'll be back for you soon. *Pob lwc!*"

Alice and Mick began clapping, and to her surprise Welly joined in. Ken brushed his hands off and gave them a shy smile as he walked back to the road.

When the applause died down, Alice heard thumping from inside the shed. "Is he okay in there?" she asked Ken. After all, she thought, it wasn't the farmer's fault he'd become a zombie.

"Don't worry. He'll settle down very quickly in the absence of any other stimulation. Zombies are like budgies."

"Large, infectious budgies with an insatiable desire for human flesh," Welly said.

"I hate budgies," Alice said.

Ken made a disgusted noise. "I'd really appreciate it if you would stop spreading your bigoted beliefs," he said to Welly. "Yes, hunger is one of the symptoms of the early stages of zombism, thanks to their chronic low blood sugar. And yes, as they lose their fine motor skills, they become messy eaters. But as the vast majority of zombies weren't cannibals before they were infected, very few of them have any active desire to eat people afterwards."

"Except when they do." Welly crossed his arms, the proverbial immovable object.

"Which is entirely the fault of negative cultural stereotypes, perpetuated by people like you." Ken's finger was in Welly's face.

"That's right, blame society. That way you don't have to own up to any responsibility for spreading this plague."

"You sanctimonious, genetically warped British thug!"

"Bleeding-heart, thumb-sucking American!"

"Excuse me," Alice said. "I hate to interrupt your very productive tête-à-tête, but Mick just went into the cottage."

*

Much to Mick's expressed disappointment, the farmer apparently lived alone and preferred tea to coffee. There was no sign of a computer, so Ken turned on the radio and began searching for a local station. Welly, meanwhile, sat down and peeled off what remained of his socks.

"How are your feet?" he asked Alice. "It's important to take good care of them, especially when you're in the field."

"Sore," she said. "But if I unlace these boots, I'll never get them back on."

Alice poked through her overnight bag, searching for anything that didn't get soaked when Welly fell into the bog. To heck with his obsolete code of chivalry, she thought, next time she was carrying her own bag. At least her Taser and everything else in her purse were still intact.

"Sugar," Mick exclaimed, rummaging in the cupboards. "Sweet crystals of life." He added the box to his salvage pile, which so far consisted of a turkey baster, a salt shaker, and a spatula. Alice could hear the Med-Trekker inside his satchel beeping regularly.

Alice looked back down at her ruined overnight bag and its stinky contents. She might as well abandon it here. Alice regretted throwing her damaged bra into the wilds of Wales, now that her spare smelled like a peat bog. Wrinkling her nose, Alice stuffed it into her purse, hoping she'd get a chance to wash it out. She didn't relish the idea of jiggling all the way to Llanwrtyd Wells.

Exiting the kitchen, Mick pulled his Med-Trekker out. A grimace of disappointment crossed his face. "Regrettably, our farmer friend possesses the same strain of zombism as the pilot."

"At least that means we're definitely on the right track for finding him," Ken said.

"Marvellous," Welly growled. "At the cost of another civilian casualty." Near the front door, Welly had found a pair of rubber boots that fit adequately, although they did nothing to complement his suit. He was now trying to brush the dirt off his suit jacket without much success.

Ken frowned at the radio, which had just died in a burst of static. "We'll get a better sense of how things are going once I get this up and working."

"I'm starving," Alice said. "Is there anything to eat?"

"I don't recommend you eat anything here," Mick said. "Looks like our farmer friend's immune system was compromised by his less than hygienic standards."

"He's still mourning his dead wife," Alice said, the information popping into her head. "The poor woman's probably rolling in her grave." She suddenly realized the phrase was in poor taste considering the woman's zombie husband wasn't exactly resting in peace. "I mean, she used to keep this place immaculate. I took a peek into the bathroom. If you give me half an hour and a scrub brush, it might be useable."

"We're not staying," Ken and Welly said simultaneously. Welly gave Ken a dirty look.

Ken shrugged and resumed digging through the desk against the far wall. "Dave can't be very far ahead of us," he said.

"Alice," Welly said. "I need you to go outside and see what sort of vehicles the farmer owned."

"Ah, batteries," Ken said. He fished an unopened pack of D-cells out of a drawer. Cracking open the back of the radio, he replaced the old batteries.

"And I'm raising the emergency level to Heavy Winds," Welly said, taking out his Oddfone.

"Don't overreact," Ken said, fiddling with the radio's dials. "We've only seen one new case."

"Isn't it already Heavy Winds?" Alice asked.

"High Seas," Mick said, tossing aside an empty coffee tin.

"Oh right, because Heavy and High aren't easy to mix up," Alice said, rolling her eyes. "Odyssey really needs to — "

"Quiet, please," Welly interrupted. "One moment..."

"For all we know, the farmer picked them up on the road and brought them back here. Dave and the pilot could be very close by," Ken jumped in. "Just wait a minute until I find — "

The radio crackled into life. "Authorities are strongly recommending that area residents remain inside until this situation has been brought under control. Do not open your doors. A gang of hooligans has been reportedly menacing people in the town centre..."

"Foxtrot!" Welly cursed.

"It's too fast," Ken said, sounding bewildered. "Even airborne the virus couldn't spread this far, this quickly. There's got to be another explanation."

The radio crackled, and then the signal returned. "...evidently in costume as zombies and chanting 'brains'."

"Maybe they're not real zombies," Alice said, hopefully.

Welly flipped open his Oddfone. "Lilith, there's High Seas in Wales." Waving his free hand at Alice, he said, "Find me a Bravo car!"

Alice frowned, trying to remember which swear word Bravo stood for.

"Now, Alice!"

"Okay, okay!" She stomped outside. "There's no bloody need to shout."

*

Five minutes later, Alice walked back inside the farmhouse and announced, "There's an ancient brown car behind the shed. Don't ask me what make or model because I have no idea. It's a car; it's unlocked. The farmer kindly left the keys behind the sun visor, just like in the movies." There'd also been a tractor and a pickup truck. Alice had rejected the tractor as too slow, and the pickup truck would be an open invitation for Ken to start collecting stray zombies.

Welly's jacket was spread out on the kitchen table, looking damp, but somewhat cleaner. He picked it up and put it back on, over his shoulder holster. "Let's get our act together," he said.

"We're not going anywhere until I visit the bathroom," Alice said, firmly. It might be all well and good for the men to relieve themselves in bushes and behind crashed airplanes and who knew where else, but Alice had standards

"If you must, but be careful," Welly said, rather needlessly in Alice's opinion, as she grabbed her purse and headed to the back of the house. Then again, she thought, it wasn't all that surprising Welly was twitchy on the subject of bathrooms as his last Sensitive had died in one.

There was an oddly fishy smell about the bathroom, which made Alice wrinkle her nose. For a moment she had second thoughts about using the facilities, but the water trickling out of the tap was clear. Alice decided she could manage well enough without actually touching anything.

After all, she thought, it wasn't as though the farmer was in any shape to complain if she didn't flush. Plus she didn't relish the alternative of going outside where zombies might be lurking behind the bushes, waiting to give her a friendly but fatal hug.

The towel beside the sink actually had a layer of dust on it. "Men," she muttered in disgust.

Alice examined her reflection in the dim yellow light of the single bulb still working in the row above the mirror. She was a bit sunburnt, her face muddy, and hair matted. But considering that in the course of the day she'd visited Odyssey's Mailroom, shopped in London, survived a plane crash, and trekked through a Welsh bog in pursuit of a pair of runaway zombies, Alice decided she didn't look too bad.

Alice splashed her face as best she could with only the dribble of water flowing into the sink. She then tried to run her hairbrush through the mats on her head. It was then she saw it. And it was not alone.

"Oh no," Alice moaned. It wasn't fair, she thought, despairingly. She was only twenty-six years old!

"I'm too young to be going grey," she told her reflection sternly, but the offending hairs refused to turn back to brown. She tried to comb the darker hairs over to cover them, but was only partly successful.

Alice sighed and reassured herself that Welly cared about her regardless of her hair looking like a silver rat's nest. There was no particular reason that fact should make her feel warm inside. After all, Enhanced Agents and their Sensitives had to get along, if their partnerships were going to last for any length of time. Still, as Alice patted her hair back into some semblance of style, she couldn't shake the feeling that there was something more going on. Maybe Welly didn't just care about his Sensitive, but actually about Alice, the woman.

"Talk about bad timing," Alice muttered. A zombie apocalypse was not a good time to indulge in an office romance. She buttoned up her jean jacket, and lifted her purse strap over her head so she wouldn't lose the purse if they had to run. Then the smell of rot and decay hit her nose. "Ewww, what died in here?"

She dug into her purse and removed the source of the offensive smell, her bog-soaked bra. She'd forgotten about her plan to wash it. She held the bra under the tap, but there wasn't enough water pouring out to make much of a difference.

"Alice, please be quick about it!" Welly called out to her.

As she yanked back the shower curtain to use the bathtub, Alice shouted, "Wait just a – Ohmygod!"

"It's really not appropriate to call on any deity in the bathroom," Welly said, sounding closer.

"Oh, yes it is. There's a naked dead woman in the tub," Alice whispered. The corpse was blackened and decayed, but was still recognizable as an older woman. Is this what the Welsh do? Alice wondered in shock. Stick their loved ones in a tub to rot?

"What was that?" Welly asked through the bathroom door.

"I said," Alice forced herself to speak louder, "there's a naked, dead…"

The woman's eyes opened, and the corpse jerked up into a sitting position. The dead woman's desiccated face was grinning. Her lips had dried and cracked, framing a set of enormous yellow teeth.

"ZOMBIE!" Alice screamed.

10

Welly and Ken Have a Frank Discussion

"**F**oxtrot!" Welly shouted. "Get away from the door!"

The zombie extended her arms toward Alice. "Bad zombie," Alice said. "No hugging!"

"Alice, move!"

"Okay," Alice said, but her legs refused to obey her.

There was a loud thump as the bathroom door gave way. It slammed into Alice and propelled her into the tub. She landed head first in the zombie's lap.

Alice screamed and tried to roll away, but the zombie had a death grip on one of her shoulders. She started to hit the corpse with the only thing at hand, her boggy bra. "Bad touch, bad touch!" she shouted, twisting free.

"Get down NOW!" Welly bellowed, and this time Alice obeyed, ducking and covering in the far end of the tub.

A thunderous boom shook the entire bathroom, and dust fell down from the ceiling.

Ears ringing, Alice huddled in the tub, whimpering. A strong arm caught her around her waist and pulled her out of the tub. Welly, smoking gun in one hand, propped her against the bathroom wall with the other. "Did it bite you?" he demanded.

Alice inadvertently glanced back at the zombie and sobbed. The old woman was face down in the tub, or she would have been if she hadn't just had her face blown off.

"Alice," Welly gave her a gentle shake, which caused her teeth to chatter. "Did that thing bite you?"

Alice looked into his eyes and blinked. She'd never seen him look so stricken. Suddenly, the meaning of his words sunk in. "No," she managed, but it sounded like a whisper, so she tried again. "No!"

Welly looked immeasurably relieved. "All right, love, you don't need to shout," he said.

"What?" Alice's ears were still ringing, and her head was starting to pound.

"You mindless MORON!" Ken bellowed.

Alice definitely heard that. Feeling dizzy, she looked down, and shrieked again. Chunks of zombie flesh and bone were sticking to her jean jacket. She reached up with a shaky hand and realized she also had zombie in her hair. Then all the lights went out.

*

Alice had passed out for less than a minute, but she felt weak and humiliated. While she was unconscious, Welly had carried her out to the living room couch and stripped off her zombie-bespattered jacket. She woke up as he was using a damp cloth to wipe away the remaining remains of the zombie farmer's zombie wife. When she felt well enough to sit up, he sat beside her, and held her hand.

"Swallow this," Mick said.

"What?" Alice asked. The moment her mouth opened, Mick tossed a pill to the back of her throat. Alice coughed and swallowed. "Gross. Tastes like iodine and garlic."

"Be thankful you can't taste the mistletoe," Mick said. "Toxic in large doses, but works wonders on the ear drums." He glanced down at the Med-Trekker. "Of course, the bad news, my molested magpie, is you're still zombie virus free."

"Yay," Alice said quietly, feeling too shaken to be more enthusiastic. However, her head was already feeling better, and the ringing in her ears was fading. "Where's Ken?" she asked.

"Burying that thing in the back yard," Welly said, contemptuously. "I should have never let you go in there on your own."

"Welly, no matter how you feel about the dangers inherent in bathrooms, I have the fundamental human right to pee alone."

"I doubt the Universal Declaration of Human Rights covers that particular point," Welly said, but there was a hint of amusement in his expression.

"A Canadian helped write it," Alice said, "so I'm sure he would have included it along with other sensible provisions like the right to drink hot chocolate after skating."

The back door banged open, and Ken stalked in. Alice immediately knew he'd buried the farmer's wife in the compost pile. She suddenly felt nauseated.

"Sunlight is the best cure for an upset stomach," Mick said. "It'll just take me a minute to jury rig a lamp out of a jam jar and your solar calculator. The calculator probably won't survive the operation, but it's for a good cause."

"Leave her alone, Mick," Welly said. He gave Alice's hand a squeeze before releasing it and standing up.

"I hope you're proud of yourself," Ken snarled. "You just shot a sick, defenceless woman."

"That wasn't a woman, it was a zombie!"

"Her name was Dorothy," Alice said, with a sniff.

"All of you are overlooking the very good news about Alice's bath-time buddy," Mick said.

Everyone stared at him blankly, and Mick shook his head. "I know none of you have my level of medical genius, but surely somebody noticed our dearly departed friend's advanced state of decomposition. Which means, drum roll please..."

"She was infected weeks ago," Ken said. "Dave and the pilot couldn't be responsible."

"So she was hiding in the bathtub all this time?" Alice asked.

Ken frowned at her. "Don't be ridiculous. When a late-stage zombie's mobility becomes restricted, they have difficulty doing things for themselves, like getting in and out of the bathtub. Someone should have installed a walk-in bathtub for her safety and dignity."

"Ken is right," Mick announced.

"Zombies have the universal right to walk-in bathtubs?" Alice asked.

"Not in the current declaration." Mick pressed a button on his Med-Trekker, and a small, plastic vial popped out. "This, ladies and gentlemen, is the strain of the zombie virus that I extracted from Dorothy's pulverized brain matter. It's completely unrelated to the airborne strain we set loose on the plane. Which, by the way, I've decided to name 'Darryl' in honour of that virus's first lucky contestant." He popped another vial out of the Med-Trekker and held it next to the first. "Darryl, meet Dorothy. May your offspring be numerous and lead to a cure!"

"Two zombie viruses," Welly said. "This is very far from good news." He snapped open his Oddphone. "Lilith, it's Stormy as all Hotel here. Get me Borislav."

Alice risked getting up and was pleased that she was steadier on her feet than she felt. She tried to focus on Welly's conversation with Borislav, but was distracted by Ken who was pacing the kitchen, broadcasting his boiling emotions.

As soon as Welly tucked away his phone, Ken lit into him. "Not only are you murdering innocent sick people, now you've called up the fascists with their firebombs to wipe out the rest! Heavy Winds was bad enough, but Stormy?"

"A Stormy emergency level for a zombie outbreak is a limited and/or controlled epidemic in a small population centre. I reported the truth," Welly said, glowering. "With a second strain on the loose, I would be within my rights to raise it to Raging Seas."

Alice contemplated digging her Taser out of her purse and firing it at both of them.

"It's just gone twenty-two hundred hours," Welly said, "and we've got until dawn to get this under control before the fascists, as you call them, take over. Personally, I think that's more than generous."

Welly stepped into the kitchen to stand in front of Ken. "I need to know you're not going to get in my way. My job is to preserve the lives of every uninfected person in Llanwrtyd Wells, and keep the zombie plague from spreading any further."

"And save the World Bog Snorkelling Championships!" Alice added.

Welly ignored her. "The quickest and only guaranteed way to accomplish that goal is to kill each and every unsecured zombie before it can infect anyone else," Welly said. "You can have your farmer in his shed, but the rest are mine."

"That's premeditated murder!" Ken exclaimed.

"I should throw you into that shed with your precious farmer," Welly growled at Ken, his fists clenching. "I've seen what a zombie can do to a person. And it doesn't matter if it's his teammate, best friend, or even his beloved spouse. It'll rip them to shreds without a thought."

"Okay, yes, sometimes zombies are violent." Ken threw his hands in the air. "But not on purpose; they can't help lashing out under stress. They're no more violent than uninfected people if you handle them with care. That's why we have to protect them."

"No, we should wipe out every single zombie for the good of the entire human race," Welly shouted, "instead of harbouring them in your Bravo Mailroom!" Welly was as angry as Alice had ever seen him, all but spitting each word at Ken.

Ken's ears had turned the color of brick. "You've set yourself up as judge, jury, and executioner of every single zombie. And what was their crime? They caught a virus."

"You make it sound like they caught a cold," Welly shot back. "The virus is what makes them dangerous!"

"Dangerous? You should talk. Zombies don't have your super strength or resilience, and they sure as hell don't age slower. And as they slowly rot to death, they don't stand around and plot genocide!"

Mick nudged Alice's shoulder with his elbow. "Isn't this marvellous? He's going to talk about me next."

Ken pointed his finger accusingly at Wellington. "When Mick enhanced you, he changed everything about you. How your heart beats, how your muscles flex, your bones, your skin, every cell in your body was altered so you could become Odyssey's perfect soldier. If zombies aren't human," Ken spat out, "what about Enhanced Agents? Tell me, *ubermensch*, do you have a shred of humanity left inside you?"

Welly turned white and stepped toward Ken.

"No, Welly, don't!" Alice yelped.

He glanced at her and then looked at Ken. "I'm giving you one chance to reconsider your words," he said,

"You're right, I should reconsider," Ken said, his voice shaking with rage. "You're not a Nazi experiment. You are a Nazi!"

Welly backhanded Ken, sending him sprawling across the kitchen floor. Alice didn't have time to think. She leapt between them, intercepting Welly before he could hit Ken again. He stopped in mid-step, the palms of Alice's hands flat on his chest.

If there was ever a time in Alice's life she needed to say exactly the right thing, it was now. Except fortune cookies didn't typically address impending homicide. Shaking, Alice opened her mouth and to her surprise, heard herself say calmly, "If we fight each other, everyone dies."

"A true prediction," Mick said. "Everyone dies. At least, everyone in a fifty-mile radius. Except for me, of course, I have my exit strategy all worked out."

"Mick, enough," Alice said, still not quite believing she'd managed to come up with an actual psychic prediction. "See if Ken's okay." To her surprise, he silently obeyed.

Welly took several deep breaths, his chest slowly rising and falling under her hands. Then he nodded.

Alice sighed with relief.

"Ouch, stop that," Ken protested.

Alice turned and looked at Ken. He was clutching his face with one hand and slapping Mick away with the other.

"His jaw isn't broken," Mick announced. "A couple of loose teeth though. If you don't want to lose them, I'd chew food on the other side of your mouth. On the other hand, brushing teeth is tedious, so I'd recommend chewing on apples."

Ken regarded Welly sullenly, cupping his bruising face. "You could have broken my jaw," he managed.

"If I'd wanted to break your jaw," Welly said, without heat, "it would be broken right now."

"That's the spirit," Mick said, cheerfully. With one hand, he pulled Ken up off the floor. "Now, shall we have peace in our time?"

"We save as many of the infected as we can," Ken insisted. "No more shooting them in the head. Zombies are people, too!"

"Zombies are most definitely not people, and I'll kill as many as necessary," Welly retorted. "We are going to save as many of the uninfected as we can."

"There now," Mick said, draping his long arms over both their shoulders. "Save the infected; save the uninfected. If we save everyone, all our problems are solved."

"Remove your hand, or I'll remove it for you," Welly said, icily.

Ken snorted in disgust and ducked out from under Mick's arm.

Alice realized that one prediction did not a peacemaker make. "Welly, you shouldn't hit Ken. You might accidentally break him." To Ken, she added, "And you really shouldn't call Welly a Nazi. After all, he fought in World War Two against them."

Welly threw his hands up in the air in blatant frustration. "I know you think I'm ancient, Alice, but for the last time I did not fight in the Second World War. It was the Korean War. The Korean War!"

"You're shouting at me," Alice said.

"It was the Foxtrotting Korean War!" Welly marched out the back door, slamming it behind him.

"Wait!" Alice called out, following him outside.

"There's no time," Welly said. He stomped across the lawn, heading for the shed.

Alice ran to catch up with him. "No, I mean you should watch where you…"

Welly yelped and staggered back. He bumped into Alice, almost knocking her down.

"I tried to warn you," she said, annoyed. "Part of my job is keeping you from injuring yourself. How am I supposed to do that if you won't listen to me?" It was hard enough for Alice to feel useful being partnered with a superman. She didn't need Welly ignoring the one talent she actually did have.

He braced himself against the side of the shed and peered at his left foot in the darkness. "I didn't expect that Foxtrotting farmer to leave a board lying around with a nail sticking right out of it."

From inside the shed there was a loud moan.

"Pipe down," Welly said. "You deserve to be a zombie."

"Do the Welsh use extra big nails?" Alice asked, recalling how tough Enhanced Agents' skin was.

"Don't be ridiculous. It's not the size of the thing, it's the angle and force," Welly said, prodding gingerly at the sole of his foot. "I'm hardly invulnerable."

True, Alice thought, remembering the time the bad guys had tied Welly to a frame above growing bamboo plants. By the time she'd found him two weeks later, the plants had completely perforated his body.

"Will you need surgery to remove the nail?" she asked, hoping not. Refilling the holes made by the bamboo had been both time consuming and disgusting.

"Obviously not," Welly said, crankily, "as it's still attached to the board." He picked up the rotting wood and leaned it against the shed.

"Some of us don't have enhanced night vision," Alice reminded him.

"Sorry," he muttered. He put his foot down cautiously and took a step, hissing through his teeth. "And I do listen to you, when you don't sound like a Chinese fortune cookie. Then I know to take you seriously."

Alice felt her face heat up. "You caught on."

Welly chuckled. "I used to call you on that horrible Psychic Hotline, Amethyst something. I remember the games you played."

"Don't remind me of that place — Hang on, you believed me when I told you the Antichrist's anarchists messed up your car. And I totally fortune-cookied you that time."

"Agitators for Antichrists. And I believed you because you were telling me what I expected to hear," Welly said, ruefully. "I'll have to watch for that."

He cautiously put his injured foot down and managed to put his weight on it. "Now, where's that car you found?"

Alice pointed behind the shed, just as the cottage back door slammed behind her.

"I couldn't help overhearing you've abused that body I put so much work into," Mick announced. "Let me see that foot so I can work my magic." He walked toward them, Ken in tow.

"Over my dead body." Welly took a cautious step and grunted.

"Isn't that the same foot you injured earlier?" Ken asked. "There may be significance in this. A message your subconscious is trying to send you."

"Clearly, my subconscious hates my left foot," Welly said, sarcastically.

"No, it could be telling you to take extra precautions in protecting it," Ken said. While he didn't sound especially concerned about Welly, at least he wasn't openly hostile anymore. Mick must have done a good job calming him down while they were alone in the farmhouse, Alice thought.

"Plus, I fluffed his aura," Mick whispered in her ear.

"What about tetanus?" Alice asked, ignoring him. "I remember in my first aid class, they said puncture wounds were really bad."

Welly began limping determinedly toward the car.

"Listening to your body's messages is important to overall well-being," Ken called after him. "Zombies have a natural understanding of the health benefits of biofeedback."

"Enhanced Agents don't get tetanus," Mick told Alice. "Unless they're already fighting another infection, and their immune system is overloaded. They sometimes have trouble handling multiple infections, especially the more virulent strains."

Welly opened the driver's side door and climbed inside. "Anyone planning on coming, get in."

Mick moved toward the door on the front passenger side, but Welly covered the seat with his hand. "No, the only one of you lot who gets to sit up front with me is Alice."

"That's very mature," Ken said, as he sat down in the back seat.

"Welly's feeling threatened," Mick explained, sliding in beside him. "And thus has to assert his dominance."

"And only Alice is allowed to call me Welly." He started the car, and they bounced around the side of the house toward the road.

Alice knew it was petty, but she liked the fact that Welly was giving her preferential treatment. While getting the shotgun seat wasn't exactly a romantic gesture, it was probably the best she could expect considering how repressed Welly was.

Her warm and fuzzy mood was broken by a sharp tug of her hair. She whipped her head around to glare at Mick. "What are you doing? You better not be molesting my aura."

"No, I was simply admiring the way your hair is changing colour to reflect your increasing maturity. It's fascinating."

"Oh no, is the grey really that obvious?"

"Don't apes do the same thing as they mature?" Mick asked, a shade too innocently. "Don't the colours of their coats change?"

"That's just the males," said Alice, sinking into her seat. "Silverback gorillas."

That's it, she thought. Even if she survived tonight, her life was officially over. She was already turning into Welly's grey-haired, hundred-and-six year old mother. Next, she'd start having all her dead pets stuffed, like so many furry zombies.

"You don't have any pets," Mick said.

"Maybe I'll have my nosy co-workers stuffed instead."

*

Under different circumstances, Alice might have enjoyed the scenic drive to Llanwrtyd Wells. Even in the dark. But much like his home and his wife, the zombie farmer's car wasn't in the best of condition. The sedan's muffler and shocks barely worked, and its maximum speed turned out to be just over sixty-seven kilometres per hour.

They weren't alone on the road anymore, but the few cars they encountered were all driving the other way. It was a bit unnerving driving toward a place everyone else was fleeing. However, Alice knew these refugees were heading straight for Borislav. Despite Welly's assurances that no one stopped by the roadblock would come to any permanent harm, given a choice, she'd still risk the zombies.

Alice was hungry, tired, in despair over her greying hair, and more than a little bit worried about being eaten by zombies. Plus the unrelenting quaintness of Wales was beginning to grate on her nerves. The large hills they'd hiked through had given way to gently rolling farmland. If Alice saw another adorable little brick house with an adorable little slate roof, she was going to... do nothing much, actually. But she wasn't enjoying the experience.

"Oh look, sheep," Alice said. Even if they were cute, it made for a nice change. "I didn't know sheep were nocturnal."

"They're not," Ken said, sounding concerned.

"Delta!" Welly slammed on the brakes.

Alice gasped, jolted forward against her seatbelt. A not-particularly-fluffy white sheep had just dashed into the middle of the road. It was followed by several of its pals, who milled around in the beams of their headlights, bleating plaintively.

Welly leaned on the horn, the raucous noise sounding especially loud on the dark, empty road. The sheep scattered, but were quickly replaced by more. Alice couldn't help noticing that none of them looked anything like the sweet, friendly creatures on the Welsh tourism posters at Heathrow Airport. These sheep had tangled dirty coats, yellow teeth, and glowing eyes. The eyes were probably due to the reflection of the light, but it wasn't a reassuring sight.

"How can you tell if a sheep is a zombie?" Alice asked, nervously.

"I'm not sure how you'd diagnose them in the early stages," said Ken, scratching his chin. "Sheep don't have particularly high mental functioning at the best of times."

"Why don't I have a little word with them?" Mick suggested, helpfully.

Welly's head snapped around. "No!"

Alice glanced back to see Mick cross his arms and grumble, "Specist."

"I'm sure they're just ordinary sheep, not zombies," Welly said.

"This doesn't make sense," Ken said. "A farmer wouldn't let his sheep roam around at night."

"Unless he'd been turned into a zombie," Welly said, grimly. "Probably some Delta'd dog chased them here."

"I don't hear a dog," Alice said.

Welly smacked the steering wheel with his palm, bending it slightly. "We don't have all night. Ken, let's clear them out of the road."

Before they could get out of the car, the sheep panicked and began to stampede, dozens of them running past, their long filthy tails swinging behind them.

"Where's that Bravo marvellous dog?" Welly asked, leaning out of the window of the car and craning his head to look around.

Alice looked out her side window, terrified she'd see a horde of zombies chasing the sheep. She sighed with relief when she spotted the dog. "There it is." She pointed as the last of the sheep raced by.

My goodness, Alice thought, that is a very big dog. A very big, woolly dog.

"I think I know how you tell if a sheep is a zombie," Alice said, faintly.

If real sheep were unappealing, this one was downright horrifying. Its drooling head flopped over its shoulder, as if its curled horns were too heavy to lift. Its ears dragged on the ground as it staggered into the headlights of their car. A single bloodshot eye stared directly at them.

"Sierra!" Welly stomped on the accelerator.

Alice shrieked as the car hit the sheep with a solid thump, the front end popping up into the air as if the car was going over the biggest speed bump ever invented. Bouncing in her seat, Alice covered her eyes with both hands. "Keep going, it's not dead!"

Welly instead hit the brakes and reached inside his jacket. "Of course it's dead. It's a Foxtrotting zombie." As he pulled out his gun, he added, "Ken, I'm going to go put that creature out of its misery, unless you'd rather turn it into a pet?"

"Very funny." Ken peered out into the darkness. "You've already run it over, so you might as well finish it off. I'm sure you don't need my help to kill something."

Alice supposed a man who would use bunnies to train his zombie partner to hunt wouldn't be sentimental about the death of a single zombie sheep.

As Welly climbed out of the car, Mick said, "I'm coming with you! And don't kill our ovine friend before I've had a chance to take a sample. I'm dying to know if he caught the bug from sneezy little droplets in the air or through direct exchange of body fluids." He hopped out of the car and chased after Welly.

Alice decided she had not heard Mick just suggest the sheep might have a zombie STI.

Tapping his fingers on the armrest, Ken said, "Even stopping at that farmhouse, we should have caught up with Dave by now. I hope we haven't passed him on the road."

Behind him, Alice could see Welly and Mick standing over a dark lump. Actually, Welly appeared to be standing on top of it, while Mick was crouched down beside it.

It occurred to Alice that she should get out of the car and help. Her next thought, that she could just as easily be psychic locked safely in the car, was far more reassuring. However, this sensible idea was immediately followed by the chilling possibility Welly might not be able to hear her if she needed to warn him.

Heart in her throat, Alice unlocked the car door and stepped outside. The sudden crack and flash of Welly's gun made her yelp.

Welly looked over at her. "Bravo Hotel, Alice, what are you

doing out here?"

"Being your partner." Alice walked toward him. It would have sounded more convincing, she thought, if her voice hadn't wavered so much.

"What's going on?" Ken asked, leaning out the back window.

See, Alice's mind gibbered, you can hear Ken just fine and he's inside the car. But then she saw them in her mind's eye. Red eyes and yellow teeth. Lots of them. Moving impossibly fast.

"Incoming!" she yelled.

"Back in the car!" Welly shouted.

For once, Mick obeyed him without hesitation. Alice ran past him toward the front passenger door.

A sheep with patchy, balding skin abruptly lunged in front of her, cutting her off. Alice shrieked.

Welly pushed her against the car and pulled the trigger of his gun. The sheep's head exploded, and it dropped on the spot.

Alice climbed into the car so quickly she didn't remember opening and closing the door. "Where is he?" she asked, frantically, realizing she'd just shut Welly out.

Welly's gun went off again and again. In the car's headlights, Alice saw him working his way around the front of the car. Then her psychic senses kicked in, and she had a terrifying vision of him surrounded by slavering, vicious sheep.

"Welly, you won't make it!" she called out, but he couldn't hear her. "Enhanced hearing, my ass," Alice muttered as she rolled down her window. "Get to higher ground!" she yelled.

Alice saw Welly hoofing a zombie sheep in the ribs, and then scrambling backward up onto the hood of the car. Alice felt the entire car sink under his weight, and she heard metal bending.

Welly fired again, and a dent appeared over her head as he climbed up onto the roof of the car. Alice was so focussed on him, however, she forgot she'd left her window open.

"Alice!" Ken yanked her back by the shoulder as a sheep's head lunged at her through the window.

"Bad sheep!" Alice shrieked. Where was her Taser? she asked herself, panicked. Followed immediately by the question, where was her purse?

"Around your neck, my scared sugar glider," Mick said, as he stabbed the sheep in the snout with the Med-Trekker's needle.

The sheep let loose a horrible, baaing wail and fell back out the window. Alice immediately rolled up her window.

Above them Welly's gun kept firing, as the roof began to buckle inward.

"Mistletoe," Mick said, sounding much too relaxed. "As I said before, toxic in large doses. And you might want to open the driver's side window so Wellington can get in."

"Right!" Alice lunged across the driver's seat and rolled down the window. She then scrambled back to her side as Welly's feet appeared, and he slid inside, thumping back down.

A sheep's grinning toothy face appeared directly beside his head, snapping at him. Before Alice could scream, Welly hauled back and punched the animal directly in the nose. To her astonishment the sheep's face crumpled in on itself, shattering around his fist.

"Oh Ken, that could have been you!" Alice exclaimed. She'd have to ensure Welly never got mad enough to hit Ken again. Welly would regret it if he permanently maimed Ken. At least, eventually, once he'd calmed down.

The car rattled to life and shot ahead. Alice held on tightly to the armrest as it first slammed into a sheep on the left and then another on the right, rocking from side to side with each impact. Welly flipped open his Oddfone, one handed. "Lilith, we've got a zombie livestock infestation here."

"Will Borislav firebomb the sheep?" Alice asked, concerned for the non-infected ones.

"That won't be necessary," Ken said, reassuringly. "Livestock culls happen all the time. Odyssey will put the word out they're infected with mad sheep disease. Worst case scenario, Wales may take a short-term hit to its wool and mutton industry."

"That's right," Welly said into his Oddfone. "We need a livestock clean up team here, ASAP. No confirmed human involvement with this incident, but it's not looking good."

"Mad sheep disease?" Alice asked. "Oh no, you're not telling me Odyssey invented mad cow disease too?"

"Unfortunately, Odyssey won't let me invent diseases per se," Mick said. "But the name 'mad cow' was the perfect cover for cow zombies."

Zombie humans, bunnies, sheep, and now cows, Alice thought, feeling overwhelmed. Had she spent her whole life surrounded by zombies and just hadn't noticed?

Alice craned her neck and looked out the car's back window. Thankfully, it appeared they'd left the horde of woolly zombies behind. She settled back into her seat, heart no longer pounding in her throat. "Where do they all come from?" Alice asked. "What caused the virus that turns people and animals into zombies?"

"Zombies are part of Mother Nature's plan," Ken said.

Welly snapped shut his Oddfone and said something that sounded suspiciously like 'bollocks'. Alice decided that she must have misheard because Welly never, ever swore.

Mick laughed. "Absolutely! We're all the Great Mother's children, born of her loins and grown in her bosom. Of course, some of us are more stunted in our growth than others." He patted the top of Welly's head.

"Welly's not stunted," Alice said to Mick, sternly. "He just ages very slowly."

"True," Mick said. "Wellington is very slow."

"Zombies are a cancer," Welly said, ignoring Mick.

"No, they're not cancer at all," Ken argued, leaning forward. "If anything, we're the cancerous tumours, while zombies are white blood cells. Human overpopulation and pollution are destroying the Earth. By comparison, zombies are completely green. They don't breed, they don't consume, they don't litter or pollute." Ken counted off on his fingers. "All zombies do is decompose, adding nutrients to the soil, and create more non-breeding, non-consuming zombies. Homo zombiens are Nature's attempt to correct the imbalance Homo sapiens have caused with industrialization."

"Put a sock in it, for Golf's sake," Welly said, keeping his eyes on the road. "You might as well say that the plague was Nature's plan to end the Dark Ages and bring about the Age of Exploration. This planet has no more use for zombies than it has for anthrax or ebola."

"Enough, already," Alice interrupted, before the conversation could get any more heated and run the risk of turning physical again. "Clearly, none of you have any real idea where zombies come from."

"I do," Mick said. "When a boy zombie meets a very special girl zombie..."

"The zombie virus is part of the natural order of things," Ken said. "You may as well ask where the common cold came from."

"There's nothing natural about zombies," Welly insisted. "Malevolent magic had to be involved at some point."

"Two little zombies," Mick sang, "impaled on a tree, k-i-s-s-i-n-g—"

"Oh look," Alice interrupted. "A cute little bridge!" In truth, she thought it was a creepy bridge, lined as it was with pointy white stones which reminded her of teeth. But the last thing she wanted to do was spend the rest of the trip to Llanwrtyd Wells listening to Welly and Ken argue while Mick spouted random nonsense.

"I beg to differ," Mick said, sounding offended. "There's nothing random about my nonsense at all."

"Zombies speak more sense than you do," Welly said.

As he drove onto the stone bridge, Alice asked, brightly. "So which river is this?" Come hell, high water, or zombie invasions, Alice was going to change the topic.

"Not sure," Welly said. "Up ahead is the river Irfon. Once we cross that bridge, we'll be in the town proper."

Alice peered through the dirty windshield. Directly ahead were lights coming from a small town. A very small town, Alice thought, more of a village really.

"That's it?" she asked.

Welly didn't answer as he turned off the highway. Their vehicle was the only one left on the road now. Alice realized she hadn't seen any other cars since the zombie sheep attacked. She hoped it was because everyone else had fled in different directions, and not because zombie livestock had dragged away the other motorists.

Distracting herself from these disturbing thoughts, Alice said. "Everything in Wales is so puny. The mountains, rivers, towns." She shook her head. "I'm just used to things being so much bigger in Canada."

"Yes, yes," Welly said. "Everything is so much bigger in Canada. But it's not the size that counts."

"Oh no," Alice said. "Size counts. Size counts for a lot." One zombie sheep was scary, she thought. A whole herd of them was terrifying.

"Size counts only if you know how to use it," he said. "I'm quite fond of Canada, having spent the war there as a child. But most of your country is under-populated and undeveloped. Exporting timber's hardly a step up from beaver pelts. Canada might as well still be a British colony," Welly said, patronizingly.

"How dare you — " Alice began, when Ken interrupted.

"Heads up!" he shouted.

"Right. Hold tight," Welly said, stomping on the gas pedal.

Alice had only a split second to see the tall figure lurching down the centre of the road. Then Ken's shoulder hit the side of her face as he launched himself into the front of the car. He grabbed the steering wheel away from Welly, and the car tipped precariously onto two wheels as it took a sharp right turn across the road.

Alice choked on a scream as the car's nose suddenly came to a jarring stop in a ditch in front of a farmhouse. She jolted forward against her seat belt and slammed into Ken, who had somehow ended up in her lap.

Welly seemed to be reciting the entire Nato alphabet. "Sierra! Bravo Hotel, Ken! Are you trying to Foxtrotting kill us?"

"You tried to kill that man!" Ken said, struggling to right himself in the tilted car. "Excuse me, Alice."

"That's not a man," Welly snapped. "It's a zombie!"

"I'm not going to let you murder another one!"

"You're both insane," Alice said. "Ken, you could have killed us, and Welly, how did you know he wasn't a drunken Welshman? You could have murdered a civilian and ended up as the Admiral's personal Tiki torch."

Mick's head popped forward. "Even Welshmen can't keep walking when their intestines fall out of their sternum. I'm a doctor, I know."

"Out of the way, Mick," Ken said, trying to climb past him. One of Ken's knees hit Alice in the ear.

"Ow!"

"Sorry," Ken said.

"You should be," Welly said. "You've cracked the Foxtrotting radiator. What are you, death to motor vehicles? You shouldn't be allowed near anything on four wheels!"

Alice belatedly became aware of a hissing noise coming from the front of the car and realized her view was obscured by more than just the darkness and Ken's large head.

"It's your own fault," Ken said, sliding into the inclined back seat. "You were about to run over that zombie. We have to go find him, he may be hurt." He unlocked his door.

"He's definitely hurt if his intestines…," Alice began.

A face slammed into her window, teeth clicking against the glass. She shrieked.

"Brainnnns," the zombie said, slobbering on her window.

"For Pete's sake," Ken said. "Everyone out of the car."

Alice didn't need to be told. She was already trying to climb over Welly's legs, clawing at the driver's side door. "My seatbelt is stuck! Help, I think the door is jammed!"

She heard a click, and her seatbelt suddenly released. Then an arm wrapped around her, and she felt herself lifted bodily out of the car. Her boots sank into the mud as Welly put her down in the ditch. She looked up and saw him aiming his gun over the roof of the car at the zombie.

Then Ken rolled out of the back of the car. "Don't shoot!" he yelled, and slammed into Welly's legs. "Ouch!"

Ken's flying tackle had absolutely no impact on Welly. He reached down with his free hand and hauled a groaning Ken up off the ground. Welly's gun remained trained on the zombie, who was just a few feet away on the other side of the car.

The zombie was a middle-aged man with a comb-over which flopped pathetically down on the wrong side of his head. Oblivious to all the commotion, he continued to try chewing through the glass window, as if under the impression they were still inside the car. "Brainnns," he mumbled, damply.

Alice climbed out of the shallow ditch into a flowerbed. From this vantage point, she could see the zombie's intestines drooping out of his belly. "I hope that doesn't hurt," she said. "Where's Mick?"

"Put that cannon away," Ken snapped at Welly, shaking off his grip. "Zombies are my job, not yours!"

"Mine, too," Mick said, suddenly popping up beside the zombie and jabbed him in the shoulder with the Med-Trekker's needle.

The zombie paused in his attack on the car. He pawed at his

shoulder with a clumsy hand. "Brains?"

"No, blood sample," Mick corrected.

Squelching around the car, Ken walked up behind the zombie. As it turned slowly toward Mick, Ken grabbed the zombie by the back of his suit jacket. "Mick, if you don't mind?"

"My pleasure," Mick said. He reached a long arm across and opened the car door. Mick then stepped to the side and ceremonially bowed to Ken and the zombie.

Ken shoved the zombie inside the car, and Mick slammed the door shut.

"This is not a viable solution!" Welly slammed his fist down on the roof of the car. A fresh dent showed in the roof where he'd hit it.

"Why not?" Ken asked. "He's safely contained."

"Until some innocent person comes along, sees him, and lets him out."

Ken climbed out of the ditch onto the road. "No one's going to try to rescue our zombie friend tonight. Most civilians during an outbreak are sensible enough to leave town or hide indoors until everything is over."

Alice looked at the only house close by. The lights were off, and no one seemed to be home. There was no car in the driveway either. She could hear the muffled barking of a large dog in the distance, but otherwise the area was quiet. Ken appeared to know what he was talking about.

"What about the police?" she asked. "Aren't they supposed to investigate accidents?"

Ken shook his head. "The local police will have their hands full enough right now, without worrying about checking cars in ditches."

Welly frowned at the zombie in the car, clearly still unhappy with the idea of leaving him in there. He then sighed and reholstered his gun. "I'm acting against my better judgement here." He climbed out of the ditch and helped Alice leap across it.

"What do you mean the police have their hands full?" Alice asked Ken. She could see the lights of Llanwrtyd Wells just down the highway. It looked like safety to her.

"One farmer doesn't mean much," Ken said, "and a few zombie sheep might just be a coincidence. Even the 'gangs of hooligans' mentioned on the radio might only be a few of the infected acting obsessively. But when zombies start acting like stereotypical zombies…" He shook his head. "It means someone somewhere has decided they are zombies."

"Someone is bright enough to notice the obvious," Welly said. "How terribly clever of them."

"Zombie isn't the first thing that naturally comes to mind when you encounter one," Ken shot back. "Usually you think he's drunk, like Alice did, or drugged. Or you decide he must be sick or injured. The natural human impulse is to assist, not condemn. Only Enhanced Agents are so divorced from their humanity—"

"How very interesting," Alice interrupted, sensing Welly begin to tense beside her. "But why does it matter if they believe they're zombies when that's what they are? I thought you were all about zombie pride or something."

"True zombie pride arises only after they've learned about their true, zen-like nature. If they're not self-actualized, however, they try to act out the worst of society's stereotypes of zombies and often get hurt."

"Tell me," Welly demanded. "Exactly how were those killer sheep back there products of social stereotyping?"

Ken rubbed his hand over his mouth. "It must have something to do with the herd mentality," he said. "Sheep aren't known for being individualists at the best of times. In fact, their primary motivation is food, so that would explain their aggressive behaviour."

"Keep telling yourself that," Welly said. "Now that you've destroyed our means of transportation, we better start walking.

It would be shame if Llanwrtyd Wells was blown off the map because we arrived too late to save it."

Alice glanced around and realized a member of their party was missing. "Mick?"

"Right here, my cuddly cuscus," Mick said, directly behind her.

Alice was proud of herself for not jumping. This time, no one would have noticed she was startled by his sudden appearance.

"Now all you have to do," Mick said into her ear, "is work on controlling your heart rate. Or even better, learn to properly regulate the release of adrenaline into your bloodstream. It's an immensely handy skill to have, you know."

"Why would it…?" Alice started to ask, then stopped herself. "You know what? I don't want to know." She ran to catch up with Welly who was already marching down the road. "Shouldn't we try to find another car? What if there are more zombies out here? Or zombie sheep?"

"As long as we stay alert," Welly said, his attention focussed on their surroundings, "they won't be able to take us by surprise. Zombies are not fast on their feet."

"Except for the sheep," Mick said. "Zombie sheep are surprisingly spry."

Alice moved closer to Welly. The too-quiet highway was definitely freaking her out. It felt like the entire human race had disappeared. "Is this how the world ends?" she asked. "An actual zombie apocalypse?"

Welly gave her a sharp look. "Under no circumstances is this how the world ends."

"I suppose fighting Nazis in World War Two gave you some perspective on the end of the world." Things could be much worse, Alice tried to convince herself. After all, zombie Welshmen weren't as terrifying as zombie Nazis.

"Alice," Welly said, with forced patience. "I've told you repeatedly, I did not fight in the Second World War. My family relocated to

Canada during the bombing of London. My contribution to the war effort consisted of participating in Boy Scout scrap metal collection drives and pestering my parents daily to buy more War Bonds. I realize the modern education system has failed your generation badly, but please believe me when I tell you that there is a difference between the Second World War and the Korean Conflict."

"Modern society is more than capable of ending the world without any help from zombies," Ken said.

"I know how the world ends," Mick said, brightly. "And it's way more fabulous than this."

"I know I'll regret this, but how does the world end, Mick?" Alice asked.

He tapped the side of his nose. "That would be telling."

Alice crossed her arms. "I don't believe you really know."

"I'm not falling for that one again," Mick said. "You can't trick me into telling my secrets."

"Again?"

"Once, when I was young and foolish and living under a red rock in a yellow desert, a toucan flew by..."

"There're no toucans in the desert," Alice protested.

"That's exactly what I said." Mick wiggled his eyebrows at her.

As Mick launched into another one of his tall tales, Alice wondered why she couldn't read his mind at all. If she tried hard enough she could get behind people's shields, even Welly's. Of course, it was usually too difficult to scan Enhanced Agents to bother trying, but she could do it.

As Mick yammered on, Alice reached out psychically and touched his mind.

Tall and tanned and young and lovely, the girl from Ipanema goes walking...

"Ah, ah." Mick shook his finger at her, chidingly. "No peeking ahead to the happy ending."

11

Dewey the Dustbin Makes Sense

Half an hour after crashing the car, they finally reached the river Irfon. They walked over a medium-sized stone bridge over the average-sized river, leading to the pocket-sized town of Llanwrtyd Wells.

Alice was too hungry and cranky to properly appreciate her new surroundings. At this moment she would have given almost anything for a nice familiar Tim Horton's doughnut shop. Or even a Canadian Tire hardware store. Alice was sure she could find lots of useful items in Canadian Tire to defend herself from zombies.

Welly turned right at the end of the bridge onto a village street. White-walled buildings that looked hundreds of years old lined the road.

"Where are we headed?" Alice asked.

"In the purple," Welly said.

Alice was concerned by Welly's apparent non sequitur. "Are you feeling okay, Welly?"

"This mission cannot end soon enough," he said.

Alice wholly agreed with that sentiment.

As Welly led them around the outskirts of the town, she couldn't help noticing that Mick kept darting off into the darkness every few minutes, only to return looking pleased with himself. He couldn't be chasing bunnies this time, she thought.

Neither Welly nor Ken showed any interest in Mick's activities, and Alice knew she should do the same. She'd promised herself she'd curb her curiosity around Mick and had regretted every time she hadn't. But after five of these disappearing acts, she had to ask, "What are you doing, Mick?"

"Posting flyers," he said

"What kind of flyers?" Alice asked.

Welly cut in. "You're not selling fake Viagra again, are you? I distinctly remember a memo from the Admiral's office forbidding it."

Mick looked offended. "There is absolutely nothing fake about my Viagharaa. I use all natural organic ingredients, including the finest powdered unicorn horn. Not only was my formula far more effective than that boring blue Viagra pill, the online sales went through the roof. People loved it!"

"For the first three hours, certainly," Welly said. "The next three, not so much. And the three days after that…"

Mick waved a dismissive hand. "Some people don't know a good thing when they've got it."

Welly shook his head and said, "Just tell me you're not inflicting any of your nasty concoctions on the general populace."

"Hand to heart," Mick said, placing his hand on what Alice was fairly certain was his appendix. "I'm not selling or inflicting anything on anyone."

"Then what?" Alice asked, but Mick had already run off again.

"Here we are," Welly said. "With any luck, our contact will still be here."

Alice stared at the café, 'In the Purple'. The lights were on and the sign in the window read 'Welcome'. It was the most beautiful thing she'd ever seen.

"What contact?" Alice asked. Then she remembered. "Oh, the

guy who reported seeing zombies here. Do you really think he stuck around?"

"Go ahead," Welly said, waving everyone on ahead. "Mick, the gentleman you're looking for is David Kevan. I'll follow in a minute, I have a personal call to make first."

Ken propped his hands on his hips. "If you're calling in an air strike on this beautiful town..."

"Don't be ridiculous," Welly snapped.

"Ridiculous? You're the one who shot that poor woman in the tub and then tried to drive over a helpless man!"

"Oh dry up! They both tried to eat Alice."

"Alice was perfectly safe both times!"

Alice stepped between them, waving her hands. "Ken, Welly's telling the truth. He just wants to call his mom." So what if she couldn't read Mick at all, Alice thought. At least she knew her own partner.

Ken frowned at him. "You're calling your mother?"

Welly bared his teeth. "Have you got a problem with that?"

Ken shrugged. "No, actually. It's just a surprise to see you acting like a human being."

Alice stamped her foot before Welly could react. "Ken, stop antagonizing him!" She spun around and stuck her finger in Welly's face. "And you, don't you dare get mad at Ken. You know perfectly well you didn't have to run over Mr. Droopy Intestines."

Welly rolled his eyes and flipped open his phone.

"Fine, I'm going to get myself a cup of coffee," Ken said.

Mick reappeared beside him. "Coffee!" he declared, in a tone of revelation. "I could definitely use several cubic metres of coffee."

Ken and Mick went inside the café, but Alice lingered, shamelessly eavesdropping on Welly's call.

"She's not home yet? Can I reach her where she's... A spiritual retreat? Brilliant, just... never mind, Lilith." He hung up and shook his head. "My mum's run off to some monastery in Québec for the weekend, and they only allow emergency calls."

"Relax, Welly," Alice said. "It's a spiritual retreat, not an all-night rave."

Welly didn't relax. "A spiritual retreat she didn't tell me about, with some man I didn't even know she was seeing."

"If it'll make you happy, I'll check in on her." Alice glanced at her watch and tried to do a quick calculation.

"Welly, what time is it there?" Alice had never been particularly good at figuring out time differences.

"Going on six o'clock," Welly said.

Alice was reassured it was still early in the evening where Mrs. Wolfe was. The last thing she wanted to spy on was Welly's mom engaged in naked sexcapades. Alice shuddered and pushed that disturbing thought out of her mind.

"*Om mani mommy* — Hey, your mother's getting a foot massage from Patrick. He seems perfectly harmless."

"He's got a foot fetish, and you think he's harmless?"

"Your mother has all of her dead cats, dogs, and birds stuffed and mounted in her living room. Compared to a bit of foot worship, she wins the weirdness prize. And I'm sure if she was in any danger, I'd pick up on it."

"I don't share your confidence," Welly said, harshly, "considering your last date tried to kill you."

"Only because he was cornered and needed a hostage," Alice shot back. "Yes, he wanted to destroy Odyssey, but let's not exaggerate how bad he was."

"Good Golf, Alice. You're a Sensitive! How can you be such a poor judge of character?"

"You're right," Alice said coldly. "I'm a terrible judge of character. I considered dating you!"

Alice wrenched the café's door open. Just inside she stopped cold. What had she just said?

Alice turned around. Welly still looked serious, except the

corners of his mouth were quirking upward.

"I never, ever considered dating you," she told him. "And don't you dare laugh at me."

Welly looked past her at Mick, who was gesticulating wildly. "Mick, what's the problem here?"

Besides Mick and Ken, there were only two people inside: a middle-aged woman with henna-red hair wiping down a Formica counter, and an older man with bright white hair, seated at a table staring at his laptop.

Mick pointed at the woman, who had an implacable expression on her face. "She doesn't sell coffee by the cubic metre. What kind of café is this? I could get better service from Starbucks!"

"Well now," the man said, looking up from his laptop at Welly and Alice as they entered the café. "More tourists." His small blue eyes examined both of them sharply. "Looks like you two started the bog snorkelling festivities early. At least you aren't in costume." He nodded at Mick, who beamed delightedly and tipped his top hat to him.

In the bright light of the café, Alice had to admit they looked pretty bad. Welly was coated with peat bog, Ken was sporting a large purple bruise on his right cheek, and she resembled something a zombie cat had dragged in. Only Mick looked halfway decent, but his bizarre outfit clearly wasn't making him any friends here.

"Dewey," the woman scolded. "Leave them alone. They look like they've had a hard night." She tucked her cloth into her apron and added, "My name is Perl. Can I get you anything? Besides coffee by the gallon, I mean. We only sell beverages by the cup."

"Cubic metre," Mick corrected. "Not gallon."

"Do you make sandwiches?" Alice asked Perl.

"I'll get you a menu, duck," Perl said, heading behind the counter.

"Don't bother, I'll eat anything," Alice said. "Could you please make up four—no, make that eight sandwiches. If you make a couple of different varieties, we can just pick what we like."

"Dewey?" Welly asked. "Is your name David Kevan?"

"I go by Dewey the Dustbin now, if you don't mind. I earned the moniker, and I'm proud of it." He regarded Welly suspiciously. "Have we met?"

Welly took out his wallet and extracted a card. Handing it to Dewey, he said, "Wellington Wolfe, Odyssey International. You contacted us yesterday."

"So I did. And you mucked that up, nice and proper. Zombies all over the bleedin' place."

"Dewey the Dustbin." Ken snapped his fingers. "You walked across Wales picking up garbage, didn't you?"

"Near enough. And I don't much care to have the rubbish get back up and start walking around."

"Zombies aren't garbage," Ken said, leaning over the table. "They're not even supernatural. They're just ordinary people suffering from a virus."

Dewey frowned at him. "You got a cure? Or a vaccine?"

"We're working on it," Welly said.

"What's this 'we'?" Mick gestured broadly. "I'm the one working on it, and my genius is being thwarted by a narrow-minded restaurant owner who won't brew more than a single pot of coffee at a time."

Dewey rolled his eyes and turned his attention back to Ken. "Well, until you got a cure or a vaccine, don't be talking to me about zombie rights. Just look what they're up to now." Dewey turned his computer toward them.

The cell phone video was low quality, but it was clear enough to make out a group of six zombies staggering down a village street.

"That's just three streets down from here," Dewey said. "Some of the kids in town are up on rooftops taking pictures and tweaking each other about it, or whatever they're calling it these days."

"They're starting to form mobs," Welly said, grimly. He flipped open his Oddfone. "Lilith, patch me through to the Cardiff office." He paused. "What? No backtalk? No jokes? Oh... Yes, I'll try my best to leave an entertaining answering machine message. Foxtrotting Cardiff!"

"Here's another one," Dewey said, clicking on a picture on the sidebar. "This one's more recent." As the video played, he added, "Most of the outside world seems to think we're launching our latest, greatest festival. They're calling it the Zombie Wobble."

"You can stop laughing now, Lilith," Welly said into his Oddfone as he rejoined them. He snapped the phone closed and stared at it thoughtfully. "Mick, is there any chance you're serious about a cure?"

"I am closer than you can possibly imagine." Mick kissed his fingertips, like a chef.

"I have a vivid imagination," Welly said.

"Really?" Alice asked. "I've never noticed." When Welly gave her a dirty look, she added, "I mean, of course you do. You're very creative and open-minded."

"Ta very much."

Ken pulled on the ends of his moustache. "While I'm not a hundred percent behind a cure, wiping out this town would be a crime against zombie-kind. I vote we give Mick a chance."

"This is not a democracy," Welly said. "You don't get a vote."

Dewey frowned up at them, looking truly alarmed for the first time. "You can't be considering a full erasure? It ain't nearly that bad yet. You don't need a tactical nuke to take out a hornet's nest."

"Where's that?" Mick asked, pointing at the building in the background of the video.

"That's the Neuadd Arms, brews some of the best ale in the district. Some of our dimmer lads actually believe this Zombie Wobble claptrap. They've headed over to the Arms to get properly started on the wobbling part. But let's get back to this town erasure business and how you ain't doing it."

"Your town has its own brewery?" Mick asked, bouncing on his heels.

"Yes," Dewey said, looking at him askance.

"Perfect." Mick rubbed his hands together, gleefully.

"Wait, rewind," Ken said, pointing at the screen. He leaned in close and peered past the faux-zombie wobblers in the foreground. "There's the pilot. And that's Dave!" Glancing up at Dewey, Ken asked, "Where are they?"

"Not far," Dewey said. "That's the town square, right across from the Neuadd Arms. Mind," he added, "that was half an hour ago. If your mate's with that lot, can't rightly say where he is now."

"But Dave's in town," Ken said, gazing rapturously at the computer. "I'm going to go find him."

"I'm going with you," Welly said. "We've got to break up those mobs before they get any more dangerous. Maybe we can keep this from spreading any further." He took a deep breath. "I don't like the idea of this town being erased any more than the rest of you. If there's any chance of containing this outbreak, we'll take it, but we need to move fast."

"Then I fear it's time for us to part ways," Mick said, melodramatically.

"Where do you think you're going?" Welly demanded.

"Did I say I was going anywhere?" Mick asked. "You are the departers. So depart! I will heroically endeavour to make do with the primitive and scanty facilities available to me here."

"Excuse me?" Perl said, pausing in her sandwich making. "I don't recall giving you permission to do anything with my facilities, heroic or otherwise."

Welly looked directly at Mick and held up his index finger. "If you're having me on about a cure, I will make it my life's mission to have you permanently removed from Odyssey employment. I don't play games when people's lives are at stake."

Mick reached over with his own index finger and tapped Welly's fingertip. "Wellington, have faith. A little patience, a lot of blood work, and the cure will be in our grasp."

Welly snatched back his hand. "Can you do it before sunrise?"

Mick nodded confidently. "With one arm tied behind my back. Although why anyone would choose to tie an arm behind their back, when two arms are much more efficient, I have no idea."

"Alice," Welly said. "Keep him out of trouble."

"Wait, what?" Alice said. "Shouldn't I stay with you?" She felt a stab of panic at the idea of being separated from Welly's reassuringly solid presence.

"You'll be safer here," Welly said. "Remember, stairs slow zombies down considerably, and don't let yourself get backed into a room with only one exit. If you're forced out of the building, it's worth keeping in mind that zombies can't climb trees. You're faster than they are and a good deal smarter. So far, you don't seem to be susceptible to the airborne variant..."

"There's an airborne variant?" Dewey exclaimed. "Since when?"

"... so whatever you do, don't let them bite you," Welly continued. "I do trust you won't be overwhelmed by a natural human impulse to offer aid and comfort to zombies."

"No, not at all," Alice said, faintly. This wasn't how things were supposed to work, she thought. They were a team, and Welly heading off on his own—with just Ken, anyway—felt as dangerous as splitting up to explore a haunted house. Alice had seen enough of those movies to know things never went well once the group broke up. "I'm never going to see you again, am I?"

"What?" Welly looked genuinely concerned. "You're not having a premonition, are you?"

"No." Even if it would convince him not to go, Alice couldn't bring herself to lie about something like that.

"Trust me, you don't want to come with us," Welly said. "We're heading right into the thick of it. You'll be safer if you stay clear."

"But I don't want to trust you," Alice protested. When he looked hurt, she quickly amended, "I mean, I'm supposed to keep you safe too, not stay behind. And you're supposed to listen to me so you don't do anything stupid. And... Stop that!" She scowled at Welly who for once wasn't shielding his thoughts. "I know you think I'm being cute, but I'm not cute at all... I mean, I'm serious. You're not indestructible, you know."

Welly's expression was reassuringly confident. "You still have your mobile?"

"Yes," Alice said warily.

"Then if you sense I'm in trouble, call me on my Oddfone. I promise I'll listen to you."

Welly gave Alice's shoulder a squeeze and turned his attention to Dewey. "You and Perl may want to leave town, just in case. I trust you know the protocols."

"Odyssey roadblocks, our memories tinkered with by Borislav and the gang, I know the drill," Dewey said, sourly. "But I won't be forgetting to never call you lot for help again. I don't care if I have to tattoo it on my chest."

"Fair enough. Mick!"

"Oh captain, my captain!"

"Don't be cute, that's Alice's job. Speaking of Alice, anything happens to her and I'll skin you alive. And I won't need a power sander or a chainsaw to do the job."

Welly looked at Alice and paused for a moment, as if there was something else he wanted to say. Then he nodded at her and turned away. "Ken, if you will."

As Ken and Welly headed for the door, Alice wanted to tell Welly that she wasn't mad at him anymore, that at some point she probably had considered dating him, and that she really wanted him to be extra careful, but all that came out was, "Wait, what about your sandwiches?"

They were already gone.

"Never mind, all the more for us." Mick walked past Perl and pushed open the swinging door to peer into the kitchen. "As I suspected, these facilities are utterly inadequate for my needs. Perl, my Welsh wallaby, do you at least sell coffee beans? The darker the roast, the better."

Mick turned and gave Alice a broad grin. "As soon as I've done some shopping, it's off to the Neuadd Arms with us."

"What are you talking about?" Alice asked, taken aback. "You told Welly you'd brew up a cure!"

"And I will," Mick said. "But what better place to brew it than in an actual brewery?"

He turned his attention back to Perl. "I'll take all your coffee beans, including the stock you keep for the café. Don't worry about me cleaning you out; you won't be allowed to open again for days anyway. Plus, I can pay twice your usual price." He waved a shiny credit card.

"But we're supposed to stay here!" Alice protested. The last thing she wanted to do was go traipsing around Llanwrtyd Wells's zombie-laden streets with Mick.

"I said I would endeavour to make the most of the local facilities." Mick took another peek through the door. "There, I've endeavoured. Now let's collect our beans and hit the streets with our feet. Anything else would hurt."

Dewey closed his laptop and slid it into a case. "Perl, love, he's right as far as leaving here goes, though he's utterly mad to want to head to the Arms."

"Just give me a moment to ring him through," Perl said. "Then I'll lock up."

Alice frowned. Mick's Odyssey credit card was glowing. She hoped that didn't mean it was past its limit.

Dewey looked at Alice. "You're welcome to accompany us. I have an idea how we might dodge the roadblocks around town."

Alice was tempted. Getting out of town was clearly the sensible thing to do, and if there was any way to slip past Borislav, she suspected Dewey would be the one to do it.

But she'd made a promise to Welly. And even if he wouldn't hold her to it, she'd still feel like she was letting him down.

"I can't," Alice said, reluctantly. "Mick is my responsibility."

*

Alice did not want to be out in the dark, zombie-filled night. And she most especially didn't want to be out in the dark, zombie-filled night with no one but Mick to rely on. Mick, who was carrying a large garbage bag filled with coffee bean packets, over his left shoulder as if it was no heavier than her purse. Between his top hat and tails and the big sack, he looked like a Voodoo version of Santa Claus.

As Alice trotted after him, clutching the bag of sandwiches to her chest, she tried to quiet her fears with logic.

She'd seen zombies get agitated. They flailed and moaned, and sometimes they got a little snappy, like the flight attendant Bronwyn. They were definitely dangerous in terms of the risk of infection they posed, but it wasn't like they were zombie sheep. They weren't fast or homicidal.

Alice felt a twinge of guilt. Ken might have been right. Falling into the tub with zombie Dorothy in the bathroom had been terrifying, but it was possible she hadn't been in much danger. Maybe Dorothy had just wanted to give her a hug.

Or maybe she'd been hungry for human flesh like Welly insisted.

Alice was feeling increasingly confused about the whole issue of zombies. Were they terrifying killers? Or just unfortunate, sick people?

Mick darted off down another side street. They were making

slow progress toward the brewery because he kept stopping to staple more of his photocopied signs on walls and telephone poles. Alice picked up one he'd dropped and looked at it. "Free Island Rhythm Drumming and Bible Study. Meeting at the Neuadd Arms tonight!"

Alice read the poster again to be sure she hadn't misread it. No, it definitely said Neuadd Arms. Pre-printed.

"Mick!" She waved the piece of paper at him.

Mick loped back to her side. "Yes, my marginally miffed magpie?"

"You let Welly and Ken think we were going to stay safe inside the café, while you were planning to go to the Neuadd Arms all along!"

"You fell for it too, so don't feel bad. It's easy to trick humans during emergencies; their minds are always addled and anxious. Now plants, on the other hand, there's a reason why the phrase is as cool as a cucumber—"

"You're stark raving mad," Alice interrupted. "And you're going to get both of us killed for no reason!"

"Nonsense," Mick said "My reasons are completely sound. Even in an apocalypse, bars are always hopping, so naturally I researched the most popular pub in town before printing up my flyers. With luck, most of this town's population will be converging on the Neuadd Arms by now. It'll be like a glorious, enormous petri dish." He dashed off again across the road and stapled another sign, this time to the front of someone's door.

Alice clutched the bag of sandwiches closer to her chest and glanced nervously up and down the street. "If everyone's already there, why are you wasting time putting up these bizarre posters?"

"To bring in the stragglers, of course," Mick called back, brightly. "Herding zombies is like herding cats, just with fewer hairballs."

"Brains!" a voice announced right behind her. Alice shrieked and turned around. A group of zombies was shuffling slowly out of the alley behind her. "Mick, help!"

The zombies burst into laughter.

"God, that was a great reaction!"

The zombie closest to her held his arms stiffly in front of him, stuck out his tongue, and let his eyes roll back into his head. "Braiiiiins."

"We want to eat your braaaainnnsss," chimed in another, enthusiastically.

More giggling.

Mick strolled up, clapping. "Very good. Did you make your costumes yourself?"

Alice realized she'd been had. "That's not funny!"

"Yes it is," said a zombie wobbler in particularly heavy eye makeup. She leaned in close, and Alice grimaced at the smell of beer on her breath. "It's really, really funny."

"Zombies aren't a joke," Alice said sternly. "They're a serious threat to health and safety. You should be inside, barricading your doors."

A tall young woman, who'd tied her hair up in scraggly bunches and dyed it red and black, patted Alice on the head encouragingly. "Way to get into the spirit! We're all going down to the Neuadd Arms if you want to join us."

"Take these," Mick said, shoving several posters into her hand. "Hand them out to your friends. There's a ten percent discount for anyone who has a flyer."

"Mick, you've got to make them listen," Alice insisted. "They don't understand the risk they're taking."

But Mick was waving them off, cheerfully. "Have fun wobbling! I'll see you all shortly at the Arms!"

The fake zombies wobbled down the street, enthusiastically chanting, "Brains!"

Alice grabbed his arm. "But they're still uninfected—"

"Oh, I wouldn't assume that," Mick cut her off. "At least one of that group appeared to be in early Stage Two. Besides, infected or uninfected, we still want to gather as many as we can in one place. In this case, the Neuadd Arms."

He shrugged off her arm, then pulled another sheaf of papers from his satchel. Brandishing his heavy-duty stapler, Mick resumed defacing the doors of Llanwrtyd Wells with posters promising free lessons in Nigerian Prince Photography.

"Wait," Alice said, catching up with him. "Welly said zombies and alcohol are a bad combination. Or maybe Ken said it. Anyway, I distinctly remember one of them saying that it's bad."

"Because both of them are wet blankets on the bed of life. Alcohol lowers a zombie's inhibitions, but they have just as much right to party as any other animal," Mick said. "Now, there are only a couple hundred more flyers to circulate. Then we can join in the infectious fun at the Arms."

"No, absolutely not," Alice declared. "We're not roaming the streets for another hour. The next mob of zombie wobblers we run into might be real! Or there could be sheep." She turned a complete circle this time, trying to ensure nothing else could sneak up on her. "Killer, man-eating, super-fast sheep!"

"Never fear, my cautious capybara," Mick said. "These streets are depressingly zombie-free. Except for that fellow over there. He's a promising candidate."

Alice spun around, just in time to see a man running up to them, waving his arms.

"Get off the streets!" the man shouted. "It's not safe out here!" He stopped in front of them, panting. "You've got to get off the streets."

"He doesn't seem like a zombie," Alice said. "He's the only sane person I've met all day." Just to be safe, however, she stepped back a couple paces so Mick was between her and the agitated gentleman.

With a flourish reminiscent of a magician's sleight of hand, Mick snapped his fingers, and a penlight appeared. He shone it in the man's eyes.

"You don't understand!" The man was tall and broad, wearing a brown tweed jacket. "It's dangerous out here."

"Pish posh," Mick said, stowing the penlight in his satchel and pulling out his Med-Trekker. "It's perfectly safe. Haven't you heard of flash mobs?"

"Flash mobs?"

"Absolutely." Mick handed a flyer to the man, and then stabbed a needle into his shoulder. "Right now, they're all in the Neuadd Arms, doing the chicken dance. And you're late for the party, my friend."

"Party?" The man stared at the flyer in his hands.

The Med-Trekker began vibrating in Mick's hand. With a huge grin, he stashed his extra flyers into his satchel and clapped the gentleman on the shoulder. Turning to Alice, Mick asked, "Shall we bring him with us? It's always a good idea to keep a fresh zombie on hand to test the cure on. It's more likely to work on the new ones after all."

Alice backed up so quickly, she nearly tripped over her own feet. "Mick, get away from him!"

Alice heard the sound of a door slamming open, across the street. "Brian!" an irritated female voice called out. "What are you doing out here? Didn't you listen to the man on the telly?"

"Ah, does he belong to you?" Mick asked.

A heavyset woman in a flowered dress marched across the road. "Yes, he's mine. Brian, get inside! It's not safe out here." She glared at Mick and Alice. "And if you two have any sense, you'll get in too."

Mick pressed several buttons on his Med-Trekker, and a new needle popped up.

"Get that away from me!" she snapped at him. "Or I'll have you up on assault! What are you? Some kind of drug dealer? I'll have you know, my Brian doesn't do drugs."

Mick pressed another button, and the needle retracted into the Med-Trekker. "I think we can safely say you're not infected."

Brian said, "There's a party at the Neuadd Arms." He held the flyer out to her. Alice could see large print on it advertising Calypso Marital Counselling.

"Oh no you're not!" The woman grabbed Brian's arm and hauled him across the road. "Never mind your mates, you're staying home tonight."

"Don't let him bite you!" Alice called after them.

The woman slammed the door, and Alice heard the loud click of a deadbolt lock.

"Oh well, there's always more zombies in the sea," Mick said, philosophically.

Alice was on her last nerve. "I've had enough! You said you wanted to go to the Neuadd Arms, so let's go. Now!"

She started walking down the road, determinedly. The brewery might be filled with zombies, but at least it was indoors. Alice had endured entirely too many people jumping out at her this evening.

Mick easily caught up with her in a few long strides. "Although, there aren't any zombies in the actual sea."

I'm not going to ask, Alice promised herself.

"They've all been eaten by fish."

No more weird conversations, no more posting flyers, and definitely no more fraternising with potential zombies. They were going straight to the Neuadd Arms.

"Occasionally a foot might wash ashore."

"Wait," Alice said, stopping. "Those were zombie feet?" She remembered reading all the news stories about the mysterious sneaker-clad feet washing up on British Columbian shores.

"Only some of them," Mick said. "You can tell by whether or

not the toes are still wiggling."

Alice tried to block out that disturbing vision. "If a fish eats a zombie, does it become a zombie fish?" she asked.

"No, at least not in the ocean." Mick patted his satchel. "I believe the answer lies in salt. I've been investigating the connection for years, but most of the zombies I've come across are already well into Stage Three. This is the first opportunity I've had to sample early stages of the virus in the wild, and in mid-mutation no less. This is so exciting!"

"I'm glad you're having fun," Alice said, peering nervously around herself. Zombies are slow, she reminded herself. All those movies with fast zombies were dead wrong.

Mick stopped briefly to stuff some flyers into a mail slot. A sudden movement in the corner of her eye made Alice scream and jump back. A boy about ten years old darted out from behind a house, shouting, "Die, zombie, die!"

Three more children followed, shrieking, "Faster zombie kill kill!"

Alice ducked as a small white projectile narrowly missing hitting her right between the eyes. "Hey!" she shouted at them.

She dodged another hail of hard white objects, and then the children scattered, giggling.

The street was empty again. Alice braced her hands on her knees. Her heart felt as though it was trying to hammer its way right out of her chest. "That wasn't funny!"

"Now this is a situation in which being able to regulate your adrenaline response would come in handy," Mick said.

Alice picked up one of the projectiles and straightened, examining it in the streetlight. "Garlic cloves?"

"Inventive, if woefully ill-informed," Mick said, flicking a piece of garlic out of his dreadlocks. "Still, I appreciate that they didn't try to stake us through the heart."

"Should they even be out at this time of night?" Alice asked.

"There's zombies on the loose!"

"Never fear, children are rarely infected," Mick said. "Strong immune systems, most of them. Wonderfully fast on their feet. And usually too clever to get within biting range of a zombie." He glanced over her head. "Now would be an excellent time to get in touch with your inner child."

"What?" Alice turned and looked.

There was a large open area at the end of the street. In the centre was a statue of a menacing black bird, and the line of iron fencing around it looked like spears lined up in a row. Alice recognized the scene immediately. She'd seen it in the video on Dewey's computer.

She walked toward the statue eagerly, hoping to see Welly, Ken, or even Dave and the pilot. Unfortunately, they were nowhere in sight. Instead, across the square, a large group of shambling figures were moving slowly in her direction. Their arms were outstretched in classic movie-zombie fashion, and there were at least twelve of them.

"Wellington was correct," said Mick. "They're definitely mobbing."

A woman screamed, nearly giving Alice a heart attack. Behind her, Brian stumbled down the street, walking stiffly. Displaying more of a sense of purpose than she'd ever seen in any zombie, he headed past Mick and Alice, straight for the mob. She could hear several of them moaning, and at least one was saying, "Braaaiins." She felt a hysterical giggle threatening to bubble up inside of her.

"Let's go," Mick said. "Unsecured zombie mobs make very poor test subjects."

Brian's wife appeared. "Brian, you get back here, this instant. Stop playing silly buggers!"

Alice ran toward her, "Get back inside!"

The woman stepped into the town square instead. She pulled

down the shoulder of her dress and pointed at a row of purple tooth marks in her skin. "Do you see that? He blacks out, scaring me half to death. Then he bites me! That nasty little toad actually bit me!" Marching into the middle of the square to face the mob, she hollered, "Brian, you're in such trouble!"

"No," Alice said, her voice faltering. "You don't understand." She's been infected, Alice thought. She'd never understand now.

Mick caught up with her. "It's best if you don't watch this."

"What do you mean?" Alice asked. She supposed a lot of zombies could be trouble, but Brian's wife seemed like she could cope with almost anything. Surely if a crunchy-granola guy like Ken could wrangle a whole mailroom full of zombies, she'd be okay.

The woman was now standing with her feet braced and her hands on her hips, letting Brian know exactly what she thought of him.

"If you keep watching, you're going to want to get involved," Mick said. "Which I don't deny could be entertaining, but the consequences will be problematic."

The first of the zombies reached the woman, arms outstretched. She knocked his hands aside and confronted him, fists clenched.

She didn't notice the young female zombie coming up beside her, until the girl sank her teeth into her neck.

12

The Townsfolk Throw a Zombie Wobble

"**O**h God!" Alice exclaimed. "We've got to help her!" She started to lunge forward, only to be brought up short by Mick's hand on her collar. Alice grabbed the front of her shirt, trying not to flash too much belly. "Let me go!"

The girl spat out a mouthful of blood. "Gross," she complained.

"Gross," another zombie in the group echoed.

"Gross, Gross, Grossss…"

The woman in the flowered dress swore and tried to push the girl away. A middle-aged man latched onto her outstretched arm and began chewing, rather more enthusiastically than the girl. Evidently he wasn't as picky an eater.

"The problem here," Mick said, still gripping Alice firmly by the collar, "is I know I'd regret letting you impulsively run into the middle of this zombie free-for-all. Right around the time Wellington decides skinning me isn't enough and begins to remove my limbs one by one, waits for them to grow back, and then removes them all again. And I really don't have the time, I've got a cure to brew, remember?"

Alice tried to hit Mick with the bag of sandwiches. "But they're eating her! We can't just let them eat her!" She wanted to scream and sob. Since she couldn't do both at the same time, she shouted, "Ken said zombies aren't cannibals!"

"They aren't," Mick said, seemingly unaffected by the horror they were witnessing. He continued to hold onto the back of her shirt. "The compulsion to chomp people is a truly fascinating part of this disease. I believe it's the virus attempting to go forth and multiply by creating new hosts. We can't put all the blame on Romero. Mobbing is a natural expression of the zombie's innate drive to create more of its own kind."

"But they're going to eat that poor woman!"

"Zombies aren't cannibals. But zombie mobs, especially in the post-Romero era, sometimes try to eat people. For a short while in the nineteen-eighties, they also occasionally broke into song and dance routines."

Alice twisted around to see if Mick was being serious. He looked wistful.

"I did enjoy the eighties," he said.

"So that's why Welly hates zombies."

"Yes, the singing and dancing was truly excruciating. Zombies have no sense of rhythm."

Despite her shock and horror, Alice almost laughed. "That's not what I meant."

Turning back she saw Tom's wife stumble and fall against another zombie, impaling him on the spiky fence. The man who'd been chewing on her arm appeared confused by her sudden disappearance and simply stood staring off across the square, his jaw moving meditatively. The other zombies milled around in confusion.

"Gross, Gross, Grosss…"

The zombie on the fence didn't appear bothered by the spike lodged in his back. He began chewing on the woman's hair.

She flailed, her screams turning hoarse.

Alice knew what she had to do. She had to get in there and save the woman before anyone else decided to chew on her. Even if Brian's wife was almost certainly infected, she still didn't deserve to be eaten. Dropping the bag of sandwiches, she kneed Mick in the crotch. Her self-defence instructor had told her this move was guaranteed to make any man release her.

Instead of freedom, Alice felt her feet abruptly leave the ground. Her whole world was upended as Mick tossed her over his right shoulder. He bent down and grabbed the bag of sandwiches, and then all she could see was the garbage bag of coffee beans over his left shoulder which kept bouncing into her face as Mick's long legs covered ground.

"Let me go!" She kicked and squirmed.

Mick stopped, but not to put her down. He gripped the bag of sandwiches between his teeth and stapled another sign to a telephone pole. When he was done, he tucked the sandwiches back under his arm. "Sacrificing yourself heroically is an Enhanced Agent's job. You, my dear, are not an Agent, you're a Sensitive. And I need you to use your abilities to secure me a laboratory tonight, not engage in pointless yet hilarious fisticuffs."

"We're supposed to be the good guys," Alice protested, her face pressed against the coffee beans. She reached back and tried twisting one of his ears, but he ignored her.

"Whatever gave you that idea?" Mick asked, resuming his loping stride.

"Put me down!" Alice kicked as hard as she could. More than once on this mission, she had felt as if she was being hauled around like so much semi-useless psychic baggage, but she'd never expected to experience the sensation so literally.

Mick stopped again, in front of another telephone pole.

"I said, put me DOWN!" Alice felt that odd sensation in her head again. A strange surge of energy followed by a sudden sense of emptiness, as if she was pouring out all of her psychic power. The last time she'd experienced it, everyone in the plane had stopped screaming.

Mick, however, just laughed and said, "You've almost got it!" And then at the far end of the square, he finally put her down.

"Here we are." He gestured expansively at a whitewashed brick, multi-story hotel. "The Neuadd Arms!" He handed her back the bag of sandwiches, which was rather battered, tipped his hat at her, and gestured at the front door. "Shall we?"

Alice glanced back across the square. The woman in the flowered dress was hidden from view by the statue and the bushes. But she could still hear her screaming.

Welly would have dashed right back across the square to rescue the woman, and never mind Mick. But when it came right down to it, Alice knew that, unlike Welly, she'd be no match for a zombie mob. The only way she could rescue Brian's wife would be to help Mick find a cure as soon as possible.

"I don't think I like you anymore," Alice told Mick, as she turned to face the Neuadd Arms, reluctantly abandoning the woman in the flowered dress to her fate.

"That's perfectly all right," he said, lightly. "I can like me enough for both of us."

When Alice thought of a pub, she envisioned a dark, smoky, hole-in-the-wall place filled with grizzled, glum drinkers all named Andy Capp. However, the Neuadd Arms had lots of windows, shedding a cheery light out onto the street. Through the glass she could see a spacious restaurant and bar with a large open fireplace, comfy chairs and couches, and people of all ages enjoying a rollicking good time. It made all the horrors Alice had just witnessed seem like nothing more than a particularly bad B-movie.

"The Baron La Croix will love this party," Mick declared, as they pushed their way through the door into the welcoming warmth of the pub. He pulled out a cigar and licked the entire length of it with his bright blue tongue, then lit it.

"God, those things stink," Alice complained. "And you can't smoke in here, there's a sign right over there. We can't party either. We need to make a zombie cure so no one else gets eaten. Remember? Zombie mobs? Trying to eat people?"

"No, you need to find me a place to work while I join these good people in a pint or two." Mick spotted a stout balding man standing a few feet away. "My good fellow! Are you here for the free..." He peered over the man's shoulder. "Island Rhythm Bible Study?"

"Music," the man said speculatively, still staring at the sheet.

"Oh, you're marvellous!" Mick said, whipping out his Med-Trekker and stabbing him in the shoulder.

"Ow!" Mick's victim was clearly not so far into zombism that he didn't notice being assaulted by a strange dreadlocked man smoking a cigar.

"Not to worry, it's just a blood sample," Mick explained. "Island Rhythm Bible Study is a wholly American-owned subsidiary of Big Rhythm. And you know Americans, they want blood tests for everything. Marriages, job applications, bible camps, voting, they're out of control, which is why we love them."

"Oh," the man said, blinking. He thought about it for a moment and then said, "I guess that makes sense."

"Ah, gullibility," Mick said, rapidly entering data in his MedTrekker. "The first and most entertaining symptom of zombism."

"That's why you were handing out these silly flyers?" Alice asked. "You were trolling for gullible zombies?"

The portly man looked back down at the sheet in his hands. "Music," he said happily.

"And you!" Mick spun around, accosting a younger, bearded man, who was also holding a flyer. "I've been expecting you!"

The bearded man frowned at him. "Are you the bloke claiming to be an Australian prince?" he demanded, waving a flyer promoting

Survival Island Time Shares. Alice assumed Mick being a prince was in the small print.

"I must be, mustn't I?" Mick agreed happily, brandishing the Med-Trekker.

"What's that thing?" The bearded man stepped back.

"I need a blood sample, of course. Otherwise, how will I know if we're related? I can't go handing out my millions willy-nilly, you know."

"You're crazy!"

"And you, sir, are not a zombie. But I suspect that gentleman over there is."

Alice looked where he pointed. A young man had fainted, and his friends were all laughing at him for blacking out after only one drink.

Mick turned back to Alice, rubbing his hands together. "It's a veritable smorgasbord of lab rats here!"

"They're not lab rats," Alice said, sternly.

"Experimental test subjects, if you insist," Mick said, rolling his eyes.

"That's not my point..."

Behind Mick the pub suddenly erupted into spontaneous cheering and all around them people were raising their glasses. Even the short, stout zombie waved his flyer in the air.

"And why do you need more blood samples?" Alice shouted over the din. "You got tons from the plane passengers!"

Mick waved the Medtrekker at her and leaned in close to her ear. "Those were samples of the Darryl virus. But the Dorothy virus is bound to be around here somewhere. And if I'm very lucky, there may even be other variants." He straightened and snagged a bottle of beer from a man walking past.

The man kept walking, his hand still held out in front of him, apparently not realizing the bottle was no longer there.

"Now, I do believe you were going to get me a brewery," Mick continued, after a swig of his newly acquired beer, "so I can start analyzing my samples."

Alice shook the bag of squished sandwiches at Mick. "Why do I have to get the room while you go on a drinking binge?"

"It's a libation to the great and mighty Baron, and you need to secure us the brewery, not a mere room, because I'll need to use the equipment to brew up a cure. And that, my nervous numbat, will require your special persuasive powers."

Alice gulped. "Really Mick, I'm not very good at that sort of thing."

"Nonsense! I believe in you. The Baron believes in you. Now, the brewmaster's right over there. Go be the best little Sensitive you can be. Go, go, go!"

Mick shoved her in the direction of a large, gregarious looking man.

"Um, hi," Alice said. "Ah, Mister... um..."

"Call me, Lloyd. Welcome to the Neuadd Arms. Here for the Bog Snorkelling Championships?"

Alice's anxiety level spiked. "I thought those didn't start until next week."

"Some come early, and there are always bikers, birders, and backpackers who come to enjoy the gorgeous Welsh countryside."

Great, Alice thought, it's not just six hundred locals in jeopardy, but countless tourists as well.

Behind her, Alice could hear the partiers praising Mick's costume. He was ordering curries for everyone in the name of Baron La Croix.

"*Om mani party hum*," she whispered, trying to centre herself and dial up her Sensitivity Amplifier implant. But she could barely hear herself, and it was hard to concentrate with all the excited, drunk people around. Focus, Alice told herself. She needed to focus, right now. Lloyd, she suddenly realized, wasn't just the brewmaster, he also owned the hotel and brewery. And he had a wife named Karen, and a corgi named Stout. When Alice realized Lloyd only used bar rags made of one hundred percent unbleached organic cotton, she knew she was focussing too hard.

"Hi Lloyd," Alice said, brightly. "I need, I mean my friend and I need, facilities where we can work on a cure for... Um, can we use your brewery?"

Lloyd's brow furrowed. "The brewery's closed for the night, but you don't need to go there to enjoy our fine ales."

"Is it close by?" Alice asked. "Because I... um, would love a tour. My friend and I." She smiled, hopefully.

"It's right behind the hotel, but we don't usually let tourists inside, even during the day." Lloyd looked her over, concern in his eyes. "It looks like you've had a rough day. Why don't I get you a pint?"

"No, I—"

"She'll have a pint of your Noble Eden Ale," Mick said, appearing beside her. "And I'll have your Innstable. I'm looking forward to its infamous kick."

"Right you are." Lloyd went behind the wood-panelled bar.

"Mick, what are you doing?" Alice asked, peeved.

"Oh, you'll love the Noble Eden Brew. According to the description, it's 'bursting with fruit and malt, with just a hint of chocolate to tickle the taste buds.' Of course, rum is more traditional for the Baron, but—"

"No, what are you doing interfering—"

"With the fabulous job you're doing?"

Alice felt her face go hot as Mick gave her a knowing look. "Our brewmaster is not infected, nor is he naturally gullible or easily led. So stop trying to persuade him with logic, it's really not your strong suit. Get in touch with your inner toddler instead, and let her rip."

Lloyd returned with their pints. "I'm sorry sir, you can't smoke in here."

"Here, you can smoke it for me then." Mick handed his cigar to Lloyd in exchange for his drink. He toasted the party-goers, exclaiming, "Eat, drink and be merry, for tomorrow at dawn we die!" This pronouncement was met with cheers.

My inner toddler, Alice thought. *What the hell does that mean?*

In theory, as a trained Sensitive, Alice knew she should be able to influence people. Her instructor had told her the most talented Sensitives could talk a fish out of water and leave the fish convinced it had been his own idea all along.

Alice knew she wasn't a talented Sensitive. She had, in fact, failed her training quite miserably. If she hadn't been set up to start dating a fellow Odyssey employee, who'd then turned out to be a dangerous mole bent on destroying the organization, she wouldn't be working as a Sensitive at all. She'd personally had a hand in saving Odyssey International, and her reward was being partnered with Welly.

That, and all the other Sensitives at Odyssey flatly refused to work with Welly.

Almost every time Alice had tried to influence anyone, she'd failed. But she remembered there had been one moment on the plane, and again when she'd tried to get Mick to put her down when Alice had felt something different. It wasn't the calm, centred feeling her instructor had described. It felt more like stomping her feet in a moment of frustrated desperation. What had Mick called it?

Her inner toddler?

"Now, can I reserve a room for you and your unusual friend?" Lloyd asked. "There's not many left."

Suddenly, everything clicked into place for Alice. She turned toward Lloyd with a big smile. "No, we need to use your brewery." She gathered up all of her pent-up anxiety and frustration, and used it like a battering ram on the defenceless brewmaster.

You have to give me what I want. You have to, you have to, you have to!

"No, I explained," Lloyd began, and then faltered.

"It's really important you let us into your brewery. Lives depend on it."

I want it now. You have to give it to me, right now. Now, now, now!

"But," Lloyd tried, looking like a deer in the headlights.

"You'll save the entire town, all the tourists, and the Bog Snorkelling, Saturnalia Wobble, Horse versus Man arm wrestling, and all of your other fantastic festivals. You'll be a hero," Alice enthused.

Give me what I want right now, or I'll scream and cry until you wish I'd never been born!

Lloyd wavered, and then slowly nodded. "All right, I'll take you there. I'll just tell my wife."

"That you need to go check on the brewery," Alice said quickly, with an extra psychic push. "You're concerned because of the reports of hooligans in the streets."

"Yes... Of course." Lloyd retreated to a back room.

Alice turned and waved at Mick, who treated her to an enormous grin. "My friends," he announced. "With regret, I must leave you for now, but the Baron's blessings are upon you. Celebrate the beauty and absurdity of life with good food, excellent ale, and really great sex!"

"Zombie Wobble, Zombie Wobble, Zombie Wobble!" everyone chanted.

Mick joined her and shrugged. "It's better than 'brains, brains, brains'."

"I doubt Ken would agree," Alice said. She wondered if they should warn everyone of the real danger they were in, but she didn't think they'd believe her even if she used her inner toddler. After all, this crowd was clearly listening to their own, thoroughly soused, inner frat boys.

Lloyd returned, holding keys. A woman accompanied him, and she looked Alice and Mick over with a very concerned expression. She opened her mouth, but Alice jumped in before she could say anything.

"You must be Lloyd's wife. Karen, right? Don't worry, your husband's just taking us out back for a quick look at the brewery. You just stay here, and watch over your customers, and everything will be wonderful. I promise."

You must believe me, Karen. You must, or I'll throw a tantrum so big it'll flatten your sorry excuse for mountains!

Now that Alice had the knack of it, she was finding it easier to access her inner toddler. She hadn't needed all that *Om mani padme* business, after all. Which was a relief as activating her implant always made her nervous that she was frying brain cells she'd need later on in life.

Karen blinked at her. "I suppose. But Lloyd, do be careful."

"He'll be back soon," Mick promised, brightly. "In one form or another," he added *sotto voce* to Alice, as they followed Lloyd out of the restaurant and down a brightly lit corridor.

"I didn't use all of my persuasive powers just so you'd have someone new to experiment on," Alice said, heatedly.

"No, no, of course not. He hasn't signed away his free will like you did when you joined Odyssey."

Alice promised herself she'd never sign another piece of paper in her life. "Then what did you mean?"

"Just that there are an increasing number of stray zombies roaming about looking for a pack to join," Mick said as Lloyd led them outside. "Speaking of which..." Mick suddenly disappeared into the night.

"Mick, get back—ow!" Alice had stubbed her toe. The back area wasn't as well lit as the front of the hotel. This was not the time for Mick to go running off posting flyers.

Alice realized Lloyd was continuing on without her. "Lloyd, wait."

Lloyd obediently came to a halt, and Alice desperately looked around for Mick. "What I wouldn't give for Welly's night vision," she muttered, but then shook her head. That would mean allowing Mick to experiment on her, and that was out of the question.

In the glow provided by the nearby streetlight, Alice could make out a two-story, grey brick building perpendicular to the hotel. She was about to ask Lloyd if it was the brewery when she noticed how he was standing stock still, staring off into space. Like a zombie.

Alice felt a stab of guilt. Her inner toddler was a lot stronger than she'd expected.

"Look what I found." Mick reappeared, dragging along a scruffy-looking man in his early twenties. He was wearing a white sweatshirt that declared 'I Survived the Saturnalia Wobble'. The sweatshirt was badly torn and stained, and stretched tight across his very round stomach.

"I'm sure this man hasn't signed away his free will either," Alice told Mick, sternly.

"Not to worry, he doesn't have one anymore. Do you, my Stage Three friend?"

With a firm grip on the back of his head, and a right arm wrapped around his chest, Mick pushed the zombie closer to her. Alice could now see the man's eyes were unfocused and some of the staining on his sweatshirt was blood.

"Stage Three?" Alice asked. "He doesn't look dead. Yet. He doesn't look healthy, but—"

"Stage Three zombies aren't dead," Mick said. "They're merely beginning to decompose. See how he's bloated?" Mick patted the young man's bulging stomach.

Alice clapped a hand over her mouth as she caught a whiff of the zombie. "Ewww. I thought he just had a beer belly."

"Nope, enzymes and bacteria multiply like gangbusters in zombies, so now he's filled with all sorts of odoriferous gasses.

Now if you could just hold him for me, I'll get—"

"Hold him?" Alice exclaimed, jumping back from Mick. "No, no, a thousand times no. I'm not getting anywhere near that thing! What do you think I am? A zombie wrangler?"

"But I've only got two hands right now," Mick said, making it sound as if he used to have more. "How am I going to get a blood sample from him if both my hands are occupied with holding him still?"

"You already have all those blood samples from the plane and from the pub. Why should I risk getting bitten?"

"Yes, you are a bitey mountain biker, aren't you?" Mick said to the zombie. Turning his attention back to Alice, he explained, "The more samples of the living virus, the better. And unfortunately, the zombie virus doesn't stay alive for very long outside of a human host. HIV is like that too. That's why it's an urban myth that people would leave infected needles in theatre seats to kill you. Although you could potentially catch hepatitis or Creature of the Black Lagoon Syndrome that way."

"Black Lagoon—? Never mind, I'm still not going to hold him for you," Alice said, firmly.

Mick sighed dramatically. "Then we'll just have to bring him with us."

"Okay, okay, we can take the zom—" Alice glanced at Lloyd, suddenly realizing she'd been talking about zombies in front of him all along. Lloyd, however, wasn't showing any interest in the conversation or his surroundings. Clearly, discretion was no longer necessary. "We can take the zombie into the brewery. Just so long as I don't have to touch him."

Lloyd led them to the grey building, and past several woodframed windows until they reached what looked like a pair of old stable doors, and Mick hustled the zombie inside. "Thank you very much," Alice told Lloyd. "Just leave the keys with us, and get back to your wife."

Lloyd shook his head slowly and opened his mouth. Before he could object, Alice visualized pouring a bucketful of her inner toddler's willpower over his head. "No, you need to go back in the hotel, right now. Stay by your wife, and don't come outside again." It was amazing how natural it felt to access her inner toddler. Now that she knew where the little brat was hiding, and what it felt like to drag her out to play, she could do it any time she wanted.

Which might be a really bad thing, Alice thought, looking at Lloyd's vacant expression with concern.

Lloyd blinked twice, handed over the keys, and began to walk away. Alice said a silent prayer that he'd be all right. She wouldn't be able to forgive herself if he'd been permanently damaged by her toddler temper tantrum powers.

Especially considering how good it felt to use them, Alice thought, pushing her concerns away. She was finally a real Sensitive, she told herself, influencing people to help save the world. Just wait until she showed Welly what she could do now.

It took Alice over a minute to figure out she could only lock the doors of the brewery from the outside, and another five to jury-rig a steel bar across the inside of both of them. There was a time, she thought, when it would have taken her a lot longer to prepare against a possible zombie siege. Alice felt it was a shame she no longer needed to update her resume with her newfound skills.

Alice went looking for Mick, more than a bit concerned at what she'd find. She walked past several stacks of wooden casks and five elevated brewing vats. Everything looked very clean and polished. The steel pipes and the wooden sides of the vats positively gleamed.

"Gorgeous, aren't they?"

She rounded the last vat and found Mick taking a blood sample from the zombie, who was now tied to the steel pipes running underneath the vat.

"They're called brewhouses not vats, my confused cassowary,

and just think of the large quantities of the zombie cure I'll be able to brew inside them." Mick's top hat was dirty, and the right sleeve of his tailcoat was badly torn, but he smiled at Alice cheerfully. "Of course, we'll have to replace them afterwards. Otherwise, the Neuadd Arms's Innstable Ale would never be the same, and that would be a real tragedy. Here, hold these."

Alice automatically took the two vials of zombie blood from Mick while he pulled another sample. She held them very carefully. She'd never wanted to get this close to a deadly virus.

"Shouldn't we be wearing protective hazmat suits or something?" Alice frowned at Mick's bare feet. "And what happened to your shoes?"

"Breaking new ground in science is always easier when barefoot. Besides, this may be an excellent microbrewery, but I doubt we'd find a hazmat suit for you here. Luckily, we have everything else we need for now. The Baron has judged our goal a worthy one." He handed Alice two more samples, and began to untie the zombie.

"What are you doing?"

"Releasing him back into his natural habitat. Don't worry, he'll soon find a mob to join. Zombies are very social creatures." Manhandling the zombie with less skill than Ken had displayed, Mick shoved him toward the entrance. "Put the vials down over there by the sink, and come open the doors for me."

Alice quickly found a large white sink at the back of the brewery where Mick had planted a white candle between the taps. The surface of the steel counter on either side of the sink was covered with syringes, rubber tubing, a small microscope and glass slides, and the Med-Trekker IV. Alice also recognized the salt shaker, turkey baster, and spatula that had come from the zombie farmer's home.

"Hustle, hustle, hustle!" Mick shouted from the other end of the brewery. "It's already past the witching hour."

"I don't think this is ethical!" Alice shouted, placing the zombie blood vials beside the microscope. She winced as she began jogging to the stable doors. Alice had a blister on each foot now. She was going to have to revise her opinion of Mock Martens. Maybe she should have paid full price after all. "If we release him, he might end up eating someone."

"Very few people are directly killed by zombies," Mick said. "Only the ones foolish enough to stand directly in front of a mob and rile them up. And if we keep him, his friends will eventually come looking for him."

Alice couldn't think of a counterargument, so she lifted up the steel bar and pushed the door on the left open.

Mick shoved the zombie outside, with a cheery, "*Mwynhewch eich bwyd!*"

"What did you just say?" Alice asked, as she pulled the door closed.

"*Bon appétit.*"

"Sorry I asked." Alice shoved the bar back in place.

"Good job on the makeshift lock," Mick commented, as they walked back to the sink. "Of course, it would never hold up to a full-scale zombie barnstorming, but maybe the larger mobs won't come here. Think positive!"

"I do my best," Alice said. She stared up at the brewhouses and acknowledged that Mick was right. They were beautiful. The contrast between the rustic charm of the building and the modern, shiny equipment was aesthetically pleasing too. She wondered if this place had been a stable before it was transformed into a brewery.

"Oh yes, a very old stable," Mick said. "The stable hands slept in the rooms on the second floor."

Alice didn't bother telling him again to stop reading her mind. It wouldn't do any good anyhow.

"I think it's a very good omen for our creating the zombie cure tonight," Mick continued. "It gives me a warm and fuzzy feeling thinking about all of the sweet, sweet pony love that's gone on inside these walls."

"Mick, please don't tell me about your pony fetish."

"But it's not—"

"Or anything else related to ponies!"

Mick looked hurt, so she added, "I'm not judging your... admiration of ponies. It's just been a very long day."

"True. And whispering about one's crushes is best suited for pyjama parties, and neither of us have pyjamas," Mick said, as they reached the sink.

Alice sighed with relief. "Now, what do you need me to do here?"

"First, listen worshipfully." He lit the candle, put his sunglasses on with a flourish, and threw open his arms. "Baron La Croix! I ask for your blessings upon this endeavour, Spirit of the Dead and Reclaimer of Souls."

These titles did not mesh with the previous image Mick had created of the Baron as a happy-go-lucky partygoer. Still, Alice wasn't terribly surprised. After all, she'd seen Mick sacrifice to Kali, so she knew he liked to worship dangerously.

"Now what?" she asked.

"Get me one of those delicious sandwiches. No reason why we shouldn't eat and work."

"Um, sanitary reasons?"

"Well in hand," Mick said, picking up a baggie of sparkly powder. First he threw a handful over the equipment on the counter, and then another handful over Alice. She sneezed hard several times, as Mick dumped the remainder of the bag over his head.

"There," Mick declared. "We're magically clean and magically delicious!"

"I'm sure any zombies that munch on us will appreciate that." Alice said, and then sneezed again.

13

Mick Reveals a Shocking Secret

Alice dumped freshly ground coffee into a bucket and poured more beans into the small electric grinder. It felt like she'd been at it all night, but a quick glance at her pink kitty watch said it had been only an hour.

"Liar," she told it, wondering if she should purchase a new, more sophisticated timepiece to match her new hair style. Of course, her hair wasn't very sophisticated right now, although she'd managed to shake most of the sparkly powder out of it.

"Watches lie all the time," Mick said. "That's why I prefer sundials."

"It's night time," Alice said.

"The sun's always up somewhere in the world."

Before Alice could think of a response, her cell began to warble Jonathon Coulton's 'Re: Your Brains'. Alice quickly fished it out of her purse, the identity of the caller popping into her mind before she answered the phone. "Welly, how are you?"

"Why the Hotel aren't you where I left you?"

Alice was delighted to hear his voice. "Did you find Dave and the pilot? You haven't hit Ken again, I hope." A brief vision flashed across her mind. "Oh, you did!" she exclaimed, disappointed. "I warned you, horrible things will happen if you keep fighting."

"He hit me first," Welly protested. "And that's not the point! Where are you? This is Mick's fault, isn't it?"

There was a loud explosion on the line, and Alice jumped, nearly dropping the phone. "Oh no, is Ken destroying more cars?"

"Of course he is," Welly said, sounding harried. "Bravo Hector! Get your hands off my weapon, and stop hitting me!"

Alice knew he wasn't talking to her.

"Now for the love of Golf, Alice, where are you?"

Alice tried to talk as fast as she could, in case there were more explosions coming. "Mick said the facilities at In the Purple were inadequate, so we went to the Neuadd Arms. There's a brewhouse, I mean, brewery behind the pub."

"You faded out. You're in the brewhouse?"

"No," she shouted into the phone. "We're in the brewery. Mick's working on the cure."

"I saved your life, you ungrateful Alpha-hole," Welly growled. "A decision I regret with—"

Another vision ambushed Alice. "Look behind you!" she yelled into the phone, but it had already gone dead. Alice almost called back, but it occurred to her that distracting Welly at the precise moment a zombie was lunging for his sore foot might not be the best plan.

"It's not like he ever listens to me anyway," she said to herself.

"Of course he listens," Mick said, scratching his right arm. "Which is why, at this very moment, he's not pistol whipping Ken, because he knows you wouldn't approve." The Med-Trekker IV made a hissing sound, and Mick returned his attention to it. The Med-Trekker currently looked less like a tricorder and more like an oversized Swiss Army knife. Everything from scalpels to glass vials had unfolded from its interior, and one end was now functioning as a miniature Bunsen burner.

"I suppose," Alice said, doubtfully. She started grinding the next batch of coffee. On the one hand, she was grateful her current task meant sitting at a table away from the sink. She didn't want to be too close while Mick tossed vials of blood around, filled the turkey baster with unknown, stinky liquids, and occasionally set things on fire. On the other hand, she wanted to feel like she was making a real contribution toward the zombie cure, instead of just grinding endless batches of coffee for some unknown reason.

"You are making a real contribution," Mick said, his attention focussed on his work. "Coffee is an essential element of any potential cure for zombism. Just think of all the incipient cases it treats every morning, all around the world."

"Coffee cures zombies?" Alice asked, half hoping he was serious. She knew it couldn't be that simple, or they'd already have a cure.

"I'm as serious as a great white shark at an All-the-People-You-Can-Eat buffet. However, coffee isn't a cure, it just slows the progress of the disease by reinforcing the blood-brain barrier."

"The what?"

"Oh dear, you should have paid more attention in grade eleven biology class instead of fantasizing about that admittedly handsome football player. He really didn't have any idea you existed, did he?"

Alice felt her face heat up. "You were explaining what the bloody barrier reef was."

"Blood-brain barrier," Mick said, using the spatula to scrape off a microscope slide. "Think of it as a filter that tries to keep nasty stuff that's in your bloodstream from entering your brain. Unfortunately, in unhealthy humans, this barrier can spring leaks, and whoopsy-daisy, the next thing you know the zombie virus is chowing down on your tasty grey matter."

Mick sniffed the end of the spatula, and nodded to himself. "Coffee, however, does wonders in plugging up those leaks and slowing the spread of the virus. That's why I always bring along a portable coffee grinder to any reported zombie outbreak."

"Would any caffeinated drink do?" Alice couldn't help but think that giving zombies a Coke and a smile would be a lot easier than grinding tons of coffee beans.

"No, there's something about coffee that's special. Even energy drinks don't work as well despite their colossally high caffeine content. Remember my Jolt Four Locos for Five Hours Energy Elixir?"

"That marvellous stuff you injected me with back in the bog," Alice said. "Do you have any more?" She could definitely use another pick-me-up.

"Ask me again in an hour. It can only be used twice in a twenty-four-hour period or the side effects become downright spectacular. Still, there's only a ten percent chance of sudden death associated with consumption."

Alice decided to rethink the wisdom of using any of Mick's wonder drugs.

"Keep an open mind," Mick chided. "While Jolt Four Locos et al. did fail as a cure for zombism, I've had great success marketing it to college students cramming for exams. Now, back to work you go."

Alice started grinding again, while Mick began singing and whistling, 'Heigh-ho, heigh-ho, it's off to work we go'. She found it very disquieting that he was able to whistle and sing at the time and couldn't figure out how it was humanly possible.

But Mick's bizarre musical skills weren't as disturbing as the noises coming from outside. She couldn't make out the individual sounds, but they had been growing louder over the last hour.

Alice cautiously peeked out of the window, but saw nothing. She frowned. The noises had to be coming from the opposite side of the brewery.

"Mick, I'll be right back."

Alice walked quickly to the stable doors, cursing both her blisters and the Mock Martens that were responsible for them.

She pulled the curtains back from the window beside the doors, and looked outside. "Holy shit," she said softly to herself.

"Mick!" Alice shouted. "Releasing your zombie into the wild didn't work."

"What?"

"He's back, and he's brought all his friends, neighbours, and passing acquaintances!"

There was a sudden, hard pounding on the stable doors. Alice leapt back instinctively.

A loud voice declared, "Thish captain speaking!"

"Mick!" Alice shrieked.

"Busy!"

"Shit!" Alice searched desperately for anything she might use to reinforce the stable doors. "Why couldn't Lloyd have installed zombie-proof steel doors?" She tugged at one of the barrels, but it was too heavy to move. "Shit, shit, shit!"

"Alice," a familiar voice said from the other side of the stable doors. "Stop using the Sierra word, and let us in."

"Welly!" She ran back to the window, but all she could see were zombies. "Are you okay?"

"If you let us in before we get eaten alive, we'll be grand."

Alice yanked up the steel bar and pushed the right side door open. Welly, Ken, and Dave tumbled inside. In Dave's case, literally. He landed on his face at Alice's feet.

A zombie wearing an orange baseball cap and clutching a piece of crumpled flyer tried to follow them, but Welly kicked him back into the mob. He then slammed the door shut and dropped the bar back in place. The piece of paper floated gently to the floor.

Welly limped over to the closest window. Alice hopped over Dave and followed him, concerned. "You hurt your foot again?" It wasn't sensible considering the raging mob of zombies trying to break in, but now that Welly was back, Alice felt one hundred percent safer. Welly would know what to do; he always knew.

"Kicking zombies isn't as much fun as it looks." Welly took out his gun and began reloading it.

"But you don't kick with your left leg…" Alice began.

"Don't you dare shoot any more zombies." Ken grabbed Dave by the back of his jacket and hauled him up onto his feet. He ran his hands over his zombie best friend, presumably checking him for damage, all the while glaring at Welly.

"I'm hardly going to break the window so they can get in, now am I?" Welly said, holstering his freshly loaded gun.

"Nice to see you two have settled your differences," Alice said, returning to the window. "But did you have to bring all your new friends with you?" She picked up the paper. It was one of Mick's posters, inviting people to come to the Neuadd Arms for exciting and lucrative opportunities in Jump Up Aerobic Franchises.

"Things didn't go exactly as planned," Welly said.

"You did find Dave, and look, there's the pilot." Alice frowned. Unlike the other zombies, who were shuffling around like lost cannibalistic sheep, the pilot was on his hands and knees, sniffing the ground.

"He's a strange one," Welly commented, echoing Alice's thoughts.

Most of the zombies were moaning, but some of them were chanting "brains" with "zombie" and "wobble" being popular runners-up. Alice suddenly felt ill. She searched the crowd and spotted at least three people she'd seen at the Neuadd Arms. Thankfully, there was no sign of Lloyd or his wife.

Welly ran a finger along her T-shirt sleeve. "You're sparkling."

"Mick decontaminated me. Or so he said. Hang on, does that zombie over there have a rifle?"

Welly glanced where she was pointing and nodded. "When we finally located Dave and our errant pilot, we unfortunately also found a disgruntled mob of Stage Two farmers. Thankfully, they're terrible shots and can't reload."

"The farmer you shot might have been self-defence," Ken said, "but you had no excuse for shooting the bed-and-breakfast owner."

"She was trying to bite me." Welly left the window and grabbed the same large wooden cask Alice had tried to move earlier. He rolled it in front of the door with ease. "And I didn't finish her off by shooting her in the head, did I?"

"Only because by then we were outnumbered by an outraged mob of zombie bed-and-breakfasters," Ken shot back.

"Bravo ingrate," Welly paused. "Which reminds me," he said, pulling out his Oddfone. "Lilith, patch me through to Cardiff."

Alice tried to shift one of the casks, but it refused to budge. She looked around for a smaller, more Alice-friendly size.

Welly, Oddfone pressed between shoulder and ear, grabbed another cask. "They what? Foxtrotting Cardiff! They can't just cut themselves off from the world on a whim, and a pterodactyl isn't any kind of excuse for neglecting their duties. A pterodactyl doesn't go around biting people and turning them into brand spanking new pterodactyls, does it? It can't create a Bravo army of pterodactyls, can it? No, it just sits there being a pterodactyl!"

"Cardiff has pterodactyls?" Alice asked. She tried to tip over a smaller cask and nearly fell over instead.

Welly sighed. "Yes, Lilith. I'm done." He dropped the cask next to the other one and closed his phone. "Ken, help Alice. We'll make a wall of casks in front of the stable doors."

"But the stable doors open outward," Ken said.

"Yes, and if your less-than-clever mates manage to figure that out, they'll still have problems climbing over the barrels. If we're lucky, they won't be able to get past them."

Ken shrugged and joined Alice in tipping over a small cask and rolling it to the door. "There, you see," Alice said to him. "Welly's not trying to kill every single zombie. He's just trying to keep them safely outside."

"And if we're extra lucky," Welly added, "they'll fall off the barrels and break their skulls."

"Zombies aren't helpless," Ken objected.

"Was Lloyd okay?" Alice jumped in.

"Who?" Welly asked.

"He's the brewmaster at the Neuadd Arms, and I'm worried about him. He's okay, right?"

Ken and Welly exchanged a glance.

"What?" Alice stopped pushing a cask.

"Hysterical people are rarely reliable witnesses," Welly said.

"Right," Ken said. "But we did hear that the brewmaster—Lloyd's his name? That his wife bit him and a whole bunch of their clientele."

Alice whimpered, and Ken rubbed her arm consolingly. "It's okay, I'm sure he's all right."

"Only you would call being a zombie all right," Welly said.

"And only you—"

"Stop it!" Alice shouted. "Welly, stop baiting Ken. Ken, stop taking the bait."

"Sorry," Ken muttered, and resumed rolling casks. Alice hurried to help him.

"Sorry," Welly echoed, and began stacking barrels on top of each other.

"Okay," Alice said. "Now how did you find us if…" She gulped, "Lloyd couldn't tell you?" She silently vowed never to use her toddler mind powers again. Poor Lloyd might have been able to defend himself if she hadn't psychically lobotomized him. It wasn't worth being a real Sensitive if it meant she would be damaging people's minds. She'd rather just be a semi-useless Sensitive, who had to chant mystical phrases she didn't understand just to do a simple psychic scan of a crowd.

"Llanwrtyd Wells's phone lines are still functioning," Welly answered. "So I rang up Dewey the Dustbin, and he told us the brewery was right behind the Arms."

"I'm so glad he's okay," Alice said, after a brief pause in which she tried to imagine how anyone could 'ring up' a person over a cell phone. For that matter, she was pretty sure Welly had meant to say the cell towers were still working, not the phone lines. She'd noticed before that Welly tended to get anachronistic whenever he was under stress.

"There," Welly said, surveying the wall of casks he'd created mostly by himself. "Far from perfect, but better."

"The zombies aren't likely to break in," Ken said. "That sort of thing only happens in the movies."

"You're the expert," Welly said, in a tone of voice that implied the opposite. He began limping toward Mick.

"But what if they try to re-enact a movie?" Alice asked Ken, as they followed Welly. "Didn't you say they're vulnerable to negative cultural something or other?"

"Negative cultural stereotyping. But they also have short attention spans, and it would take a concentrated effort to break inside here." When they reached the far end of the brewery, Ken asked in a hopeful tone, "Are there any sandwiches left?"

Alice was about to ask him how he could even think of eating at a time like this, but then remembered she'd already eaten one of the sandwiches, while Mick had devoured four. "They're right here," she said, retrieving the bag from underneath a counter.

Welly was prowling around the perimeter of the brewery, periodically pressing his ear to the walls and peering into corners. "Sandwich?" Alice shouted.

"Sandwich?" a zombie echoed from outside.

"No," Welly said, shortly. Alice supposed he was too busy making plans to concern himself with eating. For all she knew, Enhanced Agents didn't need to eat as often as normal people. Or maybe he only ate his mother's sandwiches. She watched him climb the stairs, dragging his bad leg. There was no denying he was a tough guy, but Alice knew deep down Welly was still a mama's boy.

She went back to grinding coffee for the cure, while Ken sat beside her and ate two sandwiches. Dave wandered over to Mick, who shooed him away. But as if stuck in a holding pattern, Dave circled his way back to Mick's side, only to repeat the whole process, trailing duct tape from his hands. Alice sincerely hoped he hadn't lost any more fingers. She didn't relish the idea of finding random bits of Dave scattered around the brewery.

Welly limped down the stairs, and rejoined them. "Bog off," he told Dave, who stumbled out of his way. Welly took his place beside Mick and surveyed the makeshift mad laboratory. "What progress have you made?"

"Oodles," Mick said. "And if you let..." His right hand began to shake violently, and he dropped the vial he was holding. It shattered in the sink.

"Mick, are you okay?" Alice asked, abandoning the coffee grinder.

"Nothing to worry about," Mick assured her, turning around. But he looked sweaty and his skin was a shade or two lighter than its usual ebony black. His sunglasses slipped off his nose and fell to the floor unheeded.

Dave leaned forward, his nose twitching violently. He let loose a soft moan.

"What is it, Dave?" Ken asked, getting up and joining the zombie.

Dave began to rock and moaned again. His nose was flapping so hard it looked in danger of detaching from his face and going airborne.

"What's Dave going on about?" Welly snapped.

"I don't know," Ken said. "He's confused."

Dave gave another low moan, and then suddenly lurched forward and grabbed at Mick's right arm.

Welly drew his gun, and Ken jumped between them. "No!" He

— 225 —

shouted at Welly, and then yelled at Dave, "Bad! Bad Dave!"

At a loss for what to do, Alice shouted, "What the he—H-E-double-hockey-sticks is going on?"

"I know what's confusing Dave," Mick said, rolling up the torn sleeve of this tailcoat. "I would have told you about it sooner, but I knew you would just overreact." He unbuttoned the wrist of his purple shirt and neatly rolled that up as well. A chunk of his right forearm fell off.

Alice was instantly ashamed of the little squeal that escaped her.

"Golf Delta!" Welly barked. "You should have told us straight away."

"There's no need to damn your Golf God, Wellington. It's just a zombie bite, and I'm dead close to having the cure." Mick paused and swallowed twice. "No one panic," he said, and hit the floor.

"I'm not panicking, I'm not panicking, I'm not panicking," Alice said.

"Yes, you are," Welly said. "Ken, what's his status?"

Ken was bending over Mick, feeling his bitten arm. "Stone cold and there's no pulse at his wrist. He's definitely Stage Three. Odd how he seems to have skipped Stages One and Two."

"Alice, can you continue his work?" Welly asked, in a very controlled voice.

She gave him an incredulous look.

"Sorry, stupid question. No one can continue his work." Welly took a deep breath, holstered his gun, and took out his Oddfone.

"What are you doing?" Ken asked, accusation in his tone.

"First, I'm ringing the Cardiff office one last time, and then I'm ordering an evacuation helicopter."

"You can't," Ken protested.

"I can and I will. We'll take Mick with us, and you can take care of him. As much as I hate to admit it, it's time to let Borislav clean up this mess."

— 226 —

All of Alice's internal alarms went off. "Clean up... You mean, obliterate the town!"

"I'll kill you," Ken said, with absolute sincerity, "before I'll let you kill the infected in this town."

"What about the uninfected?" Alice wailed. "And the Bog Snorkelling tourists!"

"Shut your gobs!" Welly shouted them down. "Odyssey gave us until dawn to contain this outbreak, and that's three hours from now. If either of you have a world-beater of an idea on how to pull off this miracle, I'd love to hear it. Right now, the only alternative to Borislav is allowing this outbreak to become a countrywide epidemic, or even a worldwide pandemic. I doubt either of you consider these to be happy outcomes."

Alice knew Ken wanted to shout, 'Bring on the zombie apocalypse!', but he pressed his lips together and glared instead. Alice was grateful, as Welly probably would have shot him.

Welly flipped open his Oddfone. "Lilith, I want... No, you told me the monastery doesn't accept calls." His ears suddenly flushed pink. "She got kicked out! With Patrick? For breaking rules, what rules? ... Fine, don't tell me. Just get me the Cardiff office again. Yes, clearly I'm a masochist."

He waited a moment, and then took a deep breath. "Wellington Wolfe calling again," he began, in a deceptively calm voice. "I know none of your lot care if Cardiff's overrun by zombies, and frankly, I don't care if zombies chew every last one of you to pieces. But we have an imminent Raging Seas outbreak here in Llanwrtyd Wells, which could become a Gale Force pandemic. As Llanwrtyd Wells is also a stop on the Heart of Wales Rail Line, there's a lot of people at high risk, including the over two hundred thousand souls living in Swansea."

Welly took another breath. "I'm rather fond of Swansea. I used to summer there as a child before the war. So I'm going to do my best to save Swansea, and the rest of the world while I'm at it. If you happen to give a good Golf Delta about anyone other than yourselves, do give us a call." He snapped his Oddfone shut.

Alice had always thought the phrase 'the silence was deafening' was a ridiculous cliché. Now, she wasn't so sure.

"Technically, there is no Llanwrtyd Wells stop on the Heart of Wales line." A familiar, jaunty voice said from the floor. "In fact, there's no 'Lan-wrrr-tid' Wells town either. If you want Cardiff's help, you really should pronounce it correctly."

Everyone's jaws, including Dave's, dropped open.

Mick sat up, glowing with good health. "The rail station near here is simply called Llanwrtyd." The way he pronounced it, the beginning of the word sounded as if an 'H' had married an 'L', and then given birth to a bucket of phlegm. "Now, there's a Llandrindod Wells station, but that's a good five stops north on the line."

"Mick, you don't seem…" Alice couldn't think of a tactful way to say it and gave up trying. "You're not very zombie-like."

Mick jumped to his feet. "That's because I'm not a zombie. I told you not to panic. Why does no one believe me? I'm really very truthful these days." He looked around and spotted his dark glasses on the floor. The right lens had popped out, but he put them on anyway.

"Ah Mick…"

"Yes, Wellington?"

"You appear to have left your entire right arm on the floor."

Mick looked down. "So I have. Thank the Baron. Dead limbs get so itchy before they fall off." He reached inside the empty sleeve. "Of course, it can be a bit ticklish while the new one grows in."

Alice glanced at Ken. "Your turn."

Ken swallowed. "Mick, you're not human, are you?"

Mick looked at each of them in turn. "You thought I was human?"

All of them nodded, including Dave. Mick burst into peals of laughter.

14

Welly Makes a Rash Decision

Fifteen minutes later, Mick was still dissolving into intermittent fits of giggling.

"Stop it," Alice said, handing him a piece of tubing. "It's not nice to keep a secret and then laugh at everyone who doesn't know it."

"I hid my bitten arm, I never hid what I was," Mick corrected, attaching one end of the tube to the Med-Trekker IV. "Remember when I told you about my former lover, Phil the philodendron? And I told you before that I like to vacation under water."

"I assumed you meant scuba diving!"

Mick's eyebrows danced. "And the philodendron?"

"I thought..." Alice hesitated.

"That I was a garden-variety pervert?" He began giggling again.

Alice groaned at the pun. In truth, she felt ashamed of herself for not knowing. The mind reading, the extreme pansexuality, the blue tongue: there had been dozens of clues, and she was trained to sense the unusual. Of course, Mick's explanation that he was a child of Mother Earth and first cousin to the stars had failed to clear up what he actually was.

"It's not fair. You look human," Alice pointed out.

"The Admiral is human and never looks it." Mick squinted at the liquid in the tube and frowned. "Surely, a sophisticated, over-twenty-five-now woman should know better than to judge people on their surface appearances."

"Ken!" Welly hollered. "Get your Foxtrotting zombie away from me!"

Alice looked over her shoulder. Dave was hovering rather close to Welly. She couldn't see Ken, but she knew he was fixing the latest broken window. The zombies were still milling around in the courtyard, periodically trying to get inside, but fortunately they weren't anywhere near as competent at the task as movie zombies.

Welly hadn't made his call to Borislav yet, much to Alice's relief. The dawn deadline was worrisome, but Mick was hard at work on the cure. He didn't slow down even while deriving great enjoyment from teasing her.

Right now, she was more worried about Welly. Every time he moved, his limp was noticeably worse. He would also hiss under his breath, which meant he was really suffering. No wonder he'd been baiting Ken and shouting at everyone, she thought.

"Ken, if you don't get Dave to stop staring at me, I'll turn him into a Stage Five zombie!"

"What's Stage Five?" Alice whispered to Mick.

"Dead," Mick whispered back.

"You mean... Dave's still alive?"

Mick began to snicker, and Alice felt her face going red. Was she aware of anything that was going on? "Some Sensitive I turned out to be," she grumbled.

"A learning disability is nothing to be ashamed of," Mick said. "It may take you longer to figure things out, but the end results are still brilliant."

"Thanks Mick. I think."

"Do you hear me, Ken?" Welly shouted again.

Alice glanced over at Dave, who sure enough was still sniffing at Welly. She wondered if Welly's enhancements were as confusing to Dave as Mick's dead arm had been.

She returned her attention to Mick. "It's just... I thought Ken's claim that Dave was alive was just a product of his insane obsession with zombies."

"Ken is obsessed and more than a little insane." Mick lit the Bunsen burner and suspended several test tubes above it. "However, he's also correct. Dave is alive, if just barely. He's a Stage Four zombie, which means he's no longer decomposing. Many people mistake zombies in this stage for mobile mummies."

"But..." Alice stopped herself, and then realized there was no harm in giving Mick one more reason to laugh at her. "I thought zombies rotted... I mean, decomposed, because they were dead."

"You've watched too many zombie films."

"Welly would agree with you."

Alice heard Ken stomp up behind them. "Yes, I heard you!" he yelled at Welly. "Everyone heard you. Some of the zombies outside have started chanting my name!"

"Viruses need to keep their host alive," Mick explained to Alice. "A dead host would mean lots of dead viruses." He poured green fluid into two of the vials and tsked at her. "Please don't tell me you believed a virus could raise the dead?"

"Of course not," Alice said, quickly. Then she amended that statement, "Okay, maybe after watching *Shaun of the Dead*."

"It's okay, Dave," Ken said. "Just leave the very mean man alone."

"Excellent film," Mick said. "And based very loosely on—"

"Whoof!"

Alice spun around and stared in disbelief. Dave was pointing directly at Welly. "No," she whispered.

"How can I be infected?" Welly asked, in a shocked voice.

"Did you get bitten?" Ken asked.

"Of course I got bitten. Why do you think my leg's been killing me?" Welly pulled up his left pant leg, exposing a large purple and black bite wound. "But I've been bitten by zombies before and never got infected."

"You've been bitten before?" Alice asked, faintly. Hadn't they just been through this exact same scenario with Mick? She wondered if Welly's leg was going to fall off.

Mick knelt beside Welly's leg. "Yes, your enhanced immune system should be strong enough to—You naughty zombie virus! You took advantage of the tetanus bacteria already in his system, didn't you?"

"I'm infected?" Welly asked, his voice devoid of emotion.

"Yes, indeedy. Look at this, Ken. We won't need a blood test to confirm this Stage One case. The bite wound is necrotizing. And we now have a third zombie virus variant!"

"I've never seen an Enhanced Agent zombie," Ken said, in a tone of wonder. "I bet he'll be incredibly strong."

"I'm infected." This time it was a statement of fact. "Get away from me, both of you."

Ken immediately backed off, pulling Dave away from Welly. Mick took two steps to the left, the fingers of his remaining hand drumming against his leg.

Alice desperately wanted to go to Welly's side, but the four metres between them felt like an immeasurable chasm. "We've almost got the cure, right Mick?"

"On the very brink."

"Do you hear that, Welly? We'll have the cure soon."

Welly didn't answer her. He stared off into space for a few moments, and then unholstered his gun.

Fear gripped Alice's heart. "Wellington Wolfe, put that gun away," she ordered, sharply.

"I'm your superior, I get to make these decisions." He flicked out the cylinder of his gun, checked it, and pushed it back in place.

"No, you don't. You will not shoot yourself!"

"Why not?" He met her eyes. His looked haunted.

"Because you wouldn't do that to me," she said, her voice pleading.

Welly shut his eyes and swallowed hard. "And what will I do to you when I'm Stage Two? Or Stage Three?" He began to lift the gun.

Alice felt a jolt of panic. "I'll tell your mother!"

The gun froze. "You wouldn't."

"Oh yes, I will. I will tell your hundred-and-six-year-old mother that you shot yourself in the head, and the shock will kill her!"

I will, I will, I will! Alice's inner toddler stormed.

Welly turned white, and then lowered the gun to his side.

Well done, Mick whispered into her ear. Hit him again, as hard as you can.

To hell with her promise never to use her new powers again, Alice thought, and concentrated as hard as she could.

If you shoot yourself, Welly, I will string your body upside down in Mick's office, and I'll make him experiment on you all day long and... and...

"And I'll never talk to you ever again!" Alice added aloud, stomping her foot.

Welly relaxed a bit at this declaration, and Mick snatched the gun out of his lax grip. "Yoink!"

Wait, Alice thought, confused. How'd Mick get from beside her to beside Welly without her seeing him?

I didn't. But I thought you wouldn't mind me invading your brain, just this once.

"Just this once," she said, shakily.

Grinning, Mick walked over and gave her Welly's gun. "Baron be praised."

"Alice, give me back my gun." Welly sounded exhausted.

"Not until you give me all of your ammunition." Alice felt extraordinarily powerful. Logically, there was no reason Welly couldn't just take the gun away from her. But she knew he wouldn't. Her inner toddler was six stories tall, and had a temper like Godzilla.

"Be reasonable," Welly argued. "I need the ammunition; we're surrounded by zombies. I promise I won't shoot myself."

"There are too many zombies for shooting at them to be any help," Alice said. She took a deep breath, before adding, "And I don't trust you not to change your mind."

Welly looked hurt, as he always did when Alice said she didn't trust him. But she couldn't back down this time. His life was on the line.

"Give me your ammunition, Welly. And remember, I'm a Sensitive so I know where all your secret stashes are, including the bullets you've got concealed in your underwear."

Welly's shoulders slumped in defeat, and he started searching through his clothes.

"Besides, shooting yourself in the head probably wouldn't kill you," Mick said, already back at the Bunsen burner, juggling test tubes. "And since I'm far too busy right now to put your limited grey matter back together, you'd end up with permanent brain damage. Not that everyone would notice."

Alice fetched Mick's messenger bag, and brought it over to Welly. With a sigh, Welly dumped his ammunition inside.

Alice started to hand the gun back to Welly, but Ken grabbed it out of her hand.

"Hey," Alice protested.

Without a word, Ken opened the cylinder and tipped the gun upward. Six bullets fell into the palm of his hand.

Alice felt herself turning beet red. "I'm no good with guns."

"One of the many reasons you failed Survival Island," Mick

said.

Ignoring Mick, Alice gratefully took the unloaded revolver back from Ken. She gave Welly his gun, and then gave him a peck on the forehead. "Don't worry, you're going to be fine."

"Is that a prediction?" Welly asked, a hint of amusement in his expression.

"No," Alice said. "It's a promise."

*

"Alice, my exhausted emu, please pour me a mug of coffee."

Alice picked up a ceramic mug and began jiggling the spigot of the old coffee urn. After hours of brewing literally buckets of coffee, the urn was ready to give up the ghost and so was she. But she resisted the temptation to pour a cup of coffee for herself. Caffeine boosted her Sensitive powers into overdrive, and Alice couldn't afford to lose control now. She suppressed a yawn, turned to hand the cup to Mick, and shrieked.

Mick grabbed the cup before she could drop it and grinned. "Nothing like a surge of adrenaline to clear out the cobwebs."

Alice pointed a shaking hand at him. "You... You've... There's fingers growing out of you!"

Mick casually glanced down at his shoulder, where he'd neatly cut off the arm of his jacket and his shirt, so they wouldn't get in his way. "Good thing, too," he said, wiggling the small black fingers protruding from the puckered stump. "Hands are handy, so the more the merrier."

He sipped from the mug and emptied the rest of the coffee into a measuring flask. He then passed the glass container to his finger stubs. Climbing a ladder to the top of one of the copper and wood brewhouses, Mick added, "Excellent job with the coffee. Mixed with ale, it will make a potent base for the cure."

"So, you're actually going to grow a new arm?" Alice asked, as

Mick fiddled with a large tap at the end of a long, glass tube.

"The hand is the trickiest part. Once it's out, the rest will grow much more quickly. Now back to work, my easily distracted dingo. Zombie coffee doesn't brew itself!"

While Mick siphoned ale into the measuring flask, Alice looked over at Welly. He was sitting in the corner not far from the sink. Bits of his gun were spread out on the floor in front of him. He'd taken it apart and was now putting it back together again. She was relieved to see that the zombie virus hadn't affected him yet.

She'd tried to get Welly to drink lots of coffee, remembering what Mick said about it slowing the spread of the disease into the brain. However, Welly had stopped listening when her psychic temper tantrum had lost steam. Apparently, her inner toddler was as exhausted as she was.

The thought of how close Welly had been to killing himself both infuriated and terrified her. Why the hell had suicide been his first reaction? For crying out loud, Mick was working on a cure!

Alice took a deep breath. Let it go, she told herself. Just let it go.

She picked up the closest bucket of coffee grounds and scooped some into a new filter. "Are you an alien?" she called up to Mick.

"No, I told you, I'm one of Mother Earth's children," he replied, turning off the brewhouse's tap. Mick swirled the flask, sipped from it, and made a happy sound. "I crawled out of her womb on the first day and then crawled right back in again because Father Sun was prancing around like the great flaming wally he is. You have to watch out for Sun Gods. All beauty, very few brains. "

This was why it was never a good idea to ask Mick questions, Alice thought. But she couldn't help herself.

"So, Mick, if you're not human…"

Mick waggled his stump's fingers again.

Alice cleared her throat. "Since you're not human, why do you look like one?"

"I'll give you three guesses," Mick said, climbing down the ladder. "If you're wrong all three times, I get to experiment on your first-born child."

Alice rolled her eyes. "Fine, don't tell me, Rumpelstiltskin."

"Wrong. Odyssey put an end to that hobgoblin's mischief decades ago." Mick joined her at the sink. "Two guesses left."

"I'm not guessing!" Alice shook the spatula at him. "And after this is all over, I'm going to ask Lilith to curse you. But not with a shape-shifting spell like the Admiral. No, it'll be a spell that traps you in a ridiculous, helpless form you can't escape..."

Alice suddenly realized what she'd been saying. "Except that's already happened, hasn't it? That's why you look human now! Lilith did curse you."

"Being a gorgeous black man isn't what I'd call a curse, other than the bipedalism. But yes, she did freeze me while I was experimenting with the human form." Mick sighed melodramatically. "And I was so looking forward to doing a medical study on your progeny. How about you give me permission in exchange for free babysitting?"

"Forget about my non-existent first-born child, Mick, and focus on finding the zombie cure!"

"Slave driver," he said, adjusting the flame on the Bunsen burner. "Spatula, please."

Alice gave it back to him and watched as he fiddled with the glass vials above the flame. It seemed impossible this bizarre, human-looking individual could create a cure using a hodgepodge of medical tools, brewery equipment, and kitchen utensils. And do it in time to save both Welly and Llanwrtyd Wells.

"Is the Welsh government really going to let Odyssey blow up this town?" Alice asked.

"Of course they are," Mick said. "Nobody wants to see Swansea overrun by zombies. Cardiff on the other hand –" Something popped inside one of the glass vials suspended above the Bunsen burner. Flames began licking out of the top of the vial. "Salt!" Mick demanded.

Wide-eyed, Alice handed Mick the salt shaker. He sprinkled it over the vial. Immediately, the flames changed from orange to a purplish blue.

Mick gave a relieved sigh. He carefully placed the measuring flask on the counter. "You don't really think this is the first time Odyssey has erased a town, do you?"

Alice began to nod, and then shook her head. A quick glance back over at Welly showed he was disassembling his gun once again.

"Have you ever heard of Walnut Grove, Minnesota?" Mick asked, as he pressed multiple buttons on the Med-Trekker IV.

"You mean from *The Little House on the Prairie*? Walnut Grove wasn't a real town."

"It was once, and you can find it listed on the old census rolls from the eighteen-hundreds. Thanks to the popularity of the books, the town's been recreated almost perfectly—minus the zombies, of course."

A piece of tubing popped off the Med-Trekker and began spraying blue bubbles everywhere. Alice quickly caught hold of the flyaway tube and re-attached it, this time more securely. It would be disastrous if Mick's mad scientist's lab started falling apart now.

Mick turned off the Bunsen burner, and the flames in the vial went out. "And how about Mayberry, North Carolina?"

"That's from *The Andy Griffith Show*."

Mick sniffed the vials and tsked. "Mayberry's another town that had to be erased from the map."

"But it was just a TV show! They used to play it on Family Channel all the time when I was a kid. I still have nightmares about Don Knotts's bulging eyeballs popping out and chasing me." Alice had liked Ron Howard's character, however. She couldn't decide whether the idea of a zombie Opie made her want to laugh or cry.

Mick winked at her. "What better way to convince people a town and its inhabitants never existed than to turn them into a TV show? If people find any leftover artefacts we've failed to account for, they just assume they're props from the show."

Mick was making entirely too much sense. Alice felt a chill run down her spine. In half an hour, Llanwrtyd Wells could be obliterated from the map along with everyone in it. If so, then in a few years time, no one would believe there ever was such a thing as the World Bog Snorkelling Championships, except on some bizarre British TV show.

Mick continued to rhyme off towns obliterated by Odyssey. "... Bay City, California, and most recently, Dog River, Saskatchewan." Alice noticed Mick's shoulder now had more than just fingers jutting out of it. In fact, there was a complete, brand-new hand. It waved at her.

Alice decided to go see how Welly was doing.

Welly was putting his gun back together again. Snap, snap, twist, kerchunk. The moment it was together, he started taking it apart. Ken was hunkered down in front of him, watching.

"He's locked in a pattern," Ken said to her. "Definitely Stage Two."

Welly didn't look up.

"But he can't be that far along," Alice said. "I mean, look at all the little pieces. Don't zom... I mean, wouldn't he be too clumsy to play with his gun?"

"Enhanced Agents are able to disassemble and reassemble their weapons in less than a minute. He's averaging over two minutes now and slowing down."

"Oh, Welly!" Alice felt tears prickle her eyes. She reached out one hand to comfort him.

"Don't touch him," Ken warned. "Stage Two zombies can be

volatile if you disturb their rituals."

"Volatile?" Alice snatched her hand back. "You mean, he'll blow up?" Images of spontaneously exploding zombies danced in her head.

Ken chuckled. "No, but he might bite you. And with the damage his enhanced jaws could do, I'd have to break out the duct tape early to put you back together."

Welly finished reassembling his gun, but instead of immediately disassembling it again, his right hand hovered over the weapon. Some of the glazed look was replaced with confusion and anxiety.

"I let go of my limiting beliefs," Ken said softly, "and become the zombie I was always meant to be."

Welly growled between clenched teeth and firmly took hold of his gun. Alice was momentarily scared he was going to pistol-whip Ken. But Welly began to break down the gun into its component pieces instead.

Dave woofed urgently. He was pacing by the wall of casks in front of the stable door. Ken stood up and jogged over to the agitated zombie.

Alice knelt down in front of Welly, keeping out of biting range. She wanted one last clear memory of him. A mental picture she could take with her, just in case Mick couldn't save him in time. Because Alice knew for sure now. She didn't just like Welly.

I love this big guy, Alice thought, experimentally. The thought didn't seem strange at all.

Snap, snap, twist, kerchunk. Welly's hands kept moving. But Ken was right. They were slowing down.

Welly was far from his usual well-groomed self. His dark brown hair was sticking up oddly in the back and in the front, it had fallen down over one eye. His collar had popped up over his jacket, and one wing was standing up. There was a rip at his elbow, and he was missing a button in the front. The borrowed green rubber boots looked ridiculous with his suit pants, which weren't grey anymore. They were more of a boggy brown, except for the patches of rust-coloured dried blood. She couldn't tell if it was splatter from the two-legged or four-legged zombies he'd encountered.

Alice missed the well-dressed, attractive Welly, with his dry wit and obsession with fancy cars. She even missed the bossy, bad-tempered Welly, because he always knew what to do to save the day.

She was overwhelmed by a sense of loss. He was her friend, partner, and boss. He could have been something more, given time. But now Welly would never smile one of his rare, and completely disarming, smiles at her. That thought made it hurt to breathe.

If she'd been with him, Alice told herself, he wouldn't have got bitten. True, Welly hadn't listened to her when she'd tried to warn him he'd hurt his ankle kicking in the cockpit door. Nor had he listened to her when she'd tried to warn him about the board with the nail in it, the one that had given him tetanus in the first place. And he'd hung up the phone before she'd had a chance to tell him about the zombie going for his leg.

So maybe he wouldn't have listened to her despite his promise to do so. But at the very least, Welly wouldn't have taken as many risks, because he'd also want to keep her safe.

She tentatively tried reaching out with her mind, only to hit a wall. Alice had never been able to read Welly very well, except when he was upset or angry. Besides, she had a feeling the only thought in his head right now was a recitation of the vital stats of his Magnum. Stage Two zombies, in Alice's experience, weren't deep thinkers.

She tried to imagine herself taking care of Welly the way Ken looked after Dave. Intravenous feedings, adult diapers, and full body massages of desiccated flesh — No, Alice thought, she wasn't a nurturer. She hadn't been capable of preventing an African violet from spontaneously combusting. How could she possibly keep zombie Welly healthy and happy enough to hunt bunnies with all the other Mailroom zombies?

Mick had to develop the cure in time, Alice thought.

A crash from the direction of the stable door shook her out of her maudlin musings. She stood and walked warily toward the front of the brewery.

"Mick, hurry up!" Ken shouted. "They're getting cranky out there!"

Above the stack of barrels, Alice could see the top of the doors splintering. "Ken, you told me zombies only did this in the movies!"

"It's your partner's fault," Ken said, pulling Dave away from the barricade.

"What?"

"Just like most isolated zombies have the instinct to join a pack, a pack has the instinct to pick up strays. I've told you before, they're extremely social beings."

The stable doors were groaning and shuddering in a very worrying fashion. "Couldn't it be Dave who's attracting them?" Alice asked.

"The scent of the newly infected is much stronger. Dave's so old in zombie years, I doubt they would even recognize him as one of their own."

The left stable door suddenly swung open, and voices calling for brains, sandwich, and wobble filled the brewery. Soon, there were squishing sounds and loud moans as the zombies encountered the barrier of barrels.

"Mick, if you're going to finish that cure, you better do it now!" Ken shouted. One cask rolled free of the barricade, and Ken scrambled to stop it. Dave began woofing non-stop.

"I could really use an extra hand," Mick called back. "Preferably on the end of an arm with a functioning elbow."

Alice ran to help him. He handed her one of the glass vials

filled with neon green liquid. "Pour it right in here," Mick said, using his new hand to indicate the measuring flask filled with coffee and ale.

As Alice poured the viscous fluid, Mick stirred it in with the spatula using his left hand. His new right hand now had a wrist and part of a forearm. It appeared to be conducting an invisible symphony.

There were loud crashing sounds from the front of the brewery. Over the din, she could hear Ken trying to get the invading zombies to chant positive affirmations with him to no avail.

Alice started to shake the vial to get the sticky, green fluid to pour out faster.

"Gently," Mick cautioned. "Like the rolling gait of a fat pony. If you overexcite the compound... Let's just say, I doubt your hand would grow back."

Alice swallowed and forced herself to shake the vial very gently. The smell of roasted coffee, strong ale, and rotting asparagus wafted up to her nostrils.

The moment the last drop fell from the vial, Mick tossed the spatula aside, leaned over the measuring flask, and took a deep breath. "A work of art, if I do say so myself."

Mick popped a large syringe out of the Med-Trekker, stuck it into the flask, and pulled the plunger with his teeth. The moment it was full, he hurried over to Welly, Alice following closely. Silently, desperately, praying the cure would work.

Without hesitation, Mick plunged the needle into Welly's neck, using considerably more force than Alice thought necessary. Welly's head snapped to the side, and he dropped the pieces of his gun.

Alice winced. "Shouldn't you have used a vein or something?"

"I did use a vein," Mick said, stepping back with a look of anticipation. "The internal jugular vein to be exact. The veins of Enhanced Agents are notoriously tough and prone to rolling.

There's no point being delicate with them."

"Ow," Welly said, blinking.

"Welly, you're back!" Alice exclaimed.

"Ow," Welly said again, louder. "Ow, Ow, OW!"

"Not quite," Mick said. He leaned over and moved his new index finger across Welly's line of vision. "But there are some encouraging signs."

Welly's jaw moved, and his lips tightened.

"Mainly that he hasn't tried to remove my finger from my hand," Mick continued.

Welly glared at him.

Another crash from the barricade reminded Alice there were more immediate threats to their safety than the cure not working. What would Welly do?, she asked herself. The answer was obvious.

"Let's go!" she shouted. "Up the stairs to the second floor. Zombies have trouble with stairs." Wow, she thought, astonished. She sounded just like Welly.

Ken dragged Dave toward her. Behind him, Alice could see hands clawing at the barrels, and one zombie villager had already squeezed half of his body through the barricade. Then there was an avalanche of casks.

The zombies were loose in the brewery.

15

Dave Is a Hero

"This way!" Alice shouted, as zombies stumbled and crawled over the remains of the barricade. She hoped Mick was right about Welly not being bitey as she grabbed her partner under the arm, encouraging him to stand up. Mick snatched up his messenger bag and seized Welly's other arm. Together they stumbled toward the stairs, Welly between them.

Ken tossed Dave over his shoulders in a fireman carry with practiced ease. This likely wasn't the first time he'd had to hustle with Dave in tow, Alice thought, as Ken climbed up the stairs ahead of them.

She always underestimated just how ridiculously heavy Welly was. He was like a lead-filled bean bag, except he had half a mind of his own. He kept trying to pull loose and climb the stairs by himself.

Halfway up to the second landing, Welly suddenly teetered backward. Alice held on tight, convinced all three of them were going to fall into the arms of the zombies below. "Ken, we could use some help!"

Ken deposited Dave on the landing, and ran back down the stairs. He grasped the front of Welly's shirt stopping his fall. Mick and Alice shoved while Ken heaved Welly forward. The effort knocked Ken onto his rear, and Welly tumbled down on top of him.

"Ow," Welly said again.

"Get off me, you big lummox!" Ken yelled.

Alice and Mick scrambled up on either side of Welly and grabbed him under the arms again. Welly's feet kicked against the steps, propelling him the rest of the way up the stairs. Ken grunted, as one of Welly's rubber boots caught him in the gut.

"He's shaking," Alice said. Welly was on all fours and appeared to be stuck. She heaved his elbow into the air, but that was all she could manage. "Is he supposed to be shaking?"

Ken joined her and immediately slid back beneath Welly. Grabbing his collar, Ken used his shoulder to lever him up onto his feet.

Alice looked down. Zombies were milling around the foot of the stairs, and several were beginning to crawl up the steps.

"Shaking? That's very interesting." Mick started rummaging in his bag. "I should take his temperature."

Releasing Welly's arm, Alice slapped her hand over Mick's bag. "Later!" She pushed him toward the door halfway down the hallway. "Move!" She helped Ken with Welly, while Dave trailed obediently behind. Together they stumbled into the small room.

Alice glanced around: the brewery's office. She distinctly remembered Welly telling her to never get backed into a room with only one exit, but she didn't know what else she could have done under the circumstances. "Mick, grab that filing cabinet and block the door. Ken, help him."

Mick immediately began shoving the heavy filing cabinet in front of the door. Ken propped Welly up against a wall and joined Mick. Alice could hear the zombies chanting downstairs. They were down to just one word now.

"Brains, brains, brains..."

"This is exactly what stereotyping does," Ken said, furiously. "Some joker gets them all riled up, and this is what happens."

"But we'll be safe up here, right? You said zombies have short attention spans, so they'll forget about Welly soon and go away." Alice dragged a chair over and placed it next to the filing cabinet. It wasn't much, but every little bit helped.

Thumping and bumping noises came from downstairs, and the call for brains grew louder.

Ken shook his head. "Normally I'd say out of sight, out of mind. But they've merged into a single mega-mob, and every last one of them is fixated on Wellington's scent."

"Think, think, think," Alice told herself. She looked around the office and spotted a case of bottled stout. "Wait, what if we doused Welly with alcohol?"

"I don't think setting him on fire would help us," Ken said, sounding puzzled.

"I don't want to flambé Welly! I just want to cover up his zombie smell," Alice insisted.

She glanced over at Welly, who was still leaning against the wall. He looked deathly pale and deeply confused.

"Won't help," Ken said. "Even untrained, zombies are excellent trackers."

"And evidently our zombie fan club find Eau de Welly a verrry sexy scent," Mick chimed in. "Rawr."

Alice grabbed Mick by the lapels. "Why isn't the cure working?"

"Patience, my poison-spurred platypus, de-zombification takes time." Mick sounded relaxed, but he looked worse for wear. His hat had disappeared, as had his sunglasses. On the plus side, his new arm had grown an elbow.

Behind her, she heard Ken open the office's only window. "Damn," he said. "We won't be able to go down this way."

Alice let go of Mick and hurried over to the window. In the

dim light of the approaching dawn, she could see more zombies shuffling around the corner of the hotel. They would soon completely surround the brewery. To her panicked brain, there appeared to be hundreds of them.

She took a deep breath and asked herself again: What would Welly do?

Pushing Ken out of the way, she climbed up onto the window ledge. Hanging onto the wooden frame, Alice leaned outside. Doing her best to ignore the gaping jaws of the zombies below, she looked up.

Something heavy slammed against the door, and Dave woofed. Alice shrieked and clutched the window frame tighter.

"Fuck," Welly said. "Am I a zombie?"

Sliding down off the window sill, Alice ran over to him. "You're cured!" She hugged him hard. Then she let go, suddenly worried. "Wait, you said the Foxtrot-word." Looking over at Mick, she asked, "Does that mean he's brain damaged?"

"It's possible there's some neurological damage. No way to be certain without a full workup," Mick said, breezily. "I'd still consider the cure a success regardless."

"I'm not brain damaged," Welly protested. He took a step and staggered. "But I do feel... incredibly sick."

Ken cleared his throat. He was standing by the window, his body radiating tension. "So the cure actually works?" Ken asked.

"Like magic," Mick said. "Which makes sense as it's partially magical in nature. And now that Wellington's been infected and cured, he'll be immune to the virus."

Ken didn't look happy at this news. "Will it work on all zombies?" Ken asked, looking at Dave. "Even those in later stages like... the ones in my Mailroom?"

There was another thump against the door, followed by several loud moans.

"The cure will only work on Stage One or Two," Mick said,

calmly. "Of course, if an early stage zombie has sustained any injuries incompatible with life, the cure will work, but then he'll just die. That's why the cure won't work on later stage zombies. Their autonomic systems have already sustained irreparable damage."

A low, mournful sound reverberated across the room. Alice turned and looked, fearful the zombies had broken into the office. To her relief, it was only Dave.

Alice blinked. Was it her imagination or did Dave look... heartbroken? "Can he understand us?" she asked.

"Of course he can," Ken snapped. He crossed the room and gently laid a hand on Dave's shoulder. "Buddy, you didn't want the cure, did you? I thought you were happy."

Dave moaned again, but he was soon drowned out by the zombies outside the door. The door rattled noisily in its frame as they reiterated their raucous demands for brains.

Alice shook herself. The important thing to focus on right now wasn't Dave's quality of life, but making sure they all got out of this alive. It would be a tragedy if Welly was successfully cured, only to be eaten right away by zombies.

Returning to the window, she said, "The roof is low here. Maybe if I stand on the windowsill, I could pull myself up." She peered outside and winced at the sight of dozens of zombies staring up at her avidly. "Or more likely fall to my death in the zombie mosh pit below."

Alice took another look at Welly and swallowed. He was looking healthier and was standing on his own now. "Okay, new idea. We should try to get Welly up onto the roof first. He's the strongest, and he can help the rest of us climb up. Welly, do you understand? Go up roof, yes?"

Welly glared at her, which Alice took as an affirmative. The sooner Welly got his mojo back, the better, she thought. Alice didn't like being a leader, even though everyone else seemed perfectly willing to follow her lead. The problem was if she got everyone killed, it would be entirely her fault.

Alice got out of the way as Mick and Ken steadied Welly against the window frame. She helped them hold onto his legs as he slowly climbed out the window and stood on the sill. Welly had a look of intense concentration on his face, as if keeping his balance was taking all of his mental power.

With a determined lunge and helpful shoves from the rest of the team, Welly managed to hook his elbows over the edge of the roof. He hauled himself up with a grunt, kicking the air. And Ken's cheek.

"Ouch!" Ken exclaimed. He leaned out the window and glared up at the roof. "Don't try to tell me you didn't do that on purpose!" he shouted. "I know you're still holding a grudge over those sparkplugs!"

"Okay Mick, you're next," Alice said, with forced cheer. There was no way she was going to let Welly and Ken be alone on the roof together.

With reptilian grace, Mick climbed up without help. Even the fact that his right arm was still shorter than his left didn't slow him down. He ought to have a lizard's tail and sticky pads on his feet, Alice thought.

Seated in the window, prepared to follow Welly and Mick up onto the roof, Alice looked back into the room.

"What about you?" Alice asked Ken. He'd moved away from their escape route and was facing Dave in the center of the room.

"Bravo Hotel, Alice!" Welly shouted from above. "Hurry up!"

"Welly, you're sounding like yourself again!" she exclaimed happily.

The door rattled in its frame, and the filing cabinet slid out an inch. Ken placed his hands on Dave's shoulders.

"Go ahead," Ken said, without looking at her. "I'll join you in a moment."

The door was cracking down the middle, and the shiny blade of an axe showed briefly though the gap. But Ken didn't seem aware of the danger. He pressed his forehead against Dave's and began talking quietly to him.

As Alice watched, Dave raised his hand and rested it on the back of Ken's head. Then she sensed the most astonishing thing. It was a troubling mixture of affection and regret, not emanating from Ken, but from Dave. She couldn't make out any thoughts, and the emotions felt fuzzy around the edges, but there was someone alive inside Dave's desiccated shell.

Alice also had a strong feeling that Ken and Dave were silently saying goodbye to each other. But that didn't make any sense, she thought. Surely, any moment now Ken would help Dave out the window... except Dave couldn't climb. He could barely bend his body or limbs. But maybe Ken could boost him upwards, and Welly could catch him... Except Welly wasn't very coordinated right now. He'd likely drop the fragile zombie, Dave would break in half, and enter Stage Five.

The filing cabinet tipped over with a crash. Dave and Ken separated.

Alice stood up on the windowsill and reached for Welly's extended hand. "Ken!" she shouted.

Ken hesitated a moment. Then he turned and ran toward her. Without Dave.

With Welly's help, Alice and Ken both clambered up onto the roof. The last thing she saw was Dave facing down the invading zombies with his arms spread wide.

*

"Three more hours, Borislav!" Welly shouted into his Oddfone. "All I'm asking is three more hours!"

Alice sat on the gently sloping roof and stared at the circling helicopters in the pre-dawn sky. She'd never noticed before how menacing Odyssey helicopters were. Despite their turquoise and orange colouring, they didn't look like friendly dragonflies. No, they were more like a swarm of spiteful wasps. Armed with machine guns. Plus if Mick was right, the choppers had magical town-obliterating bombs, too.

"Why three hours?" Welly shouted into his phone. "Because we've got the zombie cure. If you erase this town, you'll erase the cure too."

Ken was sitting cross-legged by the big brick chimney, looking at nothing in particular. His shoulders were bowed, as if he was carrying a horribly heavy weight. Just the sight of him made Alice want to cry. Ken without his Dave was the saddest thing she'd ever seen.

"No, you can't just pick us up. Because we're not going, that's why! This town can be saved, and I'm not leaving until every last person here is cured!"

"Did you hear that, Ken?" Alice asked. "Welly called zombies people. He finally believes zombies are people, too!"

Ken stayed slumped against the chimney, but Alice knew he was listening.

"Yes, I'll hold," Welly growled into his Oddfone. He looked at Alice and frowned. "Why are you grinning at me like a maniac?"

"Because you're wonderful."

"I am?" Welly looked concerned.

"Yes! You no longer believe zombies are undead monsters you need to massacre."

Welly looked embarrassed. "My recent experience in their shoes has changed my perspective. I couldn't think straight, I could barely remember who I was, but... I was still me."

"I was wrong too, Ken," Alice confessed. "I'm sorry for doubting Da... um, zombies were alive."

Ken lifted his head, but said nothing. His grief was like a tangible thing.

"Yes Borislav," Welly said into his phone. "Of course, I'm still here. I'm not going to jump off the roof, now am I?"

Not if she could help it, Alice thought.

Alice scooched down to the edge of the roof and looked down. Below her, the zombies continued their chanting with unflagging enthusiasm. "Brains, brains, brains!"

Mick sat down beside Alice and commented, "Of course, they wouldn't really eat our brains. They'd just chew on our limbs. Much easier than trying to break through the skull."

"I know," Alice said sharply, not wanting to be reminded of the woman in the flowered dress. She wondered if Brian's wife had gone straight to Stage Five, torn to bits at the hands of the zombies.

"It's very hard to kill someone by chewing on them," Mick said.

Alice blinked. "So if she's only missing a few chunks of flesh the cure might be able to save her after all!" She leaned over the edge of the roof and began searching the crowd for a flowered dress. She spotted several, but none of them the one she sought.

Welly was no longer shouting into his Oddfone. He was speaking in icy, measured tones. "Yes Borislav, I would be delighted to speak to the Admiral."

It occurred to Alice that this was probably the first time in his life Welly had ever been "delighted" to speak to the much-feared head of Odyssey International. Unlike zombies, there was never anything unintentional or accidental about the Admiral's decisions to eat employees who displeased him.

Mick continued blithely, "It's fortunate for our zombie friends that they don't eat brains. Brains are incredibly high in cholesterol. Very unhealthy meat. Although they can be tasty."

Alice didn't want to hear about tasty brains. She decided to focus on Welly's conversation with their boss instead. Having a cure wouldn't mean a thing to the townsfolk if Odyssey decided to obliterate Llanwrtyd Wells.

"Yes Admiral."

"No Admiral."

"Yes Admiral, I did say 'no' to you."

"Because I have a plan!" Welly began to pace, and Alice wished he wouldn't. The roof didn't have much of a slope, but the tin surface was slippery.

"Yes I do. All I need is three hours to prove it works."

"Yes Admiral."

"Yes. I mean, yes Admiral!"

Welly snapped the Oddfone shut. "Yes Admiral, no Admiral, three bags full, Admiral!" he said, irritably.

The Oddfone rang, and he paled. Putting it cautiously to his ear he listened for a moment, and then said, "No Admiral, I wasn't being disrespectful." Welly grimaced. "What was I doing? Erm… I was merely… free-associating. And I solemnly promise I will never do so again."

Welly carefully closed his Oddfone. Looking across to Alice and Mick, he said, "We've got our three hours."

The turquoise and orange helicopters slowly turned and began to fly away. However, Alice knew they wouldn't go very far.

"And you've got a plan?" Alice asked Welly, hopefully. She'd done a decent job of getting them to this point, but now she was fresh out of useful ideas. It was time for Welly to start acting like Welly again.

"I do," Welly said. "We're going to get these zombies out of town and lead them into a peat bog like the one I fell into. Once they're mired in the mud, we'll be able to walk right up and jab them with the cure." He looked at Mick. "How much of it do you have?"

"Not nearly enough," Mick said, climbing to his feet. "But I've got all the necessary ingredients. If you can get the zombies to clear out of the brewery, I'll start making more right away."

Alice stood and turned toward the chimney. "Did you hear that, Ken? Welly has a plan."

Ken didn't answer. His arms were folded over his chest and his eyes were bleak. Not even Welly's apparent change of heart from Zombie Killer to Zombie Saviour mattered to him.

Alice felt tears well up in her eyes. Poor Dave, she thought. By now, he was probably pulled to bits and trampled flat by the zombies in the room below. She began to sniffle.

Welly pulled her into a hug, and she buried her face in his jacket. It still smelled like boggy socks. "Dave was a good zombie," Welly said, patting her back awkwardly. "He died a hero's death."

"Dave's dead? For certain, dead?" Alice began to cry.

"No, don't cry," Welly said, sounding desperate.

"But we couldn't cure him, and we couldn't save him. It's so unfair!" Alice wailed.

"No, no wailing. And no more crying!" Welly took her by the shoulders and gave her a gentle shake. "Dave wouldn't want you to fall to pieces."

"No, he wouldn't," Ken said. He stood up, his back straight. "We owe it to his memory to save his people."

Welly nodded approvingly at Ken. "That's right. So, Alice, I need to you to be a good soldier and pull yourself together. We're not out of the woods yet, and I need you on my team."

Alice wiped her eyes and nose. "If you stop mixing your metaphors, I'll do my best."

"Good," Welly said. And smiled at her.

Welly almost never smiled, except when manipulating flight attendants and sometimes when he was threatening people, but this certainly wasn't that kind of smile. Alice felt warmth spread right down to her toes. "So, what are we going..." she began.

A nearby groan followed by a distant thump distracted her.

"Another zombie tried to climb through the window and follow us up here," Mick explained. "He's just joined his friends in the courtyard instead. Oh well, he can always try again. Although it'll take a while, as it looks like he's broken both his legs. No bog snorkelling for him this year."

"Bog snorkelling!" Alice yelped.

All three men looked at her. "Alice, are you quite all right?" Welly asked.

"Bog snorkelling is the answer," Alice said, excited. "You said we need to lead them to a peat bog. Why not use the one for the World Bog Snorkelling Championships? On the videos I watched, they'd cut ditches into the peat. They'd be perfect for our zombies."

"Officer thinking," Welly said.

Alice wasn't sure what that meant, but it sounded positive. "But do we know where the championship will be held?"

Welly nodded. "While Ken and I were tracking down the pilot, we saw signs pointing the way to the bog snorkelling. The only challenge will be ensuring the zombies follow me there." He rubbed his forehead. "I suppose I could attack some of them. That should get the mob after me."

"Violence isn't necessary," Ken explained. "Zombies have a distinctive scent that you still have. They'll want to get close to you."

"I smell like a zombie?" Welly asked, appalled.

Ken nodded. "It's beginning to fade, but it's still strong enough for them to recognize you as one of their own."

"Lovely," Welly said, sounding less than thrilled. "But lacking a sane alternative, I'll give it a go."

"Remember, zombies respond well to strong leadership," Mick said. "So, just be your obnoxious, bossy self."

"Right. People, listen up," Welly said. "I will lead the zombies on a merry chase to the bog snorkelling peat bog. Alice, you and Ken are tasked with finding vehicles and providing me with backup."

"There's a stable that rents ponies not too far from here," Mick said, helpfully.

Both Ken and Welly yelled in unison, "No ponies!"

Alice blinked.

"Mick can't be trusted with ponies," Welly said, darkly.

"I'm hurt," Mick said, appearing in no way hurt at all. "First off, the redoubtable Ms. Shortcake was a mule, not a pony. Secondly, a good time was had by all. Lastly, I was suggesting ponies for Ken and Alice, not for myself, although now that you mention it I could—"

"No ponies for anyone," Welly said, firmly.

"How exactly are Ken and I supposed to provide backup?" Alice asked, before Mick could start up about ponies again.

"You'll need to make sure no stray zombies go wandering off by themselves," Welly said. "But for the love of Golf, be careful. Yes, zombies are human, but they're very sick humans. They're a danger to themselves and others."

"That's an unfair characterization…" Ken began, but Welly cut him off.

"Sorry, but have you been a zombie? No? Trust me, when I was a zombie, you're lucky I didn't literally bite your head off." Welly turned toward Mick. "Much as I dislike leaving you to your own devices, Mick, you'll have to tend to your lab on your own. Make as much of the cure as you can, as fast as you can."

"Not to worry," Mick said, happily. "Alice made enough coffee to wake up all the zombies of Llanwrtyd Wells."

"Good. Alice…"

"Yes?" Her stomach did a nervous somersault. Had he figured out how she felt about him? Was he going to confess how he felt about her before risking life and limb?

"Do you still have your Taser?" Welly asked.

Alice felt her stomach curdle. "Yes, in my purse," she answered. "Unfortunately, my purse is currently under the sink on the first floor of the brewery."

"When the zombies leave, be sure to retrieve your Taser before you follow me."

"Sure. Whatever. I'll get right on it."

He stared at her without saying anything, making her nervous.

"I'm a big fan of unresolved sexual tension," Mick said, "but I do believe zombies wait for no man or woman."

Welly shot Mick a dirty look. Then he placed his right palm against Alice's face and said quietly, "Be careful. I do need you."

Before Alice could answer, Welly limped to the edge of the roof.

Silhouetted against the rising sun, Welly slowly surveyed the zombies below. Then he cupped his hands and shouted down to the zombie horde. "Hear ye, hear ye! I am Wellington Wolfe, and I am your king!"

The zombies all looked up at him, mouths gaping. The chant of brains died out.

"Follow me, my people, and I will lead you to the Zombie Promised Land!" Crouching down, Welly suddenly leapt out into the air above the zombies. He hit the ground two stories below, did a complete somersault, and then sprang to his feet, jogging toward the town square.

"He's just like Hercules," Alice exclaimed. "Except... Is his limp worse?"

There was indeed a distinct sideways list to Welly's stride.

"He's twisted his ankle," Mick said. "Good thing enhanced bones are difficult to break."

Welly waved his arms at the zombies. "Over here!" Several were already stumbling toward him. "That's right," he shouted, as he limped away. "Follow your king!"

Zombies poured out of every alley and side street to trail after him. Several of them fell out of the brewery's window, and began crawling after Welly, ignoring their broken, twisted limbs.

"Long live the king," Alice said.

16

Alice Discovers an Unexpected New Talent

When over a minute had passed without further zombie defenestrations, Mick leaned precariously over the edge of the roof and peered into the room. "Not a creature is stirring," he said. And with that announcement, he slid right off the roof and disappeared through the window into the brewery office.

Alice followed with considerably less grace. Mick helped her down from the window sill in a courtly manner that suggested he was assisting a fine lady out of her carriage. Ken climbed back inside on his own.

It was hard to say where Dave had died. Little dried-up bits of him were scattered everywhere. His remains looked like unappetizing pieces of beef jerky. His head, however, was mostly intact. Ken found it behind the knocked-over filing cabinet. He retrieved it and tenderly smoothed its tangled hair. Then he tucked the head under his arm.

"Um, Ken…" Alice began.

Ken gazed at her with bloodshot eyes. He didn't look entirely sane.

"Nothing. Never mind." Alice decided not to say anything. Hopefully, Ken just wanted to bury Dave's head, and not keep it as a *memento mori*.

Mick climbed over the toppled filing cabinet and poked his

head through the shattered remains of the door. "Looks safe enough to me," he said, and silently entered the hallway.

Ken followed quickly, but Alice did so more reluctantly. Mick's concept of safe wasn't reassuring. However, there were no zombies to be seen on the landing or the stairs. Downstairs in the brewery, she saw only one staring fixedly at a brewhouse. Wordlessly, Ken coaxed the confused zombie away from the shiny brass fixtures and shooed him out the broken stable doors.

"Mick, will you be okay?" Alice asked. His makeshift lab appeared intact. The zombies hadn't paid any attention to it in their quest to get up close and personal with Welly.

"Don't worry about me. I'll be brewing barrels of Zombie Cure Ale in no time. You two toddle along and find our newly anointed King of the Zombies."

Alice chugged down a cup of coffee undoctored by Mick's cure. She offered some to Ken, but he didn't appear to hear her.

"Ken," she tried again. "Maybe you should leave the ... I mean, leave Dave here with Mick until we can bur... um, take care of him."

Ken blinked at her. Alice reached out to scan him, but his thoughts were all jumbled and confused.

"Or we could take Dave with us," Alice said, retrieving her purse. Between Ken's bruised face and his desolate expression, she didn't have the heart to force him to leave the head with Mick.

Ken nodded, slowly.

"This is going to be fun," Alice muttered as they crossed the brewery to what remained of the stable doors.

"Almost forgot!" Mick called after her. He dug into his messenger bag and flung something white at her. Alice caught it, and realized it was the bra she'd left behind at the farmer's cottage, except it no longer stank of bog water.

"You washed my bra?" Alice asked. She was grateful, but it was a bit creepy.

"I retrieved excellent samples of Dorothy's brain matter from it after your adventure in the bathtub."

Make that a lot creepy, Alice thought. She looked it over and sniffed it, but there was no trace of zombie brain matter.

"Don't worry," Mick assured her cheerfully. "I sterilized it in the Med-Trekker. Now off you go. I'm counting on you to launch the new sport of bog bra flinging today!"

"Thanks, but I plan to keep my clothes on this time." She slipped her bra on under her T-shirt.

Alice led Ken to the doors, and then cautiously peered outside. "All clear," she said. "Or at least as clear as it's going to get." The zombies wandering around the courtyard weren't looking at them at any rate.

Alice took a deep breath and jogged across the courtyard to the back door of the hotel. She was grateful Ken seemed content to follow her. She would have been happier if he'd left Dave's head behind, or at least wrapped it in a towel or something. Every time she glanced back at Ken, Dave appeared to be staring at her.

Alice tugged on the door and discovered it was locked. They were going to have to make their way around the building to where the pub faced the town square. Alice could hear Welly shouting and knew he was on the far side of the square.

More and more of the zombies around them were heading in Welly's direction. However, some were moving far too slowly for her comfort. She was tempted to take her Taser out of her purse, but didn't dare draw the weapon in front of Ken.

"Scoot!" Alice waved a hand at two lollygagging teenaged zombies. "And you too!" she barked at an old man zombie shuffling along in his slippers. She rocked forward on her toes, prepared to bolt if they so much as looked in her direction. She hadn't forgotten what they'd done to the woman in the flowered dress.

But these zombies showed little interest in her. They kept tilting their heads back as if they could scent something in the air. Probably Welly, Alice thought. She hoped Ken was right, and it was comradeship drawing them toward him, and not because they thought he smelled delicious.

"Don't excite them," Ken said, as they rounded the corner of the building. "You need to project calm, positive energy."

"Oh Ken!" Alice exclaimed. It was the first time he'd spoken since finding Dave's remains. Turning, she spontaneously hugged him. Then she realized her elbow was resting on top of Dave's head, and she jumped back with a yelp.

Ken merely regarded her with one eyebrow raised. "No excitement," he repeated. Looking perfectly relaxed, he approached the small group of zombies transfixed by an overturned car. "Follow your king," he told them calmly, but firmly.

"King?" a female zombie without an ear asked.

"That's right, king. Follow his voice. Follow your king."

"King, king, king," the zombies chanted, and began heading off in Welly's direction. Even the slippered zombie picked up his pace.

Alice took a deep, shaky breath. "Okay, calm, positive energy it is." The woman in the flowered dress had been anything but calm. Maybe that's why they'd tried to eat her.

Only it was difficult to relax when her heart was racing. "Mick was right," she said. "I should definitely learn how to regulate my adrenaline."

As she very calmly directed another zombie toward the bog outside town, she focussed on the reassuring fact that Dave had been a zombie, too. A good zombie. Who had died protecting them from other zombies.

Even those zombies had just wanted to get close to Welly to be friends, Alice reminded herself. Unfortunately, that meant tearing anyone who got in their way into beef jerky strips. Alice felt her heart speed up again. "I'm not calm."

"You're doing fine," Ken said.

"No, I'm really not." Alice knew she wouldn't be doing fine until she was back with Welly. His suicide attempt had scared her half to death, and she didn't want to let him out of her sight for very long.

"This is lucky," Ken said.

A bike with a large wicker basket strapped to the handlebars was lying in the middle of the road near the entrance to the Neuadd Arms. It was a bit damaged, and Ken immediately began to work on straightening the bent wheel and rethreading the chain. "Alice, see if you can find — "

"Right over there, in that garage," Alice said, without waiting for him to finish. She ran across the street to retrieve another bicycle, glad to have a task she could easily handle. Finding things was the one psychic task Alice had excelled in during her Odyssey training. It required no thought, just a willingness to be open to letting useful information pop into her brain.

For some inexplicable reason, her fellow trainees had found 'not-thinking' a difficult task. Alice, for her part, had never been certain whether or not she should be proud of her talent. It was awkward to be asked, "What are you best at?" by other Sensitives when her only answer was, "Not thinking about things."

She'd ultimately decided it wasn't a topic worth thinking about.

Alice stood on her toes and peered through the dirty glass window of the garage door. Nothing appeared to be moving inside. Bending down and grasping the handle, she pulled up on the door. It stuck, and for a moment she was worried the garage was locked. Then with a loud screech, it began to move on its tracks.

"Back off, zombie!" A light flicked on inside.

Startled, Alice froze, the garage door now travelling up by itself. She was facing a teenaged boy wielding a baseball bat. "I'm not a zombie!" she yelled at him.

"Prove it!" He shook the bat menacingly, but the intimidating effect was undermined by his cracking voice. He looked all of thirteen years old, and had about a dozen carefully nurtured hairs on his upper lip.

"Prove it?" Alice asked, exasperated. "I'm holding a conversation with you, aren't I? How many zombies do you know can do that?"

The teenager nodded, but didn't lower his bat. He was wearing jeans, a blue T-shirt, and a bright red cap advertising the Man versus Horse Marathon. "So you're a thief then. Just because we're in the middle of the zombie apocalypse, lady, doesn't mean you can go around helping yourself to anything you want."

Alice crossed her arms. After everything she'd been through, she was not going to be intimidated by a baseball bat wielding teenager. "This isn't the zombie apocalypse. Or at least, it won't be, if you let me borrow your bike."

"I'm not letting you steal my bike!" The boy's voice cracked again. "If the zombies break in, I'll need it to get away!"

"I'm not stealing your bike." Alice said, offended. "I'm borrowing it for a good cause." She glanced around the garage. "Besides, I'm leaving you the motorcycle right over there. And that's way cooler than a bike, right?"

He nodded, but then shook his head. "Until I run out of petrol and the zombies eat me. Or my older brother catches me on his motorbike and feeds me to the zombies."

Of all the teenage boys she had to run into, Alice asked herself, why did it have to be a practical one? "The zombies aren't going to eat you if you lend me your bike. I need it so I can lead them all out of town and save everyone from being eaten."

He rested his bat on his shoulder. "What kind of plan is that? If you're going to survive a zombie apocalypse, you need a shopping centre. You seal off the exits and live on canned goods, or you could even start a farm on the roof."

Alice didn't have time for a debate on zombie survival plans. She marched over to the bike rack and lifted the bike off. The boy made no move to stop her. "That's a great idea," Alice said, climbing on. "You get right on that."

"Are you mad? There's no shopping centre in this pathetic town. I can't even convince my friends to take over the local pub. My dad got drunk and went to bed," the boy said disgustedly. "He says he'll see what things look like in the morning, but he won't be up until noon, and then he'll still be too knackered to do anything anyway. You know what?"

Alice's foot was on the pedal. She knew she would regret asking, but couldn't help herself. "What?"

"You and me, we should join forces," said the boy, eagerly. "We're survivors. We might end up being the only two uninfected left in this town. Maybe even the world!"

Alice bit down on a laugh. She remembered what it was like to not be taken seriously by adults. Half the time she still wasn't. "There's not going to be any need to repopulate Llanwrtyd Wells. Just stay inside and take care of your dad, and leave the professionals to handle the zombies."

The boy's face fell, and he flushed red. "I've changed my mind. I don't want to join forces with you, and I'm not letting you have my bike."

"By the powers vested in me by Odyssey International, I hereby confiscate it. After the zombies are cured, check with the Cardiff office about getting it back," Alice said, standing on the pedals. "Oh, and you don't want to wear that hat either. Zombies are attracted to bright colours." She snatched the cap off his head and began peddling flat-out. The bike shot out into the street.

Behind her, she could hear the young man shouting, "I hope you get eaten, you mad cow!"

Alice skidded to a stop beside Ken who was seated on the ground with Dave resting in his lap. "Check out my new bike," she said. "Plus I got a brightly coloured, zombie-attracting hat for you." Alice held the red cap out to him.

Ken took the hat and then returned his attention to the bike in front of him. He tested the tension of the chain. "Are we going to have a problem with the locals?" The chain slipped, and he made an irritated sound under his breath.

Alice looked back at the garage. The boy was yanking the door closed. He made a rude gesture in her direction. Alice stuck her tongue out at him. "No," she said. "He's too sensible to come outside while there's still zombies around. We, on the other hand, are mad as hatters." Alice's belly rumbled. "And very hungry," she added.

Ken grunted, completely absorbed in repairing the bike.

Alice decided to risk venturing back inside the Neuadd Arms. It seemed quiet enough, as most of the zombies had headed off after Welly. Leaving her new bike with Ken, she walked to the front door and peered inside. It was a mess: chairs and tables overturned, bloody scratches on the walls. There were also numerous copies of Mick's flyers scattered around the room. Evidently his plan to attract all the local zombies to the Neuadd Arms had been successful. She wondered if Odyssey would owe zombie Lloyd and his zombie wife compensation for the damages.

Alice took a deep breath and cautiously entered the inn. She tried to reassure herself that zombies didn't ambush people. Brian's wife had got into trouble because she'd confronted them; they hadn't lain in wait and attacked when her back was turned.

Alice spun around, but there was no one behind her. She tried to relax, but the broken furniture provided too many perfect hiding places for errant zombies. Alice couldn't get the image of a zombie snacking on her wrist out of her head. She really hoped it was just her overactive imagination and not a vision of the future. "Many a false step is made by standing still," Alice told herself. "So get moving."

She managed to reach the bar without incident, where she spotted some small bags of chips. They looked like the most wonderful breakfast in the world. She tore open the closest bag and quickly shoved several chips inside her mouth. Then she realized there was something squishy stuck to the underside of the cellophane package. She put the bag down and lifted her hand away. It was a detached ear.

Alice spat out the chips. "I'm calm," she said, backing away from the bar. "I'm really, really, really calm."

A loud moan issued from a moving pile of debris by the couch. "I'm calm!" she yelped. Fumbling inside of her purse for her Taser, Alice added more quietly. "Radiating calm, positive energy, as I try to find my fu—got it!"

Alice yanked the Taser out of her purse and saw it was coated with Bloody Merry Red lipstick. Cursing under her breath, she aimed it at the moving debris under the booth's table. Alice pressed the Taser's button, and the weapon made a disturbing sizzling sound. Then it began to smoke. She quickly dropped the Taser and began to stomp on it as flames appeared.

"Since when is lipstick flammable?" Alice asked, frustrated.

A loud moan from the couch answered her, and an arm emerged from underneath the damaged seat cushions.

"Ken, help!" Alice hollered.

He ran inside, Dave's head tucked under his arm. "What?"

"Zombie!" She pointed at the booth.

"Is that all?" He placed Dave's head carefully on the floor. Alice noticed it was now wearing the red cap she'd taken from the teenager. As Ken righted the booth's table, Alice scanned him and despaired. He was deep in denial, still holding onto the idea that Dave was working with him.

They both looked down at a groaning zombie wedged firmly between the cushions of the couch and the table. The zombie was a young, heavy-set man with red hair. His head was thrashing from side to side, and he'd begun to grunt frantically. Alice had never heard a zombie make sounds like that before.

"What's wrong with him?" She took a cautious step back, in case this was how zombies acted just before they exploded.

Ken shook his head and sighed. He climbed up onto the table and crouched there, facing the young man. He watched for a moment, and then abruptly grabbed the zombie's jaws, forcing his mouth open.

"What are you doing?" Alice asked, shocked.

"I learned this move years ago when Dave and I were dealing with drunks and nutcases on a daily basis. If you get your thumb right back behind their teeth and press down hard, they don't have any choice but to stop biting." Ken peered into the zombie's mouth. "Yep, there it is." And without further hesitation he plunged his whole hand down the man's throat.

Alice was horrified at the idea of getting anywhere near a zombie's nasty, infectious mouth, let alone digging around inside of one. "I'm calm," she whispered to herself. "Totally and completely calm." She braced herself for the moment the zombie's jaw would snap shut, sawing Ken's hand off at the wrist, blood spraying everywhere just like in a Romero film.

Instead, Ken pulled his hand out, holding what appeared to be a whole lot of very soggy stuffing. "You shouldn't eat upholstery," he told the zombie. "It's not good for you. Now repeat after me, I think before eating, as much as my zombified brain will let me."

"Brainn… mmeee?" the zombie asked.

"Can we go now?" Alice asked, plaintively. "Welly's out there alone, and we should really catch up with him." The sooner they caught up with Welly, the better. Alice didn't like being alone in this town with just a pacifist zombie rights advocate to defend her, regardless of how handy he was at fishing around in zombie mouths. Sure Mick had invented a cure, but Alice didn't particularly relish the thought of becoming his second test subject.

Ken's red-headed zombie pal seemed much calmer, if still confused.

"I suppose Big Red's safe enough where he is," Ken said, climbing off the table and retrieving Dave's head.

"Big Red?" Alice asked.

"Names are an important tool in preserving a zombie's sense of identity."

"Goodbye, Red," Alice said. "Don't eat the furniture."

Ken didn't smile, but Alice could sense he was pleased. "The next one's yours," he said.

"The next what?" Alice asked, crossing to the doors of the pub and peering out cautiously. Ken had evidently finished repairing his bike, as both of the bicycles were now leaning up against the front of the building. Alice stepped outside and reached for the one without the basket.

"The next zombie," Ken said, following her. "He's all yours."

Alice gave him a startled look, letting go of the handlebars. The bike fell back against the building with a thud. "No offense, but I don't want a zombie."

She wondered if Ken was embarking on a new campaign to make sure everyone in the world got their own Zombie Dave. "I wouldn't be a very good owner," she tried to explain, as tactfully as she could. "I'm hardly ever around. Plus I don't think my apartment building allows pets. Unless zombies count as live-in houseguests, in which case if he stays longer than a month he'd have to be on the lease. Can zombies even sign leases?"

Ken's moustache got spikier like an irritated hedgehog. "This isn't the first zombie outbreak, and it won't be the last. They're rarely identified before Stage Two, so even with a cure, you'll need to know how to handle zombies for your safety and theirs."

Alice wondered if there was any point to trying to have a rational conversation with a man who was now putting his zombie partner's decapitated head into his bicycle's wicker basket. "But wrangling zombies is your job," she said. "I'm just the psychic."

"Alice, you're a Sensitive which means in your partnership

you're the voice of reason. Enhanced Agents have a tendency to overreact to zombies. It'll be your job to keep everyone on an even keel and show them how to handle zombies safely."

"Welly won't overreact anymore now he's been in their shoes," Alice said.

"Even if he thinks your life is threatened?" Ken asked.

"Okay, no," Alice admitted. Welly did tend to act like a big, overly protective dog when it came to her safety.

A zombie shambled around the corner of the pub, arms outstretched in the classic pose. Ken made a tching sound of disapproval.

"Is that one mine?" Alice asked, relieved to change the topic.

However, her relief was short-lived when a second zombie followed the first. "Or that one?" Alice asked in a smaller voice. Then a third zombie appeared, moaning, "Braaainnsss."

Ken turned toward her with a stern expression on his face. "What do we do?" he asked.

"Why are you asking me? Oh right, it's my turn." Alice took another look at the slowly approaching zombie mob. Horrifying images of the woman in the flowered dress being ripped to pieces flashed across her mind. Screaming and running for their lives was the first suggestion that sprang to her mind.

Except, Alice reminded herself, she hadn't actually seen Brian's wife torn to bits. Yes, she'd been attacked and bitten several times, but most of what Alice imagined happening came from movies she now wished she'd never watched. Besides, running around screaming would only overexcite the zombies. And the woman in the flowered dress had clearly demonstrated that overexciting zombies was a very bad idea.

"We should get on our bikes and…" Alice began, really wanting to add 'ride the hell out of here'. Instead, she said, "Slowly and calmly lead them toward the bog?"

"Very good," Ken said. He got onto his bicycle and asked, "Ready to wrangle some zombies?" Ken gave Dave's head a quick pat.

Alice was about to answer when she realized Ken hadn't been talking to her. Fine, she thought, Ken wasn't the only one who could converse with zombies.

"Okay, zombies," she addressed the three who were staring at them, looking confused. "Time to play follow the leader."

"Brains?" one of them asked.

"No. No brains. Follow. Folllllow."

"Follow brains," the zombies agreed.

"Close enough," Alice said, climbing onto her bike.

As Ken and Alice slowly rode away, a movement in the upstairs window of one of the houses caught her eye. She glanced up to see the teenaged owner of her bicycle staring at her and the three zombies with his mouth open in astonishment. Alice waved cheerily.

*

"Hey," Alice said, pointing ahead of them. "Isn't that the airplane pilot?"

Alice and Ken were still on their borrowed bikes. They'd spent the last half hour inching through town with an ever-increasing zombie mob behind them. It was currently just over fifty zombies strong.

Alice had given up trying to pedal her bike and was now straddling the bar and walking it. Ken was walking beside his bike, but Alice wanted to keep her options open. Specifically, the option of jumping back on and peddling for the peat bog as fast as she could if the zombies decided to get bitey.

Unlike every other zombie they'd encountered so far, the pilot wasn't trapped or doing his best to follow the zombie herd. He was shuffling slowly along all by himself, headed away from the bogs and down a side street.

Alice hopped back onto the seat of her bike and picked up speed to get in front of him. She stopped a few metres away from the pilot.

Ken stopped next to her. Dave's head bounced once in the wicker basket before settling. Dave appeared to be staring at her accusingly. Alice kept expecting the head to suddenly come to life and bite her on the wrist. She'd been tempted more than once to use her toddler temper tantrum powers on Ken to make him abandon Dave. But ethical questions aside, she figured Ken couldn't afford to lose any more of his mental faculties right now.

The pilot turned toward them. "This-shhh captain speaking," he mumbled. "Fassten. Fasten lap ssstraps."

"He's remarkably lucid for a Stage Three zombie," Ken said.

"Are you sure he's Stage Three?" Alice asked.

"Completely," Ken said. "See the way his stomach is bloating and his extremities have begun to darken?"

"I thought he was just fat and tanned."

"He's rotting, Alice."

"Oh, poor..." Alice looked for a Fly Me name tag on the pilot's ripped uniform, but couldn't see one. "Is that why he's not following the rest?"

"No, that's what's so remarkable. Stage Three zombies are especially vulnerable to mob psychology. If their friends jump off a bridge, they won't think twice about joining them in the water. But he's doing his own thing. In fact, he's paying more attention to us than any of his fellow zombies."

"Um, yes, I noticed." In fact, the pilot had spread his arms wide as if asking for a hug as he shambled toward them. "Shouldn't we do something?" she asked, nervously.

"I'll definitely run him through some tests once I get him to the Mailroom."

"No, I meant right now." He was barely a metre away. Ken was undoubtedly expecting her to wrangle this zombie, and she hadn't a clue where to begin. Not only that, but the zombie mob behind her was also getting closer and had started moaning "brraiinns" again.

"I'm going to get bitten," Alice said, despairingly.

"Positive, not negative energy," Ken corrected her, climbing off his bike. "I'll take care of him. You go keep an eye on the rest."

Alice felt guilty about abandoning him to a frisky zombie, but she supposed if anyone could handle the pilot, Ken could. She pedaled away from the pilot and stopped on the side of the road.

"This way!" she called out, calmly but loudly to the zombie mob. "This way to your king!" Alice waved her arms at them. "C'mon, can't you smell him yet?" She hoped Welly wasn't so cured he was no longer attracting zombies.

A handful of zombies in the front turned toward her. "That's right!" Alice encouraged. "Pay no attention to the zombie in the uniform."

One by one they turned toward her, and a few began to tentatively step toward her.

"Everyone follow me," she said calmly. "Follow me to your king. You remember your king."

"King, king, king," the chant began again, and in short order, all fifty or so zombies were heading in her direction.

Alice gulped. It was too late for second thoughts, so she began to cycle slowly in the direction of the bog, leaving Ken and the pilot behind.

As the zombies continued to follow her like moaning, decomposing cows, Alice's confidence gradually increased. She began biking around the zombie mob, looking for stragglers. As long as she periodically showed up in front of them to wave her arms and shout encouragements, they could be trusted to keep moving more or less toward the competition bog. Perhaps, she thought, they were finally on Welly's trail.

In front of an old stone church, Alice spotted two zombies trying get through the front door. Apparently, they'd forgotten how doorknobs worked, so they were knocking on it with their foreheads.

"Stop that," Alice told them. "You're going to need your brains in one piece after you've been cured." She shooed them toward the mob and was about to follow them when she heard moaning from inside the church.

Cautiously, Alice climbed off her bike and opened the door. There was no one in the lobby, but following the groaning, she found one stray zombie at the bottom of a stairwell. "Brains?" he asked her, appearing unsure he was doing the zombie routine correctly.

Zombies, Alice recalled, weren't good with steps. "The problem with these old churches is nothing's accessible to the disabled, or virally enabled as Ken would say," she told the zombie.

She couldn't think of any way of safely getting him up the stairs, so she decided to leave him there. She made a mental note to tell Ken about him later. "Peace, not brains," she advised the zombie, before abandoning him.

As Alice left the church, she spotted two more zombies who had wedged themselves into some shrubbery across the street.

Alice almost left them there as well. Then it occurred to her they might eventually free themselves and bite someone. And if that bitten person left town and somehow slipped past Borislav, she'd be wrangling zombies tomorrow in another town facing obliteration due to an out-of-control zombie infestation.

Alice grimaced. "I don't want to do this," she said aloud. "I really, really don't want to do this." But even as she was saying these words, she was abandoning her bike and clambering over the bushes.

"This is Ken's job," she told the nearest zombie, a youngish woman with blue-striped hair. "Or Welly's."

"Brainssss," the woman said, agreeably.

"In any case, it definitely shouldn't be my job," Alice said, as she positioned herself behind the zombie. "I'm just the girl who knows whether or not there's true love in your future. And if you've lost something, other than your brains, I can usually find it for you." Alice placed her hands on the zombie's shoulders and shoved as hard as she could. "The time is right to make new friends!"

The woman toppled forward out of the shrub and landed on her face in the road. "Sorry," Alice called after her. "Now go! You're going to be late." That hadn't sounded calm at all. She tried again. "Follow your king."

Another zombie tripped over the prone woman. "Late…"

"Brains…"

"Kinnnng…"

The zombies were starting to cluster, zeroing in on the woman, who was clumsily trying climb to her feet.

Alice ducked behind a bush. "I'm not here. I'm totally not here. Just keep walking, zombie folk." She scrubbed her hands in the dirt. "I can't believe I just voluntarily touched one of them." She wiped her palms against her jeans, hoping the virus wasn't transmissible on contact.

The "brains" and "kings" sounded a bit further away. Still crouched down, Alice lifted her head and peeked cautiously at the road. To her relief, the former hedge zombie had joined the pack who were all still heading down the road.

"Brains?" a voice asked directly above her.

Alice looked up. To her horror, the second hedge zombie had worked himself free of the bushes and was now staring down at her quizzically. He was wearing a soccer jersey and had an excessive amount of wild, curly hair on his head. More alarmingly, one of his eyes had come out of its socket and was bouncing against his cheek. Alice shrieked and scrambled backward. "Welly, Ken, anybody, help!"

"Brrrainsss!" the zombie growled, sounding more aggressive.

"Got to stay calm," Alice reminded herself. But then she tripped on a root and landed on her rear, just as the zombie lunged at her, arms outstretched.

Alice rolled to her side, as the zombie fell on its face, narrowly missing her. She jumped up. "I'm totally calm!" she yelled.

A chorus of voices from the road answered her. "Calm…" "Brainnns…" "Late…"

"Stop it!" she shouted at them.

"Stop," mumbled the zombie on the ground. He tried unsuccessfully to push himself up.

"Stop," several of the zombies on the road repeated. Worse, others seemed to take this as a suggestion, and they stopped. They started turning toward her. Her nice, bovine herd of zombies was no longer headed toward the bog, they were now staggering straight into the hedge.

Alice had an alarming vision of dozens of zombies, all stuck in the hedge. She'd be spending the next several hours trying to extract them all, until Odyssey got tired of waiting and firebombed them all right where they stood.

Screw calm, positive energy, Alice thought. "No, no, no!" she shouted at the zombies. "Follow your king!" She focussed hard on the mob and let loose her inner toddler.

Follow your king right now! Now, now, now!

To her relief, the zombies had enough of their minds left to be influenced by her psychic temper tantrum. One by one they turned back, and a few began to tentatively step in the right direction.

Follow your king right now, or he won't be your friend anymore!

With low moans of distress, the zombies began staggering toward the competition bog again.

"Thank God," Alice said. "Now where's Mr. Dangly Eyeball?"

The zombie was halfway up onto his feet, but was beginning to topple over. Alice ran behind him and grabbed him under the armpits. With an enormous effort, she hauled him up, only to feel his mouth clamp down on her right wrist.

"Oh no, you don't!" Alice snatched her wrist out of his mouth and then shoved him as hard as she could. Mr. Dangly Eyeball toppled right over the hedge to land among his brethren on the road.

There was no time to stop. Running as fast as she could, Alice bolted around the hedge and grabbed her bike. Hopping on, she quickly pedaled around and through the disorganized mob, dodging their outstretched arms until she was ahead of them on the road. "That's right," Alice called to them. "Follow me to your king!"

Alice was shaking so hard, it was difficult to stay on her bike. She wanted to fall down and start crying. "I got bit," she said aloud. "I'm a zombie now."

She didn't feel particularly zombie-like, but then she was only Stage One. Hopefully, Ken would catch up with them soon so he could take over the zombie wrangling. He could have her carry Dave and shamble along with the other zombies.

Her wrist was throbbing. Alice forced herself to look at it.

No blood. That was something, at least, Alice thought. She slowed down the bike, so she could take a closer look. Alice turned her wrist over. A bruise was blossoming, but she couldn't find any tooth marks.

"Wait, where's my watch?"

Her lucky Hello Kitty watch had vanished.

"That zombie ate my watch!"

17

The Cardiff Branch Makes a Belated Appearance

As Alice herded her zombie horde through Llanwrtyd Wells, she spotted a number of non-zombified villagers stranded up on rooftops and in trees. She tried shouting reassuring things such as, "Don't worry, we've got everything under control!" at them, but they didn't appear particularly grateful. The Welsh, she decided, were a very grumpy people.

Alice was sure she was an impressively intimidating sight to the uninfected villagers. A mysterious woman in black jeans and a purple T-shirt, single-handedly saving the entire town from a zombie invasion. Alice sat up straighter. She was grateful Mick had returned her bra to her. It would have been embarrassing to heroically jiggle her way across Llanwrtyd Wells.

When they reached the end of town, Alice took another spin around the herd. Two backpacking zombies had split off, distracted by a rabbit. Alice redirected them and started to follow when she was distracted by a bizarre sound.

Happy peals of childish laughter?

Dropping her bike, Alice peered over a stone wall. In the yard was a woman in a blood-soaked, flower-print dress flailing and snapping at two small boys.

One, blond and freckled, was standing in front of the woman, waving his arms with so much enthusiasm he could have been signalling passing aircraft. "Over here, over here!" the boy shouted.

Slowly the zombie turned toward him, jaws gaping. "Brainnns…"

The children howled with glee. "Brains! Brains!" the dark-haired boy chanted, jumping up and down.

Alice was suddenly furious. Even when she was a child, she hadn't liked children. At least, not the bullies, which had been the majority of them in her experience. "Leave her alone!" Alice shouted.

"She's only a zombie!" the freckled boy protested. His expression clearly said he thought she was a hysterical idiot.

"Zombies are bloody awesome," his darker-haired companion declared, dancing back out of the zombie's reach.

Finding a gate a few feet down, Alice pushed her way into the yard. "You shouldn't be teasing her. She's got a virus," she told them, sternly. "She's very sick, and I have to take her to get a shot."

"Yeah, right," the blond said, scooping up a handful of mud. He flung it at the woman.

"Bugger off," his friend suggested, turning his back on her.

Alice saw red. Back at the tavern, she'd resolved never to use her new toddler powers again, but she'd already broken that resolution with the zombies. Besides, she thought, if there was ever a legitimate use for her psychic brainwashing, this was it.

"No, you two are going to bug—go home. And you will treat any zombies you see with the respect and compassion they deserve. If you don't, I will so tell on you."

I'll tell your parents, your teachers, your mayor, your prime minister and the chief of Odyssey's Mailroom. You'll be in so much trouble you'll wish you were zombies!

Both boys turned and stared at her, eyes wide open.

"Now scram, both of you!" Alice stamped her foot on the soft ground and pushed hard with her mind.

The boys ran off immediately.

Her tormentors gone, the female zombie staggered toward her, mouth still hanging open. She looked well chewed on. Alice spotted a bloody bite mark on her neck, and another on her arm. Her floral dress was torn and bloody.

"You're Brian's wife!" Alice exclaimed, delighted. "I'm so glad you're not dead."

The woman's head fell over on her shoulder, and she groaned.

"No, you're only mostly dead." Alice held the gate open. "C'mon, let's get you on the road."

The woman's transformation into a zombie hadn't decreased any of her stubbornness. Brian's wife shook her head and began hobbling toward the house.

"I do not have time for this," Alice grumbled. This time she was more careful about grabbing a zombie. She took the woman by the scruff of her neck, keeping her wrists well away from the snapping jaws. Alice didn't have another lucky watch to lose, and she didn't want to show up at the bog just another shambling, drooling zombie.

Brian's wife was having difficulty keeping her balance, so it was easy enough for Alice to turn her around and guide her to the road. Unfortunately, the moment Alice let her go, the zombie toppled over. There was a loud crack as she landed in the road, among the shuffling zombies.

"I'm sorry," Alice said, wincing. The woman's arm was now dangling limply as she struggled to her feet.

"Don't worry," a familiar voice called. "Zombies never hold grudges."

"Ken!"

He was cycling up the road behind her zombie pack. Following him were at least a dozen zombies.

"Hi ho, zombies!" Ken called, shepherding his flock to join hers.

"Hiiii…" they called back, amiably.

Delighted, Alice picked up her bicycle and joined Ken. When they were side by side, she noticed that Dave's head was no longer in Ken's basket.

"Um, where's the—Dave?"

"Dave's looking after the pilot. I locked both of them in an abandoned car," Ken said. "I'll go back and get him out later."

"Okay," Alice said. Because why not? It wasn't the craziest thing anyone had done in the past twenty-four hours. Not by a long shot.

Besides she had much more important things she needed to tell Ken. "I wrangled zombies! I totally wrangled tons of them. You must have seen me shove that lady into the road. I walked right up to her, I grabbed her and did it all by myself. Do you see that zombie over there? He actually ate my watch, right off my wrist!"

"Which wrist?" Ken asked, interested.

Alice held it out to him. "I guess you would have fished the watch out of his throat, but I don't want it back, even though it was my lucky Hello Kitty watch."

"I don't see any broken skin," Ken said, inspecting her wrist closely. "You probably haven't been infected."

"Oh, and I should tell you," Alice continued. "There's a zombie stuck at the bottom of a stairwell a few blocks away in the old stone church." She waved her arm vaguely in that direction. "Also, there was this other zombie who nearly fell right on top of me. I've got so much to tell you! I really have a handle on this whole zombie wrangling thing now. I can shove them around almost as well as you do."

"Wrangling zombies is about recognizing that they're human beings," Ken said, in a quelling tone. "As such, they are entitled to the same respect and dignity as any other person on this planet."

"Oh," Alice said, feeling a sudden stab of guilt. She'd been thinking of the zombies as slow-moving, bitey cattle, and not as people at all. "I stopped some boys from teasing one of them," she said in her own defence.

Ken nodded approvingly and then paled.

"What's wrong?" Alice asked. Then she saw it.

A bunny was staggering down the field beside them.

"I suppose it's too much to hope that Flopsy just has a bad case of mange?" Alice asked. She looked all around them, but to her relief, there weren't any other rabbits in sight. Alice couldn't cope with a horde of zombie bunnies, not after her experience with the sheep.

"I am never going to hear the end of it if I don't nip this in the bud," Ken muttered to himself. He climbed off his bike and gave her the handlebars to hold onto.

"But we need to guide the zombies—the human zombies, I mean, to the bog," Alice protested.

"They have Welly's scent now, they'll be fine." He strolled over to the bunny.

Alice glanced up the road. Ken was right; the zombies were happily trundling along by themselves.

The zombie bunny, however, appeared very far from happy. With a low growl, it lunged at Ken's toes.

"It's definitely been infected," Ken said. Bending down, he grabbed it by the ears and picked it up. He held the bunny out at arm's length while it kicked and squirmed in his grasp.

"What are you doing?" Alice asked. "Shouldn't you put it out of its misery?"

"We need to know whether it's got the same variant of zombism as the human population. It needs to be alive for Mick to get a good blood sample." Ken started walking toward her, holding the struggling, snapping rabbit away from himself.

Alice cringed, but didn't drop his bicycle. Ken shoved the

bunny into his bike's wicker basket. He pinned it down with one hand and began trying to pull his serape over his head with the other.

"Here, let me help," Alice said, mystified by what he was trying to accomplish, but willing to follow his lead nonetheless.

"Actually, if you can hold the rabbit for a minute."

"That's not what I meant." Alice tried to retreat, but Ken already had her hand and was wrapping it around the bunny's disgusting, rotten ears.

"Just hold him there," he said. "Don't let go and don't let him bite you." Ken released his grip on the animal, leaving it entirely in Alice's grasp.

"Ken, I'm really not comfortable with this," she protested.

"You've handled human zombies all by yourself," he said, unbuttoning his embroidered denim shirt. "Don't tell me you're scared of a little bunny rabbit."

The bunny's jaw was working steadily, yellow incisors scissoring up and down in a vain attempt to gnaw on her hand. Alice tightened her grip and felt something squishy give way in the bunny's ear. "It's meaner than a zombie person and unspeakably gross, and why are you getting *naked*?"

Ken had just shrugged out of his shirt. He draped it across the handlebars of his bike. "I need to secure the rabbit. I doubt you have any bunny-sized handcuffs on you, so my shirt will just have to do." He slipped his serape back on over his head.

"I could have found you some rope," Alice said. "I'm good at finding things. Oh my God, one of its ears just came off!" The remaining ear slipped through her sweaty hands, and the bunny was loose. Alice tried to lunge after it, but Ken's bike knocked hers over, and she fell on her rear.

Ken threw his shirt over the bunny and began quickly wrapping the arms around it, until he'd created a denim bunny mummy. "There," he said. "A present for Mick."

"I'm sure he'll be thrilled," Alice said, kicking herself free of her bike and climbing back to her feet. "And I'm not even being sarcastic." She pointed at a scrap of rotten flesh on the ground by Ken's feet. "Do you think he'll want that ear too?"

"He might." Without any hesitation, Ken picked up the ear and tucked it into the basket with the zombie bunny mummy.

When this was all over, Alice promised herself, she was getting into a tub with a bucket of soap, and she wouldn't come out for at least twenty-four hours. "We better catch up with the zombie horde," she said, picking up her bike.

"Horde is a negative term. Try referring to them as a moaning of zombies instead," Ken said.

"What?"

"Like a bellowing of bullfinches or a gaggle of geese," Ken explained, his expression serious.

Or an insanity of zombie wranglers, Alice thought as she climbed onto her bike. Aloud she said, "Whatever. Let's just get going before they moan their way out of sight."

They had to peddle hard to catch up with the zombies. The group was moving much more quickly now, and several were making strangled, excited sounds.

"What's got into them now?" Alice asked. "And please don't tell me they're about to go on a wild bunny hunt."

"No, look." Ken pointed at a large vinyl banner strung between two trees and brought his bike to a halt in front of it.

Alice stopped alongside him and read the sign. It welcomed them to the Annual World Bog Snorkelling Championships in English and what she assumed was Welsh.

"Finally," Alice said, walking her bike past the banner. "I was beginning to think we'd never... Wow, it's huge."

The competition bog was very different from the lumpy mess they'd trudged through the day before. The land was flat and covered with coarse, tall grass. There were long, deep trenches cutting through the middle of the soft earth, with white wooden poles at both ends. Each trench was filled with the brownest water Alice had ever seen. She didn't feel the slightest urge to snorkel in it.

"There's Welly!" Alice exclaimed. She dropped her bike and waved enthusiastically. "Hey, Welly!"

Down in the center of the bog, Welly waved back.

All around him, zombies flailed their way across the marsh, determined to reach him. One particularly robust individual managed to stagger right up to his king. Welly grabbed him by the front of his shirt, lifted him up into the air, and then dropped him into a bog trench with a splash. The zombie sank like a stone, disappearing from sight.

Alice was afraid the zombie would drown, but then his head broke the surface of the water. Then she realized all of the trenches were full of wet zombies.

Welly grabbed an old lady and unceremoniously dropped her into the trench, next to the previous zombie. The old lady zombie proved just as buoyant as the fat one.

"We should get down there and give him a hand," Ken said.

One of the slower zombies shuffled past Alice, dragging a broken leg. When he reached the edge of the road, he tripped and fell onto his face.

"Oh, you poor thing." Alice ran to him and grabbed the back of the man's shirt to pull him up onto his feet. The zombie's head twisted to the side, and he snapped his teeth at her. "Stop that!" Alice said sharply, dropping him back on the ground. "I'm trying to help you."

"Can I borrow your bra?" Ken asked.

Alice stared at him, and he turned red. "No, you may not! Bog bra flinging is not a sport, no matter what Mick says."

"Never mind," Ken said, pulling his belt out of his pant loops. Stepping over the zombie now trying to crawl across the soggy peat, Ken slipped his belt under the zombie's jaw and fastened it tightly on top of its head. Ken grabbed the now-muzzled zombie by one arm and hauled him up onto his feet. Alice seized the zombie's other arm to steady him.

"Mrrraayyns," the zombie said, rolling his eyes at her.

"Are you going to have any clothes left by the time this is over?" Alice asked Ken, concerned.

He ignored her. "*Shwmae?*" Ken asked the zombie.

"Bless you," Alice said. She hoped Ken wasn't going to pick this moment to come down with a cold.

Ken shook his head at her from the other side of the zombie. "I just asked him in Welsh how he was feeling."

"I don't think your enunciation is wet enough," she said. Her left boot sank into a puddle and made a sucking sound as she pulled it out. "It should sound like that."

"Mmat," the zombie agreed.

When they shoved him into a trench, their zombie did not land neatly like the ones Welly had tossed in. Instead, the muzzled zombie toppled straight forward and landed on his face. He slowly slid headfirst into the water, his legs kicking in the air.

Alice jumped back as the brown water erupted into a froth of flailing limbs. "Will he drown?" she asked.

"No, zombies don't need much oxygen," Ken said.

Alice felt overwhelmed by the sheer number of zombies in the bog. "It looks like half of Llanwrtyd Wells was zombified," she said.

Ken shook his head. "Nah, I'd say only thirty percent of the population. There's maybe two hundred zombies here, tops. I've seen worse." Ken headed over to another zombie, an overweight middle-aged woman struggling across the grass toward Welly.

Alice didn't doubt it. "But where do we begin?"

He glanced back at her and smiled. "One zombie at a time," he said.

*

An hour later, all of them were coated in brown muck. Alice felt on the verge of collapse. Ken, bare-chested since he'd wrapped an injured zombie in his serape, was staggering with fatigue. Welly, however, was grinning like a lunatic. All the zombies were safely tucked away in the trenches. Now they just had to wait for Mick to show up with the cure.

"Aren't they marvellous?" Welly said, surveying his subjects with pride.

"You're not really their king, you know," Alice said. She wondered if being a zombie had addled Welly's brain.

"Of course not," he said, equably. "But I am responsible for them."

Alice shook her head. Not forty-eight hours ago, she'd been concerned Welly never unwound and fully enjoyed himself, even on vacation. Now here he was, as happy as could be, neck deep in mud and zombies. Maybe this explained how Welly could read all the fine print in his Odyssey employment contract, even the bits about being recycled after death, and still choose to sign on.

Movement on the road above them caught Alice's eye. A large black car was slowing down alongside the bog.

Alice pointed out the car to Welly. "They're from Odyssey's Cardiff office. Looks like your message about saving Swansea all by yourself worked."

"What message?" Welly asked.

"Don't worry," Alice said. "I mean, you probably just forgot because of the emotional trauma of having been zombified, not because you're a permanently brain-damaged ex-zombie."

"I'm not emotionally traumatized or brain damaged! I remember calling Cardiff." Welly's brow wrinkled. "Don't think I mentioned Swansea."

Alice was torn between concern about Welly's brain, and relief he probably wouldn't remember how she'd used her inner toddler powers on him to keep him from putting a bullet in his brain. Damaged or not, it was still better in one piece.

The car came to a stop. A large man with an alarmingly bushy, black beard emerged from the back seat. Alice instantly knew this was the infamous head of Odyssey's Cardiff office. He marched across the bog, accompanied by a shorter, younger man in a dark suit. Alice realized the escort was an Enhanced Agent, for despite his smaller stature he was sinking into the soft earth as much as Welly did.

Two more people exited the car, Dewey the Dustbin and a woman Alice didn't know. However, they appeared content to watch from the road. Alice waved at Dewey, and he waved back.

As the head of the Cardiff office neared, Alice could see his long moustache ended in two sharp points curling up into corkscrews on either side of his nose. She could also see he didn't look at all pleased.

"Of course they show up after all the excitement is over," Welly said, sourly.

Behind her, Alice could hear Ken practicing his Welsh on the trapped zombies.

"*Iechyd da! Brysiwch Wella! Gwellhad buan!* Alice, heads up!"

Alice turned to see a naked zombie, coated from head to toe in mud, heading her way. She slogged over and gave him a firm push. He fell and slid back into the trench, landing on top of several other zombies. After a moment of grappling and moaning, they sorted themselves out. Then there was nothing to see but peat-coated heads sticking out of the stinky water. It looked like a bunch of bog bodies were holding a hot tub party, Alice thought.

She rejoined Welly, just as the two men reached him. Welly spoke before either of the Cardiff contingent could. "Wellington Wolfe, acting head of the External Investigative and Enforcement Division." He did not offer his hand. "Good of you to eventually come around."

"Graham Broch, head of the Cardiff branch. We'd have been here sooner if you hadn't sent us to the wrong bloody location!"

"I told you exactly where we were," Welly ground out. "Llanwrtyd Wells on the Heart of Wales rail line."

"There is no Llanwrtyd Wells on the Heart of Wales line. It's simply called Llanwrtyd, and due to your feeble pronunciation, we thought you'd said Llandrindod Wells, which is on the line. We've been up all night, checking every rail stop between there and here, searching for your zombies!"

Welly frowned, as if trying to remember something. Alice thought Graham was an ungrateful bastard, but his mastery of phlegmy syllables impressed her.

"Hi, I'm Trevor," the local Enhanced Agent said to Welly. "We met once, during my Head Office orientation last year."

"There is, however, a Llanwrtyd Wells on the National Cycle Route," Graham continued, sarcastically. "Perhaps you were concerned the zombies might invade Swansea by bicycle."

"Okay, there've been some misunderstandings," Alice said, trying to be a peacemaker. "But on the plus side, we now have a cure for zombism."

"And whose brilliant idea was it," Graham barked, "to stick all the zombies in the Bog Snorkelling Competition Bog? Don't you realize there'll be hundreds of people descending on this town next week, wanting to swim in these trenches?"

"And we saved the entire town!" Alice was determined not to be ignored.

"As soon as the zombies have been injected with the cure, they can be cleared out of the trenches," Welly said, quietly but forcefully. "I've been reassured by a reliable... enough source there'll be no risk of infection for next week's tourists because bog water is sufficiently acidic to kill viruses. Trust me, everything is under control."

Trevor, meanwhile, had backed away from the confrontation.

Alice was about to warn him that he was too close to the trenches, when one of the zombies grabbed him by the ankle. Trevor slipped in the mud, and the zombie bit down hard on Trevor's calf.

"Get it off! Get it off!" he screamed.

Ken was at the opposite end of the trenches, so Alice shouted, "I've got it!" She ran to Trevor's side, and to her surprise, recognized his attacker.

"Lloyd," she said sharply to the former brewmaster. "Let go of Trevor right now."

"Please God, get it off!" Trevor thrashed in the mud, trying to kick the zombie.

"Hold still," Alice ordered, crouching down. She grabbed Lloyd's jaw the way Ken had demonstrated on Big Red back in the Neuadd Arms. She pressed hard, and the zombie's mouth popped opened, releasing Trevor's leg.

"Don't do that again," she told Lloyd, sternly, as the zombie slipped back into the trench.

"Oh God, am I a zombie now?" Trevor asked, curled up in the muck.

"Don't be such a baby," Alice said, standing up. "You're enhanced, remember? And even if you do catch the virus, we've got a cure now."

"God, it hurts!"

"Here comes your Sensitive." Alice pointed at the woman running toward them. "She has aspirin in her purse."

Alice tramped back to Welly, wiping her muddy hands on her equally muddy pant legs. Welly's stoicism could be exasperating at times, she thought, but she was very glad he wasn't such a drama queen.

"Under control?" Graham yelled at Welly. "Everything is out of control here!"

Welly smiled in a way that was not friendly at all. "If that's your opinion, Graham," he said, "then I'm more than happy to formally surrender my authority to you."

"What?" Graham paled. "You can't abandon your assignment."

"Yes, I can," Welly said. He yanked up his pant leg to reveal a peeling, black bite wound, surrounded by a nasty purple bruise extending all the way to his knee, which was badly swollen. "Injured in the line of duty. So you're in charge now."

Graham began to splutter. "Absolutely not!"

"No need to go spare," Welly said, calmly. "Borislav's already called off the helicopters. I'll also leave my colleague Ken with you. Certainly, he looks like the madman of Borneo right now, but he's our resident expert on zombies and will help you manage the infected townsfolk."

Alice looked at Ken and frowned. Was he taking off his jeans?

"And Mick," Welly continued. "I'm sure you've heard of Mick— He's cooking up more of the cure, which I can guarantee works."

At that moment, a merry cry came from the road. "Here I come to save the day!" It was Mick, perched on several wooden barrels in a small pony cart. The brown and white Shetland pony pulling the load whinnied at them.

"Mick, I expressly said no ponies!"

"But Tea Bear volunteered!" Mick shouted back at Welly. The pony bobbed his head up and down, as if in agreement.

Welly grabbed Alice by the arm. "Come along, we're done here."

"Graham, you great Welsh bustard!" Mick called out, cheerily. "I've been wanting to work with you for such a long time. And I brought loads of extra syringes, so you can join in the fun!"

"What did you call me?" Graham demanded.

As they hiked back to the road, Welly kept up a steady stream of complaints about the uselessness of the entire Cardiff office.

"I don't know how you can walk on that injured leg," Alice said, cutting him off.

"Too much dashing about," Welly said. "Nerves all decided to go on holiday." He rapped his knuckles on his left thigh. "Can't feel a thing."

"And when they come back from their vacation?" Alice asked.

"Won't be much fun," Welly said, but he didn't sound worried.

Considering in the short time they'd worked together, Welly had managed to get himself frozen, perforated, and flambéed, Alice supposed the sensation of agony was relative.

Welly stopped in front of Dewey the Dustbin. Holding out his hand, Welly said, "We couldn't have done it without you."

They shook hands. "Graham Broch is none too pleased," Dewey said. "Ran into him in Builth Wells where Perl and me were laying low. Had to tell the fool he was a twenty-minute drive from the largest zombie outbreak in Wales since the Tonypandy Zombie Riots of nineteen-ten. Thinks it's my fault because I called Head Office, instead of notifying him first. But you lot got us a cure, so Graham can get stuffed. That reminds me..." He went back to the car and retrieved a brown paper bag and a thermos. "Perl sent along some tea and scones for your brekky."

"Thank you!" Alice seized the bag while Welly accepted the thermos. She bit into one of the raisin scones. Heavenly.

"You'll keep an eye on things here?" Welly asked.

"That I will," Dewey said. "I'm not up to running around anymore, like you young folks. But I can still keep my town clean."

"Thank you," Welly said. "I feel better knowing you're here."

"The bicycles," Alice interjected, her mouth full. She swallowed and explained, "The one with the basket is from the pub, and the other belongs to a kid down the street. We can't return them because Welly can't ride them with his injured leg, although he probably couldn't anyway because he's so heavy he'd — What?"

Welly was giving her an incredibly dirty look, while Dewey was grinning. "I'll take care of it," Dewey said. "Good luck to you both."

As they walked away, Alice said, "I didn't mean you're fat, because you're not."

"Let's not talk about it."

"Okay." Alice finished off her scone. "Is Dewey a retired Agent?"

"Agents never retire," Welly said.

"Odyssey really needs a union." Alice handed him a scone and helped herself to another.

"Feel free to mention it to the Admiral. If you're lucky, he'll only be a small mammal at the time and unable to eat you."

"Oh no, I almost forgot! Dewey!" Alice ran to where she and Ken had abandoned their bikes.

"Alice?" Welly hurriedly limped after her.

She reached Dewey, who thankfully was still in one piece. "Zombie bunny!" she gasped at him.

"A zombie what?" Dewey asked, looking at her like she'd gone mad.

Ken's bike had been knocked off its kickstand, and Ken's shirt was on the ground in shreds. The zombie rabbit was nowhere in sight.

"A bun—" Alice began, but was cut off by a scream. "Never mind," she said, "Trevor just found it."

"Son of a bitch, get it off me!" Trevor yelled loudly.

Welly opened his mouth to shout, but Alice put her hand over his lips. "I don't think Trevor would appreciate your 'swearing causes dire consequences' lecture right now. Besides, I doubt calling a zombie bunny a son of a female dog will bring down the wrath of God."

Welly smiled against her hand. "Probably not," he conceded.

Her fingers tingling, Alice snatched her hand away. "I think we better go before the zombie sheep show up."

"The what now?" Dewey asked again.

"Never mind," Alice said. "A pleasant surprise is in store for you. You will inherit some money or a small piece of land," Alice said, quoting two fortune cookies for good measure. Then she walked away before Dewey could ask another question.

Even limping, Welly caught up with her quickly. "Should I be worried about a horde of zombie rabbits?"

Alice looked around the surrounding fields. "I sure hope not. And it's a moaning of zombie bunnies, not a horde."

"If you say so," Welly said, sounding unconvinced.

In the light of a peaceful, sunny day, Alice had to revise her opinion of the Welsh countryside. It really was pretty. The sky was blue, and the hills rolled gently under a lush carpet of green. Maybe you could call them mountains, Alice thought, feeling generous. She still believed Canada was far better, but Wales wasn't bad after all.

Welly handed her a thermos cup of tea. She gulped it down, burning her tongue. "Where are we headed anyway?"

"We're going to the train station," Welly said. "Which is called Llanwrtyd, even if there's no Wells tacked onto the end. They should have figured out I meant Llanwrtyd, after not finding us in Llandrindod. Sheer incompetence!"

Alice ignored his grumpiness. Instead she enjoyed the feeling of breakfast in her belly, the sun on her face, and the lack of zombies nipping at her heels. She also felt good because she'd finally figured out she wasn't just baggage, partnered up with a superhero for no discernable reason other than her dubious psychic abilities. She was an actual, useful part of a team. She'd faced down zombies, acquired a brewery so Mick could cook up his cure, and she'd forced Welly to give her his gun when he was suicidal. If it weren't for her, Welly'd not only be a zombie, he'd also have a great big hole in his head.

"What are you grinning at?" Welly asked.

"Me. I'm awesome," Alice said with a laugh.

Welly chuckled. "You are, at that."

*

After half an hour of trudging along the road in the increasing heat of the day, Alice's buoyant mood had evaporated. Wales might be pretty, but she was too exhausted and sore to enjoy the view anymore. The blisters on her feet felt like they were multiplying, and the soles of her Mock Martens were coming loose where the acidic bog water had eaten away at the stitching. Never again, she promised herself, would she buy cheap, knock-off shoes.

"Graham could have at least offered us a ride to the train station," she griped. "We saved the town. And the world."

"What do you want?" Welly asked. "A ticker-tape parade?"

"Wouldn't be a bad start," Alice said.

"Virtue is its own reward."

"No, it's not," Alice said. "I have blisters on my blisters."

A big red bird soared overhead. It looked just like the bird statue in Llanwrtyd Wells's town square. She watched it for a minute, then asked, "Wait, what was I saying?"

"Life owes you a living."

"You're funny. Can we steal a car?"

*

Walking across the large stone bridge, Alice remembered driving over this river only the night before. It felt like a million years ago.

"Are you going to call your mother?" she asked.

Welly looked peeved. "It's the middle of the night in Ottawa."

"You're afraid she might tell you why she and Patrick got kicked out of the monastery," Alice said. She reached out to Mrs. Wolfe with her mind.

"Don't be ridiculous. I simply don't want to wake her. She is one hundred and six, you know, and needs to be in bed, asleep." Welly paused. "Maybe she should move back to England. Canadian winters can be very hard on the elderly."

"Seniors have sex lives in London, too,"

Alice decided not to tell Welly his mother was awake. After all, he was right in one sense, she was definitely in bed.

"I'm not having this conversation with you," Welly said.

Alice agreed with that sentiment. "So was there a real zombie outbreak in Lla-whatever Wells?" she asked, desperately trying to cut her psychic link to Mrs. Wolfe.

"It certainly seemed real to me," Welly said.

"No, I mean did Dewey see real zombies roaming the streets, or did we bring real zombies here when the plane crashed?" Alice focused very hard on this issue, desperate to block out the images of Mrs. Wolfe and her seventy-five-year-old boy toy. "I know the farmer's wife was already a zombie, but do we know for sure she infected anyone else? Oh, that's a relief," she added, finally free of Mrs. Wolfe's love life.

"What's a relief?" Welly asked, sounding puzzled.

"Uh, nothing. It's just Mick said the airplane pilot infected the farmer. Maybe his wife was the kind of zombie who rots away quietly in bed without spreading the disease. "

Welly came to a sudden halt in the middle of the bridge. He appeared stricken.

Alice said hastily, "No, I'm wrong. The pilot couldn't have infected all those people in only a few hours, even if it was an extra-virulent airborne infection. Besides Dewey's reliable, right? He wouldn't have called unless he'd been sure."

"Yes," Welly said.

He still looked depressed, so Alice added, "I'm so proud of you, my King of the Zombies." She squeezed his arm encouragingly. Nice biceps, she thought.

He raised an eyebrow.

"No, really," she said. "You used to hate zombies—"

"Too many of my mates have been killed by them," he said.

"—but you didn't climb up into a bell tower and start shooting them. You didn't even let Odyssey rescue us and obliterate the town. You gave Mick time to find a cure, and then you made sure all the zombies would get it."

Welly grinned. "I rather like the bell tower idea. Wonder why I didn't think of that earlier."

As they stepped off the bridge, Alice thought that Welly's kindness, bravery, and sense of humour more than compensated for his enormous age and occasional bossiness. She decided she wanted more from him than just an occasional smile. Alice wanted a real romantic relationship with Welly, and it wasn't just because she'd nearly lost him for good.

Okay, maybe that was a part of it, Alice admitted to herself. But since when were near-death experiences a bad reason to start a relationship?

However, Alice knew if they were to have a romance, she'd have to make it happen. If she waited for Welly to make the first move, she'd be ancient too. Especially as he'd apparently forgotten everything that had occurred while he was zombified.

Recalling what had happened to poor Lloyd, Alice rejected the idea of using her evil toddler powers to seduce Welly. She was confident with a bit of time and effort, she could make Welly realize that they were meant to be more than just partners. Of course, the trick would be letting him think he was still the boss, while she'd really be the one calling the shots. Alice smiled to herself; she loved challenges.

"How about that car, can we steal that one?" she asked.

"It does look in pretty good sha—"

Through the windshield, they could see the zombie pilot. He was chewing determinedly on something wearing a red Man versus Horse Marathon cap.

"Is that a head?" Welly asked.

"Don't ask," Alice said. "Seriously, don't ask."

Epilogue

Wherein Alice Gets Jabbed With a Giant Needle

"**W**hy do I have to do this?" Alice wailed as Welly dragged her down the hall to Odyssey's cafeteria. "I survived the zombie outbreak!"

"Yes," Welly said. "But if you want to survive the next one, you'll have to be immune."

They rounded a corner. Alice found herself facing two of Borislav's armed guards standing in front of the bright orange doors. The right-side door was decorated with a new poster that warned: 'Food fights can lead to permanent injury or death!' The stick figure in the illustration appeared to have been lobotomized by a banana.

"Names?" the tall woman on the right asked in a bored voice, as she waved a turquoise and orange metal wand over them.

"Wellington and Alice, Section Five."

The shorter male guard entered their info into his handheld computer. He frowned.

"I know, I don't match my ID photo," Alice blurted out. "I really wasn't going to dye my hair again, but seriously, I'm too young to be a silverback gorilla. Sophistication is overrated."

"Procedure is to update your records every time there's a major alteration to your physical appearance or DNA," the taller guard said, sternly.

"I didn't lose a limb, I changed my hair colour," Alice protested. "But you're absolutely right, I'll go take care of updating my file right now." She tried to turn around. Welly tightened his grip on her left arm.

"Compare your scan with her records now. We'll take care of the paperwork later," Welly ordered.

"We're just doing our job," the woman said, resentfully.

"Yes, of course," Welly said. "And you're doing an excellent job of obeying the letter of the law."

"I really am okay with postponing this," Alice whispered.

"You've already postponed it for three days," Welly said.

"She's clear," the shorter guard said. "Enter on your right and line up to your left."

"And do us all a favour and kill Kenny," the female guard added with a sneer. Her partner snickered.

"Ken is Odyssey's Mailroom chief," Welly said, fixing both guards with a stern look. "You will treat him with the respect he deserves."

Alice was so surprised that she didn't protest as Welly hauled her through the push doors.

Ordinarily, the Head Office cafeteria resembled its high school counterpart. The same cheap plastic chairs, graffiti-covered folding tables, and seating determined by status. Now it had been transformed into a completely different kind of hell. Nurses were dashing about carrying trays of suture needles. Groaning patients were laid out on cots against the walls. A line-up of terrified Odyssey employees was guarded by more of Borislav's black-uniformed guards.

The entire scenario felt and looked very fascist, Alice thought. But she didn't point that out to Welly. World War Two veterans tended to overreact if you implied they belonged to a fascist organization.

Instead she said, "It was really nice of you to stand up for Ken." She was proud of Welly for finally letting go of his contempt for the zombie activist.

"It's wicked to mock the afflicted," Welly said, piously.

Alice gave him a dirty look. "And it's wicked to imply your fellow employee is afflicted. Even if he is."

Welly guided Alice into a line behind Emma from Maintenance. At the head of the line was the cute guy from the Admiral's office whose name Alice could never remember. Between them were a bunch of people she didn't recognize at all, although she wouldn't have been surprised if Welly knew them all by name. Welly knew everyone in Odyssey.

Mick was on the other side of the room, perched on top of a table, injecting a sobbing woman with an unbelievably huge needle. She was clutching her bleeding arm tightly to her chest. Mick looked over and waved cheerily at Alice. "Love your new hair!" he shouted.

The line Alice was in, however, led to a different table. Seated behind it was Ken, and...

Alice blinked. "Hey, isn't that the zombie pilot?"

"Next," Ken called.

The cute secretary stepped up and held out a shaking arm.

"Closer," Ken said. "Dave's not a giraffe."

"Did he just call the pilot 'Dave'?" Alice asked.

Welly leaned in close. "Ken always has a Dave," he said, quietly. "I believe he's on his fourth now." Welly pushed Alice forward several steps to close the gap in the line.

"Who was the first Dave?" Alice whispered.

"I don't know," Welly said. "Ken arrived here with him. There's a rumour they used to be police in California, but I don't know how likely that is. Odyssey recruited them in Minnesota."

The cute secretary screamed.

"Oh, this is going to hurt!" Alice started chewing on her nails until she remembered just how much trouble this kind of cannibalism had gotten her into last year. She yanked them out of her mouth and put them behind her back. "How about if I just quit Odyssey?" she asked.

"Nobody quits Odyssey," Welly replied. "And you really don't want to know what's happened to people who've tried."

Another scream. The line moved forward.

Alice noticed there was a stack of T-shirts on the table next to Ken with a sign saying, 'Zombies Are People Too! Buy a shirt, bumper sticker, or button today. All proceeds go to the Incurable Zombies Support Fund.'

"I should have read the fine print on my health plan," Alice whimpered.

"Come now," Welly said. "Odyssey takes excellent care of its employees. While I don't approve of Mick's *modus operandi*, he has taken every precaution to ensure there are no unintended side effects."

"Which is why I had a tetanus booster yesterday, and I'm on antibiotics now," Alice said. "I feel so much better." She felt nauseated.

Just this morning, Alice had been working on her grand seduction plans against an unsuspecting Welly. Now, thanks to him, she might not make it through the next hour alive.

A grey-haired man behind her tried to make a break for it. Two guards grabbed him and frog-marched him right to the front of the line.

"Hey, that's not fair," Alice said. "Now the rest of us have to wait longer." Since she couldn't escape this nightmare, she now wanted to get it over with as fast as possible.

"And you can't beat the job security," Welly added, cheerfully. "If the cure doesn't take, you'll have an exciting career in the Mailroom."

Alice glared at him. "You're not helping." It was easy for Welly. He was already immune. She wondered if he'd take care of her if she was a Stage Four zombie.

He smiled, something he'd been doing a lot more since Wales. "Just try to get through this with your dignity intact." .

"I have no dignity. I'm a coward, I freely admit it." Alice was having a hard time staying angry. She loved Welly's smiles, and she particularly loved the fact that they were all directed at her.

"You're no such thing," Welly said, firmly. "A coward wouldn't have stood up to me about Tasering airline employees, nor been willing to help Ken herd zombies into the peat bog. And it was very brave of you to save that prat Trevor from being eaten."

Alice felt warmed by Welly's words. "Maybe I'm a contextual coward. This context, for instance."

Welly didn't try to argue. Instead, he pulled her forward and planted a kiss on her forehead. "There's my brave girl," he said. Before Alice could respond, he winked and gave her a gentle push forward.

Without realizing it, Alice had arrived at the front of the line.

"Alice," Ken said. "It's so nice to see you. I love the color of your hair." His plaid flannel shirt was unbuttoned, and underneath Alice could see he was wearing a 'Zombies Are People Too' T-shirt.

"N-N-Nice to see you too," Alice stammered, still discombobulated by Welly's kiss. Did he remember she'd kissed him the same way when they were holed up in the brewery? And since when was kissing okay in the workplace? However, seeing New Dave the Zombie Pilot up close was enough to banish further speculation on the state of Welly's mind.

New Dave looked different, and not just because he was more decayed. His hair was darker and curlier than she remembered. She decided not to ask if Ken had given him a perm so he'd look more like old Dave. It was better not to know.

"I should buy one of your T-shirts," Alice said, in a last-ditch effort to avoid the inevitable. "And a bumper sticker for Welly's car."

"No, you won't," Welly said, forcefully.

"I'm disappointed, Wellington," Ken said. "I'd hoped after your time as a zombie, you'd move past your racism."

"I don't object to the message," Welly said. "But no one is defiling my car with a bumper sticker. She's only just recovered from the abuse you put her through back in London."

Alice rolled her eyes. The first thing Welly had done when they'd returned to Head Office was check on his beloved Aston Martin.

"Get on with it!" someone shouted from the line.

"No wait," Alice said, quickly. "What happened to the zombie bunny? Mick didn't know."

"That's because the rabbit went missing shortly after Mick finished his tests." Ken looked at Welly accusingly. "Rumour has it an Enhanced Agent shipped the zombie rabbit to the Agitators for Antichrists' headquarters in a gift basket."

"Provoking the enemy is a very serious accusation to make without proof, Ken," Welly said. "And Alice, get on with it. That's an order."

Alice took a deep breath and shoved her arm in New Dave's face.

He sniffed politely, but did nothing.

"Dave's not biting," Alice said. "Does this mean I don't have to get the cure?"

"Hang on," Ken said. "He's just not excited enough to bite." He bent down and began rummaging among the boxes under the table.

"But I dyed my hair an exciting shade of purple," Alice said, and then had an idea. "Maybe he could just lick me instead," she suggested.

"Biting is the most reliable way to transmit the infection," Ken said from under the table. He sat up with a battered guitar in his hand and settled it in his lap.

"You're going to play that?" Alice asked, in disbelief.

"Wait until you see what Dave can do," Ken said, happily. He strummed a few chords and then launched into a song.

"Don't give up on us, baby!"

Dave opened his mouth wide and began to yodel.

Ken reached the end of the first verse and commented, "He's very musical," before launching into the second.

"Don't give up on us, baby…"

"Ow-wow-wow-ow!"

Alice was so distracted by this spectacle she almost failed to notice the gleam in Dave's eye as he took another sniff of her arm.

"OW!"

Thanks to

The Workhorsery, for allowing me to drink their Kool-Aid and embrace the dream of bringing non-depressing Canadian fiction to the world.

Nik Ditty, for giving wonderful advice and valuable encouragement on the earliest stages of this novel. She made me the writer I am today! But she's not to blame for the grammatical mistakes I still make.

Dr. Maureen Korp, for giving the second draft its first professional edit. She's also not to blame for all the times I ignored her excellent advice.

Jocelyne Allen, for gently killing all my clichés and finally correcting all those grammar mistakes I'd stubbornly refused to give up.

Collected Works Bookstore in Ottawa, for employment, encouragement, and giving me a coveted Saturday evening for the launch.

Trish Slater, for believing in my writing long before I did, and handselling the heck out of this book!

My husband, for letting me disappear for seventy-two hours

every September.

My daughter, for generously allowing me to take over her bedroom for seventy-two hours every September.

My son, for allowing me to ignore him for seventy-two hours every September.

My godchildren, for loving me despite being ignored for a lot longer than seventy-two hours every September.

Melissa and everyone else at the International 3-Day Novel Contest, for providing me with the most insane and yet efficient way to produce a complete first draft of a novel every September.

Speaking of insanity, I'd also like to thank everyone at Stand-Up for Mental Health and its founder, David Granirer, for giving my depression an outlet that was much more fun than group therapy. Also, for allowing me to shamelessly promote this novel at SMH events by telling jokes that coincidentally happened to be about Welsh zombies.

When author Victoria Dunn's not busy writing, she's the ultimate Bond girl: intelligent, accomplished, and stunningly beautiful. She doesn't just blow smoke off her pistol—she blows smoke rings.

In a parallel universe, Victoria Dunn is the evil hive mind of Victoria Higgins, stand-up comic and tree-hating pagan, and Meghan Dunn, Sunday School teacher and reading tutor. Find one or both of them at www.aliceheartsbooks.com.